DEATH OF A DIPLOMAT

Also by B.M. Allsopp

Death of a Hero - How it all began
Death on Paradise Island
Death by Tradition
Death Beyond the Limit
Death Sentence
Death Off Camera
Death Of A Diplomat

B.M. ALLSOPP

DEATH
OF A DIPLOMAT

FIJI ISLANDS MYSTERIES 6

Coconut Press

Paperback edition first published in Australia in 2025 by Coconut Press

www.bmallsopp.com

Contact the author by email at bernadette@bmallsopp.com

Paperback ISBN 978-0-6488911-9-2

E-book ISBN 978-0-6488911-8-5

A catalogue record for this work is available from the National Library of Australia

Exclusive to Fiji Fan Club members

One of the things I've learned about *Fiji Islands Mysteries* readers is that they are just as fascinated by the lovely islands of Fiji as I am. If you enjoy this book, I invite you to join our Fiji Fan Club. I'll welcome you with something new to read that you won't find in any book store. I'll tell you more after you've solved this mystery.

THE PRINCIPAL ISLANDS OF FIJI

AUTHOR'S NOTE: The village of Tanoa is fictitious, as are Paradise and Delanarua islands. Other places on this map are real, but nearly 300 exquisite small islands are omitted.

THURSDAY 12th July

1

For the rest of their lives, the boys in the Junior Shiners Training Squad would remember the Australian High Commissioner showing up to their Thursday training session at Albert Park. Anyway, that's what Tevita predicted, and he reckoned himself a pretty fair judge of people, having survived on the Suva streets since he was a little kid.

Tevita's earliest memory was watching the other runaways and throwaways as he scrounged for food scraps. He soon decided the shoe-shine trade was for him, as he was too small to push a wheelbarrow laden with vegetables. He got by all right, but when the greatest rugby player of all time, Josefa Horseman, stopped for a shine, Tevita concluded God had sent him, like an angel. Maybe he was eleven or twelve at the time but he'd never known his birthday.

Now, Tevita was as good as grown up and his life was wonderful, all thanks to his special friend, Joe. He was in the Junior Shiners team, with the best rugby coach in the world, worked in the police garage washing nice cars, and only yesterday had moved into Junior Shiners House, where he had his own bed in a beautiful room high off the ground, with louvres that opened and shut and taps that worked.

Anyway, that Thursday, when Joe blew the whistle to end their dodging drill, Ms Armstrong was beside him, the top of her head level with his shoulder. She'd come to training before, when Joe had introduced her, explaining Ms Armstrong gave them the piece of land to build Junior Shiners House, so she was their benefactor and friend. Joe said in Fiji, she was like the Australian chief, who spoke to the Fiji government about how the two countries could help each other. Her chiefly title was Her Excellency. A cool title, Tevita thought.

Today, all the boys ran to greet her, clustering around. She laughed.

'*Bula, bula*, hello Shiners. I'm so excited to hear about Junior Shiners House. Joe tells me most of you have already moved in. How do you like it?' She spoke in English and Joe translated into Fijian.

The boys went overboard, shouting, jumping around, cheering and hooting, but Ms Armstrong understood they were happy. She laughed, looking up at Joe.

Then Joe blew his whistle. 'Calm down, boys. Ms Armstrong wants to speak to you.'

'Shiners, I'm so glad you're celebrating. I've brought a small present to remind each of you of moving into your own home. I want to give them to you now. Sit down, and I'll call out your names.'

In the end, the boys sat down and shut up. Ms Armstrong called 'Samuela' from a list. Samu jumped up, a bit shy as he was the first. She shook his hand, said a few quiet words and gave him a paper bag with a big smile. When Samu looked in the bag, his eyes all but popped out of his head, and he stared down at Ms Armstrong.

'Show them, Samu!' she said. He held up a pair of black rugby socks, the most expensive non-slip ones from Khan's Sports Emporium. None of the boys could afford them, even second-hand. They couldn't believe their luck when Ms Armstrong presented each Shiner with his own pair.

Tevita, like most Shiners, saved his boots and socks for games and trained in bare feet. That didn't stop all of them pulling on their new socks and prancing around until Joe called out, 'Do you want to play your next game with holes in those new socks, boys?'

'Just trying on, Joe,' Pita called.

As they pulled their socks off and rolled them up carefully, Ms Armstrong said, 'Shiners, I must leave you now, but I'll see you again on Sunday. I'm thrilled Joe asked me to your Junior Shiner's House grand opening ceremony. I'll be there if it's the last thing I ever do! So, I'll say *moce mada*, see you later.'

Tevita knew the Shiners would never forget that Thursday's training. Not only because of the socks, but because of what came after.

SUNDAY 15th July

2

Horseman scanned the guests trickling through the gates. He took a deep breath and straightened his shoulders. Along with many others, he'd doubted his ambition for his ragtag rugby team of Suva's shoe-shine boys. Yet Junior Shiners House stood behind him, undeniable. To one side, the Fiji Police Band's conductor raised his baton and the jaunty tune of Fiji's welcome song put a grin on every face and a spring in every step. The grand opening ceremony had begun.

The boys of the Junior Shiners squad, proud in their black and tan uniforms, formed a guard of honour on either side of the front gates. A few shuffled their feet and dropped their eyes as the well-dressed guests smiled at them, but most stood tall. Horseman moved across to greet the guests at the head of the guard of honour. Although he didn't know most of them, they all knew him and shook hands with enthusiasm.

He smiled and extended his hand to a slim woman in crisp naval whites. '*Bula*, and welcome, Lieutenant Connolly.'

'I'm happy to be here, Detective Inspector. What an achievement! Congratulations!'

'I've had little to do with it. Others have done all the work. And without the support of you all at the Australian High Commission, Junior Shiners House would still be a castle in the air.'

'Not at all! You're the driving force. These boys would still be on the streets but for you. You've met our First Secretary, Hugh Forester, haven't you?' She turned to the good-looking man in a smart linen jacket beside her.

'Yes, briefly, when we signed the lease, I think. Thank you for coming, Mr Forester.' Forester's handshake was brief but firm.

'Good to be here, and to see you again, DI Horseman.'

'Excuse me, I'm keeping an eye out for the High Commissioner,' Horseman said, glancing at the guests streaming in.

Lt Connolly looked about. 'Oh, isn't Helen here?'

'Not yet.'

'I haven't seen her today, but I wouldn't expect to on a Sunday. Let me give her a call.' Lt Connolly stepped aside and fished a mobile phone from her uniform pocket.

She soon rejoined Horseman, shrugging. 'I can't think what's happened. She didn't pick up. I left a message and a text, but I'll keep trying. There's time yet.'

A volunteer escorted Lt Connolly to the VIP seating beneath a flapping blue tarpaulin.

Horseman felt awkward glad-handing the great and the good of Suva society, even if it was his own charity project. He spotted the publicist, Meri Street, looking happy, chatting to the Deputy Commissioner of Police and his hangers-on. He joined them, uneasily accepted their congratulations until Meri caught his anxious sideways glances.

'Gentlemen, please excuse me. I need to update Joe on a few last-minute tweaks to our program.' Meri beamed at the senior officers, fished a file bound in fake leather from her shoulder bag and led Horseman away.

'Something the matter, Joe?' she asked as they skirted the makeshift marquees.

'The Australian High Commissioner's not here yet, Meri. Her naval attaché's trying to reach her, but no luck. And it's what—fifteen minutes to kick-off? It's not like Helen. She only has to travel one or two hundred metres, but I thought she'd arrive in the official car and show the flag.'

'Look, why don't you continue with the meet-and-greet. I'll check with the naval attaché—what's her name?'

'Lt Patricia Connolly.'

'In case Helen doesn't arrive, we can delay no more than fifteen minutes or people will get restless. Who should we ask to do the honours instead?'

'Helen's second-in-command. That's Hugh Forester, the first secretary. I assume he's used to speaking with no notice. Part of his job.'

'No problem, I'll brief him.'

Horseman pictured the official High Commission car flying the Australian flag pulling up beside the open gates, Helen Armstrong leaping out, not waiting for the driver to open her door. She would greet him effusively, full of apologies and a laughing narrative of a mechanical problem, a boiling radiator or a blown-out tyre. But the white Mercedes did not pull up.

The police band played on, while the caterers kept the drinks coming, then brought out trays of finger food intended for after the ceremony: curry puffs, dainty sandwiches, bright cubes of pineapple and papaya speared by toothpicks. That should keep the guests content to wait a bit longer.

Meri's smiling face weaved through the crowd. Could she have news of Helen?

'Sorry, Joe, neither Pat nor Hugh has been able to track down the High Commissioner. We must start now while people are still happy. The Deputy Commissioner will introduce you, then Gloria will tell the story of the Joe Horseman Foundation. You will respond and introduce Hugh from the High-Com, who'll unveil the plaque. Then Mosese and Pita will speak for the Shiners. Gloria will wind up with an appeal for funds. Finally, more refreshments while the nosy guests can inspect the building with the architect.'

'Great.' Meri's fair skin was flushed. She pushed her glasses up and dabbed at her forehead with a handkerchief, but the afternoon heat did nothing to dull her shining blue eyes. Her commitment to the Shiners hit him hard. Why should a foreigner care as much as he did?

Meri and Gloria effortlessly herded the VIP guests to chairs on the low platform. The crowd clustered around as the Deputy Police Commissioner approached the microphone, resplendent in his dress uniform with its red and gold braid.

'Five years ago, when our national rugby hero Joe Horseman returned to us, his friends in the Fiji Police Force, I wondered how he would settle down to procedure and paperwork after injury ended his international career too early. Well, I soon saw his discipline and determination would serve him just as well in bringing criminals down as tackling the opposing team. However, the boys living by their wits on the streets of Suva disturbed him. The shoe-shine boys avoided the police, but they idolised Joe and flocked to join his rugby training squad, which has now developed into one of the top teams in the junior third-grade. The boys are due to be promoted to second grade next season. Congratulations, Shiners! Congratulations, Detective Inspector Horseman!'

Horseman sat with the other officials, smiling and nodding to acknowledge the unbridled applause, his gaze fixed on the entrance, willing the High-Com car to pull up, or any vehicle carrying the High Commissioner. Or the lady herself on foot. When he focused on the stage again, the Deputy Commissioner lifted his arms and the clapping died down.

Gloria Chung, the svelte restaurateur and Action for Children director, took over the microphone to tell the story of how the Joe Horseman Foundation began two years ago with the single aim of providing hostel accommodation for the homeless youth of the Junior Shiners training squad. She was generous in her thanks to everyone associated with the charity—the list went on while Horseman stared at the road helplessly.

He heard his name and forced his attention to Gloria, who turned towards him, clapping. He'd never felt less like speaking. Short of a miracle, he wouldn't be introducing Helen Armstrong now.

After voicing the elaborate courtesies expected, he spoke what he felt. 'I will never forget what my late boss, Superintendent Navala, said to me a few years ago. "Joe, rugby isn't enough. It's good, but not all a child needs." This was a shock to me, a childless man. The next year, a brutal criminal bashed our own Mosese, an original Shiner, as he slept under the Albert Park grandstand, sending him to hospital. That's when I decided being their coach was not enough—I must find safe shelter for our squad. Even with the success of the fund-raising magicians of the Foundation, it's been a struggle to find a building suitable for adaptation to our purpose and the Shiners' modest needs. One day, Her Excellency Helen Armstrong, the Australian High Commissioner, rang to request a meeting, the first of several. The outcome was that Australia leased to our Foundation, for a peppercorn rent, this unused corner of High Commission land across the road from the official compound. Ms Armstrong introduced us to designers and builders and worked with us to build what we see today—a simple, good-looking building that will be home for up to thirty teenage boys and is outstanding value for money. So much so that we are mortgage-free.'

The audience broke into spontaneous cheers and claps until Horseman raised his hand. 'I'm glad you approve. This means that the Foundation can allocate all funds raised today and in the future to the running costs of Junior Shiners House. Eighteen boys have already moved in, and are paying for their lodgings by doing all the cleaning, gardening and assisting the cook.'

The resident Shiners suddenly stood up, turned to face the guests, and burst into the rugby victory song, 'We Have Overcome' in Fijian. Their fervent, untutored voices blended in natural harmony, piercing Horseman's soul. He controlled his emotion by singing along with the boys.

'At this point, I was to invite Her Excellency to open Junior Shiners House. I'm sorry to report that at the last minute, she was unable to join us. However, her staff are here in force, and I'm delighted to ask her First Secretary, Mr Hugh Forester, to unveil the plaque in her place.'

Many in the audience glanced at each other, frowning in confusion as the First Secretary stood, buttoning his crisp linen jacket. The applause was polite but tentative.

'Her Excellency is devastated at missing this occasion. The entire High Commission staff are proud that Australia has played a key role in getting this innovative project off the ground—indeed, by providing the ground on which Junior Shiners House now stands. May God bless all who dwell here.' Meri led him to the plaque by the front door, hidden by a black curtain. The First Secretary pulled the cord, revealing a burnished brass plate engraved with the details of the opening. 'I declare Junior Shiners House open.' This time the applause was whole-hearted.

For the next noisy hour, while the guests fanned themselves, ate and drank, and the band played and the architect showed groups around the hostel, Horseman kept checking the gate, as if Helen was more likely to appear if he was watching. Despite her absence, the opening had happened. It had even been successful, going by the number of guests reaching into their pockets or purses to pop a donation into the baskets handed around by some Shiners players. Most were shy, but Horseman had persuaded some to ignore how they felt and take on this duty.

Hugh Forester and Lt Connolly approached him. 'Any news?' he asked.

Forester shook his head. 'I've contacted Helen's driver. She told him yesterday afternoon that he could have the whole day off today. I asked the security guard to check and her car's in our garage. I suppose we should ring the hospital. I can leave now without offending national pride, I think.'

'Absolutely. Thanks a lot for stepping in to unveil the plaque,' Horseman replied. 'But leave the hospitals to us—we've got a system. I'll alert foot patrols and traffic to be on the lookout. You could ring around her friends, her favourite restaurants, anywhere she might have gone and fallen ill.'

'Do you really think so, Detective Inspector? I don't think we should advertise that Helen's missing. All too mortifying when she turns up, which I'm sure she will soon.'

'Mr Forester, if she's met with an accident or illness, she'll need our help. Here's my card. Please call me when you can. I'll ring you after we've checked the hospitals and clinics. What's the best number for you?'

Forester produced a leather cardholder and passed Horseman an official High Commission card. 'Try the mobile first. Good luck, Inspector Horseman.'

3

It was eight o'clock and Horseman couldn't wait any longer. 'Hello, Mr Forester. Has Helen turned up?'

'No, Pat and I have rung her friends—those known to us, anyway. I'm afraid we decided not to call random restaurants as you suggested. Who knows what wild rumours we could start by doing that? You must be even more familiar with the coconut wireless than me. Helen's the Australian High Commissioner—we must be discreet.'

'I understand. But it's my duty as a police officer to protect diplomats while they're in Fiji. If there's a conflict between Helen's safety and her privacy, her safety must take precedence for me.'

'Of course, you're right. I just can't believe that she's come to any actual harm.'

'Until she shows up somewhere, we can't know she's safe. We've now checked all medical facilities on Viti Levu. None of them has treated Helen, nor anyone matching her description, in the last two days.'

'The entire island? That's drawing a wide net! Well, you're thorough!'

'The only way to investigate, sir. And for Helen, that's even more important. If it weren't for her, the Shiners wouldn't have a safe roof over their heads tonight. But it's more than that. During those months of negotiation, I got to know Helen. I hold her in the greatest respect.'

There was a second's pause. 'As do all the High Commission staff, Inspector.'

'Yes, of course. Look, it's my job to think ahead. I'm already planning what to do if Helen doesn't return or get in touch tonight, and that doesn't include wishing and hoping. There's one thing you can do now that will help.'

'Ye-es?' Forester sounded wary.

'My advice is to report Helen to the police as a missing person. I hope she walks through the door while we're speaking, but the fact is, each hour that passes makes it more likely that she's unable to return because she's been injured or taken ill. Let me email you a form now, or fax it if you prefer. You can fill it in and send it back. That way, the police can start an official search for your High Commissioner in the morning. If you delay notifying the police until tomorrow, a search won't get going until lunchtime.'

A pause, then a sigh. 'You're right, I'm sure. Fine, email the form and leave it with me. I'm still hoping, though.'

'Me too, Mr Forester. My motto is *hope for the best and prepare for the worst*. Remember, call me the moment you get any news—doesn't matter what the time is.'

'I will, Inspector. Goodnight.'

***

When he left Suva Central Police Station at half-past eight, Horseman's head was spinning, refusing to operate by logic, step by step, as he willed. Like Forester, he supposed, his mind still hadn't taken in the fact that Helen Armstrong had missed the opening of the Shiners hostel, an appointment she was very much committed to. Only last Thursday, she'd visited the Shiners at training and told the boys she wouldn't miss the opening for the world.

He bought a pumpkin-and-pea roti from the barrow that was a fixture outside the police station in the hour before and after the change of shift. The warm, spicy mush would settle both his stomach and brain. He would walk home, hoping the fresh evening air and physical movement would produce cool, orderly thinking.

He crossed the threshold of his flat in the Seaview Apartments, Suva's only high-rise residential building, and shut the door. The familiar sense of isolation and order washed over him. He knew this comfort was an illusion, but he needed it to function. He dropped his bag on a chair and went out to the balcony. The view, whatever time of day, always filled him with pleasure. There was no moon but lights carved out the shape of the bay and mapped the town streets.

He got a Fiji Bitter from his fridge, rolled it around his face a bit and took a swig. His mind settled down as the icy beer reached his stomach. He sat on the balcony floor, stretched his legs out to brace them against the rail and let his thoughts come.

First, he'd do what Forester regarded as indiscreet: call the restaurants he thought Helen was most likely to patronise, both in the city of Suva and the outskirts. He jotted down the names and rang them right away, while dinner service was still at its peak. No luck.

Next, he made a list of all the other eateries for the constables to call in the morning. Misper procedures were standard, but they would need to go further for Helen, including other Suva diplomatic missions. Really, the First Secretary should be the best person to approach the embassies, but if Forester persisted in his policy of discretion, or rather secrecy, then Horseman would have to do the job himself.

He needed sleep. As he did his routine stretches before bed, he remembered he hadn't thought once about the Shiners hostel opening since he walked out the gates when it was all over. Now he relived it. Despite the absence of the guest of honour, the event had gone off with a bang, thanks to Meri and Gloria, and their team of helpers, including his mother, whom he'd persuaded to take on the role of hostel house-mother. And not least, the boys themselves. At the end of the afternoon, as the guests departed, there were few dry eyes when the boys sang a heartfelt '*Isa Lei*', the Fijian farewell song.

MONDAY 16th July

<h1 style="text-align:center">4</h1>

Insistent phones rang in Horseman's dreams that night, waking him repeatedly. While it was still dark, he gave up on sleep and staggered to the shower. He pulled on rugby shorts and a tee-shirt and jogged over to Dr Matt Young's house to pick up Tina for their morning walk. Seaview Apartments' zero-tolerance policy on pets dictated that when Horseman moved there, his dog, Tina, continued to live with his friend and former landlord. The temporary arrangement had now operated for a few years to the satisfaction of all three parties.

They walked to the waterfront east of the Suva Bowling Club, where Horseman sat on the seawall while Tina nosed among the tangles of seaweed piled up on the beach, turning up crabs that scuttled for freedom. She barked happily as she bailed up a sea snake heading to the water's edge, its silver bands glinting in the rising sun. Another mongrel trotted up and greeted her with a sniff. The two took off, prancing and capering around each other, dashing in and out of the small waves together.

Horseman set to work with his phone, calling all the hospitals and clinics in and around Suva a third time. Again, none had admitted or treated Helen Armstrong or anyone matching her description. No ambulance had transported her anywhere. The First Secretary had not returned the Missing Persons form that Horseman had sent him. Still, he could hardly nag the man about it—yet. He had no idea how closely the Australian government monitored High Commission activity, but surely Hugh Forester could report missing staff to the police without taking advice from Canberra.

He whistled Tina, then threw her ball into the sea. She darted away from her playmate, into the waves and swam out. In no time, she dropped it at Horseman's feet and shook herself with vigour, spraying him with sandy salt water. He threw her ball twice more, then said, 'That's it, Tina. Back to Matt's. Time for work for me.'

***

He climbed the stairs to the first floor where the detectives worked. His shattered knee had been slow to come good, but after five years of a dedicated exercise regime, he no longer needed the support of the banister and was mostly free of pain. Detective Constable Apo Kau was already at work, frowning at the computer screen, a mug of tea beside his keyboard.

'*Yadra*, good morning, sir. The opening went well yesterday, don't you think? The Shiners were in seventh heaven!'

'*Yadra*, Apo. I'm grateful for your support yesterday. And every day. The team wouldn't exist but for you volunteers.'

Kau smiled broadly, his eyes lighting up behind his black-framed glasses. 'I'm glad to do it. All of us are. But is there any news of the High Commissioner? Has she turned up?'

'No, she hasn't. I sent Hugh Forester a misper form, which he hasn't returned yet. I'll chase that up now. Can you get cracking with Traffic? Get a printout of all road incidents reported on the weekend, for the whole island, and go through them. Get full details on any involving a woman.'

'*Io*, yes, sir. But if she wasn't injured seriously enough to go to hospital, why wouldn't she have shown up by now?'

'I don't know, Apo. I can speculate, but that's not going to lead us to the answer. The High Commissioner hasn't returned, or Hugh Forester would have let me know. She must be somewhere. We'll only find her by being systematic and thorough.'

'*Io*, sir.' Kau's worried frown returned. 'She's an impressive lady, isn't she? Taking such an interest in the boys the way she does. Popping in to training every so often, chatting to them. Then, giving them all socks on Thursday! She's my idea of a top diplomat.'

'Not mine either.' Horseman stood by his desk, picked up the phone and dialled Hugh Forester.

'Good morning, Mr Forester. Any news?'

'No, Inspector. The diplomatic staff are very concerned now. None of her close associates has any idea of her whereabouts. Only Lt. Connolly saw her on the weekend at all. None of them got a call, text or email from her.'

'Did any of them try to get in touch with her?'

'Two of her friends called and then texted her. She didn't reply.'

'Did you get the Missing Persons form?'

'Yes, I did. I've filled in the basics, but I'm still thinking she must turn up this morning.'

'Of course. But now we've got to take immediate action to find her. I think the best plan is for me to come to the High Commission, get the misper form filled and filed, and talk to all the staff who worked directly for Helen.'

'I agree, we all want to do anything possible to help. When would you like to come?'

'I'll be there in half an hour, Mr Forester.'

Horseman turned to Kau. 'See if you can get us a car for the day, Apo.'

DC Lili Waqa walked in, all smiles, and dropped her bag on a chair.

'*Yadra*, both of you. What've we got?'

'The Australian High Commissioner's gone missing, Lili,' Kau replied.

Waqa's jaw dropped. '*Oi lei*, oh no!'

'I'm off to the High Commission now. Grab your notebook and come with me, Lili. I'll fill you in on the way.'

Kau put the phone down and grinned. 'You're in luck, sir: I've nabbed the last free car.'

'*Vinaka*, thanks, Apo, you'll need to fill in the Super when he comes in. No speculation, remember. Stick to the facts.'

5

The police sedan laboured up steep Edinburgh Drive behind a bus emitting a fog of diesel exhaust and Pacific reggae music. DC Waqa overtook at the crest of the hill, turned right onto Princes Road, skirting the white wall of the Australian High Commission compound and drew to a stop at the open iron gates. The Fijian security guard stepped forward with a clipboard, nodding when Waqa held out her ID. His sombre face broke into a smile when he recognised Horseman.

'*Bula*, officers. Please park on the left in front of the office wing. The First Secretary is expecting you. I pray you can help us.'

'*Bula*, Saula. We'll do everything we can to find Her Excellency. When did you last see her?'

'On Friday afternoon, sir. I signed off at six o'clock. I had the whole of Saturday and Sunday off. Now I wish I hadn't. If only I'd been on duty ...'

'That sort of thinking won't get us anywhere, Saula. The best way you can help is to keep a sharp watch now you're on duty again and report anything remotely unusual to your boss.'

The car park bays were arranged so as not to block the view of the High Commissioner's Residence at the top of the drive. Later additions, such as an entry porch, hadn't obscured the original timber house, one of the oldest surviving in Fiji. Helen had held several meetings planning Australia's support of the Shiners hostel over lunch in the Residence dining room. Horseman had enjoyed the century-old ambience, the cross-breeze through the wooden shutters, and the spectacular view along the coast. Helen's delight in her temporary home and eagerness to share it had forged a bond between them, as it must have done with many others.

Today, however, he mounted the steps to the office building. The receptionist picked up the phone as they entered. By the time they'd reached her desk, Hugh Forester emerged from his office opposite, his hand outstretched.

'Come in, officers. Let's sit down.' He gestured to a sitting area near the windows. 'We're all getting rather anxious. What can we do to help?'

'It would be a good start to tell us who you've rung so far.'

'I'm afraid we've just called whoever popped into our minds. Regrettable, but if you excuse me, I'll ask Losana, our office manager, to compile a complete list.'

'Thank you. My own priority is to fast-track Helen's misper registration. DC Waqa can assist you or whoever you delegate.'

'Hmm. We do have a few Australian Federal Police officers based here, but they would hardly be familiar with your processes. If that's your first priority, I'll fill in the form now with DC Waqa's advice.' Forester gave DC Waqa a friendly smile.

'Good, I'll ask Losana to put the list of phone calls together with Lt Connolly. You can add your own when they're finished.'

'Sure. Well, let's get started.'

'One more thing. I wasn't aware you had AFP officers working here until you mentioned them a moment ago. It'd be good to meet my counterparts, if they're available.'

'Certainly. They should still be in the office—it's rather too early for their official liaison appointments. Ask Losana to let them know you're here and I'm sure they'll make time to meet you.'

'Thanks, Mr Forester. After that, we'll need to interview other staff who worked with the High Commissioner.'

'Anything to help, Inspector. Drop in at my office when you're ready. I hope DC Waqa and I will have your form complete by then.' Forester smiled. He didn't look particularly worried. Horseman supposed he'd cultivated an imperturbable diplomatic manner.

The office manager seemed calm, too. She stood smiling in a sunny yellow dress. Her wavy hair and honey-coloured skin placed her home in the Polynesian-influenced eastern islands. She held out her hand and shook his firmly.

'I'm Losana Tuwai, Detective Inspector Horseman. So pleased to meet you.' Her smile was playful. 'I'll be the envy of my rugby-mad husband and brothers now! Tell me what I can do to help you.'

***

At ten o'clock, the Australian High Commissioner was officially registered as a missing person, and the list of all the friends her colleagues had spoken to was completed. Horseman joined Forester, Lt Connolly and DC Waqa at the conference table in Forester's office. Losana wheeled in a tea trolley, poured tea and coffee from shiny pots, then unwrapped a basket of scones. The warm aroma made Horseman weak at the knees; if there was one thing he could not resist, it was a fresh scone. Unasked, she placed one on a plate with large dollops of cream and strawberry jam, together with a knife and passed it to him.

'*Vinaka*, Losana.' He made himself wait politely, sipping some tea for a few minutes before tackling the scone, but it was torture.

'Perfect,' he said. 'I think your cook must be Fijian.'

Lt Connolly smiled. 'He is. We're all putting on weight. There are still Australians who can bake a good scone, though.'

While Losana was still serving, there was a tap on the open door and a tall middle-aged man loomed into the doorway. His thick hair and cropped beard were rich brown, his skin fair and scattered with light freckles. He wore the pale blue AFP uniform shirt, complete with badge and patches.

'Come and have a cuppa, Bob,' Forester said. 'Meet DI Horseman and DC Waqa from Suva Criminal Investigations Division. Officers, this is Chief Inspector Bob Browning.'

After the introductions, Browning joined them at the table and asked, 'Is the High Commissioner now officially registered as missing?'

'Yes, sir,' Horseman replied. 'Her disappearance is worrying. I need to talk to Mr Forester and Lt Connolly in more detail before organising the search. Of course, it would be great to get your advice, sir.'

Browning smiled. 'Bob, please. I'm sure you've nothing to learn from me. I'm working with your head of Training Division on courses in new communications technology equipment that Australia is donating to you.

'Thank you, Bob, we're in need of that. I'd like to gather the staff together in one room and get them to write down their most recent sighting of Ms Armstrong.'

Browning looked eager. 'I'm happy to herd everyone into the reception room with the help of my two colleagues.'

Horseman looked to the First Secretary, who nodded. 'Fine by me, Bob. Let's get that done.'

6

Horseman put the sheaf of A4 papers in his satchel. Browning had offered to escort DC Waqa around the public counters to get statements from the staff who couldn't leave their posts.

'I hope your staff have confidence that the police will do everything possible to find Helen,' Horseman said to Forester as they walked back to his office.

'We're all confused and shocked. I had my doubts about your statements tactic, but now I realise it was helpful for people to take some practical, physical action, no matter how small or even, in most cases, irrelevant. Doing it together was reassuring.'

'Good. Even if most statements are irrelevant, there are always some that need following up and can even give us leads. Could I impose on your time now to ask you a few more questions?'

'Yes, of course. Though I don't think there's anything relevant I haven't already told you.' Forester ushered Horseman into his office, this time to the low armchairs around a coffee table by the window.

Horseman took out his notebook. 'Well, let's review what we've got and get a timeline going. It would speed things up if I could see Helen's official diary.'

'Losana keeps that. Of course, it's confidential.'

'I imagine most of the information that will lead us to Helen is confidential, Mr Forester.'

The First Secretary looked unhappy. 'I suppose so.'

'Let me reassure you, I won't need to take it away. After I go through the last week or so, I'll ask for photocopies of any pages I need.'

'Helen must be one of the last heads-of-mission in the world with a diary book. She argues that knowing when people have cancelled or changed appointments can be important. However, our admin assistants keep a parallel e-calendar.'

'I agree with her. I'd like to see the book first, if I may.'

Forester picked up the phone and asked for the High Commissioner's diary.

'When did you last see Helen, Mr Forester?'

'Friday afternoon around half-past five. Most of the staff finish up when the doors shut at half-past four, especially on a Friday. However, Helen chaired a meeting of diplomatic staff that continued for a further hour. That's quite normal. I came back here then and worked for about another hour before packing up, but I didn't see Helen again after the meeting disbanded.'

'Do you drive to and from work, Mr Forester?'

The first secretary looked surprised. 'No, some of us live in the compound. I'm lucky to be one of them, so I walk. Our houses are behind the Residence, tucked away out of sight.'

'So, you walked home around half-past six?'

'Yes, but not for long. I had a reception at the US Ambassador's to attend, so I showered, changed and left again. I got home around ten. After that, I stayed in.'

'Did you notice anything unusual when you got back to the compound?'

'Nothing. Australia wasn't hosting any parties, so all was quiet.'

'And Saturday?'

'I got up late, saw Pat driving out the back gate from my kitchen window, settled down to catch up with the news over coffee. It was nearly noon when I went out to the Morris Hedstrom supermarket further up Princes Road to stock up on supplies. I stayed home all afternoon, took a nap. Saturday night was the Bastille Day Masked Ball, hosted by the French Embassy, the highlight of the diplomatic calendar. I have to hand it to the French.'

'Was Helen at the ball?'

'I assumed she was, but I didn't see her. Mind you, that's not surprising. There are hundreds of guests, crowds of them in the ballroom, on the roof terrace, the lawn at the waterfront, all wearing masks. No one misses that party by choice.'

'And yesterday?'

'I slept until lunchtime, then made coffee. I met Pat and we walked out the back gate just after two and across the road to your reception at the hostel.'

'Who do you think Helen would ask for help, perhaps if she got sick?'

'Only those on the list you have, whom I've already rung. But I wasn't close to her outside of work. Pat Connolly knew her better.'

'Many thanks, Mr Forester. I don't want to keep you from your work any longer. May I sit in the reception area while I look at Helen's official diary?'

'We can do a bit better than that, Inspector. There's a little office just off reception for visitors who need a desk and privacy. Losana will show you. No doubt I'll see you again before you go.'

'Yes, I'll look in. Thanks again.'

The First Secretary stood and Horseman returned to Losana at reception. She handed him a thick foolscap volume bound in navy blue with the Australian coat of arms embossed on the front in gold. On this occasion, she didn't smile. The gravity of the situation was now sinking in.

Horseman flipped the pages back a few weeks. Mondays to Fridays were crowded with appointments within the High Commission, with other diplomatic missions, and Fiji government bodies. Weekends were less densely packed, but Horseman only spotted one blank page, the day following a flight to Canberra, presumably for discussions with the Department of Foreign Affairs. She flew back to Suva the next morning. The previous week showed nothing out of place with the usual pattern. On Saturday, there was a morning tea with the Fiji Association of Women Graduates at the University of the South Pacific and in the evening, the Bastille Day Ball, which Hugh Forester had also attended. On Sunday, unusually, Helen had only one appointment—the opening of Shiners House at two o'clock. As Helen had given the driver the day off, she must have intended to walk from her house down the slope to the back entrance, then cross the road to the hostel, just as other High Commission staff had done.

There was a tap on the office door, then DC Waqa appeared, smiling cheerfully. 'All done, sir. Everyone who's at work today, that is.' She brandished a thin bundle of A4 sheets of paper.

'Good work, Lili. I'd like to squeeze in a chat with Lt Connolly before we get back to the station. I think she might have known her boss on a more personal basis than Hugh Forester did.'

7

Horseman returned the appointment diary to Losana, asked her to email him the electronic version and check if the naval attaché was free.

'I remember passing Lt Connolly's office. No need to escort us,' DC Waqa said with a smile.

'That's quite all right. This building's rambling. Just give me a moment to get this email off to you.'

No one could have been friendlier or firmer, so they looked at a large Australian Aboriginal painting on the wall until the office manager bustled out and led them away.

'Thank you for seeing us, Lieutenant. I'm hoping you may know more about Ms Armstrong's plans for this last weekend than the three appointments in her diary.'

'Not a great deal, I'm afraid. You can understand that those of us who both live and work in the compound guard our privacy as much as we can, without being obsessive about it.'

'Yes, I remember what it was like to live in the police barracks. However, I imagine your accommodation is much more spacious and more private.'

'Indeed, we're very lucky.'

'I'm rather hazy about what a naval attaché does, Lieutenant. Do you organise the annual war games we have with the Australian Navy?'

Lt Connolly looked surprised. 'I'm involved in those, yes. And a lot more. If you had an hour, I could tell you about my job, which I love. But I imagine you haven't got all day to chat.'

'True, but I need to learn more about Helen's life here if we're to mount a successful search for her.'

A frown creased Lt Connolly's forehead. 'I've only been here one year, and Helen's been here six—an unusually long posting. As the longest-serving head of mission in Suva, she's the respected head of the diplomatic corps and the diplomat with the closest knowledge of the players in the Fiji government and politics. She knows this place intimately. Loves it, too. So, when I arrived I was dependent on her to show me the ropes, even though I represent the Defence Department, not Foreign Affairs. She's been a great mentor, but her own circle of friends and acquaintances was well-established years before I arrived. I'm still a newbie.'

'I see on Saturday she had a meeting at USP with the Fiji Association of Women Graduates. Do you know any more about that?'

Her face lifted. 'Yes, I was there, too. Helen's particularly interested in women's organisations here. FAWG welcomes foreigners, so by joining she shows her support and also gets to know Fijian women who are likely to be influential in a range of spheres. She suggested I join and go with her to the meetings, so I did. They're fun and the best intro to Fijian society for a female expatriate. My counterparts in the military here are all men, so I'd hardly meet a woman outside of our compound but for FAWG.'

'I'm glad to hear they've made you welcome. When did the meeting finish last Saturday?'

'People tend to hang on a bit. It's officially morning tea, but in Fiji that's a spread more like the main meal of the day to me, so no one's rushing off for lunch. I left at around half-past twelve, as I had a meeting at the naval base at two o'clock. The socialising was still going strong, but Helen wanted to leave then. I got a lift both ways with her.'

'Did you come back here after your visit to the naval base?'

'I called into the market for some vegetables—oh, I was driving one of our cars, by the way. Then on to the supermarket, then home. It must have been half-past four by then. I relaxed until it was time to get ready for the French Embassy bash.'

'Did you drive yourself there?'

'No, Vuki, the driver, took me with three other staff.'

'How about Helen?'

'Helen left earlier. She said she was having a drink with friends first, but she didn't say where. I assume Vuki drove her, but I really don't know. It's not my job to keep track of Helen's social life.'

'Do you know who the friends might have been?'

'No, as I said, we all respect each other's privacy here.'

'Did you see Helen at the ball?'

'No, I didn't—just assumed she was around somewhere—the ball took over the whole Grand Pacific. As I said, she knows everyone in top government and international circles in Suva. She would have been circulating among them, not chatting to her own colleagues.'

'You make the ball sound like it was work for her.'

'Oh, definitely. She was the consummate diplomat: a role model for me.'

'Did everyone wear masks?'

'Yes, all kinds, from full-head rubber to dainty Venetian-style lace ones on a stick. Of course, the rubber was insufferable in the heat, and people who wore those took them off before too long or shoved them up to their foreheads. Many were woven from grass, inspired by different Pacific Islands. The masks are a lot of fun. I was a bit surprised that most guests kept them on, I guess out of respect for our hosts' intentions.'

'When did you leave?'

'Around two. The ball was still going strong, but probably half the guests had left. I spotted Hugh and Walter, the Third Secretary, and we got a taxi at the front of the hotel. Helen believed it wasn't fair to expect drivers to pick us up after eleven at night, especially from social events.'

'So, was the last time you saw Helen when she drove you both back here from the FAWG meeting?'

Lt Connolly paused, frowning. 'Yes, I think it must have been.'

Horseman's phone vibrated in his pocket. It was probably Superintendent Ratini, but he couldn't possibly interrupt this interview. He reached into his pocket and switched the phone off. 'You reminded me Helen's been a leader of the diplomatic scene here for years. I imagine in her briefings, she's mentioned some diplomatic tensions. Has she warned you about missions hostile to Australia?'

'Naturally, there are rivalries. But hostile is going too far. You're surely not thinking Helen's been kidnapped, are you? That's not possible. I mean, rivalry, yes, but violence? It's unthinkable.' She shook her head slowly from side to side.

'As we have no clues at all as to her whereabouts, Lieutenant, we can't close our minds to any possibility yet. Can you think of anyone Helen knew who disliked or resented her, no matter what the reason?'

The naval attaché shook her head faster in denial. 'No, the idea's ridiculous. I admit she would never stay away so long—what is it now, say 35 hours? She wouldn't stay away so long without getting in touch if she could. Perhaps she met with an accident and has amnesia, or is injured or ill—perhaps a heart attack or seizure—and is lying helpless somewhere. That's the only possibility that makes any sense. Maybe her taxi ended up in a ditch, something like that.'

'You may be right, Lieutenant. My team are thoroughly checking out those possibilities as we speak. We know that Helen has not been treated at any medical facility on the whole of Viti Levu, that's how thorough our checks are. I'm looking for a shortcut here. Do you know anywhere or anyone Helen may have gone to as an escape, to get away?'

'No, I can't think of anywhere or anyone. And it's never occurred to me she wanted an escape—she gave every impression that she relished her life here at the High Commission in Suva. She's told me more than once how she's dreading retirement.'

Horseman placed his business card on the table in front of the naval attaché. 'In that case, DC Waqa and I will leave you and join the officers searching for Helen. Remember that you're in shock now. Later, when you think of anything Helen said or did over the last few days that now seems a bit odd, please give me a call without delay. Even if you think it's trivial. Let the police be the judge of relevance.'

'I will, Inspector. Without fail.'

As they left the building, DC Waqa's radio buzzed. She turned aside and answered, catching up with Horseman at the bottom of the steps. 'Sir, Apo's trying to reach you. You should call Superintendent Ratini right away. He's asking why you've switched your mobile off.'

8

Superintendent Ratini thumped the desk with his fist. 'Good God, man! You didn't bother telling me the Australian High Commissioner went missing yesterday? It's well past eleven in the morning, and I had to hear about that *trivial* incident from the Deputy Commissioner, who got it from an AFP officer seconded to the High Commission! Made me look like a prize fool.'

'I apologise, sir. It's been tricky. Last night, I strongly recommended that Mr Forester, the First Secretary, file a misper report with us, but he decided to wait, believing that Ms Armstrong would return by this morning. DC Waqa and I have been at the High-Com all morning, speeding up the notification, which was done by ten o'clock. Mr Forester is most reluctant to attract public interest.'

'How does the idiot think we're going to find her, then?'

For once, Horseman agreed with his senior officer. 'Indeed, sir. Discretion and reputation rate very highly with Mr Forester.'

'Hmmph. Why did you ignore my calls? I get the news from the Deputy, then I find DC Kau the only one of your team at work …'

'I did ask Kau to explain the situation, sir.'

'Which he did. Then I called you. You didn't answer. I want to know what's happening, Horseman!'

'It was bad luck that when you called, it would have been rude to interrupt my interview, sir. I need to build trust with the High-Com senior staff if we're to find Ms Armstrong. The High Commission compound is technically Australian soil. The Fiji Police hold no jurisdiction there.'

'*Oi lei*, man, aren't they desperate for us to find her?'

Horseman frowned. Although Ratini never lost a chance to goad him with insult and sarcasm, Horseman couldn't deny that once again, his super had put his finger on a key question.

'The diplomats are a bit hard to read, sir. I was surprised at their lack of emotion. Maybe appearing calm and in control is deeply ingrained in them. Unlike Chief Inspector Bob Browning, the AFP officer, who seems straightforward. He could be useful as a direct contact for us on this case.'

'Hmm, *io*, yes—especially as he's working directly with our Deputy Tauvaga on some training project. Well, you talked to a few diplomats. What did they have to say for themselves?'

'No leads for us, except the list of Ms Armstrong's contacts whom they've already called with no positive results. They claim the High Commissioner kept work and leisure separate, as they all do.'

'You don't believe them?'

'I believe they try. They're just hoping Helen will turn up soon so they can continue to keep their diplomatic reserve.'

Ratini shook his head, thinking. 'What else did you do up on the hill?'

''We got statements from everyone who works there, including locals.' He patted his satchel, still hanging over his shoulder. 'Reading these is our next task.'

'Hmmph, give that job to DC Waqa. What about the search?'

'I'm going to step that up right away, sir. Ms Armstrong was last seen 36 hours ago. While we're the Aussies' guests at their High Commission, they're our guests in the rest of Fiji. We have a duty to protect them, and they must not restrict our efforts to find Ms Armstrong. I propose a full-scale media appeal for information, including a public hotline. For that, I'll need more resources, sir.'

Ratini grimaced as he ran a hand inside his shirt collar. 'I brought that on myself, I suppose. I'll see what I can do.'

'Sir, if I could request DI Vula and his team, and DS Taleca, as well as experienced uniforms for the hotline—'

'Don't want much, do you?'

He felt his stomach clench with the stress of staying calm under Ratini's relentless hostility. '*Io*, I want to find the Australian High Commissioner, sir.'

Ratini scowled. 'Leave it with me, man. Go and mount a proper search!'

As Horseman closed the Super's door behind him, he reflected that Ratini was mellowing. Three years ago, when Ratini arrived in Suva from the Western Islands district, he'd gone ballistic whenever he set eyes on Horseman, who still hadn't a clue why. Mystified as he was by the super's bullying, he tried to ignore it, but he didn't always succeed. Singh, his much-missed sergeant, believed Ratini was simply jealous of Horseman's rugby-star popularity. Horseman thought there must be something more.

9

Horseman jogged onto the Albert Park field at half-past five, exactly one hour late for Junior Shiners training. Sergeant Lemeki from Traffic, his reliable deputy coach, had clearly not spared the boys. Divided into Shirts and Skins teams, they were well into the short practice game that ended their training sessions, and many looked like they'd played a full match. As Horseman watched, Pita caught the ball but stumbled as he took off. He managed to pass to Tevita, who fumbled it before accelerating into an average lope for a few metres until Sitiveni brought him down in a tackle. Lemeki blew the whistle. Tevita stayed on the ground, his chest heaving. Sitiveni stood over him, bent double at the waist.

Lemeki and Horseman shook hands. '*Vinaka*, Lemeki. Yet again, I'm sorry I had to ask you to fly solo.'

'No problem, Joe. No matter what division we're in, all police understand what emergencies mean. Any news on the High Commissioner?'

Horseman shook his head. 'Not yet. But the Police Commissioner himself appealed to the public at a news conference an hour ago. They'll show that again on the evening TV news. Our press release didn't make the afternoon papers, but it's the dominant story on the internet news sites and will be the morning headlines tomorrow. Radio stations have talked about not much else since lunchtime. The hotline's been operating for a few hours now. Ratini's come up with some uniforms and extra detectives will join us in the morning.'

'Before training, we prayed for her safe return. What a terrible business!'

'True. You've been working the boys hard, I see. A lot of them have had it.'

'No harder than usual, Joe. They can't summon up their strength this afternoon. In my opinion, the disappearance of the High Commissioner has hit them hard, like a body blow.'

'You think so? I should have realised.'

'You know, Joe, in these rascals' eyes, that lease is a personal gift to them, not a donation to your charity. That lady is their very own saint, an angel who will always look after them. And they feel just as committed to her. That's my theory, anyway.' Lemeki trailed off, embarrassed. He was a hard taskmaster as a coach, but Horseman knew his total reliability over the years spoke of a deep commitment to the boys he called rascals.

'*Vinaka*, Lemeki. You're a better psychologist than me.'

Lemeki bent his head under the assault of praise. 'You see a lot in Traffic, Joe.'

Horseman nodded slowly and muttered, 'True, true.' Then he said, 'The boys are right, you know. I believe Ms Armstrong did regard that land as a personal gift to them. Her challenge was finding a way to help them that met her government's guidelines for aid projects.'

'*Io, io*. We know all about guidelines in the police now, don't we? Used to be called rules, in the days when things were simpler. Well, time to get these lazybones back for their second half!' With that, Lemeki blew two sharp blasts on his police whistle.

The Shiners got their wind back during the break and put on an energetic show for Horseman. This half built to an exciting ending as Tevita intercepted Sitiveni's pass, tossing the ball to Pita, who sped to the try line, throwing off two challengers who hurled their bodies at him. Mosese took his time, teasing out the moment until he kicked an impressive goal from the side to secure a win for the Skins. Sweat trickled down their bodies, despite the freshening breeze. Both teams flung themselves on the grass, rolling like puppies, then raced for the taps to sluice themselves and have a drink.

As they made their way back to their coaches, Horseman thought about what he would say to them, especially with Lemeki's words in his mind.

'Junior Shiners, you pulled yourselves together well just now. You showed me that even when you're tired, you can concentrate and work well with your teammates. Great goal, Mosese! Well done, Shiners!'

Cheers and hoots erupted, but less raucously than usual.

'We were all shocked when the Australian High Commissioner, Ms Armstrong, didn't turn up to open your hostel yesterday. She would have been there if she could. We're worried because she still hasn't returned to her home and we don't know why. Her friends and the police are searching for her. You'll see her picture on TV and in the papers and hear about the search on the radio. If you saw Ms Armstrong anywhere on Saturday, Sunday or today, put up your hand. Think carefully.'

Pita's hand shot up. '*Io*, I saw her on Saturday afternoon, coach. Driving her nice white Mercedes past the market. That car stands out, man. I waved but she didn't see me.'

Groans broke out and calls of 'Man, as if she'd notice you!', 'Why didn't she stop?', and other witticisms. Tevita laughed out loud. 'You hitched a ride from Ms Armstrong? Unbelievable, Pita!'

Horseman smiled indulgently. '*Vinaka*, Pita. That's good information. Anyone else? No? Remember, we are worried Ms Armstrong may have had an accident and can't get home. You can help her by keeping your eyes open. If you see her, please come to see me or Sergeant Lemeki at our station.'

'What about Apo and Tanielo?' The Shiners looked up to Horseman's young DCs, who also volunteered as assistant coaches.

'*Io*, you can ask for them, too. They couldn't come to training today because they're working on the search.'

'We'll search very hard, Joe!' Tevita shouted.

'No, boys. I don't want you to search for Ms Armstrong. That's our job, the police. I want you to keep your eyes open, notice what's around you. If you see something related to Ms Armstrong, come and tell us without delay.'

'*Io*, Joe.'

The boys ran off to set up the trestle table for the post-training snacks. Their own team physician, Dr Pillai, had provided a substantial meal after training since the squad got going, but now that the hostel was a reality, the boys in most need would go back to their new home for dinner. So last Thursday, the dinners had changed to snacks of milk and fruit.

Dr Pillai kept watch at the trestle table as the older boys handed a carton of milk and a couple of oranges to each boy. He beamed at Horseman as he approached. 'They're all here again, Joe.'

'*Io*, another good decision of yours, Doctor.' Horseman looked down at Dr Pillai's luxuriant thatch of coarse black hair.

Dr Pillai was nothing if not self-effacing. 'Oh no, goodness me, Joe. We're exactly on the same page about this.' The two men, one tall and solid, the other short and thin, watched their protegés sprawled on the grass in threes and fours, peeling their oranges and slurping their milk to the sound of relaxed talk and laughter.

'I don't think any of them are seriously worried about Ms Armstrong,' Dr Pillai said.

'No, they're still just boys,' Horseman agreed.

'It looks like someone wants to talk to you, though. A colleague? Oh, I see now—someone much more important.'

<h1 style="text-align:center">10</h1>

Horseman turned around. Although the man approaching must have been heavily muscled and fit in his youth, in middle age he had run to fat, like many senior police officers. However, Ratu Usaia Tuilau was the revered President of the Fiji Rugby Union. He'd been invited to the hostel opening but had declined politely.

After exchanging greetings, Horseman introduced Dr Pillai, then looked up at Ratu Usaia.

'May I introduce the Junior Shiners training squad, Ratu?'

'Delighted, Joe, delighted. I was sorry I couldn't make your opening yesterday. Looking forward to seeing the High Commissioner again, too. What a dreadful business!

'*Io*, it is. We've mounted a full-scale search, so ...'

'*Io*, a matter of time, eh? But how much time has the unfortunate lady got? However, I know you're doing everything possible. I assume you'll be returning to the station after training?'

'*Io*, Ratu. I slipped out to catch the last half-hour. The boys need to know they can rely on me.'

The chief lifted his eyebrows in agreement. 'That's wise, they need heroes more than most. But now you're out, I wonder if I might detain you for another half-hour or so?'

Horseman worried about what the 'or so' entailed. He really must get back.

'You have to eat, Joe. How about we stroll across the road to the Grand Pacific Hotel and eat some pizza, or whatever you like? We won't have to wait long. There's a matter I'd like to discuss with you, even though this may not be the best time. But when would be the best time? Unfortunately, increasing crime in our islands means you're perpetually stretched.'

Horseman knew Ratu Usaia would get instant service. Anyway, how could he refuse?

'*Vinaka*, I'd be delighted, Ratu. As you say, CID is always busy.'

'Good. Now, will you please introduce your team, whom I've heard so much about?'

A few of the boys had recognised Ratu Usaia and everyone knew their visitor was not only the Fiji Rugby Union boss but also a chief by the time Horseman stepped forward. As one, the boys sat on the ground and clapped in a show of respect. Horseman raised his hands for silence, but before he could speak, Ratu Usaia stepped forward.

'It's my honour to meet you today, my friends. Many of you are growing up without the love and support or even the knowledge of your families, your clans and your chiefs. But you've shown you're tough, you're survivors, and now, under the tutelage of Inspector Horseman, Sergeant Lemeki, your assistant coaches, and the care of your team physician, Dr Pillai, you are showing you can also be winners. I congratulate and salute you!'

Unusually for a chief, Ratu Usaia kept his address short, but Horseman knew this visit from the pinnacle of Fiji rugby would lift the boys' morale sky high.

***

Ratu Usaia must have notified the hotel of his order, as a waiter immediately showed them to a secluded table on the waterfront terrace. The south-easterly breeze cooled Horseman down after his anxious day, rustling the palm fronds just enough to isolate them from the close-packed tables around the pool. The sinking sun reminded him that this day, like all others, would soon glide into the past.

Another waiter brought Fiji Bitters, the glasses already running with condensation. Horseman decided not to press the glass to his face in front of the chief. As they clinked glasses and toasted the Junior Shiners, he felt himself relax.

Again, it was as if the chief had read his mind. 'No matter how vital the task, Joe, you'll do it better if you take a moment or two to relax.'

'I've always been unable to relax until the game is over.'

'Well, this game could be a longer one. You must conserve your energy and that of your team, too.'

'*Io*, you're right, Ratu Usaia. Of course.'

'I'll come to the point, Joe. Have you heard that Owen Jones, our national coach, has decided to return to Britain at the end of his contract next year?'

'No, I haven't. What a loss he'll be.'

'*Io*, he had a stellar career on the field and he's proved to be a fine coach. He quickly adapted his approach to our conditions in Fiji and our culture. His family settled in well and they've loved their five years here. However, his parents are ageing, his children are in high school already, and he feels it's the right time to return to his native land, Wales. We, who prize our links to our islands so highly, can only agree that he has made the right decision for his family.'

'I wish he could stay on for the World Cup, though. Our national teams have upped their game under him, last year especially. Both Sevens and Fifteens. Owen's done more than train the boys—their spirit seems stronger, too.'

'I agree, Joe. I'm pleased you've noticed. Because that spirit is so vital, but can be quite fragile. We need Owen's successor to nurture that.'

The waiter placed a wooden platter between them. The spicy, cheesy aroma set Horseman's salivary glands into overdrive. He swallowed. The waiter cut the pizza, sliding two pieces onto each plate. A colourful garden salad came next. 'Enjoy your meal!' the waiter said cheerfully.

Horseman waited, head bowed. Would the chief want to say grace? He did, but like earlier, kept his words brief.

'You and the Board have a tough job ahead of you, then,' Horseman said.

'Well now, Joe, that depends. We've selected our first choice, and if he accepts, our job is done.'

Horseman swallowed before he spoke. 'Great news! Dare I ask who you've chosen?'

The chief chewed slowly, as if considering the question. 'You may indeed. The entire board agreed to offer the position to you, Joe.'

Horseman spluttered, almost ejecting his mouthful. Hastily, he reached for his beer and took some cautious swallows.

Ratu Usaia gave him a benign smile. 'Take it easy, man. We can't have you choking to death before you've even started.'

'Ratu, I never imagined such an honour. You know I returned to the police force more than five years ago. My only coaching has been with the Shiners; my only international experience during that time has been as a TV spectator.'

'Joe, I understand our invitation comes as a shock. This may not surprise you, but the Board members have examined your qualifications for the position minutely. Not only yours but also those of a few others on our short list. And having done that, we agreed that you are the man most likely to lead our teams to even greater heights. Remember, there are a couple of years until the next World Cup.'

'*Vinaka vakalevu*, Ratu Usaia. I'm shocked and overwhelmed. I don't suppose you'll be surprised if I say I need time, perhaps considerable time, to decide if I'm up to the job. Not to mention whether I should abandon my commitment to the Force. Criminal investigations are rather like rugby matches in a way.'

'No doubt you have promotion ahead of you in the Force. We understand this will be a big decision for you. Eat up now. You've got an international emergency to get back to. Don't let me cause any delay in finding the Australian High Commissioner.'

Horseman finished his pizza and beer while he listened to Ratu Usaia expound on what the new coach should prioritise, in his humble opinion, of course. The instant Horseman wiped his mouth on his starched linen napkin and placed his knife and fork together on his plate, the waiter swooped in and cleared their table.

Ratu Usaia bent to his briefcase and withdrew a buff foolscap envelope, which he handed to Horseman. The contents were bulky. 'Here is the Board's offer, Joe. Tied up with red tape and complete with details of your duties, remuneration, terms and conditions, etc, etc. Naturally, there's room for negotiation about most of these items, except for the coach's duties. When you've had time to go through it all carefully and think about it, give me a call and I'll try to answer your questions informally. That should be more successful than handing over negotiations to the lawyers, don't you think?'

TUESDAY 17th July

11

Horseman mounted the stairs to the detectives' floor and regarded his busy team with pleasure and a certain amount of pride. With the extra uniforms working the public hotline, and the cables bundled around the hastily assembled carrels where the telephone operators worked, the room was packed. Kau and Waqa had done well to reserve space for the detectives in the corner furthest from the banks of phones, marking the boundary with cabinets that normally stood against the walls. They enclosed one table, six folding chairs, a tea trolley with a computer and peripherals. A phone sat on top of one filing cabinet and a tray with tea-making things on another.

Horseman squeezed past the whiteboard forming part of the improvised office walls. Lili Waqa plonked the open case file on the table just as the newest recruit, probationary DC Isireli Pareti, entered bearing a tray with a steaming aluminium teapot, milk, sugar, mugs and spoons.

Pareti nodded to Horseman and smiled. '*Yadra*, sir. Would you like tea before we begin, or later?'

'*Yadra* Izzy. Haven't you learned yet that detective constables must multi-task? Whatever the job in hand, you must be able to drink tea at the same time! So, we'll have tea during our review meeting to give you more practice. Oh, by the way, DC Pareti, see if you can book us a car for the day.'

DC Kau set his mug on the filing cabinet abutting the whiteboard while he led off with the limited facts about the Australian High Commissioner's disappearance. Helen's official photo in the middle of the board shocked Horseman. She was businesslike in her jacket and collared blouse, her round, smiling face friendly and open. But as the head of a diplomatic mission, she must keep many secrets.

Just as Kau rapped his marker on the board, a head popped around, followed by a body untidily dressed in a faded polo shirt missing a button and rumpled cargo pants. Superintendent Ratini had favoured them with his presence.

'*Yadra* all. Started yet?'

Horseman stood. '*Yadra*, sir. We're just about to start now. Will you join us?'

'*Io*, I will. This situation gets more desperate by the hour. I need the latest.'

'Would you like a cup of tea, sir?' DC Pareti asked, lifting the teapot.

Supplied with tea, Superintendent Ratini signalled to Kau to begin.

Given that Ratini had just transformed the friendly review meeting into a nerve-racking assessment task, Kau performed well. He identified Ms Armstrong's principal colleagues and outlined her known appointments, both official and recreational, in the days before her last sighting on Saturday and her failure to attend the opening of Junior Shiners House on Sunday afternoon.

'So, how well do you know this lady, Horseman?' Ratini asked, a sneer lurking in his voice.

As usual, Horseman pretended he was unaware of Ratini's innuendo.

'We're well acquainted. She approached our charity to explore ways Australia could help with the hostel project. Between then and the signing of our lease nine months ago, I met her quite often, but I don't know her personally at all.'

'Aha, you've got your feet under the dining table at the High Commission now, have you?'

Horseman smiled. 'Just once or twice, sir. Her Excellency invited the Foundation's board members to lunch at her residence following the signing of the lease.'

Ratini frowned while slurping his tea. 'You see, and here I'm addressing all of you, especially the junior detectives, you must take great care to avoid investigating people you have strong connections with. Difficult in many islands where everyone knows everyone, but it should be possible in Suva. Horseman, have you considered whether you're too close to Ms Armstrong to keep an open mind?'

'*Io*, sir. I've formed a favourable impression of Ms Armstrong during our meetings, but we're not friends. My determination to find her may have an extra edge because of our acquaintance, but I believe that's a benefit.'

Ratini's brow furrowed again. Eventually, he said, 'Okay, then, I'll leave you on as Senior Investigating Officer. Anyway, DI Vula's committed to the drug importation case that seems to be going nowhere fast, just chewing up good officers. Mind how you go, though. Well, where are you up to? Anything from the hotline?'

Horseman nodded to Kau, who pointed to the timeline on the board. 'Callers have reported sightings later than this, sir, but none have been substantiated so far, or even reported by more than one person. We can rule out some, like the man who said he saw her in the back seat of a limousine passing through the gates of the President's residence at three o'clock on Sunday morning.'

The constables laughed. Ratini rubbed his unshaven chin and smirked. 'Needs checking, Constable.'

'*Io*, sir. We've checked. The guards on duty reported no one entered after the President returned from the Bastille Day ball at half-past eleven when the gates were shut. The guards on the next shift opened them at nine o'clock to admit the President's physical therapist.'

Ratini wagged his head back and forth. 'Well, that will do for now, I suppose. I agree it's not enough for a search warrant on the President's house. What are your plans for the rest of the day, Horseman?'

'We're going to finalise them at this meeting, sir. What I propose is to continue to monitor all medical centres, initiate follow-up with all police stations and posts on their search efforts and continue to check all hotline calls. Public relations will continue to issue releases to all the media.'

'Goes without saying, man. Did anything come out of your day at the High Commission yesterday?'

'Two for immediate follow-up, sir. Both came from Ms Armstrong's official diary. Today she had an appointment with Dr Sergei Orlov, a computer scientist at the University of the South Pacific.

He's not on the list of acquaintances her colleagues gave us, so he hasn't been called yet. Looking back in the diary, Ms Armstrong also met Dr Orlov a few weeks ago. Before I go to see Dr Orlov, I'll ask Ms Armstrong's colleagues what these meetings were about.'

'Hmm, and the other?'

'Two weeks ago, an entire afternoon was ruled across and the single name Joshua was written in capitals. I'll also see if the staff can identify this individual.'

'That's it?' Ratini turned these two innocent words into a damning evaluation.

DC Waqa raised her hand, her face eager. 'Sir, I've summarised the High Commission staff statements in a table if you're interested.'

'Excellent work, DC Waqa. Any potential leads out of that?'

'Sir, after what DI Horseman has just said, maybe yes. One colleague who was at the Bastille Day ball said she hadn't seen Ms Armstrong there. She wondered if the High Commissioner actually attended.'

'Really? Interesting. Well, you'd better get on with it and good luck! Report to me at the end of the day, Horseman.'

'I will, sir.'

After Ratini left, Izzy Pareti made another pot of tea while Horseman produced a packet of Paradise Biscuits' most popular product, Coconut Creams. The team's mood changed from anxious to cheerful in an instant.

'Well done, Apo and Lili,' Horseman said. 'Superintendent Ratini put you on the spot and you rose to the occasion. He's also sped up our meeting, even if it wasn't so convivial. Lili, have you got that statement from the Bastille Day guest handy?'

'*Io*, sir. Two full pages of details.'

'Like a gossipy interviewee, she could be invaluable.'

'There's another I remember who mentioned the name Joshua, sir. I didn't think much of it until you mentioned the name in Ms Armstrong's diary just now. I hope I wrote it down.'

'Really? Sounds promising. Then you and I will go and surprise the High-Com again, and then on to USP. Apo, you'll be in charge of the hotline follow-ups. Get Izzy to help you. Call me if any news comes in. While you're setting all that up, let's finish the tea and biscuits.'

12

Lili bubbled with excitement as they drove up the hill to the white walls of the Australian High Commission compound, draped with purple bougainvillea.

'Just think, sir, if I hadn't taken those statements, we mightn't have paid much attention to the mention of Joshua in the diary. Especially as that was two weeks ago when Ms Armstrong allocated him a whole afternoon. I wonder who he is?'

'Well done, Lili, you've got an impressive memory. A second mention of Joshua makes the lead more promising.'

'DI Singh taught me how to sort and tabulate a pile of statements, and that's so useful I'll never forget that. She taught me so much else, too.' Lili glanced at Horseman, grinning.

Horseman was surprised by a twinge of resentment—hadn't he imparted as much as Singh to the three successive probationers? He dismissed the unworthy feeling. He had to admit her instruction was more regular, more consistent and more direct than his own more intuitive methods. And anyway, how could he possibly feel envious of Singh, his former sergeant and friend, whom he'd missed every day since her promotion and move to Labasa? She deserved all the honour and respect that the DCs held for her, and more. Perhaps it wasn't envy he felt, but guilt that he had let Singh go. But she had every right to choose where she went. He was never sure of emotions, and he certainly didn't trust them. It was evidence that he could handle best. So far, there was no evidence to speak of regarding Helen's disappearance. With each passing minute, her safety was more doubtful.

They approached the reception desk, today staffed by an equally well-groomed but much younger woman than Losana. To Horseman, she looked like a high school kid in her starched white shirt. Her ponytail was immaculate, and her wide smile revealed even white teeth. They presented their credentials.

'Good morning, officers, I'm Kirin. Losana said you might be coming,' she said. 'I'll just let her know you're here.'

'No need to interrupt her, Kirin. I should have a word with Mr Forester first, if he's available.'

'I'm afraid he's not here at the moment. Is there any news of the High Commissioner?' Horseman shook his head as she picked up the phone, pressed a single button and murmured into the mouthpiece. In a moment, Losana emerged from the inside office, looking fresh in a bright patterned *bula* shirt and white skirt.

She was polite but grave. 'I gather there's no news, Inspector?'

'No. Is there anything from your end?'

'I fear not. Just hearing the police appeals in the media drums it in. I think we're all accepting at last that something serious has happened to Her Excellency. Forgive us if it seemed we didn't take you seriously yesterday.' Her mouth turned down, and her eyes filled with tears.

Horseman smiled. 'We both understood you were in shock, and living off hope. We're all still expecting Ms Armstrong will turn up. There's no need to apologise, Losana.'

Losana nodded, then managed to speak. 'Please come into my office, and I'll do everything I can to help you. I suppose Kirin told you Mr Forester isn't here.'

'Yes, she did.'

'Would you like tea or coffee, Inspector?'

'*Vinaka*, nothing at all. We've had a few cups of tea at the station already.' They sat at Losana's small conference table. Horseman showed Losana the photocopied page from Helen's diary with today's appointment with Dr Orlov pencilled in.

'Oh yes, I've rung Dr Orlov already. Of course, he's heard about the search for Ms Armstrong, so he'd already decided not to come.'

'The meeting was here, then?'

'Yes. If meetings are in Ms Armstrong's suite, we don't write a place in the diary.'

'I'd be grateful for Dr Orlov's direct number, if you've got it.'

'Certainly, just a moment, please. Here we are— his direct line at USP and his mobile number.' She wrote the numbers on her own business card and handed it over.

'Another favour please, Losana, and we'll be on our way. I don't want to disturb Mr Forester while he's in a meeting, so could you tell me when he's likely to be back?'

Losana consulted her computer screen, squinting a little as she scrolled. 'I'm not sure, his diary doesn't say, but he has an appointment for lunch. He's taking over as many of Ms Armstrong's appointments as he's able to.' Her eyes welled again.

'I understand. Don't worry about it.'

Losana brightened a little. 'Don't hesitate to leave a message for Mr Forester on his mobile, Inspector. His phone will be on silent if he can't answer it, so you won't be interrupting him. I know he'll want to help you.'

'*Vinaka*, Losana, I'll do that. We may see you later today.'

'Good luck! I'll call you when Mr Forester returns in case you don't hear from him.'

As they went down the steps, DC Waqa was frowning. 'What's the matter, Lili?' Horseman asked.

'I expected we'd be chasing up the identity of Joshua, sir.'

'If Mr Forester had been available, we would. I had to think on my feet. Perhaps Joshua's like a codeword for a project or person that Helen was involved with unofficially. If that's the case, Mr Forester may not take kindly to us bandying the name about with the local office staff.'

They got into the car. Waqa turned to him, eyebrows raised in disbelief. 'You mean something top secret, like spies?'

'I guess it doesn't seem likely, but it's possible. Rightly or wrongly, I decided that was a matter to raise with the First Secretary. We'll see him later today. I'll leave a message for him now.'

Waqa's eyes rounded with anticipation.

13

Dr Sergei Orlov chose to meet the detectives at his house on campus. It was one of about a dozen semi-detached bungalows housing single academic staff. Each unit had only one bedroom, but an extra-spacious living room and study made them desirable, especially as the rent charged by the university was half that of the private market in Suva. Academics on the waiting list frequently served their contracts and returned to India, New Zealand or America before reaching the top of the list. Dr Orlov was lucky. Horseman wondered how long he'd been on the staff.

It was always a pleasure to drive through the main campus gates, following the winding drive through the former botanical gardens dotted with low-rise buildings. The temperature dropped several degrees beneath the huge overhanging figs and banyans, which in their maturity formed a canopy over damp gullies of vines and ferns. Towering royal palms bordered the formal grass quadrangle, like a tropical version of medieval cloisters.

Horseman pulled up at Unit 23, overhung by flowering pink frangipani trees, whose sweet scent wafted over them as they got out of the car.

Dr Orlov waited at his open door. He was short and wiry, with a greying wispy goatee, narrow blue eyes and hair pulled back in a ponytail. Probably in his forties. He scrutinised Horseman carefully as they shook hands, merely nodding at DC Waqa.

'Come in, please. I cannot believe what I read in the papers about Helen. Do you know now where is she, please?'

'I'm sorry, we haven't found her yet, Dr Orlov.' They went into the spartan living room and sat on frayed cane armchairs beneath a whirring ceiling fan.

'Please call me Sergei. Helen has sat here often to discuss her project. I refuse to accept she just vanished.' Dr Orlov's voice was deep, with a marked Russian accent which Horseman found pleasant.

'The police are conducting a systematic search, Dr Orlov. We don't believe Ms Armstrong just vanished either. Let's cut to the chase. Have you got any ideas about where she could be?'

'None. Believe me, I would tell you if I knew.'

'Were you at the Bastille Day Ball on Friday night?'

Dr Orlov's mouth twitched. 'No, I don't get invited to Embassy balls, and would not go even if I were.'

'How long have you known Ms Armstrong?'

'About two years. The Vice-Chancellor was in discussions with the Australian authorities about a major donation to develop the university's IT capacity. Most people interpret that as computer equipment, but Helen understands that is mere surface cosmetics, although essential, of course. The VC's background is law, so he asked me to sort out several options for a complete upgrade with the High Commission. I imagined they would send some tech expert, but Helen wanted to drive this project herself. She usually had a young IT specialist with her and sometimes deferred to him, but she had a broad understanding of both our deficiencies and options for redress. Most of all, she was determined to plan an aid project that would solve our real problems.'

'Out of interest, what is the project about?'

'Essentially, improving communication between all twelve of our member countries: from the Marshall Islands in the north to Tonga in the south, from the Solomons in the west to Cook Islands in the east. USP has its own satellite to deliver classes to students, but the IT capacity of the small member countries is limited. But you are well aware of all this—I heard you were a student here?'

'Yes, but I decided I'd made the wrong choice. I joined the police a year short of completing my degree.'

Dr Orlov shot him a speculative glance and said nothing.

Horseman attempted to get the meeting back on track. 'What did you recommend to Ms Armstrong?'

'Oh, yes. We're depending more and more on the internet, even in the Pacific islands. Our first giant leap in speed and connectivity came some years ago when Australia allowed us to plug in to their undersea cable to the States. That cable is about to be duplicated. The additional one has multiplied capacity, and Fiji needs access too. It's not quite as simple as it sounds and very costly, but Helen saw the necessity and told her government so.'

'That makes sense.'

'I can't go into details. The proposal is nearly ready now. Helen consults me about minor adjustments coming from the Australian government departments involved.'

'The details don't concern us, Dr Orlov. You probably got to know Ms Armstrong pretty well after numerous meetings over two years.'

'Yes, somewhat. We worked together well, were on the same page, as she used to say. I must say, she has an easy personality—I guess that's essential for a diplomat. I was suspicious at first, but she won my trust over time.'

'Why were you suspicious of her?'

Dr Orlov's mouth twisted wryly. 'Huh! Because I am Russian, Inspector. Experience has ingrained in us a deep distrust of government officials.'

'I always find that when I work with someone over an extended period, like you have with Ms Armstrong, I get to know them personally. Did you meet her on social occasions also?'

Again, the wry smile. 'If you're implying a romantic involvement, the answer is no. I'm not attracted to older women, not even attractive and clever ones like Helen. However, I did attend the occasional cocktail party and lunch at her residence to celebrate milestones in the project. She was hospitable, and I got the sense she enjoyed what were really working meetings.'

DC Waqa, busy with her notebook, looked up. 'Who was present at these parties, sir?'

Dr Orlov, who'd been addressing himself exclusively to Horseman, looked at her, surprised.

'Why do you want to know?'

Horseman let Waqa answer for herself.

'Sir, until we find the High Commissioner, we must contact every person who was in contact with her recently, no matter how slight.

However, guests at her residence qualify as more than slight contacts.'

'Wouldn't her own staff be a more reliable source for guest lists?' He shrugged dismissively. 'Well, if you insist, the last occasion was more than a month ago. Going by my vague memory, the VC was there with his wife and someone from his office, along with Professor Prasad, who's head of our IT department, the Bursar, and several High Commission staff, including the First and Second Secretaries and an IT specialist from Canberra. Most were accompanied by spouses, which seems to be the critical factor designating a meeting *social* rather than *working*. Believe me, they're all *working*.'

'Thank you. Was there anyone present not from USP or the High Commission?'

'Interesting negative question. Not that I can remember.'

Horseman sensed a slight softening in Dr Orlov's attitude. 'Whether working or social, did you ever meet anywhere else?'

The academic was silent. Was he dredging his memory or deciding whether to tell what he knew?

'I don't think—but wait. It's more than a year ago now, but Helen did invite me one Sunday afternoon to go sailing on her yacht. I guess she intended it as a team-building exercise, or some such management-speak. Just within the reef, but I found it very exciting, as I had never been sailing before.'

Horseman avoided exchanging glances with Waqa. 'I've never tried sailing, but I'd love to. I imagine it's exhilarating.'

'Indeed, it is. Lots of urgent action and shouting to change the boat's direction. Yet it's peaceful too, with no engine sound, just the wind in the sails. I was sorry Helen didn't invite me a second time, but that afternoon was special. Alex, her ex-husband, was visiting and he was at the wheel much of the time. He did use the motor to manoeuvre out of the marina. Then Helen and someone from the High Commission raised the sails, Alex cut the motor, and Joshua took us far from the cares of the world.' Dr Orlov smiled at Horseman, warm with nostalgia.

'Sounds like a special memory. Is Joshua on Ms Armstrong's staff?'

'Oh no, Inspector. *Joshua* is the name of Helen's yacht.'

Horseman tried to hide his astonishment. 'Ah, I see. Did you leave from the Royal Suva Yacht Club?'

'I suppose so. There's only one yacht club here, isn't there? I didn't know it was royal.'

14

Horseman thumped the steering wheel. 'Good God, Lili, why didn't they tell us at the High Commission that Helen had a yacht? And that her ex-husband was around somewhere? That's pretty basic information.' Although overjoyed at the revelation, he couldn't understand why none of her colleagues had suggested that Helen might have gone to her yacht.

'It's still possible *Joshua* is a code word, though, isn't it? That would explain why no one's mentioned it.'

'Possible but not likely. That afternoon blocked out in her diary probably means she was just doing some work on the boat, or seeking some quiet time away from the compound.' Horseman pulled out his mobile. 'Let me check if Forester's replied to my message.' He glanced at his messages. 'No, nothing. I'll call him again.'

Horseman left another message when Forester didn't pick up the call once again, then started the car.

'Lili, I can't leave this. I'll go back to the High-Com. There'll be someone senior I can talk to without putting the office staff on the spot. You take the car, pick up Apo at the station and go to the yacht club. Find out if the *Joshua* is berthed there. I imagine the manager would keep keys for their resident boats—if so, take a look. If not, take a look at the outside and find out what you can.'

'Aye, aye, sir!' Lili beamed and continued to do so the entire journey, even while radioing DC Kau. Her frank enjoyment of the chase reminded Horseman of Singh, but so far Lili lacked her mentor's relish for cat-and-mouse interviewing tactics. Maybe that would come with more experience.

When Horseman pulled up, she dashed around the car and was waiting to take over the wheel before he got out. As he climbed the steps, he was still racking his brains about those strange omissions in what Helen's colleagues had told him. How many more were there, and why? Only one way to find out, but he must play the diplomat himself, not a role that came naturally.

Kirin was behind the reception desk again and looked up eagerly at him. 'Have you any news, sir?'

'I'm afraid not yet, Kirin. We just checked with the station. There's a big team working on this, following up every call on the hotline. We'll find her. I wanted to speak with Mr Forester, but I understand he's not back. I need to speak to one of Ms Armstrong's close colleagues as soon as possible. Is Lt Connolly in, or the Second Secretary?'

'Please take a seat while I check, Inspector. Would you like to help yourself to some water from the dispenser over there?'

Horseman followed Kirin's polite ruse to get him out of earshot while she made her calls. But at his first sip of ice-cold water, he realised how thirsty he was and downed two cupfuls at the dispenser before retreating to the visitors' seating with a refill in hand. He put it down when Lt Connolly walked in.

'Good afternoon, Inspector. I'm sorry to hear you still don't know what's happened to Ms Armstrong. Let's talk in my office. Bring your water, but would you like tea or coffee?' He detected a note of accusation in her voice.

He remembered the excellent coffee he'd had here yesterday. 'Thank you, Lieutenant. Coffee, if I may.'

'Please call me Pat. Follow me, please.'

Lt Connolly's office lacked a conference setup. She sat behind her desk, waving an open palm to the chair opposite.

'Have you thought of any more of Ms Armstrong's acquaintances to contact, or any more places she might have gone to?' Horseman asked.

'None at all.'

'I talked to Dr Sergei Orlov this morning at USP. He told me that just over a year ago, he went sailing on Ms Armstrong's yacht, *Joshua*. Among the crew was her former husband, Alex.'

'That could well be true. I wasn't there.'

Kirin came in with a tray of coffee things, which she placed on Pat's desk. Again, wrapped warm scones leaked their aroma into the air. Horseman wondered if they baked scones on the premises every morning and, if so, why weren't all the staff overweight.

'Thanks, Kirin. We'll serve ourselves.' The naval attaché seemed perfectly calm as she poured coffee.

'Pat, until an hour ago, the police had no idea that Ms Armstrong had either a yacht or a former husband.'

'Really? As far as I know, Ms Armstrong's ex-husband is in Australia, so what could he have to do with her disappearance?'

'Nevertheless, he's someone we need to talk to. Can you give me his details, please?'

Lt Connolly looked down in confusion. 'Well, his details must be somewhere, possibly on Helen's file. I have no authority to look at that. I imagine Losana may be able to supply that information to you. All I know is his name is Alex.'

'And her boat, *Joshua*?' Surely Helen had invited her new naval attaché for a sail.

'Ah, a beautiful 36-footer. It's actually the *Joshua Slocum*, named after the first man to sail alone around the world—that was in the late 1890s, can you imagine? I've been sailing with Helen often, out beyond the reef where you feel free as a bird. And there are plenty of those.'

'I don't understand why you didn't tell us. She might have gone there, don't you think? After the noisy ball, for some solitude?' He heard resentment in his voice and stopped.

'Well, it's just possible, I suppose.' Lt Connolly's tone was doubtful. 'But Ms Armstrong is not an impulsive teenager. She's a safety-conscious, experienced sailor who would never take out her boat in the middle of the night.'

'She may not have been alone,' Horseman said before he realised he shouldn't share his thoughts with Lt. Connolly. Either she was not prepared to share her own, or she was unimaginative.

He spread half a scone with jam, topped it with cream and took a bite. Heaven.

Lt Connolly looked relaxed as she sipped her coffee. 'I should mention that, as far as I know, Helen hasn't taken the yacht out for a few months. The engine's unreliable and needs a major overhaul, apparently. She was trying to find someone she could trust to do the job. Sometimes, the wind's just right so that you can manoeuvre the boat out of the berth under sail, but not very often. As I said, Helen's a cautious, safety-conscious sailor, so she prefers not to take the risk of damaging her own or neighbouring yachts.'

'Is it possible she may have wanted to spend some solitary time at peace in the yacht's cabin?'

Lt Connolly grinned. 'Peace? You won't find that at the yacht club on a Saturday night. There's a bunch of serious drinkers there that get louder and louder as the night wears on. Some can get obnoxious. That's not Helen's scene at all.'

'Do you know where the boat's keys are kept?'

'No.'

Horseman forced a smile. 'You'll appreciate, Lieutenant, that our success depends on Ms Armstrong's colleagues and friends telling us everything they know. Don't hold back information that you believe is irrelevant. We need all the facts.'

'I apologise, I didn't think of the yacht.'

Horseman nodded. 'Thanks for the coffee and scone. And of course, for your time. I'll be off now.'

'Good luck again, Inspector.'

He made two quick calls in the corridor, then stopped at reception. 'Is Losana free for a minute or two, Kirin?

Kirin smiled, pressed a button, and Losana emerged in a moment, beckoning Horseman. 'Come in, Inspector.'

They sat in armchairs. 'Losana, I've just found out there was an oversight on the Missing Persons form Mr Forester filled in yesterday. Ms Armstrong's next-of-kin field remains blank. Can you give me that information?'

Losana's face clouded. 'Actually, I don't know who that would be. I'm sorry.'

'Even the High Commissioner must have an employment file. Could you check that, please? Obviously, we should have informed her family, but searching for her took precedence.'

'I understand. The file may be in Canberra. I'll have a word with our own personnel manager here and get back to you, or she may prefer to call you directly. Oh, by the way, Mr Forester apologises, but he has back-to-back meetings all day as he's taking as much of Ms Armstrong's load as possible. He'll call you when he can.'

Horseman stood in the car park, wondering whether to go out to the road to hail a taxi when his phone buzzed. It was DC Kau. 'Sir, Lili and me are here at the yacht club. Security won't let us through to the marina. They say it's all private property, highly valuable, et cetera, et cetera. I explained about the search for the High Commissioner, but they won't budge. I'm pretty sure her boat is moored here—they didn't look surprised when I asked. Can we come and pick you up?'

'No, go back to the station, Apo. A taxi's just pulling up now. Meet you back there.'

15

The Fijian public, or ninety-five per cent of them, recognised Horseman. He was grateful for the interest of discerning rugby fans, but wished he could go about his business as a citizen without being stopped by strangers who wanted to replay games with him. But occasionally, he had no hesitation in using his fame to pursue a case. This was such an occasion.

He approached the glass door of the clubhouse, DC Kau a step behind. The doorman smiled, saluted and opened the door with a flourish.

'Welcome, it's good to see you, Josefa Horseman.' The man wore a name badge.

'I'm happy to be here again, Samuela. It's been a few years, I admit.'

'I can sign you in if you're here for a drink or some lunch or—'

Horseman showed his ID. '*Vinaka*, another day, Samuela. But we're on business today. We're here to inspect a yacht, a permanent mooring here at the marina, the *Joshua Slocum*. We'll require the keys.'

The smile left Samuela's face. 'It would be an honour to assist you, Josefa, but I will have to call the marina security.'

'Fine, we'll get ourselves a glass of water at the bar while you're doing that. I'll pick up a brochure too. I've always wanted to learn to sail. How about you, DC Kau?'

***

Five minutes later, Samuela escorted the two detectives into the club manager's office, where they squeezed past the immense bulk of a khaki-uniformed security guard to sit on two tiny folding chairs. The manager's wary face was marked by dark circles around his eyes.

'Welcome to the Royal Suva Yacht Club, officers. I'm Ajit Patel. How can we assist you?'

'Mr Patel, you'll be aware that the police are searching for the missing Australian High Commissioner. Ms Armstrong has a yacht, the *Joshua Slocum*, berthed at your marina, I believe.'

Mr Patel glanced at the guard. 'Yes, I believe that is so. Is she currently in her berth, Ilai?'

'*Io.*' The enormous guard nodded.

Horseman's smile embraced all three club staff. 'We're here to examine the yacht for evidence to help us find Ms Armstrong. I'd be grateful if you could show us to the boat and open it up for us.'

The guard's jaw stiffened as he glared at Mr Patel.

'My goodness, Inspector, you'll appreciate that security can be a problem for us. Only owners have keys.'

'Really? What happens when a boat gets damaged, whether by accident or malice? Or comes adrift? Or an owner orders maintenance by your tradesmen? Surely management must have keys to attend to emergencies?'

'In these cases, we contact the owners. Club staff may only access boats on direct instructions from the owners.'

'Mr Patel, I understand how careful you must be with your duplicate keys. Your security measures definitely have police approval. However, such a prudent man as yourself will understand how exceptional this case is. Ms Armstrong is the most senior diplomat in Suva, a guest in our country whom we are duty-bound to protect. There could be an international scandal if we fail to find Ms Armstrong fast. This is an emergency where your help may well be vital. What a feather in your cap that would be!'

Mr Patel tilted his head from side to side, considering. Horseman counted to five before bringing out the stick. 'A warrant to search your premises is on the magistrate's desk. There's a backlog, and it probably won't be signed until tomorrow. Please don't make us wait until then. Such action would slow down the official nationwide police search for your most important club member. A police prosecution for obstruction wouldn't help the club's reputation, would it?'

Mr Patel tilted his head again. 'My goodness, I understand now. Ilai will take you to the *Joshua* and open up for you, if he can. Many times, the owners change their padlocks and forget to give us the new key, so we can't carry out their orders anyway. Sometimes the owners tell us to use bolt cutters to gain access. So I can't guarantee the key will work.'

'Then I suggest Ilai brings your strongest bolt cutters to save time, Mr Patel. Just in case someone has changed *Joshua*'s padlock.'

'Yes, Ilai, take the bolt cutters also, please.'

Ilai scowled at them all.

'I appreciate your good sense, Mr Patel. You've made the right decision. We'll wait outside while Ilai gets his tools.'

Horseman wondered about the guard's antipathy. Many security guards were former cops, sometimes earning more than they had on the force. When Ilai reappeared in a few minutes, still scowling, Horseman tried to win him over.

'You've got such a straight back, Ilai, I wonder whether you've got parade-ground training. Maybe the military, or the police?'

'Police, sir.' Ilai turned and led the way to the steel marina gate, inserted a hefty key that resembled one made for a prison, and opened the gate, locking it on the inside after Horseman and Kau had passed through. There was room on the walkway for two abreast, so Horseman kept pace with Ilai.

'A good policeman is always in demand, eh? Did you retire from the force? I have a mate who found his pension couldn't cover his family obligations. He's really pleased to have some private security work, like you.'

Ilai stopped his lumbering walk and looked at Horseman. He panted. 'I don't have a pension, Inspector, that's why I have to work when I'm too old. Some sneak accused me of stealing evidence. I don't know who, or he'd be dead. I denied the charge, but the Board took no notice. How could I actually prove I was innocent? Innocent until proven guilty, my arse! Doesn't apply to internal police investigations, did you know that?'

'What happened, Ilai?'

'They discharged me with a clean record because they couldn't prove anything. But no pension, so I had to get other work. That's a terrible punishment. I'm diabetic, you know.'

'I'm very sorry to hear that, Ilai. I don't want to pry, but what was the missing evidence?'

'Money. Quite a lot. Do I look like I've got thousands of dollars?'

Ilai abruptly turned away and continued plodding along the floating walkway.

'No wonder you don't feel friendly towards the police.'

'It's the injustice that angers me so much,' Ilai muttered, looking straight ahead.

They took a right turn and headed away from the shore. The boats along here were bigger, both sailing yachts and motor cruisers. They must have deeper keels. The breeze was fresher. Horseman couldn't help but enjoy the glittering water, the clanging rigging, the rhythm of the pontoon beneath their feet and the salty smell. And of course, the sleek white boats, trimmed with dazzling metal fittings.

'Here we are,' Ilai said. The single-masted *Joshua Slocum* occupied the second last berth, but the final berth was empty. The hull was dark blue; the cabin was varnished timber that looked overdue for a repaint; the decks were timber, too.

'*Joshua*'s a sound boat, but varnish is an awful choice for superstructure—or anywhere on a boat. You've got to sand back and do it all again every year in the tropics. Looks nice for a short while, though.' Ilai looked and sounded less angry as he gazed at the yacht.

But moments later, his face compressed in grievance again. 'Australian owners, though! What would you expect?'

'What do you mean, Ilai?' Horseman asked.

'More money than sense but mean with it! That High Commissioner could choose a paint that would last five years easy. I told her that, just like the painters did. But she insists on varnish, which needs doing every year. But you know what? She told me she can only afford to get it done every second year, so it looks a mess like now half the time!'

He gestured at the empty berth next to the *Joshua Slocum*. '*Seeker* must have left last weekend when I wasn't working. Now, she's a workmanlike vessel. They do diving charters.' Ilai grabbed a stanchion to step aboard *Joshua* when Horseman laid a hand on his arm.

'*Vinaka vakalevu*, Ilai. I'm sorry, but only DC Kau and I may go on board, as this is an official police search. If you give me the keys, I'll check if they open the hatch padlock.'

Ilai's face froze with offence once more, but he handed a small bunch of keys linked to a yellow float and waited sullenly with Kau, swinging his bolt cutters.

Horseman stepped over the stern rail and into the cockpit. He stepped over coiled ropes and sundry fittings. The cabin hatch had two plywood shutters secured by a heavy-duty brass padlock. He rapped on them and shouted, 'Police! Open up, please!'

He waited, then rapped and called once more.

'How can there be anyone inside if the padlock's locked?' Horseman glanced over his shoulder to see Ilai looking smug, his arms folded over his enormous belly, the handles of his bolt cutters resting against his shoulder like a rifle.

Horseman nodded, while wondering what other shortcuts Constable Ilai may have taken if he favoured entering before knocking. The second key he tried fitted. As he slid the hatch back to pull out the shutters, the unmistakable stench of death hit him. He swallowed with an effort and slid the hatch shut. He returned to the stern rail. Had the others caught a whiff? The breeze was in his face, so maybe not. He raised his voice.

'*Vinaka*, Ilai, we won't need your bolt cutters. The hatch opens easily. I'm sorry, but I'll have to hang on to *Joshua*'s keys, though. I'll need you to let some search officers in and point them in the right direction, if you'd be so good. They could turn up within half an hour and will have police identification. No one else is to enter the marina, even club members.'

'*Io*, Inspector. I can manage that.'

'I'm grateful, Ilai. I'll rely on you.'

Ilai left with a purposeful stride, swinging his bolt cutters. Horseman beckoned Kau on board.

Could he rely on Ilai? He didn't want the media to get hold of the news before the police could make an official announcement. Ilai would be glad of a media gratuity. But he was jumping the gun. What if the smell was rotting cheese or a rat?

16

Horseman slid back the hatch on its runners, lifted out each timber shutter and placed it in the cockpit. The smell made him gag, even when pressing his handkerchief over his mouth and nose. He peered down the steps into the gloom of the cabin, making out a glass on a table glinting in the shaft of light from above.

'I can't see much, Apo. When the stink dissipates a bit, I'll go down and open the curtains, find a light switch.'

Kau dived into his backpack and handed Horseman a torch. 'Be careful, sir. Here's a mask too, if you think it will help.'

'*Vinaka*, probably not, but how can it hurt? How are you?'

'Getting acclimatised, sir. Shall I follow you?'

'Wait till I can see what we've got here.' He shone the torch down the steps. As he swung it to the right, it lit legs in loose black trousers, then swept over a shiny royal blue torso and short grey hair. The woman's pale arms were swollen, her skin shiny, but he knew he was looking at Helen Armstrong, the Australian High Commissioner to Fiji.

For a few moments he stared, unable to move as a great pity surged through him. The torch beam quivered, then shook wildly, and he saw his hands were trembling. He turned off the torch, then took three deep breaths as he gripped the sides of the hatch. But it wasn't the stench of death that made him retch.

He turned around to face an expectant Kau. 'It's Ms Armstrong. Dead some time, I think, although the heat of the sealed cabin may have accelerated the process ... Make the calls for me, please, Apo. Ratini, SOCOs—you know who. I'll speak to Forester at the High Commission when I'm ready, if he ever answers his mobile. Get Lili to contact our Public Relations, put a suppression order on the media until the next-of-kin are notified. God, we don't even know who they are yet; we really slipped up there. I'll call the pathologist now.'

'Right away, sir.' Thoughtful Kau turned away from Horseman to switch on his radio.

'You've got her, Joe?' Dr Matthew Young's unsurprised tone calmed Horseman's jitters a little. He took another deep breath, held it, then exhaled slowly. His old friend dealt with death every day, and none handled it better.

'Yep, I'm in the companionway of her boat at the yacht club, looking down. I know it's Helen, and she's dead. I'm about to go down, open up and have a closer look. How are you placed?'

'Fifteen minutes to close up the current post-mortem, everything else can wait. Any idea if it's suspicious from where you are?'

'No.'

'You've got gloves and bootees with you, just in case?'

'*Io*, Matt. You've trained me well.'

'Under the circumstances, I can't say I'm glad you've found her. I'm sorry, Joe. She was a good woman, wasn't she?'

Horseman nodded and ended the call, unable to speak. Kau was still busy marshalling the troops, but broke off when Horseman tapped his shoulder and dived into the kitbag. Gloves and overshoes would do—he had to survive in the cabin, which would be like an oven. There was a head torch, which he grabbed too. He put them on, went back to the hatch and stepped down backwards. Thanks to the head torch, he avoided what might be a smear of blood on the handrail and a potential reprimand from Ash Jayaraman, the SOCO sergeant. But a wave of dread all but knocked him off his feet again, even though the viscous smear could be lots of things. Jam, for example.

First things first. One step to the desk where a ruler and a greasy spanner lay on top of a sheet of perspex. Beneath the perspex was an open chart of Suva Bay. This must be the navigation table. He leaned over a bevy of small monitors, recognising the chart plotter as he did so. He could reach the curtain and yanked it back, flooding the cabin with light. Swallowing against the horrible reek, he did the same on the other side. Refusing to look at Helen's body, he stepped carefully past her and down two more steps into the forward cabin. Light came from another roof hatch, which he opened wide. The gust of fresh air in his face instantly settled his stomach. He opened the curtains here, too. He could see electric light fittings, but where were the switches? Never mind, it was bright enough for him; the SOCOs could turn on the lights. All seemed in order here, so he returned to the upper cabin where Helen lay.

Opposite the navigation nook was a dinette. A blue-and-white striped cloth covered the table. A wine glass lay on its side, with what looked like red wine spilled on the cloth. There was a plate with cheese that had melted into a puddle. In the galley beside the dinette, the sink held two more plates, some cutlery and a couple of tumblers. A plastic bin on the draining board held food scraps and supermarket packaging. Well, he'd leave that to the SOCOs, but he was satisfied that Helen had shared her last meal with a companion

He could delay no more. He took two more deep breaths and turned from the galley to face his benefactor. She sprawled against the side of the wooden bunk, as if she'd fallen forward, but twisted her head and upper body as she fell. Was she trying to recover her balance or to see her attacker?

She must have come here either before or after the Bastille Day celebration at the Grand Pacific because she was certainly dressed for the ball. He'd never seen her in such a glamorous outfit as these full, shiny silk trousers and loose blue tunic edged with wide bands of glittering sequins. Leaning over, he saw that her half-turned head rested in what must be congealed blood. He'd leave it to Dr Young to lift her head. He couldn't possibly bring himself to touch her if he had any choice in the matter. And thanks to the reliable specialist teams available to detectives in Suva on a weekday during business hours, he wouldn't need to.

He looked around the cabin again, this time for potential weapons. Apart from the spanner, there were tools in a rack at the back of the navigation table and knives in the galley sink, but he resisted the temptation to pick them up. Rotating back to Helen's body, he caught a flash at the end of the bunk. He leaned over and saw it was a beaded satin evening bag wedged between the mattress and the bulkhead. He thought of the SOCOs and left it in place.

He bowed his head and stumbled over a prayer before climbing the steps to the cockpit again. Kau was sitting on the bench writing in his notebook. He looked up at Horseman, his face anxious.

'It could be murder, Apo. Head wound, and there's nothing hard or sharp that I can see that she may have fallen against if she tripped or became dizzy. I guess boat builders take care to avoid that. Where are we at now?'

'Superintendent Ratini exploded, but he thanked me in the end and said he'd divert the uniforms on the hotline to secure the scene. SOCOs and a photographer will be here as soon as they can.'

'Good. I'm ready for some fresh air here under the tarp. Go down to the cabin and look around without touching anything. Come back and tell me what you've noticed, especially anything that could be used as a weapon. The stink's a lot better now.'

DC Kau looked eager and stepped carefully to the companion-way. Horseman also took some notes, much briefer than those of his promising apprentice. When he returned, he listed everything Horseman had noted, except for the evening bag. 'The spanner on the desk is the only potential weapon I could see, sir'

'Chances are it's not what the killer used. He most likely threw the weapon into the sea or took the weapon away with him.'

'Or her, sir,' Kau said with a smile. 'DI Singh always insisted we shouldn't assume murderers were men.'

Horseman smiled too and felt a little better for picturing Singh's upturned mouth and quizzical lift to one eyebrow. '*Io*. Just think of the Champion murders. DI Singh would be proud of you, Apo.'

'Shall I wait at the marina gate, sir?'

'Not yet, I want to check if Ilai's got an alibi. When you hear the story of his dismissal from the Force, his hostile attitude to us is understandable. But he's also got a grudge against Aussies, and especially Helen. He's a person of interest who needs to be eliminated.'

'*Io*, what a weird reason to take against Ms Armstrong! The guy's mad. He could be capable of anything.'

'Let's not jump the gun. He feels humiliated and ignored, and maybe if I can give him some responsibility, he might cooperate. After all, we don't have the keys to the marina gate, so his resentful stonewalling could make life difficult for us. I've asked Ilai to let our team in and keep everybody else out. When the first of our lot arrive, I'll go to the gate and have a chat with Ilai. If I can clear him, he could be useful.'

Kau clenched his jaw. 'The less I have to do with Ilai, the better, sir. What more can we do here?'

'Let's each take one side of the decks, looking for any disturbance.'

The decks seemed shipshape, with the rope ends neatly coiled in spirals and no stray tools lying about. No sign of violent struggles up here. But Horseman was scarcely more qualified to notice whether anything was missing than Kau.

17

At last, Ilai rang to say the SOCO team was at the gate. 'I'll escort them to the *Joshua*, if you like,' Ilai offered.

'*Vinaka*, Ilai, I'd appreciate you staying on guard at the entrance. There'll be more people arriving soon, and I need you there to let them in. Just give the SOCOs directions, I'm sure they'll find us. After I brief Sergeant Jayaraman, I'll come to consult you about security for the scene.'

Horseman turned to Kau. 'Apo, we've both had a shock. As a Shiners volunteer coach, I know you feel like I do about Ms Armstrong. Our benefactor is dead. If she was murdered, we owe it to her to find her killer quickly and calmly. We treat everyone in her circle as a suspect, no matter how unlikely they seem, until a watertight alibi excludes them. I won't rest until we find the culprit.'

'Me neither, sir. I'm with you.' Kau sniffed but his voice was resolute.

The two detectives waved when they saw the search team approaching. Sergeant Ashwin Jayaraman didn't smile, but shook hands firmly with Horseman and Kau.

'What a terrible loss. Unbelievable that such a lady ... but here we all are.' Ash's deep brown eyes shone as he held Horseman's hand. 'I know this one is personal for you, Joe. And for you, too, Kau. We SOCOs always do our best, but for her, we'll give two hundred per cent. Promise!'

Horseman couldn't speak at first, so touched was he by the sincerity of the normally business-like SOCO sergeant, who had never called him by his first name before. Finally, he cleared his throat.

'*Vinaka*, Ash. I know you will.'

Horseman's former DC, Musudroka, now a qualified SOCO officer, also shook hands and patted both Horseman and Kau on the back in a semi-hug. The two other constables stood back, awkward when faced with sentiment by their superiors. One carried a rigid box in each hand, and the other shouldered a long black case the size of a golf bag.

'Well, to work now. What have we got, Inspector?' Ash's tone was brisk.

Horseman surprised himself by relating his observations systematically and briefly.

'You should have limited yourself to shining a torch down the stairs, but I understand, so no reprimand today,' Ash said with a half-smile.

Horseman fished his gloves and overshoes out of his pocket, holding them up in his defence. 'Believe me, you should be kneeling in gratitude that I opened the hatches. The reek nearly knocked me over. These yachts are as good as airtight.'

'Right you are, sir. You're forgiven.'

'Extra uniforms should turn up any minute. How big an area should we cordon off, do you think?'

'Ideally, the whole marina. At least, tape off the gate. I wouldn't mind closing the clubhouse too, but I haven't anything to justify that. Yet. Other than the smell, was there any indication when she died?'

'My guess is Saturday night or Sunday morning. She's all dressed up and was supposed to be at the Bastille Day Ball at the Grand Pacific on Saturday night. So, I think she died either before or after the ball. Look, there's no room in the cabin for me to watch while you work, and I need to talk to the security guard.'

Horseman found Ilai on guard. '*Vinaka* for directing the SOCOs, Ilai. Before we get on to how you can help me here, I've been thinking about what you said back at the *Joshua*. I'm curious about why you seem to dislike Ms Armstrong. It can't really be because of the varnish, I think.'

Ilai narrowed his eyes, then shifted his gaze over Horseman's shoulder. 'She was always friendly to me when I ran into her here. Then I got the idea I should make a new start, go to Australia like one of my nephews. I asked her if she would help me, but she said she had no part in the visa application process. She said the Visa section at the High Commission would help me with advice and the forms. What a liar! Of course she can say who gets a visa and who doesn't. Treating me like an ignoramus!'

'Did you go ahead and apply to migrate?'

'*Io*, my application failed. She was never so friendly after I asked her for help.'

'I understand how disappointed you must have been.'

Ilai stared at Horseman and shrugged. 'Tell me what you want. Who's coming next?' He was not going to confide any more now.

'Dr Young, the pathologist, a police photographer, Detective Superintendent Ratini and some constables, possibly someone from the Australian High Commission. Possibly others. Call me before you let anyone in. Absolutely no media, Ilai.'

'*Io*, I can recognise those bastards. The liars gave me hell, destroyed my life.'

'*Vinaka vakalevu*, Ilai. I'm relying on you.' Would Ilai come to recognise that with a common enemy in the media, Horseman could be his friend? Now they knew Helen had died violently on board the *Joshua*, Ilai's status had changed from an obstructive gatekeeper to a potentially vital witness or maybe a potential suspect. Right now, he must jeopardise Ilai's cooperation by tackling him head-on about his whereabouts last Saturday.

'Ilai, I know you'd prefer me to be direct. If you're going to help us with security here, I'll have to trust you. To do that, you need an alibi for the weekend. You've already said you weren't working here. Where were you and what were you doing?'

Ilai stared for a moment, then pulled himself up straighter. 'I understand, sir. Fortunately, that's easy. I went with my Lami Methodist Church choir to Lautoka for the annual competition there. We performed on Saturday afternoon, attended worship and dinner on Saturday evening. We slept with other choirs on mats in our host church. On Sunday morning, we performed again in the finals and went to service in the afternoon. You can ask anyone!' Ilai beamed with pleasure.

'Sounds wonderful. Congratulations on your success.'

'We didn't win, but yes, we count the finals as success.'

'Very well done! I'd be grateful for the names of your pastor and choir master, Ilai.'

'No problem. I don't like it, but there's no point resenting a cop doing his job properly.'

***

Horseman delegated checking Ilai's alibi to Kau, who set off to Lami Methodist church immediately. But he couldn't delegate reporting to Ratini yet again. He sat in the *Joshua*'s cockpit and took three deep breaths before making the call. Ratini answered immediately.

'Anything new, Horseman?'

'Sergeant Jayaraman and his team are just setting up. Dr Young will be here soon. However, it's likely Ms Armstrong was murdered.'

'How can you say that before the pathologist has seen the body? I fear this impetuous jumping to conclusions precludes you from the job of SIO on this case. Your friendship with the victim is affecting your judgment. This is a national disaster, man! We need absolute caution. We can't afford to make the tiniest mistake!'

'I appreciate the reminder, sir. But Ms Armstrong's body is inside the cabin with a head wound, and the yacht was padlocked from the outside.'

Horseman looked up as Alisi, the photographer, climbed on board. She stepped into the cockpit, patting him on the shoulder in passing.

'I'm coming over to take a brief look at what you're doing there. Lili and Izzy have just left with the extra constables from the hotline.'

Horseman could well do without Ratini's presence, but said, 'Good news, sir. See you soon.'

18

As Horseman turned the corner onto the main walkway, Dr Young appeared at the other end, striding towards them, his face shadowed by his wide-brimmed straw hat. They met and shook hands, Horseman's old friend expressing his condolences with genuine sympathy. Dr Young listened intently to Horseman's summary of what he found in *Joshua*'s cabin.

'Murder sounds probable, mate. I'm obliged to keep an open mind and come to my own conclusions, of course. I'm glad you didn't lift her head.'

'More than my life's worth, Doctor.'

The pathologist raised one eyebrow. 'I've taught you well, then.'

'Matt, I'm in a race with the media on this one. They won't be far behind despite our suppression order. You'll have more dead bodies on your hands if the lunatic fringe releases shots of Helen being carried out. Could you do me a favour and take her away as soon as you can?'

'Great minds, Joe. The mortuary van's already outside. No need for you to kill anyone, mate. I'll ring you when I've finished the post-mortem. You won't want to witness that, I assume?'

'No, I couldn't. As you told me once, you do your job and I'll do mine.'

'Exactly. You mentioned Helen was going to the Grand Pacific on Saturday night?'

'*Io*, the Bastille Day ball.'

'I should tell you I was there myself for a few hours.'

Horseman's jaw dropped. 'Really?'

Dr Young looked down. Could he be nervous? 'Yeah. Gloria asked me along.'

'Gloria Chung from the Shiners House committee?'

The pathologist looked Horseman in the eye. 'The same. I could hardly refuse on the grounds that I wanted to watch the Pacific Cup semi-final on television, could I? Actually, it was fun, and Gloria was in her natural element. Half the fun was watching her enjoy herself.'

Horseman's heart beat faster. 'Did you see Helen there?'

'No, Joe. But that doesn't mean she wasn't. There were hundreds there, in the ballroom, on the roof terrace, outdoors—all masked. And don't go speculating about Gloria, mate. I was helping her out as a friend. We do that for each other occasionally, when invitations include partners. I'll get going to the yacht. See you soon.'

Horseman came to the gate, which Ilai was holding open to admit DC Waqa, probationer DC Pareti and four serious-faced uniforms. He thanked Ilai, then led his extra forces along the walkway until they were out of earshot of the gate.

'*Vinaka* to you all for your part in the search for the Australian High Commissioner. You may be feeling some relief that the search is over. But a tragedy has happened here. Ms Armstrong died on board her yacht at the end of the marina. We hope the pathologist and the SOCOs will be able to tell us how that happened soon.'

The uniforms bowed their heads. One of them crossed himself.

'We haven't been able to get in touch with Ms Armstrong's next-of-kin yet, so there's a media embargo in place. Still, you all know the coconut wireless. Do not admit any reporters. Don't tell anyone about this case, no one at all, not even your family or friends. That's an order.'

'*Io*, sir,' the constables chorused and stood straighter.

'Until we know how she died, we are treating Ms Armstrong's death as suspicious and excluding everyone from the marina. You'll appreciate that this is difficult, as we can't cordon off the water with police tape. DC Waqa will oversee securing the *Joshua Slocum* and its surrounds as far as possible. DC Pareti and three constables are to go with her.'

'Sir, in Lautoka, I once saw a fishing boat at anchor cordoned off with rope and buoys. The buoys had police signs on them, but they turned out to be a navigation hazard in the harbour, so they upgraded the buoys to ones with flashing lights.' The speaker was in his mid-forties, medium height, fit-looking and clearly experienced.

'Sounds like a suitable solution, Constable ...'

'Rosiga, sir. Tomi Rosiga.'

'*Vinaka*, Rosiga. You come with me and DC Waqa to talk to Ilai, the club's security guard. By the way, I want all of you to be extra courteous to Ilai without disclosing anything about the case. He may not like us on his territory, but he's a former cop and we need his cooperation.'

When they got back to the gate, Ilai greeted Horseman with a nod and a half-smile, then nodded to Waqa and Rosiga when Horseman introduced them.

'*Vinaka vakalevu*, Ilai. You're doing a great job directing our personnel. But you can't do it forever, and you can't do it without a break. When does your shift end?'

'Four o'clock. I don't mind helping you until then, Inspector.'

'I would be grateful for your help, Ilai. I'd like Constable Rosiga to guard the marina gate while you take your usual lunch break, and after you finish your shift this afternoon. He'll need a duplicate key. Can you authorise that, Ilai?'

Ilai frowned, his bushy eyebrows flattened in an unbroken straight line. 'You'd better clear it with the manager.'

'*Vinaka*. Before I do that, there's a practical problem I'm sure you can help me with—how to prevent the media, especially TV people, approaching the *Joshua* by boat. Do you ever close water access to the marina, or parts of it? Perhaps when there's maintenance going on.'

Ilai's eyebrows lifted. 'Not really. We close off a section of walkway with portable barriers if necessary.'

'You see, I've never had to do this before. But Constable Rosiga here saw boat access closed off in Lautoka by ropes strung between buoys. The buoys had lights and police warning signs. Do you think we could rig up some similar barrier here?'

'*Oi lei*! What else do you expect of me? We have plenty of polypropylene rope, and we have floating buoys we set up for races. Maybe something could be done. You'd need to ask the manager.'

'*Vinaka*, Ilai. I'll do that right away.'

But just as Horseman opened the clubhouse door, a police car pulled up with a squeal of brakes right at the marina gate. Ilai roared his protest, his meaty hand held up to signal stop. Superintendent Ratini got out of the car.

'What are you doing, man? Want to get yourself mowed down?' Ratini yelled at Ilai.

'Are you blind? Can't you see No Parking in metre-high white letters?'

'Where?'

'On the bitumen underneath your car, idiot! Reverse slowly and park in the public car park beside the drive.'

Ratini fished his ID out of his frayed jeans pocket, thrusting the badge under Ilai's nose. 'Detective Superintendent Ratini, on urgent police business. Who are you?'

Horseman shut the clubhouse door, and he and Waqa retraced their steps to the marina gate.

'*Bula*, Horseman, what's going on?'

'All going according to plan, sir. Ilai here has been efficient in admitting the accredited crime scene personnel, who are all now at work on the High Commissioner's yacht, *Joshua Slocum*. I'm not satisfied with the security of the marina from the water, as a keen reporter could easily get photos from a dinghy.'

'Bastards, the lot of them.'

'We've come up with a plan for a floating rope barrier secured to buoys with police signs and lights. Waqa and I were on our way to talk to the manager about it when you arrived. What d'you think, sir?'

Ratini liked being consulted. He rubbed his stubbly chin. 'Anything to keep the press out. Fiji's good name with Australia is at stake here, quite apart from respect for the High Commissioner herself and her family. Incidentally, have you informed Ms Armstrong's colleagues?'

'No, sir, still waiting for someone there to ring back with her next-of-kin details. Setting up the crime scene was the first priority, but liaising with the High Commission can't wait any longer.'

'*Io*, you do that, Horseman. Why don't I pull my weight here? I'll have a word with the manager about erecting a water barrier double quick.'

'*Vinaka*, sir. We also need the manager to issue gate keys to us, so Constable Rosiga can take over. Ilai hasn't left his post for hours now and needs a break.'

'Makes sense. Everyone's in now, eh? Ilai, you come with me and Waqa to see the manager. You'll be better able to explain your barrier plan to him.'

The furious tension in Ilai's face vanished, the muscles beneath the fleshy folds relaxed, and he looked positively benign as he said, '*Io*, Detective Superintendent. I'll help where I can.'

Ratini was the rudest, most inconsiderate and sarcastic superior officer Horseman had ever come across. Yet had he succeeded in winning over the hostile security guard? By accident, of course. Perhaps Ratini and Ilai were two of a kind.

His mobile rang while he mused. He narrowly avoided dropping it and was happy to see the caller was Kau. 'Sir, I found Ilai's pastor, who will vouch for him all weekend. His memories are quite specific and detailed, so I'm entirely satisfied he was in Lautoka.'

'Do you think DI Singh would be satisfied, Apo?'

Horseman heard Kau smiling. '*Io*, I do.'

'Great work. Come back to the marina now. Ratini's here with four extra constables. You can help Lili organise the security barriers to keep the press at bay. Ilai and Constable Rosiga have the most experience in water barriers. I'll need the car to go to the High-Com.'

'Fifteen minutes, tops, sir.'

Less than two hours ago, Horseman had been knocked flat when he'd shone his torch on Helen's dead body. Now the calm routine of police procedure had taken over, the first alibi had been offered and checked, and the miracle of Ratini offering practical help had happened. Was it possible that things were looking up?

<h1 style="text-align:center">19</h1>

It didn't seem right to break such momentous news to Australian officials from the yacht club carpark, amid the rumbling, grinding gears and squealing brakes and angry honks of container trucks heading west from Suva's port. No, he'd be at the High Commission in five minutes if he went the back way. And if Helen's second-in-command wasn't available, who should he talk to? Of those he'd met already, he most trusted the AFP officer, Chief Inspector Bob Browning.

Near the foot of the stairs to the office building, Horseman noticed Hugh Forester standing, his head back. He opened his mouth and blew out a cloud of vapour. Was he smoking? As the First Secretary brought his hand to his mouth, Horseman realised he had a vape between his fingers. He'd rarely seen an e-cigarette before and only in the hands of foreigners: they'd not taken off at all among Fijians.

'Ah, you've discovered my secret vice!' Forester said when he noticed Horseman, then faltered at the sight of his grave face. 'Let's go to my office.'

The First Secretary opened his office door. 'I apologise, I couldn't get back to you this morning. Not a free moment. Have you found Helen, Inspector?'

'Yes, but it's not good news, Mr Forester. I suggest we sit down.'

'Of course.' Forester waved him to an armchair facing the window, then seated himself on a matching sofa on the other side of the coffee table.

Horseman took a deep breath and exhaled. 'We found Ms Armstrong not long ago. I'm deeply sorry to have to tell you she died on board the *Joshua Slocum,* her yacht.'

Forester froze, one hand gripping the arm of his sofa. After moments of silence, he blurted out a single word. 'Where?'

Had he not heard Horseman, or already forgotten in shock? 'On board her yacht, the *Joshua Slocum*.'

'I heard. I meant, where was the boat?'

'Oh, I see. Berthed at the yacht club.'

'The staff at the club keep an eye on things. Someone there should be able to tell you when she took the boat out and returned.'

'Thank you for that. The investigation is just beginning. The pathologist has attended, the specialist search team are working at the scene now, the marina has been closed, and police are securing access by water, as much as possible.'

'Is all that necessary?'

'Mr Forester, Suva may not be a paparazzi hotspot, but our media are just as invasive, aggressive and shameless as yours in Australia. We're trying to protect Ms Armstrong's dignity and privacy, and that of her family and the High Commission. We've placed a police embargo on any media announcement until we can notify her next-of-kin. However, nobody here can tell me who that is. Unscrupulous reporters sometimes break these embargoes for a scoop. The Australian High Commissioner is a VIP in Suva, and Ms Armstrong especially so because of her long service and active role. We in the Fiji Police Force are grateful to her for many practical aid projects. None more so than me, as you know.'

Forester nodded slowly, then rubbed his hands over his face. 'My apologies, Inspector. I've been covering Helen's appointments and my own, while still expecting her to turn up. I'll ring Canberra now with the news and get you the information about her next-of-kin.'

'Ms Armstrong will be in the mortuary at Suva Colonial Memorial Hospital very soon, if not already. As I knew her, I don't have any doubt about the identity of the dead woman I found. Nevertheless, someone from the High Commission will need to formally identify her. There's no urgency, though. Dr Young, the chief pathologist, will conduct the post mortem this afternoon.'

'What? Don't you need official permission for that? Canberra may prefer that to be done in Australia. Foreign Affairs may want the immediate repatriation of Helen's body.'

'At this stage, no one knows how or why Ms Armstrong died. We are classifying her death as suspicious until the pathologist reports his conclusions. That procedure is a requirement of Fiji law. It may reassure you to know that Dr Matthew Young is Australian and highly regarded internationally.'

'Well, I can certainly visit the mortuary and confirm her identity. But first, I hate to eject you so rudely, but I will need privacy for a few minutes while I call Canberra. You've had an awful morning, obviously. Have you eaten? Cup of tea while you wait in reception?'

'Yes, please. I'd appreciate that.' Forester lifted the phone as Horseman left.

Losana stood by her office door. 'Come in, Inspector. Kirin's back from lunch and has gone to rustle up some refreshments for you. Come and wait in my office, she won't be long.'

'*Vinaka*, Losana. I know you're busy. I'm fine here in the waiting room.'

Losana smiled. 'If you're sure.' She left her door open, and when she noticed Kirin returning with a tea trolley, she emerged and hovered.

'I forgot to ask whether you'd prefer tea or coffee, so Kirin's made both,' she said cheerily.

There was a teapot and a coffee plunger, a jug of water, dainty sandwiches, flaky sausage rolls and iced cupcakes. '*Vinaka*, Kirin. This is excellent. I can serve myself from the trolley.'

He hadn't realised how hungry he was. He wheeled the trolley as far from the reception counter as possible, turning a chair to face the window. His hands trembled as he poured coffee. A delayed reaction, he guessed. He recalled the scene in the yacht cabin once more, scanning clockwise from the companionway, but his stomach protested. Anyway, he was confident that he and Kau had captured the details in notes and mobile shots. And if they hadn't, Alisi and the SOCOs would do so. What he needed to do now was eat and drink. He hoped Forester would be on the phone long enough for him to do that.

He'd demolished all the food and emptied the coffee pot when his mobile buzzed.

'I've got instructions from Canberra, Inspector. Can we resume our meeting?'

Horseman carried the water jug and two glasses back to the First Secretary's office and placed them on the coffee table.

'I hope you've had something more than water.'

'Yes, thank you, and there's nothing left. I was hungry.'

'Gets you like that when you're running on adrenaline hour after hour, doesn't it?'

Forester sounded sympathetic for the first time. He shifted back on the sofa and drew his spine up straighter.

'Canberra's in shock, as are we all. I'm to be Acting High Commissioner until they make a new appointment. I'll fully cooperate with the Fiji police and comply with your rules and procedures. Chief Inspector Bob Browning and his small AFP team here will assist you as and when you need. The disposal of Helen's body, funeral and so on is solely the decision of her next-of-kin. Helen had few relatives. Both her parents died years ago, she divorced even longer ago, and her son tragically died in a motorbike accident at the age of twenty. She has a much older sister in Queensland and nieces and a nephew who all have grown children themselves.'

'How sad,' Horseman felt tears in his eyes and blinked.

'It's a little surprising that Helen's next-of-kin is her former husband, Alexander Scala. Perhaps because her sister is over seventy, I don't know. Perhaps Helen forgot to update her particulars. However, Foreign Affairs will notify both Mr Scala and Helen's sister.'

'Good, and can you tell me the moment that's done, please? This news is going to leak soon, and the story's going to be big. It's not right to hear of the death of someone close on the television news. Even if you're an ex-husband.'

'Yes, Canberra will let me know.'

'One thing more, please. I will need to speak to Alexander Scala as soon as possible. I hope you're cleared to share his contact details with the police?'

Forester pursed his mouth. 'Canberra hasn't passed them on to me yet, I'm afraid.'

Horseman felt annoyed and let it show. 'I wonder what Canberra means by full cooperation, then. Perhaps you can give me the name and number of the person in Canberra I should ring.'

Forester took one look at Horseman's face, wrote an Australian mobile phone number on one of his own business cards and handed it over.

'Thanks. You'll want to break the news to your staff, of course. When you've done that, I'd like to talk one-to-one with Ms Armstrong's closest colleagues. When could I start doing that?'

'Let's say four o'clock. The High Commission closes to the public then, which is when many staff knock off for the day. However, the ones you'll want to interview aren't in that category. We're all bound to help the police, aren't we?'

'I appreciate that.'

'We'll postpone all our appointments for tomorrow as a mark of respect. A small team from Canberra will arrive tomorrow, early afternoon. I think they'll want to meet you. I assume you'll be leading the investigation, Inspector?'

'That's possible—should be decided later today. I'll let you know. Tell me: did Ms Armstrong invite many staff on board her yacht?'

'I really don't know. Senior staff have all gone out at least once, probably. I've been three times in three years, and each time she also had a few guests from other missions or walks of life.'

'You'll understand that for elimination purposes, we need the fingerprints of anyone who's been on board the *Joshua Slocum* this year. Please make that clear when you're talking with your staff. To make it easier for you all, I'll bring a constable with me at four o'clock, who'll take prints. The SOCOs will have lifted all the prints from the boat by then. Thanks to the processing equipment Australia gave us, Sergeant Jayaraman will have them matched quickly.'

Forester raised one eyebrow. 'I can hardly object then, can I?'

Horseman smiled. 'Not if you want to help the investigation, sir. I can't lift the media embargo until Ms Armstrong's sister and former husband are informed, so please instruct your staff not to speak of this to anyone until the death is announced in the press. I'll get back to the station now.'

20

Forester's Canberra contact picked up Horseman's seventh call. He'd imagined a grumpy old bureaucrat, so the friendly voice of a young woman surprised him.

'Danny Porter, Foreign Affairs Public Relations. What can I do for you, Detective Inspector Horseman?'

'I'm anxious to know if Ms Armstrong's sister and ex-husband have been notified of her death, Ms Porter.'

'What's your interest in this matter?'

Horseman felt like slamming the phone down. He needed another deep breath, in and out, before he could explain in another lengthy recital. 'Surely Mr Forester told you all this?'

'We need to be careful, Detective Inspector. Just like you. However, I can confirm that both relatives have now been notified, not without difficulty, I might add.'

'Thank you, Ms Porter. I'll lift the media embargo immediately, and the Fiji Police will release the tragic news to the press. Your department and the Australian High Commission may issue your own bulletins reporting Ms Armstrong's death. Another request—may I have both relatives' telephone numbers, please? I'll need to provide them with updates as they happen. But I must speak to Mr Scala fairly urgently.'

'It's a little irregular, Detective Inspector. However, I'm authorised to help the Fiji Police with information. To avoid error, I'll email them to you right away if you give me your address.'

'Certainly. But read them out first, please, just in case the email gremlins are lurking.'

Danny Porter chuckled. 'Right you are. You'll also get all my contact details in the email.'

***

Horseman shut himself off from the blare of the radio, always the first to break news in Fiji. He didn't mind the DCs keeping up with the media coverage. It could even be useful when the press misreported the details. But he needed to concentrate now.

He grabbed one of the hotline headsets for himself and called Alexander Scala's mobile number, only to listen to an announcement that the device was turned off or out of range.

His next call was to Dr Young. 'I'm going to start proper interviews at the High Commission later this afternoon, Matt. There's a team from Canberra coming up tomorrow, and I want to get in before they arrive, in case they advise staff to restrict what they tell us. I'm hoping the radio and television news will blast through the wall of reticence I always seem to get from the diplomats.'

'It's probably just their default position, mate. Best line of defence is to pretend everything's business as usual.'

'I hope that's all it is. Look, I know you haven't finished the post-mortem yet, but I'd like to tell the High Commission people something. Is there anything you can give me about the time and cause of death?' He swallowed, feeling he was betraying Helen by speaking of her in police jargon. Yet the jargon helped him suppress his emotion. Maybe that's what it was all about for the diplomats, too.

'Sure, I can. I've actually finished the post-mortem—we started as soon as we got Helen back here. Not just because she's a high-profile death, but because, just like you, I could cope better if I didn't put it off and the prospect of what I had to do just nagged at me more and more. Not good for the soul, mate.'

'True.'

'There's one right way to approach a post-mortem, and this might help you when you're forced to rummage through the personal possessions and even the secrets of someone you knew and liked and admired ... where was I?'

The pathologist sounded worn out, and Horseman gave him time to gather his thoughts.

'Oh, yeah. You've got to look at it as the last service you can ever do for your friend—to find out how and why she died. And there's no one else who can do that better than a pathologist and a police detective. And you know what? Unfortunately, that means you and me, as far as Helen's concerned.'

'*Vinaka*, Matt.'

'As you know, I'm happy to share my pearls of wisdom any time! You can pass on these facts, which aren't going to change, no matter what we discover in our lab or from toxicology. The High Commissioner was a healthy woman for her age who could be expected to live for another twenty years at least. She was murdered, probably where her body was found. She died from the first of two blows to the head from a blunt instrument. Not just blunt, but I would suggest something smooth. Various tools on board the yacht would be candidates, but the weapon could also have been brought on board by the murderer if the attack was planned.'

Horseman's stomach heaved in protest. 'Could she possibly have fallen by accident?'

'Afraid not, because there are two distinct, overlapping wounds. If it's any comfort, I think the first was lethal. It probably stunned her instantly and killed her within a minute or so.'

'When?'

'Rigor has already come and gone. Everything fits with your idea that it could have been before or after the Saturday night ball. Difficult to be more specific because of the conditions on board. I would have said early Saturday evening from the process of decay, but the environmental conditions, that is, a small, sealed cabin in a yacht, would hasten decay by several hours at least. Lab analysis of some of the tissue samples may allow me to narrow that window a little, but not yet.'

'*Vinaka*. Anything else you've got I haven't thought to ask about?'

'Stomach contents are consistent with the scraps found in the galley and the wine dregs. She certainly ate that meal.'

Horseman thought for a bit. 'Still, she could've gone to the ball, couldn't she? Maybe she didn't eat anything there. Anyway, smoked fish and cheese are highly likely to have been on the French Embassy's menu.'

'Yeah, they were. I was there, remember.'

'Of course. Anything else significant?'

'Not yet, but you'll be the first to know, if and when.'

***

Horseman tried Scala's number again and failed to get through again.

Next on the list was Sergeant Jayaraman. 'How are you getting on, Ash? Still on the yacht?' Horseman asked.

'Yes, sir. There's a lot packed into a small space on a boat. We'll be through here within the hour, though.'

'Anything promising?'

'First, Ms Armstrong's mobile phone was in her handbag. I don't think it was her only mobile, or perhaps she routinely deleted all her calls and texts. I'll get our guys to retrieve what they can, but we may need to pass it on to Telecom, which will be slower.'

'I guess she'd be cautious about leaving a trail. I'll check on protocol for High-Com staff's use of mobiles.'

'Second, I've got lots of fingerprints to match when you can get me some—inside and outside. Smears of blood from around the cabin, not including the pool around the victim's head, which Dr Young sampled. I'm taking the cutlery, plates and glasses, an under-sink rubbish bin, and the tablecloth to the lab. Not hugely hopeful of anything additional to the prints, but you never know—our new microscope's fantastic.'

'Is it too much to hope for a weapon? Dr Young says Ms Armstrong died of a blow to the head from something smooth and weighty.'

'He said as much to me, too. There are plenty of candidates in the cabin and the cockpit. Nothing with blood on it, though. I'm not familiar with yachts, that's the problem. I don't know what should normally be here, and what's out of place.'

'Good point, Ash. Me neither. And we certainly can't take any of the yacht club members or staff into our confidence. But I think I know someone who may be able to help—a friend in the navy. I'll see if he's around and get back to you tomorrow.'

'Right, sir. Keep in touch.'

Horseman tried to call Alexander Scala once more and once more listened to a recording announcing that the phone was turned off or out of range. But now it was time to brief his team before heading off to the High Commission.

<h1 style="text-align:center">21</h1>

The conference room buzzed as staff exchanged their reactions with their neighbours. Horseman allowed this to go on for a minute before interrupting.

'Ladies and gentlemen, you now know as much as we in the investigation team do. I reiterate that the pathologist is certain Ms Armstrong was murdered. Standard police procedure requires that we record the fingerprints of the High Commission staff, with your consent, naturally. We will then compare them with fingerprints found on the *Joshua Slocum*, in Ms Armstrong's office, and in any other places in the compound that we need to examine for evidence over the next few days. Then we can immediately eliminate you from our enquiries. After that, we'll know which fingerprints may lead us to the murderer. Any questions?'

Horseman hadn't met the man who raised his hand. 'What happens to our fingerprints? I, for one, have concerns about a foreign government possessing them.'

'Understandably, sir. All fingerprints taken for elimination purposes will be destroyed when that process is complete. Police only retain fingerprints of people who are charged with a crime.'

'What does that mean in our digital age?' the man persisted.

'Sir, it's your right to refuse to be fingerprinted. However, I would appreciate your cooperation. Let's have a chat in private before you make up your mind.' The man waved his hand dismissively. Those around him showed no reaction.

Horseman continued to address the entire room. 'We'll need to talk to some of you who worked most directly with Ms Armstrong and anyone who's been on board her yacht, for any purpose, this year. Please don't underestimate the importance of your observations—what you can tell us may be critical. We will disrupt your work as little as we can, but I know you agree with me that nothing is more important now than finding out who killed Ms Armstrong. I need your help to do that.'

The subdued clapping that followed surprised Horseman.

'Thank you. If you'd like to talk over the issue of consent, I'll see you here at the front of the room. If you agree to be fingerprinted, Detective Constables Waqa and Kau will do that in the next room on the right. You don't need to wait in line. Detective Constable Pareti here will usher you in. While you wait, please help yourself to refreshments from the trolley at the back.'

After a second or two of uncertainty, some people rushed to DC Pareti, who smiled, checked their names on his list and waved them through the door. Others wandered over to the refreshments while the rest stayed in their chairs, slumped and lethargic.

The man who'd queried the fingerprinting came up to Horseman, holding out his hand genially. 'Walter Friend, Inspector. Third Secretary.' He was young, too pudgy and wore large, green-framed glasses.

Horseman shook hands, wondering what the man's game was.

'Thanks for answering my questions, Inspector. They do need to be asked and answered, I'm sure you'll agree.'

'Yes, certainly. However, you strike me as a man well acquainted with the relevant law, Mr Friend.'

'Well, perhaps. To be frank, I intended my question and your answer as a demonstration for our junior staff who may not realise they can't be compelled to give you their fingerprints.' He beamed. 'I will comply with your request, by the way. I don't object on my own behalf.'

Horseman dismissed the man from his mind as a self-satisfied time waster, but could not be rude, so decided to ask a few questions. 'Have you ever been on the *Joshua Slocum*?'

'No, no such luck. I've only been here two months. I heard Her Excellency usually invites new diplomatic staff for a sail, so I was looking forward to that. Someone said the boat needed some work and hadn't left the marina for a while. So you can see my fingerprints won't be any use to you.'

'You never know, Mr Friend. As I explained, the prints are for elimination only. At this stage, we have no suspects. As you're new to Suva, I imagine Ms Armstrong spent quite a bit of time with you, introducing you to Fiji?'

'Some, but I'd hoped to work with her more closely, actually. I had so much to learn from her, but she was very busy, very hands-on with every project and initiative. Possibly too much so, for the head-of-mission. Most of the time, the Second Sec showed me the ropes; sometimes the First Sec, Hugh Forester. Her Excellency was always cordial, but I can't say she took much interest in me, Inspector.'

'Thanks for explaining, Mr Friend.'

'I'm wondering about your surname, Detective Inspector. I apologise for being personal, but you look Fijian ...'

'Your Fijian colleagues could probably tell you, but I don't mind. Legend has it that my European ancestor was shipwrecked on a reef off Vanua Levu, maybe in the late eighteenth or early nineteenth century. A few men managed to get ashore, where they were clubbed and prepared for the ovens. My ancestor clung to some timber and washed up in a different bay. He came to on the beach as he was being nuzzled by a horse, part of his ship's cargo. The club-wielding warriors were keeping their distance, terrified. You've got to remember, none of them had ever seen a land animal bigger than a pig.'

Horseman enjoyed Friend's wide-eyed amazement.

'When the chief came along to inspect the flotsam and jetsam for himself, it was true love at first sight. The chief would have given anything for the horse—guns, war canoes, slaves, women—anything and everything. My ancestor soothed the traumatised animal, and kept repeating the word horse, trying to placate the Fijians. Desperate to convince the chief of his value, he demonstrated his riding skills. Up and down the beach. Bareback. Trotting, galloping, wheeling and rearing. Can you imagine?'

'I can, indeed. I can picture it exactly.'

'The upshot was my ancestor became the chief's horseman, groom and riding instructor. He was given a house and at least one wife, and lived long enough to have several children. His only son adopted his father's title as a surname, which has been passed down in the European way until today.'

'You tell a terrific story, Inspector Horseman. Thank you.' Walter Friend was a little embarrassed. He was just beginning his diplomatic career, after all.

'As there's no one else hovering to debate fingerprint procedures, I'll grab myself a cup of tea. Nice to meet you,' Horseman said.

He took his tea and poked his nose into the side room where Waqa and Kau were taking fingerprints. Pareti was on top of the marshalling, admitting only one person as each exited. A young Fijian man got up from Kau's table and held out his hand to Horseman.

'I'm Vili Naulu, sir. You may want to talk to me as I was on the *Joshua Slocum* quite often. I helped crew for Ms Armstrong.'

'*Vinaka*, Vili. Let's talk over here.' He led Vili to a small table in a corner where they wouldn't disturb the fingerprinting process. Pareti rushed up with a couple of chairs.

'Tell me more, Vili.'

'I'm a bookkeeper. Two years ago, Ms Armstrong sent around an email asking for volunteers to learn to sail in return for crewing on *Joshua Slocum* when required. I jumped at the chance. She took on four of us and two remain.'

'Did Ms Armstrong train you?'

'Sometimes she did, but she doesn't have much time. More often it was Mr Scala, when he was in Fiji, of course. He spent more time here back then. He was Ms Armstrong's husband, but they're divorced now.'

Horseman tried not to react. 'Was Mr Scala a good teacher?'

'*Io*, sir. Tough as, though. A hard taskmaster. I think two dropped out because they couldn't take his shouting and swearing. I don't mind that at all. You've got to jump quickly to be any use sailing.'

'*Oi lei*! I'd like to learn one day. How recently have you seen Mr Scala?'

'Not sure ... about a year ago.'

Horseman nodded, thinking. 'How often did you crew for Ms Armstrong?'

'Oh, it wasn't regular. Twice a month sometimes, then not at all for a couple of months. Once a month at other times. So much depends on the weather with sailing, you know.'

'When did you last go out?'

'Probably two months ago. She complained the engine wasn't ticking over properly—said it needed an overhaul. It was risky to go out until that was done. She was very safety-conscious.'

'Did you go every time Ms Armstrong went sailing?'

'I wouldn't know if she took the boat out without me, would I? You soon learn not to ask questions when you're a local employee at the High Commission. Still, it's a great place to work and I know I'm lucky. You can ask about your job, of course, but not about other people's jobs, and not just out of curiosity. No one tells you not to ask; they just don't answer you. Australians aren't chatty like us Fijians, are they?'

'I've met Australians who're just as curious and chatty as Fijians, Vili. Perhaps diplomats are different. Did any of the diplomats go sailing with her regularly?'

'I don't know about regularly, sir. The naval attaché, Pat, often comes along. The others come maybe twice a year, if they like sailing. Often there are guests from other embassies too, and I have no idea who some of them are.'

'What about the other volunteer who trained with you?'

'*Io*, that was Taufa from the Visa section. We often sailed together, other times just one of us went, depending on how many guests were on board. Taufa got married and now she has a baby, so she doesn't come anymore. She must have given it up about nine months ago, because Ms Armstrong was worried about her falling. There's so much to trip you up on the deck of a yacht.'

'*Vinaka vakalevu*, Vili. You've been very helpful. Did you give your phone number to the constable? I may need to speak to you again.'

'*Io*, I did. I'm happy to help anytime if I can. But I must say, I can't wait to tell my dad I shook your hand!'

22

The next two guest sailors Horseman spoke with supplied the names of some diplomats and Fijian notables who'd been on the *Joshua Slocum* in the last year. When Horseman looked in the fingerprint room again, there were only two people waiting.

'Good work, Pareti. This has all gone smoothly. Are these two the last?'

Pareti frowned and studied his clipboard. 'I think there should be a few more, sir. But three people turned up who weren't on the list—I wrote them in.'

'Don't worry about it, Izzy. We'll follow up tomorrow.'

The First Secretary, Hugh Forester, approached him to offer a glass of water, tinkling with ice. Horseman was surprised at the thoughtful gesture. 'Thanks, Mr Forester, just what I need.'

'Few objectors to fingerprinting, I hope?'

'None at all. Not even the Third Secretary, Mr Friend. He told me he spoke out because he wanted junior staff to be aware of their rights.'

Forester raised one eyebrow sceptically but said nothing.

'Do you want me to provide a list of my co-guests when I last went out on the *Joshua*?'

'Yes please, sir. D'you know if Helen kept a guest list for her sailing parties?'

'I've never seen one, but she was businesslike with records.'

'That brings me to another request, Mr Forester. We'll need to search Ms Armstrong's office here and her private apartment, which I believe is in the Residence. Those rooms, together with her yacht, are the most likely places to find clues that will lead us to her killer.'

Forester smiled. 'That's fine in theory, but we come up against the question of jurisdiction, don't we? The Fiji Police are only here on Australian soil at our invitation. I'm pretty sure a Fiji magistrate's warrant can't get you through our gates, let alone searching rooms.'

'True, true. We're grateful guests on your property. The news that Canberra has offered the Force full cooperation and assistance was welcome indeed.'

'Thank you, Inspector. The Canberra team flying in tomorrow might define for us both just where the boundaries of our assistance lie. Until then, I can't see my way clear to permit our rooms to be searched by Fiji police officers.'

'I understand, but the sooner we find documents like guest lists for the yacht, the better.'

'I appreciate all that. You're welcome to visit tomorrow morning. Any staff member here may talk to you freely—I don't need to know who chooses to do so nor what they say.'

'I understand, Mr Forester. Would nine o'clock tomorrow be too early?'

'Not at all. You can come earlier if you like—say half-past eight?'

'See you then. Good afternoon, Mr Forester.'

***

The pizzas were still warm when Izzy put the boxes on the table and opened the lids. They sniffed the appetising smell of yeast and garlic with pleasure. 'Help yourselves,' he invited. Horseman was pleased the probationer had also bought a few rotis from the vendor outside the station. He gobbled his favourite, pumpkin and pea, while the DCs dived into the pizzas.

'Someone boil the kettle while I make a few calls,' he said. 'Mr Forester didn't allow us to search the High Commissioner's office, nor her apartment, but he agreed that Ms Armstrong could have kept lists of guests she invited to go sailing on her yacht. If those records are at the High Commission, Losana may know about them. But if they're on the yacht, we should be able to find them. Maybe she kept a Visitors' book on board. I know there's one at the Residence because I've signed it myself more than once. I'll ask if the SOCOs found anything like that.'

'Don't all boats keep a logbook?' DC Kau asked. 'Ms Armstrong might have listed guests there.'

'Good idea. We can check that tomorrow if Ash didn't lift it today.'

Izzy had placed a steaming teapot on the table and poured a mug for each of them by the time Horseman finished his call. 'Ash says he didn't see a Visitors' book, but documents weren't their primary focus. He noticed the storage around the navigation table was full of books, charts and references like tide tables and so on. He's happy to return first thing in the morning and go through the drawers and cupboards thoroughly. I'll tell him Lili and Izzy will go along too. Apo, you can come to the High Commission with me. When we finish our paperwork, let's focus on getting a good night's rest. It's been a hell of a day.'

But Horseman tossed and turned that night. He couldn't shift the image of Helen, her head in a congealed mess of blood, dead on the cabin floor of the boat she loved. She shared his concern for Suva's homeless shoeshine boys and other street kids, at the bottom of the city's rubbish heap. How could he rest until he discovered who killed this good woman, to whom he owed so much?

WEDNESDAY 18th July

23

Tina loved her run on the beach, but now tugged on her lead as Horseman walked her up the slope to Dr Young's house and her bed on the deep verandah. The pathologist had left home for the hospital extra early to work on Helen Armstrong's post-mortem report. He also wanted to supervise all the forensic and toxicology analyses of tissue samples, which had been divided between three laboratories. He would never forgive himself if some detail were overlooked or a result wrongly calculated.

Horseman replenished Tina's water bowl and set off on a slow jog to Seaview Apartments, predicting he'd spend most of today sitting on his backside in meetings and interviews. He'd only gone two hundred metres when his phone rang.

'Bob Browning here, Joe. I've been doing a bit of digging and unearthed whole clumps of dirt on our friend Alex.'

'Great! I'm just jogging back home after taking the dog for a run. I can talk now or call back when I get home.'

'Call me back. I'll need your full attention, mate.'

Horseman sped up, and half an hour later, showered and dressed for work, he put his feet up on his balcony rail and rang Browning.

'Helen Armstrong's former husband is a person to command our interest, Joe. He's also a keen sailor, veteran of many blue water offshore races like Sydney to Hobart, Sydney to Mooloolaba, and he even crewed on the winner of the Admiral's Cup around the Isle of Wight one year. He used to be Alexander Scala QC, until his rising star crashed to earth when he was disbarred following his conviction on cocaine possession charges fifteen years ago. The couple divorced the following year.'

'*Oi lei*!' Horseman rubbed his hand over his face. 'What's he been up to since?'

'You may have to dig some more. From what I can piece together, he's a professional yachtsman, delivering boats to owners all over the world, competing in offshore races, many of which have rich prizes. He writes for yachting magazines, too. He buys and sells boats for himself and others. How much he makes out of all this I've no idea: as a humble AFP officer, I don't have access to the Australian Taxation Office records.'

'That would be a useful resource, wouldn't it?'

'You bet! I'm speculating that *Joshua Slocum* was transferred to Ms Armstrong in the divorce settlement. Scala's current boat is a 12-metre cruising yacht, *Pot of Gold*, which must be a capable ocean racer because he regularly enters prestigious events, including the Auckland to Fiji annual race, I might add. Is the name of the boat intended to be ironic? Anyone I've met who owns a sailing boat says the experience is like standing under a cold shower, tearing up fifty-dollar notes.'

Horseman grinned. 'I get the picture. Foreign Affairs has already spoken to Mr Scala, but he's yet to pick up my calls or reply to my messages. I wonder where he is right now? He could be on the high seas or in any port in the world. In the meantime, I'll get on to Customs and Immigration. If they're doing their job, Alex Scala couldn't anchor in Fiji without filling in an Arrivals Form and being issued a Visitor's Visa. However, I know from bitter experience that some officers are slipshod in applying the rules to those who enter Fiji by sea.'

'Even if they were all punctilious, it's not hard for a yacht to avoid official ports of entry and drop anchor in a secluded inlet in Australia. I imagine it might be even easier in Fiji.'

'Not hard, no. Fortunately, most people want to do the right thing. In a few hours, I should be able to find out whether Mr Scala belongs with the majority.'

'His conviction makes me doubt it.'

'*Vinaka*, Bob. Look forward to seeing you later today.' From Horseman's point of view, the AFP officer had dug up gems, not dirt.

24

As Lt Connolly walked along the corridor to the High Commission's reception room, Horseman thought how flattering the crisp naval whites were: the glaring whiteness, knife-edge pleats, the touches of braid and gold providing just the right amount of decoration. Not that this woman's slender figure needed flattering. She'd seemed defensive when they'd last spoken, but he understood that shock and confusion could easily create that false impression. Would the tragic end to their search for the High Commissioner make her more ready to open up?

She invited him to her office again and asked Kirin to bring them tea. 'Or would you prefer coffee, Inspector?'

'I'd be grateful for either, but if you really want to know, I'd love a cup of coffee if it's no trouble.'

'None at all,' smiled Kirin. 'Give me fifteen minutes and I'll make you the best coffee you've ever had.'

'I think Kirin likes you, Inspector,' Lt Connolly said as she opened the door to her office. 'Take a seat and tell me how I can help you further.'

'Lt Connolly, it's less than twenty-four hours since we found Ms Armstrong's body on board her yacht, and we're at the very beginning of our investigation. I want to emphasise that the best way you can help is to be completely frank. It's never helpful when people assess the relevance of each piece of information they know and reject half of it. We need to hear everything you saw or heard or know. And, as I've heard you were one of the most frequent guests at Ms Armstrong's sailing parties, I believe I can learn a lot from you.'

The naval attaché smiled and nodded. 'I understand, and I'll try to help.'

'Good. Why did Ms Armstrong invite you to sail more often than other colleagues?'

'I was happy to crew, but I was hardly an expert at first. Helen liked teaching, and after six months, I was confident to skipper *Joshua*. This was useful for Helen as she could devote more time to her guests. She always mixed business with pleasure. She thoroughly enjoyed her sailing parties, but they also allowed her to get to know people from different walks of life and different countries, cultivate connections, you know. Sailing's much better than golf or tennis in that way. You can't play golf or tennis without quite a bit of training and practice, but anyone can sit in the cockpit of a boat, wearing a lifejacket and holding on if you're scared. Unless you were a colleague, like me, nothing else was expected of guests. In reality, nearly everyone loved the experience and was keen to repeat it.'

'Vili told me Mr Scala taught him and Taufa how to sail.'

'That would have been before my time.'

'Did you see much of him?'

The naval attaché compressed her lips. 'No. He never stayed here in the compound and never appeared at High-Com functions. But he's a first-class sailor, you've got to give him that, and he really loved the *Joshua Slocum*. He checked her over, did any maintenance himself that he could, and arranged for the best specialists here to do what he couldn't.'

'Do you know where he stayed?'

'On his own yacht if he sailed here, I think. Or a client's yacht if he was delivering.'

'Does he often come to Fiji?'

'I can't give you dates, but he's been here three times that I know of in the last year.'

'When was the last time you saw Mr Scala?'

'Three or four months ago—February or maybe March. He was delivering a yacht, I believe, and was only here for a few days. He and Helen took the *Joshua* out, and she asked me along to crew. They had a serious discussion, and Alex gave her a list of maintenance jobs for her to get done as soon as possible.'

'Does he have a land base here, Lieutenant?'

'I don't know—neither he nor Helen ever mentioned that to me.'

'Would you say they had a good relationship?'

A tap on the door signalled the arrival of their coffee. Horseman jumped up and opened the door wide to admit an overladen tea trolley propelled by Kirin.

'Thanks, Kirin, it smells delicious. Park it alongside my desk. We'll serve ourselves. No scones for Inspector Horseman today?'

'Not today. You'll like the mini-muffins, though.' She nodded to a cane basket and whisked off a protective white tea towel. I've got banana with nuts, as well as pineapple and ginger. Please enjoy them.'

Lt Connolly poured their coffee while Horseman put one of each kind of muffin on his plate. They were mini-muffins, after all. One bite confirmed Kirin's prediction that he'd like them. After half a cup of very good coffee, but not the best he had ever tasted, Horseman continued.

'What was your impression of Ms Armstrong's relationship with her former husband?'

'They always seemed to be friends, but not close friends. You know, maybe more like colleagues who were comfortable with each other. I couldn't understand it.'

'Why not?'

'After what he'd done? I suppose you've heard about his conviction?'

Horseman nodded. 'I found out two hours ago. Two days ago would have been better.'

A pink flush appeared at the naval attaché's open collar and deepened to crimson as it rose up her neck.

'That man recklessly destroyed his own career, a disgrace to the legal profession. He would have brought Helen down with him if she hadn't divorced him as fast as she could. Then the death of their son ... I don't know how she coped. Yet she treated him and spoke of him like a friend.'

'Did Helen keep guest lists for her sailing parties, Lieutenant? Either here or on board the boat—maybe even a Visitors' book?'

'Well, I haven't seen a book or a file, but I wasn't involved in planning the sailing parties. Helen was very organised, I can't imagine her not keeping one.'

'Who helped her organise it, send invitations and so on?'

'You'd better ask Losana. If she didn't look after that, she'll know who did.'

Horseman made a note. 'Could you consult your own diary and let me know the date when you saw Mr Scala last? You said February or March.'

'Sure, I can work that out and ring you or email you.'

'Great. Finally for now, in the months since you last saw Mr Scala, has Ms Armstrong mentioned in your hearing that he had plans to come to Fiji?'

'Hmm, I'll need to think about that, Inspector. I don't think so. But you've got to understand that while Helen was friendly and generous, she protected her status in Suva. She never gossiped and always observed protocols, even here.' The crimson flush reappeared on Lt Connolly's neck, this time rising above her jaw and into her cheeks.

'Would Helen expect you to observe the protocols of a murder investigation, do you think? I believe she'd want her killer caught.'

The naval attaché put her hands to her cheeks, which must have been burning. He understood her prevarication, but only to a point. 'Please don't conceal anything, Lieutenant. Even if you're not totally sure.'

She took her hands from her face and looked at him. 'It was last Saturday morning, so I'm sure. We were driving to the FAWG meeting at the university, and talking about the Bastille Day Ball, what we were going to wear and our masks. I suggested we might go together with some colleagues. She said Alex was in town and wanted to meet her on board the *Joshua* to discuss the quotes she'd got for the overhaul of the engine. She was hoping he'd approve one quote and she could go ahead with the work right away. I said I'd see her at the ball and we could get a taxi back together if that suited her. She said we could decide that later. Vuki, the driver, would take some of us to the ball, but would have the rest of the weekend off. She was always considerate of local staff's family time.'

'Anything else?'

'No, Inspector. After we got back from the FAWG lunch, I never saw Helen again.'

'*Vinaka vakalevu*, Pat. You've been an enormous help. I'm afraid we need what you've just told me in writing.' He retrieved his laptop from his satchel, took a business card from the box on Lt Connolly's desk and started typing. 'I'll email you a Witness Statement form now. Please fill it in as soon as you can, leaving out nothing you've just told me, and adding anything more that comes back to you. I'll print it out, and you can sign it when I'm here next, probably this afternoon. Thanks for the great coffee.'

On the reception counter, a vase of white arum lilies had replaced yesterday's bright orange and blue strelitzias. He complimented Kirin on the mini muffins and asked if Losana was available. Kirin invited him to go through with a wave of her hand.

Losana was wearing black, relieved only by a white frangipani flower in her hair. Dark shadows beneath her wide eyes told of a sleepless night. Horseman suddenly realised that Losana may have been closer to the High Commissioner than any of her Australian colleagues.

'*Yadra*, Losana. It's a sad day for you, and I'm sorry to intrude. But I hope you can help me.'

'I'm happy to help any way I can, Inspector.' Her smile was strained.

'Did you help Ms Armstrong organise her sailing parties in any way?'

'Not much, just some clerical work.'

'Did you ever go yourself?'

Losana smiled broadly, gazing past Horseman, remembering. 'Once only. It was windy and choppy, even though we didn't go beyond the reef. Most people on board found it exciting, but my stomach said, "No, sailing is not for you, Losana".'

'Did you send out invitations?'

'Ms Armstrong wanted the guests to feel special, like a chosen few, so she preferred to ring them up herself to invite them. She'd give me the names of those who accepted. She liked to have six or eight guests besides High-Com staff who'd be helping.'

'It would help us enormously if you could send me those lists, Losana.'

'Really? Well, that's straightforward enough. I keep them in a folder. I'll email it to you right away, sir. Anything else I can help you with?'

'That's it for now. You must have a lot to do with the Foreign Affairs team arriving in a few hours.'

'Oh, I can cope with them! Chief Inspector Browning mentioned that you should attend a briefing meeting about the investigation. Until they arrive, we won't know when that will be, but I'll call you.'

'*Vinaka*. I've got a lot to do between now and then, so I'll dash off now.' Losana gave him a small smile as he stood up, then turned her eyes to her computer screen.

What to do next? He needed to check on the SOCOs, on the divers who should have been looking for a weapon around the marina for nearly two hours, on his DCs who were dredging up info on Alex Scala, and Dr Young, who could tell him more if he visited the morgue in person. If only their mornings were as fruitful as his was proving to be.

25

Horseman drove down the steep lane by the side of the Colonial War Memorial Hospital, turned left and pulled into a parking bay near the discreet sign, Pathology Department. He pressed the buzzer, and one of Dr. Young's white-coated interns let him in. 'Go through, Inspector Horseman, he's in the lab,' the intern said.

The pathologist's lanky body stooped over a monitor, then straightened and bent the other way to look through his microscope eyepiece and adjust a knob or two.

'Hello, Joe. How's your morning going?'

'Promising, so far.' Horseman briefly related the news about Alex Scala and Losana's guest lists for the *Joshua* parties. 'I'm hoping you're making progress with your side of things, too. From the way you're hopping from the microscope to the monitor, I'd say something's caught your attention.'

'I'm looking at a specimen of congealed blood from our friend's head wound. Look at the screen and I'll show you. Don't be squeamish, mate. This is only a drop of blood here.'

Dr Young moved his cursor, circling several particles scattered among the blood. 'These are, well, microscopic fragments of metal, not sure what yet, but not iron or steel.' His friend was a compulsive teacher, so Horseman stepped forward obediently, but barely glanced at the screen. He couldn't. 'So, are we thinking a boat tool?'

'That's my guess, especially if it was a spur-of-the-moment strike. One thing I know is that boat builders avoid steel fittings in the cockpit because the magnetic field makes the compass inaccurate. My guess is these specks could be brass, bronze or aluminium. We'll find out. But I'm intruding into your realm, detective.'

'There are plenty of heavy metal tools stowed away on board. A spanner was on the chart table, and more were in a rack. On the other hand, if the murder was planned, he might have brought a weapon with him, something quite unrelated to boats.'

'Not enough for you, mate?'

'Enough for now, what can I tell the Foreign Affairs team this afternoon?'

'Only what I said earlier. The victim was a healthy, mature woman, killed by two blows to the head with a smooth, blunt metal object, probably last Saturday evening or early Sunday morning.'

'*Vinaka*, Matt. Be sure to call when anything else comes up.'

***

Desperate for action after more fruitless calls to Alex Scala, Horseman drove to the yacht club to review the crime scene. The Fijian flag hung limply at half-mast. Ilai was on duty at the marina gate and held out his hand as Horseman strolled up to him.

'*Bula*, Ilai,' Horseman shook the guard's hand firmly. 'How are things going here?'

'Pretty busy, sir. Your young constables are a help to me and the other guards. Not so many would-be intruders as I thought. I reckon our makeshift water barrier has made some stickybeaks think again. No one gets through this gate without the SOCO sergeant's say-so. Some of the boat owners are pissed off. Of course, they understand why the marina's off limits, but they feel better if they grumble and whine. Sergeant Ash is a good cop.'

'True, Ilai. I'm lucky to work with him. *Vinaka vakalevu* to you, too. When did the divers get here?'

Ilai consulted his watch, lifting his eyebrows in surprise. 'About two hours ago, Detective Inspector.'

Horseman nodded. 'I'd better go and see what's happening. See you later, Ilai.'

DC Izzy Pareti was pacing the pontoon near the *Joshua*. He waved when he saw Horseman. The divers' tanks and buoyancy vests lay on the pontoon near the yacht, and the divers themselves sat in the cockpit, drinking mugs of tea. Wetsuits peeled off to their waists, they were enjoying drying off in the sunshine. They greeted Horseman and shook hands. One man held out a plastic box of sandwiches.

'*Vinaka*, they look good, but I've been well catered for at the Australian High Commission. Who's looking after you guys?'

'Courtesy of the yacht club—unexpected and welcome. Good corned beef. Your man Izzy fetched it from the kitchen.'

'Glad to hear it. Have you found anything yet?'

One diver shook his head. 'Not yet. Man, it's a sad sight down there. A rubbish tip. We've covered half, and we'll be able to do the rest after our break. The sand's so fine here, quite muddy, so any heavy metal potential weapons are likely to get buried quickly. Still, there's a fair chance something dropped or thrown in last Saturday night will still be visible. One thing in our favour is that there's very little seagrass or algae—the constant churning from the outboard motors sees to that. And the visibility isn't bad today, because the marina's out of bounds.'

The other diver nodded and gave a cheerful thumbs-up.

'I've just learned the weapon was metal but not steel.'

'Good to know.'

'Is that the boss I hear?' Ash's disembodied voice came through the hatchway, followed after a few seconds by his head and shoulders. 'Come on down. Lili's with me, cataloguing our last haul.'

'Ash, I can't be bothered robing up. Can you and Waqa take a break in the fresh air?'

They soon emerged. Horseman was absurdly pleased to see both of them, as if he'd not seen them for days. It was always like this—time stretched to breaking point in the first few days of an investigation. The twenty-four hours since he'd found Helen's body seemed like a long week to him. Later, time would switch, and a week could race by like a day on steroids.

Horseman beckoned Izzy to the empty berth next to the *Joshua*, where they could perch on the raised timber fenders. As he told them about Lt Connolly's reluctant revelation about Alex Scala, all three leaned forward eagerly, their eyes widening in surprise.

'It's got to be this Alex Scala then, hasn't it, sir?' Waqa asked.

'He's certainly a suspect if he was in Suva last Saturday, Lili,' Horseman said. 'What I need most is to talk to him. I've called so many times. He picked up when a Canberra official rang to tell him of Ms Armstrong's death, but he doesn't answer when I call.'

'Have you got his fingerprints?' Sergeant Jayaraman asked. 'You said he's got a Class-A drugs conviction.'

'*Io*, in Australia, though. I want to ask the AFP senior officer at the High-Com to help get them this afternoon. He's delivered already with Alex Scala's background this morning. We know Scala was here with Ms Armstrong a few months ago, so his prints will be on board. No, to nail Scala, we need to find evidence like the murder weapon with his prints.'

'I see what you mean, sir,' Waqa replied.

'DC Kau's already gone to the Immigration Office to get a history of his comings and goings to Fiji. You know what a nightmare those records can be, Lili.'

Waqa chuckled. 'I'll never forget DI Singh's tales about the Jona case.'

Horseman smiled too, remembering Singh's outrage at the indolent Immigration clerks. Then he snapped back to the present. 'How much longer do you need here, Ash?'

'Forty minutes, tops. Thanks to Lili! We'll get most of the cataloguing done here, saving us a lot of time back at the lab.'

'No problem, as long as you haven't monopolised her. How're you going with the yacht club staff statements for Saturday, Lili?'

Waqa jutted her jaw. 'Only got one so far, sir, and he saw nothing. I've got the details of all the staff who worked on Saturday. It's just that only one of them's rostered this morning. I'll have to try phoning them from the station. Some are casuals and only work weekends, so it'd be too slow to wait until their next shift.'

'I think we can release the crime scene when the divers have finished. Do you agree, Ash?' Horseman asked.

'Yes, we've done our level best.'

'Izzy, relieve Ilai on the gate when he has his lunch break, then come back on guard here when the SOCOs leave. I'll send a couple of uniforms to relieve you after the divers leave and the marina is open to members and workers again. You can all help Ilai remove the floating barriers and signs, too—that's our job, not the club's—but I know Ilai will want it done his way. A constant watch over the *Joshua* will be even more necessary when it's not a protected crime scene.'

Izzy frowned as he thought that one through, then nodded. '*Io*, sir. I hadn't thought of it like that.' He brightened. 'Do you reckon the murderer will return to the scene of the crime?'

'That's always a possibility. We can only hope so. Probably most people who drop by will be just sightseers, but we'll get everyone's names and addresses.'

'*Io*, sir. I understand.'

'I'm heading back to the station. Keep up the good work here. Ilai's attitude to the police has transformed, and that's because of the courtesy you and the others are showing him. I'd never have thought yesterday he'd be complimenting me on my promising constables!'

26

DC Kau had not yet returned to the station, so Horseman knocked on Superintendent Ratini's door. He entered at his boss's barked summons, 'Come in!'

At first glance, a different man stood beside the Super's louvred window. His hair shorn neat, his face shaved smooth, Ratini wore a new white short-sleeved shirt and pressed grey trousers. The only jarring note was the scuffed brown leather belt. Horseman wondered, with a sinking heart, if Ratini was going to represent the Fiji Police investigation at the High-Com meeting with the Australian Foreign Affairs visitors.

'*Bula*, sir. I hope you've got time to hear my report.'

'*Io*, sit down. Progress, dare I hope?'

'Some, and a plausible suspect.'

'Go on, man!'

Horseman related their actions of the last twenty-four hours, ending with an account of all his teams' current whereabouts and tasks. 'You'll understand how understaffed we are for such a high-profile case, sir.'

'Sure, the Aussies are going to be howling about our laziness and incompetence any minute.'

'Sir, Hugh Forester, First Secretary and now Acting High Commissioner, asked me yesterday whether I was heading the investigation into Ms Armstrong's murder. I had to put him off a bit, saying you'd be making a decision on personnel immediately.'

'Quite right, too.'

'The people at the High-Com need to know who to communicate with, sir. They'll expect me to brief them on the team this afternoon, along with our progress to date. I'd like to announce a more appropriate allocation of staff than we've got now, or they'll be right to think the Fiji Police can't cope with the case. The AFP senior officer, Bob Browning, has offered assistance, but I don't know how that stacks up officially.'

Ratini stared at him. The super's professional barbering and fresh shirt took years off his age. Was Ratini going to be the SIO, at the request of Forester at the High-Com or the AFP or the top brass of the Fiji Police?

'I won't beat about the bush, Horseman. The Deputy Commissioner has discussed staff allocation for this case with me at some length. As you know, I had doubts about your suitability as SIO because of your personal relationship with Ms Armstrong through your charity business. However, taking everything into account, the Deputy thinks you're the best choice, so consider yourself SIO as of yesterday.'

'*Vinaka*, sir.'

'You need another DI on the team, but DI Vula is over-stretched with the cocaine seizure case, and we're hesitant to bring any less experienced DI from outside the Central District. I'm pulling in DS Taleca from Training—you two go way back, don't you? He'll report here tomorrow.'

'*Vinaka*, sir.'

'DCs Kau, Waqa and Pareti will devote one hundred per cent of their time to this case, overtime authorised. Kau's as good as a sergeant, anyway. When's he going for his exam?'

'The next one scheduled, in two months. I agree he's ready for it.'

'I can be generous with uniforms, as long as you've got jobs for them to do. At the moment, keep the two you've got guarding the yacht club marina; they've worked well for us before. You'll have to make sure you're not giving your DCs jobs that an experienced uniform can do just as well.'

'*Vinaka*, sir.' Ratini was treating him like a raw detective-sergeant, but Horseman suffered in silence.

'About the meeting this afternoon. The deputy and I will attend, as a courtesy to the status of the victim and the Australian High Commission. The Deputy is content to leave the assistance of the

AFP at an informal level, at least for now. You're free to consult Bob Browning whenever you think his connections may be useful.'

'Good. That's the best way, I believe,' Horseman replied.

'The Foreign Affairs team is due to land in an hour. The Deputy will advise me of the time of the meeting, but probably around three.'

'I'll be ready, sir. In the meantime, I'll be hunting down Alex Scala.'

***

After listening to the usual 'out of range' announcements, sending more texts and email messages which would be ignored like all those before them, Horseman retrieved Forester's business card. He rang the phone number of the Foreign Affairs officer who had notified Alex Scala of his former wife's murder.

'Danny Porter, Foreign Affairs Public Relations.'

'Good afternoon, Danny. It's Detective Inspector Joe Horseman. I spoke to you yesterday.'

'Oh yes, in Fiji.' Her voice still sounded friendly, but a little guarded.

'Danny, you may remember you gave me the mobile number for Mr Alex Scala, Ms Armstrong's next-of-kin.'

'I sure do. Any luck?'

'I'm afraid not. All I get are "out of range" notifications. He hasn't responded to my texts or emails either. It would be a great help to know where that mobile was when you spoke to Mr Scala. As far as I know, he could be anywhere in the world.'

'Well, I don't know either, nor how to find out. But I suppose that's a simple matter for our Comms guys.'

'It is indeed. We could do it here if only you'd rung Scala from a Fijian phone!'

Danny chuckled. 'I'll talk to my manager and see what we can do. Call you back on this number?'

'Yes, please. If I don't answer, try my mobile and leave a text.'

'I'm on it. I hope I can get back to you today, but no promises.'

'What? And it's still morning in Canberra! Just joking,' he added when he remembered it was never a good idea to joke on the phone with someone you didn't know.

Feeling restless, he made a cup of tea for himself in the kitchenette, wondering what to make of Ratini and the Deputy Commissioner's attendance at the High-Com meeting later on. Was it just diplomatic protocol or a lack of trust in his own ability? He wasn't surprised Ratini thought he needed to spy, but he'd believed he had the Deputy Commissioner's vote of confidence. Horseman had also believed he'd have spoken to Alex Scala before the meeting, but there was little chance of that now.

At least Ratini had made an effort today, shedding his usual slovenliness to look neat and clean. Horseman glanced at his own clothes, considering whether his floral-patterned *bula* shirt and black jeans were good enough. He decided they may not inspire confidence in the Australian visitors, who would probably wear suits. Maybe he should go down to his basement locker and check the clean clothes he kept there for a sudden summons by the top brass. Like now. Yes, he'd do that as soon as he finished his tea.

The phone rang. It was DC Kau. 'Apo?'

'Great news, sir. Alex Scala flew from Savusavu to Suva last Friday afternoon. I've got more to tell you when I get back. Got Scala's entry-departure history on a USB, too.'

'*Oi lei*! Who'd have guessed? Great work, Apo. I'm going to my locker to change for the High-Com meeting right now. See you when you get here.'

His thoughts jumbled as his mind reframed the sequence of events since Sunday afternoon, when he stood waiting at the gate of the Junior Shiners hostel to greet Her Excellency Helen Armstrong, who never arrived. Three days later, he mourned her brutal death, but the discoveries today encouraged him a little. Too experienced to seize on Alex Scala as Helen's killer, he knew the man clearly had questions to answer. If only Danny Porter in Canberra would ring him back soon. Knowing Alex Scala had flown from Savusavu in Vanua Levu last Friday gave the man opportunity, but did not help them with his whereabouts now. He could still be in Suva or anywhere else.

27

Kirin and Losana greeted the police delegation of Tauvaga, Ratini and Horseman, and escorted them to a large room cleared of furniture. They took off their shoes and left them with dozens of others in a neat row beside the door. Horseman hadn't been expecting a *yaqona* ceremony to welcome the Australian visitors. But when he thought about it, he understood how the Fijians on the High-Com staff would feel responsible that the High Commissioner had been killed in Fiji, that they had failed in their hospitable duty to keep an honoured guest safe. They could show their sorrow by conferring special status on her compatriots who had come not to avenge, but to investigate her murder.

About twenty foreigners, some of whom Horseman recognised as High-Com staff, sat on woven pandanus mats which covered the floor in the centre of the room. Hugh Forester beckoned the police officers over to sit near him. Horseman wanted to get down to business and guiltily hoped the ceremony would be brief.

A dark wooden *tanoa*, the *yaqona* mixing bowl, stood on the raised dais at the front. Behind the *tanoa*, around fifteen Fijians sat cross-legged on pandanus mats. Horseman assumed they were local staff of the High Commission. A huge rectangle of decorated *masi*, the Fijian tapa-cloth, hung behind them on the front wall.

A middle-aged man he recognised as the Tamavua village chief entered and sat down on the dais behind the *tanoa*. He was dressed like Horseman, in a tailored *sulu*, the Fijian wraparound skirt, dark jacket, white shirt and black tie. The chief clapped once.

'Welcome, honoured guests, to our poor land...' He continued in Fijian for a few minutes of ritual welcome, emphasising the unworthiness of his people, and the greatness and generosity of the Australian guests.

A black-suited guest then placed a bunch of *yaqona* roots before the wooden bowl, and murmured, 'Ratu, please accept this token of our thanks for your kind welcome.'

A young Fijian man, crouching low, picked up the *yaqona* and sat beside the chief. 'Ratu accepts your most generous offering with humble thanks, and grants you and our Fijian police officers the status of Tamavua villagers for the duration of your duties here.'

The chief clapped three times. The young man added ground *yaqona* and water to the *tanoa*, stirring the contents thoroughly. He kneeled to serve the chief *yaqona* in a coconut shell cup. The chief drained the cup, and the other Fijians clapped three times. '*Maca*', empty, they responded. Two servers then offered bowls to the foreign guests, and then the other Fijians, who all clapped their thanks before downing the beige liquid. After two rounds, the chief signalled his refusal to the server, who retreated on his knees.

Hugh Forester stood up. '*Vinaka vakalevu* to the chief of Tamavua village and to all our wonderful Fijian staff who organised this ceremony. We are all in shock and grief at the death of our beloved High Commissioner and are pleased to welcome our Australian government colleagues, who will support us as we continue her work. Before we all return to our duties, please enjoy afternoon tea here.'

Some of the Fijian staff quickly folded the mats while others set up trestles, spread starched white cloths and helped Losana and Kirin lay out the spread from trolleys that appeared as if by magic. The chief circulated among the gathering, cup of tea in hand, speaking briefly to everyone. A good diplomat, Horseman thought, puts everyone at ease. He happily left that role to Deputy Commissioner Tauvaga, while he turned his own attention to the tea table of curry puffs, dainty sandwiches with the crusts cut off, flaky sausage rolls, butterfly cream cakes, treacle tartlets, cubes of tropical fruit on toothpicks and more. It seemed the Australians had fully adapted to the Fijian custom of substantial mid-afternoon refreshment. He loaded his plate, accepted a scalding-hot cup from Kirin, which he placed beside him on an empty trestle abutting a wall. After all, he'd missed lunch. But a proper full-Fijian afternoon tea was worth two of his usual snack-lunches. Maybe three. Ratini, looking like a fish out of water, soon joined him and slumped against the wall.

<h1 style="text-align:center">28</h1>

A more select group than Horseman had expected gathered in the conference room: the three Australian visitors, five High-Com diplomats, two AFP officers, and the three Fijian Police officers. After Deputy Commissioner Tauvaga expressed solemn condolences, he introduced Superintendent Ratini and then Horseman as the senior investigating officer.

'Detective Inspector Horseman has already spoken with some of you. It's because of his concern when Ms Armstrong failed to attend his own charity function last Sunday afternoon that an official search began so soon. And it's thanks to your cooperation that he has already uncovered significant facts that have identified one person of interest. For the benefit of our visitors from Foreign Affairs in Canberra, I'll ask DI Horseman to brief you on his progress to date.'

Horseman was succinct, but thorough, omitting only his request to the department's telephonist in Canberra to trace the location of Alex Scala's mobile phone on Tuesday afternoon. When he invited comments and questions, he was met with silence, which seemed to him to go on for minutes, although it could only have been ten seconds. Hugh Forester glanced around the table and eventually accepted his responsibility as Acting High Commissioner to respond.

'Many thanks, Detective Inspector. I've spoken with you several times since Sunday afternoon and am grateful for your diligence.' He glanced around again, his eyes lighting on the black-suited visitor. 'Mr Phillip, as you've only just arrived, I wonder if you have a question for the Fiji Police.'

Despite the efficient air-conditioning, Mr Phillip looked tired and hot, his face florid and damp. He ran a finger under his pale blue collar. 'Geoffrey Phillip, Pacific Secretary. I endorse the cooperation Hugh and his staff have already given to your investigation.'

Phillip paused, rubbing his chin. 'Far be it from me to interfere in operational matters, but I'm puzzled why you suspect Alex Scala? The first thought in Canberra yesterday was that Helen was attacked by opportunistic thieves who spotted an open hatch on her yacht. A robbery gone wrong, as it were. Isn't that more likely?'

The Deputy Commissioner smiled. 'Your idea is highly plausible, Mr Phillip. Mr Scala is currently a person of interest because of evidence DI Horseman's team has discovered. We need to locate and speak to him urgently.'

Tauvaga looked at Horseman, who nodded. 'Yes, sir, we do.'

Nods and soft murmurs rippled around the table, then again an awkward pause lengthened. Horseman attempted to cover his embarrassment. 'In the next few days, we may find evidence that leads us in a different direction. Our minds are always open.' He bit his lip to stop himself uttering more useless truisms.

Horseman's floundering seemed to boost Phillip's confidence. 'Perhaps I should ask how the Australian High Commission can best help you, Inspector Horseman.'

Tauvaga inclined his head to Horseman. 'Thank you, Mr Phillip. It's most important for staff to be completely open in answering our questions. Please resist your natural impulses as highly educated people to filter what you have observed or experienced through your own judgment of relevance. You can't know what's relevant or irrelevant right now. Please tell us the lot.'

More nods and murmurs greeted this request.

'Second, although our search team has now examined the crime scene, Ms. Armstrong's office here, and her own apartment in the Residence might reveal much more. Our forensic team needs to search those rooms without further delay.'

Murmurs escalated to grumbles, accompanied by lifted brows, frowns and open mouths. Again, no one was sure who should voice the collective consternation.

Hugh Forester said, 'We will need to confer about this request, Inspector. A police search of the High Commission is quite out of order.'

This group had no established leader or hierarchy yet, and Forester had assumed his acting role only yesterday. The time to press them was now. Horseman smiled in a friendly way. 'For criminal investigations, Mr Forester, it's quite routine here, as in Australia. Detectives and forensics officers always thoroughly examine a murder victim's home and workplace. What they find is often critical to identify the perpetrator. If Ms. Armstrong did not live and work in a diplomatic mission, detectives would have already examined her private spaces. I did make this request yesterday and hoped you would have discussed the matter.'

The Australians around the table exchanged glances.

'I remember now, yes. But other tasks have taken priority,' Forester said.

'Are the rooms locked at least?' Horseman asked.

'I don't know about her apartment. Does anyone? Walter, please step out and ask Losana.'

Horseman could see the young Third Secretary was reluctant to miss out on what was said in the meeting, but he quickly obeyed. 'Is her office in this building secured?'

'No. How do you mean? Since Ms Armstrong was missing on Monday, I've been in and out of her office, working on tasks that couldn't be put off, on Ms Armstrong's diary, consulting files and so on.'

Horseman was about to protest, but caught warning glares from both Ratini and Tauvaga.

'Has anyone else entered the High Commissioner's office?' Ratini asked in his gravelly voice before Horseman could go further.

Lt Connolly and the Second Secretary half-raised their hands, glancing at Forester, who said, 'Both my colleagues here informed me they needed files they'd left for the High Commissioner to read and comment on. Oh, of course, the cleaners have been in there.'

Ratini drew in his breath noisily through his mouth, no doubt preparatory to the heavy, deliberate sigh he used on his underlings at Suva Central. To Horseman's relief, he must have recalled where he was and exhaled normally. Horseman sensed from the tone of the murmurings that not everyone approved of Forester's disdain for security.

Walter Friend reappeared with Losana by his side. Friend addressed himself to Forester. 'Losana tells me Ms Armstrong's apartment was cleaned on Monday. Do you have any other questions for her?'

'Why was it cleaned?' Forester asked.

Losana's face was serious. 'It's routine on Monday morning, sir. All of us, including the housekeeper, expected her to return very soon, any minute, so it was cleaned quite early, to be fresh and welcoming, especially if the High Commissioner was ill.'

'Thank you, Losana, you may go now.'

Forester then asked what Horseman wanted to, but couldn't. 'Bob, can we have your professional opinion on this matter?'

Chief Inspector Browning looked up with a smile. 'What DI Horseman has said is correct: police procedure in a murder inquiry includes a search of the victim's home and workplace. If the police are refused entry, a search warrant can normally be obtained. You'll need a legal expert to advise whether a warrant would be granted to search the Australian High Commission in Suva. Possibly there's an issue of diplomatic immunity, I'm not sure about that. I understand that the Fiji Police would strongly prefer to look through the relevant rooms with your willing consent. In their position, I certainly would.'

'We would indeed,' Tauvaga said.

Forester stood. 'As I've not had a chance to discuss this question with my visiting colleagues, I'd like to propose that we do so now, in the absence of the Fiji Police team. I'm sure you understand no slight is intended. We will let you know the moment we make a decision.'

'Perfectly understandable, Mr Forester,' Tauvaga assured him. 'But it would be better for us to remain in your building, if we may. I know if I return to my office, I may not escape again, and it's always better to communicate face-to-face, don't you agree?' Tauvaga beamed around the table, ending with an avuncular chuckle to Forester, as if he merely confirmed the Acting High Commissioner's view. Ratini and Horseman followed his lead and left the room.

They stood at the edge of the car park, their eyes inevitably drawn by the gabled porch of the century-old colonial weatherboard house, which was the High Commissioner's residence. On the side wall, the original push-out wooden window shutters remained. Apart from its size, there was no sign of luxury, and the only mark of officialdom was the Australian flag, flying at half-mast above the porch.

Deputy Tauvaga spoke first. 'Dreadful business, this. Her Excellency was such a warm hostess, made everyone welcome and meant it. An astute and effective High Commissioner, too. May God grant her peace and guide us to her killer.'

'Amen to that, sir,' Ratini said. 'Do you think this Forester is up to the job?'

'You never know. He's in charge for now, but he may not succeed Helen. However, we need to search that apartment, so let's pray they agree, while Forester's not sure of himself. You both may as well know I'm not prepared to apply for a warrant. Far too confrontational. That would imperil our relationship with Australia and never be forgotten.'

Horseman knew Tauvaga had decided. At least he knew where he stood. 'Did you go to the Bastille Day Ball, sir?' he asked.

'No, the Commissioner went. It's mainly a diplomatic community thing. I've attended in the past, but now I'm too old. I passed my invitation along this year.'

Horseman's phone buzzed. 'Inspector Horseman, it's Losana. Mr Forester is ready for you in the conference room now.'

29

Back at the station, the three DCs listened to their chief's report, their eyes wide.

'You agreed to that?' DC Kau asked.

'My agreement wasn't required, Apo. Our Deputy Commissioner will not permit a police search of High-Com premises without the willing consent of the Australians. I don't know whether the visitors or Hugh Forester were more influential, but it doesn't really matter. The Aussies have agreed to secure the relevant rooms while we pursue the Alex Scala lead. Clearly, they hope that what we discover from him will make the High-Com search unnecessary. If nothing comes of the Scala lead, my bet is that they'll agree to us searching Ms Armstrong's rooms.'

'But sir, how useful will it be? Sounds like the cleaners and other staff may have removed or destroyed evidence already, whether deliberately or not.'

'True, Apo, but we have no choice. What we have to do now is find Alex Scala. What do the Immigration records have to tell us?'

'Sir, Scala visits Fiji twice or more each year, most recently a week ago, at Savusavu, on board *Pot of Gold*, his cruising yacht. We know he flew from Savusavu to Suva last Friday on Fiji Airways. Immigration has no record of his leaving the country since. And he hasn't travelled on any internal flights.'

'Have you checked the ferries?'

'Izzy is doing that, sir. You know how hard it is to get recent passenger lists.'

'*Io*, or any passenger lists. No pressure, Izzy, but we need to find Scala now.'

Lili Waqa said, 'One impression I got from working at the scene was that the sailing people are quite a fraternity. I heard about members crewing for each other and so on. And Scala's a member. I looked at the book to see if he'd signed in recently, but he hasn't. So far, I've only asked Mr Patel, the manager, and Ilai, the guard, but they haven't seen Scala recently. I could ask around more if you think it's worthwhile.'

Horseman didn't need to consider. 'Yes, it certainly could be. He could have sailed back from here to Savusavu on a yacht if a mate was going anyway. Does the Yacht Club keep a record of long trips like that, leaving from the Club? As a safety register of some sort, maybe? Check that first, Lili. See if anyone at the Club can tell you who Scala's friends were in Suva. He could be staying with one of them.'

'*Io*, sir, I'll give it my best shot.'

'Apo, if you've sifted through the Immigration records, you'd better start checking Suva hotels. If Scala hasn't left Suva, he must be staying somewhere.'

'*Io*, sir. Give me fifteen minutes, and Izzy and I can look after that.'

Something so obvious pierced his thick skull that he clapped his hand to his temple. 'You know, we can go at this from another angle. I can phone the Savusavu police or the Immigration office there, and get them to check if *Pot of Gold* is still moored there. And someone can knock on the hatch and see if Alex Scala is at home. Why didn't I think of that before? We're so tied up in the digital world now, I couldn't see beyond it.'

While Horseman checked that the DCs were clear about their tasks, his mind wrestled with the details of his own spur-of-the-moment idea. He knew no Immigration officers in Savusavu, which was a minor shipping port but the favourite of foreign yachts because of its calm anchorage in the lee of Nawi Island, a natural sea-wall. However, the arrest of a yachtsman there for importing drugs had sparked rumours about officials being on the take. His colleague DI Vula would know more. He picked up his phone.

'Siale, I want someone to check on a yacht that entered the country at Savusavu recently. Just someone to look out the window and tell me if she's still there. I don't want to advertise I'm checking, though. Who can I trust in our station there, or in Customs?'

'*Oi lei*, what a question, Joe! The people seem cooperative, but I couldn't vouch for anyone, I'm afraid. It's such a small place, everyone's connected. Go yourself, if you can.'

'*Vinaka*, Siale. I'll think some more.'

As he put the phone down, a solution came to him, his mind now alight with the promise of salvation. He snatched up the phone again and after a few redirects, he heard the familiar voice he'd missed every day since she'd left. He smiled; her tone implied callers better not waste her time.

'*Bula* DI Singh, it's been far too long. I hope you can spare me a minute or two.'

A moment's silence. 'DI Horseman, I can indeed.' As cool as ever, but he heard her smiling. Neither asked about the other's health, or the health of their families, as was the custom for friends who had been apart for some time. This was not her way. So he recounted the case briefly, explained his present quandary and asked for her help.

'Have you got a map on the wall, Joe? You do know Savusavu's ninety kilometres by road from Labasa, where my window is?'

'Really? I thought there may be someone you trust, whose window is closer.'

'Ha, ha. As luck would have it, I know Savusavu quite well. There's a case that has tentacles everywhere, much bigger than just Labasa. You'll understand when I say Siale Vula's involved, too.'

'Good. At this stage, I just need to know if *Pot of Gold* is anchored in Savusavu now, and whether Customs searched the boat before granting clearance a week ago.'

'Siale's advice to you is wise, but there are people in Savusavu I can trust as long as I initiate and control the operation. Let me think it through for a bit, make some enquiries and ring you back.'

'Sure. Is it premature to ask Ratini to authorise travel?'

'Hmm. How are you two getting on these days?'

'Much the same. Maybe he's mellowing a bit.'

'Planting the idea wouldn't do any harm. Up to you.'

'Sure. I wish we could nut this out together at the Arabica, Susie. But as we can't, I'll wait for your call.'

'I'm homesick for Didi's mother's rock cakes already.'

***

Horseman decided to defer mentioning Savusavu to Ratini until he was certain of his next move. Even if Scala's yacht was now moored there, he needed to know if it had been there on Tuesday when the Foreign Affairs officer in Canberra had notified Scala of his former wife's death. Danny still hadn't called him back, so he picked up his phone once more and dialled.

'Hello, Inspector Horseman. You're next on my list! I don't suppose you believe that, do you?' Danny Porter chuckled. It was clear she didn't care whether Horseman did or not.

'Why would I doubt you? I understand how long it can take to get things done, especially when one has to rely on others. Does my position on your list mean that you've got an answer for me?'

'Absolutely! Mr Scala's phone was in Savusavu in Fiji when I spoke to him yesterday. I hope that helps.'

'It does, Danny. *Vinaka vakalevu* to you, that's "thanks very much" in Fijian.'

'No problem, Inspector. Let me know if I can help you with anything else.'

***

This additional fact confused the issue of Scala's whereabouts. Horseman tore a fresh sheet from his notepad, turned it around to landscape format and sketched a timeline for Alex Scala. Although there were only a few confirmed incidents, ordering them on paper gave him a mental snapshot.

He called the DCs to gather around his desk. 'More news, guys. Foreign Affairs has traced the call made from Canberra to inform Scala of Ms Armstrong's death. Scala's phone was in Savusavu.'

The DCs stared at each other. 'But if he was in Suva on Friday, he must have got back to Savusavu on Tuesday morning at the latest.' Waqa shouted in frustration.

'Exactly, Lili. Checking whether Scala sailed over with a yacht club mate is even more important now. And I'm expecting to learn any minute whether Scala and his yacht are in Savusavu now. So it makes sense to call a halt to the Suva hotel checks, Apo, at least for now. I've just made a rough timeline for Alex Scala. I'd like you to add this to our official timeline. Don't fit Scala's incidents in the main line for now; draw a separate, parallel one for him. Put it on the whiteboard and in the case file, please, and get Izzy to help you.'

Apo grinned. Singh's methodical flair had rubbed off on him. Horseman handed over the sketch.

30

As the team settled into late-afternoon desk work, Apo Kau sent Izzy to pick up the late edition papers from the newspaper stand and make tea for everyone. When the probationer brought the tray, Horseman produced a packet of Paradise ginger biscuits from a desk drawer. 'Share these around, DC Pareti. Persistence is what we need with this sort of work, and the late-afternoon mind is just that little bit more alert with a shot of sugar.'

He scanned both *The Fiji Times* and *The Sun*. A horrific collision of a bus and two cars had supplanted the High Commissioner's murder on both front pages. The editor had included short stories about the visiting Australian delegation from Foreign Affairs; Horseman guessed taken word-for-word from a government press release. And predictably, a *Times* page-two article and *The Sun*'s editorial demanded that the Fiji Police step up their pathetic efforts and make an arrest. Horseman bristled, although he knew he shouldn't be such an easy target. He had found Helen's body just thirty-two hours ago! He got up and put the papers on the DCs' table.

He snatched up the handset on the second ring of the phone. Relief flooded through him when he heard Singh's voice, unless it was the sugar hit from the three biscuits he'd scoffed.

'Joe, *Pot of Gold* is moored here at Savusavu. My source hasn't noticed if the yacht has moved out of port and back again. There's a dinghy tied at the stern, so it looks like someone's on board, but he can't be sure until he sees someone on deck. He'll keep a lookout for that from now on, when he can. My friendly Customs officer confirms that they cleared the yacht for entry ten days ago, but they skipped searching it as owner-captain Alex Scala supplied them with all the information they needed.'

'*Vinaka*, Susie.'

'What do you want to do?' Her voice was alert and eager for the fray. More than any colleague he'd encountered, Singh had a hunter's instinct deep in her soul—not what you'd expect of a sugar-cane farmer's daughter.

'Hmm, it's getting late. It'll take you two hours to drive there, won't it?'

Singh paused. 'Ninety minutes if I'm lucky, but you're right, slower in the dark. There'll be an equal element of surprise in the early morning, anyway. How about I go in with a small team to search, on the grounds that no search was done, and the police have just become aware of Scala's drug conviction? I could persuade my Customs guy to be present as a witness, but this would be a police search, and Customs can do nothing to stop us. No time for a warrant, but if Scala has nothing to hide, he won't object.'

'But if he does object, he can get rid of whatever he has to hide before we can get a warrant. I don't like the risk, Susie. How many SOCOs in Savusavu?'

'None, everything comes to the lab here in Labasa. I could take a SOCO with me, two if there's nothing else on.'

'How long should it take to get a warrant signed there? Quicker than Suva, I hope.'

'Usually same-day service. If the magistrate's off sick, you just have to wait.'

'I want to be there. Ratini watches the budget like a hawk, for better or worse. I can't see him approving an air ticket for me when you're on the spot, though. Are you happy to interview Scala if he's on board?'

'Sure am. If he's willing.'

'If Scala's on board alone, and you and the SOCO find something suspicious, like a bloody weapon, which Scala fails to explain satisfactorily, you can arrest him for suspected drug-smuggling or murder, then bring him back to Suva, where we can interview him together...'

'You know what you always told me about wishful thinking?'

'I do. Just my feeble attempt at humour. Look, I'll email you the case file and put it to Ratini.'

'Be pleasant, Joe.'

'Who, me? Aren't I always pleasant?'

'Not always. You get your rugby face on and tackle anyone in your path, no questions asked. If you can bring them down, all the better.'

'I'll call you,' he replied.

His rugby face? Surely she was joking. Still, her flippant remark reminded him he'd not had a single minute to think about the bombshell proposal the Fiji Rugby Union President had made to him a few days ago. Except when he was drifting off to sleep, when the ghosts of his glory days would trip him up for a few moments, before the horror of the High Commissioner's death took over.

He planted his palms on his desk and pushed himself up before noticing he'd reverted to his old crutch, using his hands to stand up. This tactic became ingrained during years of rehabilitation after he'd smashed his knee and career in an instant. He didn't need to use it now; he must be more on guard against slipping back into old habits.

So he tried to relax his face to appear more pleasant to his Super as he pitched his proposal. He knocked on Ratini's door and entered at the shout of 'Come in!'

'Horseman, sit down! What are your thoughts on our meeting with the Aussies, eh?'

'A mix of wins and losses, sir. Given Deputy Commissioner Tauvaga's refusal to apply for a search warrant for a diplomatic mission, the outcome's acceptable, I guess.'

'Hmm. I was surprised at how defensive the High-Com people were, I must say. They behaved like well-educated criminals.'

'The more time I spend there, the more I think that's their instinctive behaviour, sir. They don't know what their counterparts have up their sleeves, so they throw up a beautifully decorated, well-mannered firewall.'

'Hmm, maybe. Got anything new?'

Horseman outlined Scala's phone trace to Savusavu, where his yacht was now moored.

'The best way to question Scala is for me to fly there first thing in the morning, sir. If he's involved in this smuggling racket DI Vula and DI Singh are working on, we need to surprise him. Although I've emailed the case material to Singh, I strongly prefer to be present. I'm responsible as SIO and know all aspects of the case. And of course, I want to support DI Singh.'

'Surely you don't think our brilliant DI Singh needs support, Horseman?' Ratini leered and set Horseman's teeth on edge, as always.

'I don't know, sir. It depends on whether Scala is on board his yacht, and if he is, how he responds to being woken up by the police in the early morning. Scala's an unknown for us, apart from his drug conviction.'

'A long time ago, wasn't it? No record of violence?'

'Fifteen years, sir. No violence recorded.'

'I'll save your plane ticket for when it's needed, then. Stay in close communication with DI Singh.'

Back at his desk, Horseman reflected on the day's wins and losses, trying to concentrate on the wins and how to generate another. Were the High-Com officials united in rejecting the police request to search Helen's rooms? He thought that was unlikely. Maybe the time was right to ask a favour of someone who might be embarrassed by the High-Com's decision: a fellow police officer. It was already six o'clock. He picked up the phone again, dialled Bob Browning's mobile number and waited, hope in his heart.

'It's Horseman, Bob.'

'How are you, Joe?'

'A bit frustrated, I admit. I'll come to the point, Bob. I rang to ask a favour. Whether you help me is entirely up to you. There's a good chance we'll get Scala to an interview room tomorrow, but I expect he could be uncooperative. He's a struck-off barrister, after all. We need his fingerprints to compare with several unknowns we lifted from the *Joshua Slocum*.'

'Understood.'

'Can you get them for us, please? I'm asking so we can avoid requesting them through official channels. We can get them that way, but I know it will take days, if not a week.'

'Waiting that long's not going to help any of us, is it?'

'No, it could wreck our investigation.'

'Do you know anyone in the Queensland Police?'

'Not particularly. I've met a few at conferences or training, but I've had no follow-up with them.'

'Yeah, I know how it is. Leave it with me. I'll do my best. To stand up in trial, I'll need an official "elimination purposes" request form, though. I know one or two people. I'll call when I know how they want to do it.'

'I'm grateful, Bob.'

'No worries. Don't sit up all night at the station. I've got your mobile number.'

31

Horseman needed to stretch his legs after so much sitting. He grabbed his mobile, said goodnight to the team, hurried down the stairs and out the front door. He ignored the cluster of food vendors around the station gates and crossed the road to Hare Krishna's. The warm aromas of spices made his mouth water, but he kept on going, lengthening his stride as he turned left to walk a few hundred metres along Victoria Parade, then crossed over to Ratu Sukuna Park. As darkness fell, fairy lights strung along the spreading branches of the old rain trees added an easy glamour to this overused space, popular at all times of day and night.

Enticing smells wafted from even more food stalls catering to both evening picnickers and takeaway customers: barbecued meat, curries, deep-fried cassava chips blended together with the diesel from the road and the salt from the sea air. Those for whom the blend was too much could always dine in McDonald's or KFC across the lane. But Horseman liked the unique smell of this part of town and lingered in the park, exchanging a few words with the vendors he knew. Each one greeted him with a joyful smile. Some threw up their hands or shrugged their shoulders helplessly, promising Horseman he would hear their detailed opinions on the performance of the national team next time they met.

He crossed to the stone seawall and walked west along the footpath, back towards the station. These days, the concrete path was well lit, bordered by struggling native hibiscus and other salt-resistant plants, interspersed with palms. The light breeze off the sea freshened, and with it he breathed in more salt and less diesel. How liberating it must be to leave human habitations behind and sail before the wind on a yacht. The life of ocean cruising and racing that

Alex Scala lived intrigued him. So far, Scala's single past conviction and the guarded opinions of Lt. Connolly and young Vili Naulu were the only clues to this man. He hoped he would learn much more tomorrow. But Singh hadn't yet told him if her lookout had seen Scala on board *Pot of Gold*, so all was in doubt.

He jogged back to the station, stopping at the roti stand to buy his dinner: one pumpkin-and-pea, and one beef and potato. Only Kau remained in the office. The loyal DC had made a pot of tea and poured a cup for Horseman before resuming the never-ending task of updating the case file. Back at his desk, Horseman was tucking into his roti while checking his emails when one message made him bite his tongue. The sender was Sergeant A. Jayaraman; the subject was Interim Scene-of-crime Analysis. 'Good on you, Ash,' he said to himself. Then, to Kau, 'I'm sending Ash's interim report, Apo, but you can file it tomorrow.'

'*Vinaka*, sir, but I'll read it before I go.'

Ash's first matching exercise had eliminated all the High-Com staff who'd stated they'd been on the *Joshua* this year. However, one of the drivers, Vuki Maya, had volunteered his fingerprints but had not stated he'd been on the yacht. As Maya's prints matched a set the SOCOs lifted from the cabin, Horseman put him first on the list for interview the next day.

That left two clear prints from two unknown individuals. One of those was found on the used plates and glasses in the yacht's aft cabin. Horseman thought it likely those prints belonged to Alex Scala, if he'd kept his date with Helen. What could be more natural than a woman on civil terms with her ex-husband providing a meal for him on her yacht, which formerly belonged to both of them? Two colleagues knew that Helen wanted to consult Scala about engine repairs. This was no secret. It was also understandable that, because of Scala's criminal conviction, Helen avoided inviting him to her residence within the High Commission.

However badly he needed Scala's prints, Horseman wouldn't ring Bob Browning again about his request this evening. He believed the AFP officer would do his best.

The SOCO lab report had not identified any possible weapons from the yacht. Clearly, there were many candidates among the non-ferrous tools, but the on-site detection of blood residue had drawn blanks. He made a note to have a word with Ash about that tomorrow. To his disappointment, all the blood samples collected from the yacht belonged to Helen.

Horseman made a few more calls, then realised it was now too late for anyone to welcome his requests for favours and special exemptions. He was washing his cup at the sink when his mobile buzzed. He dashed back to his desk.

'Singh! I'm just packing up to go home. I'd given up hope of hearing from you.'

'Me too. I called your mobile because I thought you'd be home already. My guy just texted me. Someone's emerged from *Pot of Gold*'s cabin, looks like a man. At the moment, he's not getting in his dinghy. My guy's been eating at a café with a view of the yachts, but he has to go now.'

'Thanks so much! I'm afraid I can't join you tomorrow. Ratini said you're perfectly capable and there's not enough evidence. Yet. He'll wait to see what you turn up there.'

'He's right on both counts—Ratini's improving! I might see you later tomorrow, then. Keep you posted however it goes, Joe.'

'You'd better. Good luck, and Singh ... please take care of yourself. *Moce mada.*' She had no time for his protective urges, but he couldn't help them. No matter how gladly she ran towards risk, it was he who had invited her to do so.

THURSDAY 19th July

32

Detective Inspector Susila Singh enjoyed the spectacular descent from the heights of Vanua Levu's Cross-Island Road to the shores of Savusavu, surely the most beautiful of Fiji's towns, wedged on a narrow strip of flat land against a steep hillside. She could take in the beauty of her surroundings because her constable, Ravin Banerjee, was driving. SOCO Joni Bavadra lounged in the back seat of the Land Cruiser beside Customs officer Lusi Wing. It was just after half-past eight, an hour later than Singh had planned. After completing the paperwork to search Alex Scala's yacht, *Pot of Gold*, and emailing it to her superintendent and the court magistrate, she'd spent a restless night, knowing how risky email was, how unaccountable many official recipients of messages marked URGENT felt themselves to be.

She couldn't deny she was thrilled that Horseman needed her help, and excited at accepting his challenge. Absolutely, she must eliminate the colossal risk that someone in the magistrate's office would ignore the emailed warrant application.

But Labasa had two advantages over Suva; everyone knew everyone, and many government buildings included residences for top officials. So, at six in the morning, she collected the police vehicle at the station, drove to the Courts compound, and knocked on the door of the Magistrate's residence. A maid ushered her into a roomy, book-lined office, where the white-haired magistrate welcomed her with a benign smile.

'Thank you for agreeing to see me, Mr Simpson. Here's the envelope with the completed documentation for our proposed search of the yacht *Pot of Gold*, moored near Nawi Island off Savusavu. We must conduct the search as early this morning as possible, before

Mr Scala is aware of our presence. I'm sorry I've already flouted procedure by knocking on your door at daybreak, but I'll make that even worse, I'm afraid. If you do approve the proposed search, would your staff please fax the warrant to the police station at Savusavu? An officer there will see I get it. His details are in the envelope also—in fact, I've written a fax cover-sheet so your secretary needs only to attach the warrant itself.'

'Yes, everything's clear. Are you sure you can't wait, though? While I go through the application? I trust you implicitly, Inspector Singh, but it would be quite wrong of me to sign off on an approval without a thorough reading.'

'Of course, I'd be horrified if you did that, sir.' She caught herself, but not in time. How arrogant he must think her, to judge his official conduct. And how stupid of her to blurt out her opinion like that. She must think before she speaks for the rest of the day, at least.

The magistrate's eyes twinkled behind his gold-rimmed glasses. 'If you can't wait, Inspector Singh, I'll certainly pass on your instructions to my clerk, who starts work at half-past eight. There are legal advantages in producing an original signed document rather than a facsimile, you know. When the proprietor of targeted premises is inclined to refuse entry, an original warrant document gives him less scope to challenge it. No scope, in both fact and law.'

My goodness, Mr Simpson was all but telling her there was a risk to faxing the warrant to Savusavu police station. She was grateful, but incredulous. Singh rapidly recalculated her plan as the magistrate continued.

'There's also the delay inherent in a document being handled by several individuals. Believe me, few officers are as quick and efficient as you, Inspector. My maid will make you a cup of tea while you wait, if you decide to do that. I'm afraid my wife is still asleep,' the magistrate said.

Singh only hesitated for a second. 'I'll accept your generous offer, then, Mr Simpson. As they say, a bird in the hand ...'

'Exactly. I'll get on with it now if you'd like to find Maria in the kitchen.' Singh handed him the envelope with a grateful smile.

Having the signed warrant in her backpack obviated the need to visit the Savusavu police station at all, but she made a courtesy call to let the sergeant know Labasa officers were on their territory. After that, they went to meet the Customs officer who would board the *Pot of Gold* with them.

Leaning on a post at the Customs jetty, a tall, beefy young man waved as they got out of the vehicle. He walked over to them, leading an eager small dog. Not that Singh liked dogs much.

'Seru Kubura, Customs officer, and with me my secret weapon, detector dog Sami. She's a beagle and proud of it.' After they'd introduced themselves and patted Sami, Kubura gestured to a picnic table in the shade of the Customs office. 'How about you familiarise me with your plans before we head to *Pot of Gold*'s mooring?'

'Great, Seru,' Singh answered. 'Searching boats is your specialty, not mine. We're relying on you and Lusi Wing to set us straight.'

'Would you like tea or coffee after your long drive?'

'Just some water, please. We're already an hour late.' Kubura called for water through the open louvres of the Customs office window.

'Have you sighted Scala this morning?' Singh asked.

'No. One or the other of us has been around the jetty since first light. And his dinghy's still tied to the stern, so I think he's still on board.'

Within a minute, someone placed a jug of water and paper cups on the table. By the time they'd emptied the jug, they'd also reviewed and tweaked their plan for the operation.

'Thanks for the water, Seru, and your advice, too. Let's go, shall we?'

They boarded the Customs speedboat, sat where Seru told them to sit, and motored away from the jetty.

33

Kubura filled Singh in as they approached their target. 'The yacht is anchored in the narrow stretch of water between the town and Nawi Island. It's a perfect anchorage—always calm, whatever the wind direction. What's interesting is there's a marina there now with top-class services, but Scala chose not to take a berth there. He could just want to save money or want peace, quiet and privacy. But at the marina you've got power, showers and toilets, laundry, it's so convenient. So, anchoring further away does raise suspicion in a suspicious man like me. That's *Pot of Gold* up ahead now, sixteen metres, fibreglass ketch. She's a beautiful yacht, isn't she?'

The Customs officer pointed to a streamlined boat flying the Australian ensign at the stern and the Fiji flag from the mast. Singh knew there were special protocols for flags on boats, all a mystery to her.

She called Scala's mobile number as they approached their target. No answer. Kubura handed her a loud-hailer. 'Detective Inspector Singh and officers are coming alongside *Pot of Gold* and request permission to board to interview Mr Alexander Scala, skipper.' They waited in silence until Singh repeated her call. After several moments, the entry hatch rolled back, and a man in a white tee-shirt and frayed denim shorts climbed out into the cockpit. His feet were bare and his face was weatherbeaten.

'What's this? Please explain yourselves.' He didn't look or sound angry. They were now alongside the cockpit. Kuruba stood up, holding on to a stanchion to keep the speedboat steady.

Singh introduced herself again. 'Are you Mr Alexander Scala, sir?'

His gaze assessed her. 'Yes, what is this about?' His grey curly hair was unkempt, but his short beard looked recently barbered.

'Mr Scala, we can speak more easily on board, with your permission.'

'Why should I invite the police on board?'

'Mr Scala, I have a magistrate's warrant to search *Pot of Gold*. You can choose to let us board and conduct the search in your presence. The alternative is I arrest you now for obstructing a police enquiry, and we take you to Savusavu station for questioning. While I'm doing that, search officers from both the police and Customs will search your yacht.'

'Why? *Pot of Gold* was cleared for entry the day after I made port here on 9th July.'

'Mr Scala, I'm not one for small boats. I'm holding on here, and I'm still not happy. Your yacht is much bigger and steadier. May we talk on board?'

'I see I've got no choice.' His tone was grudging. Kubura tied the speedboat's bowline to a stanchion and Scala fitted a boarding ladder over the gunwale. When everyone except Constable Banerjee, who was to guard the speedboat, had climbed up, Kubura tucked Sami under his arm and was on the deck in two strides.

They sat on the cockpit benches. Singh retrieved the warrant from her backpack, unfolded it and handed it to Scala. He put on thick spectacles which hung round his neck on a string and examined the document.

'I see this seems to be in order, and is the original. But I'm entitled to know how and why this came about. I remind you once more, Customs cleared *Pot of Gold* for entry to Savusavu on 9th July.'

'It's come to police attention that you have an Australian conviction for possession of a prohibited Class A drug, Mr Scala. You sail to Fiji quite often, and your yacht has been cleared without a Customs inspection on your last four entries.'

'I'm known here, yes. But I haven't met you two before,' he nodded to Kubura and Wing.

'No, sir.' Kubura said.

'So, putting those two facts together, the police decided *Pot of Gold* should be searched, and we applied for a search warrant, although not required for a routine Customs search, which is simply being done rather late.'

Scala stared at her. She hadn't a clue what he was feeling.

'I understand this may be a difficult time for you, sir. I understand your former wife was the Australian High Commissioner to Fiji. My condolences on her death.'

This seemed to surprise Scala—his eyebrows shot up. 'Well, go ahead and get it over with, then.'

The two Customs officers and the SOCO had already decided on their procedure. One took the forward cabin, one the saloon, and Kubura and Sami dealt with the aft cabin. Singh stayed in the cockpit.

Scala moved between each section of the boat, trying to watch each officer as they opened and inspected the contents of every compartment, drawer, locker and container. He opened his small safe when Constable Bavadra asked him, but like everywhere else, the officers found nothing to object to. The beagle sniffed around the cockpit, then went on deck with Kuruba and inspected every nook and cranny without apparent interest, her tail slowly wagging. Then Kuruba took her down the companionway and let her loose inside, with all the cupboards and drawers still open and mattresses upturned. Once again, the dog was thorough but detached.

Singh thought the exercise was a duty for the dog, rather than a pleasure. Sami had inspected the full length of the boat, but in the forward sail locker, Kuruba turned around and directed the dog to search again in the opposite direction. In the carpeted saloon, where upholstered settees could serve as bunks, Sami paused. She bounded up onto the settees and nosed into the open lockers above them, then jumped back on the floor, nosing around the edge of the carpet. Then she sat, her tail thumping madly, and uttered a low growl, all the time gazing expectantly at Kuruba.

Kuruba called Lusi to join them. 'Did you take up the floor panels?' he asked.

'No,' she said. 'I didn't realise they were removable, sorry.'

'The ballast comes up to the floor here. And under each settee is a water tank. They occupy the entire space through to the hull,' Scala explained, unperturbed. 'Perhaps the dog is reacting to the smell of fresh water.'

'Perhaps. Humans make errors, so do dogs. Not as often as humans do, in my experience. So we'd better have the floor panels up, please. I don't want to lever your floor up, so if you could show me the catch?'

Scala frowned, but squatted down and pulled up one corner of the carpet, revealing a flat brass ring pull. He lifted the floor panel on the port side.

'Neat, I'll do the other one,' said Kuruba. The space beneath was sealed with black plastic. Underneath, they found dozens of sealed plastic packages, each the size of a one-kilo packet of flour.

'What's in here?' Singh asked.

'I don't know,' Scala replied.

'Right. Lusi, count each brick into our crates. Inspector Singh, count aloud as she does it, then sign and seal.' Kuruba looked at Scala. 'Sir, how many layers did you pack in here?'

Scala ignored him. But Scala had been almost right—there was only space for one layer between the floor and the top of the ballast. That was forty packages.

'Let's see those water tanks now, please, Mr Scala.'

'They're welded to a steel cradle, bolted through the yacht's frame. They can't be taken out.'

'Show me, please. Now.'

Scala was right about the construction of the water tanks. But stuffed behind, beneath and beside them were another eighty plastic-wrapped packages, each the size of a packet of flour.

Singh arrested Scala for offences relating to the possession, import and export of prohibited goods. Constable Bavadra handcuffed him and read him his rights. A wave of joy surged through Singh, even while her mind knew it was too soon.

<h1 style="text-align:center">34</h1>

Horseman had just stepped on board the *Joshua Slocum* when the call came. He listened intently, his smile growing wider. He tipped his head back and laughed.

'Singh, you're a wonder, I always said so. What fantastic news! I'm back on Helen's boat now. Remember Timo Vodo, from the navy?'

'Of course, say *bula* from me.'

'He's here to scrutinise the boat's tools and tell me if anything's missing. I'm still trying to identify the weapon. The divers didn't come up with anything. I don't know what should be here.'

'Creative!'

'Desperate, you mean. You've made my day. Have you told Ratini?'

'Yes, and our air charter costs are coming out of his budget, so that tells you how elated he is. We're landing at two o'clock. That's the plan, anyway.'

'Oh, has Ratini booked you accommodation?'

'He offered, but a cousin of mine is renting my flat in *Seaview*, so I'll squeeze in with her. We'll be neighbours again for a bit.'

'Is Ash up to date on this? The sooner we identify the drugs, the better. What about Siale Vula and Narcotics?'

'Yes, they'll be looking after our precious cargo after we land.'

'I just had an idea, Singh. If Scala was here on *Joshua Slocum* last Saturday, it's possible he involved Helen's boat in the smuggling, too.'

'The SOCOs found no drug traces, did they?'

'No, but they didn't employ a sniffer dog. We had a murder victim on the cabin floor and no reason to suspect drug involvement. I'll ask Ash to review any samples for drugs and get the dog team's best canine detective on the job.'

'Good idea—without Customs officer Sami, we wouldn't have found Scala's hoard. See you this afternoon, Joe.'

'*Vinaka vakalevu*, Susie. Can't wait to see you.'

When Horseman picked up Singh's call, Lt Vodo had discreetly moved to the yacht's bow and started inspecting the metal fittings and tools stowed on deck. When he got to the cockpit, Horseman told him Singh's news.

His eyes widened. 'No pressure, then.'

'None at all. You're here to tell me what's not here, that's much more difficult.'

'Everything on the port side is present and correct. Come with me and we'll check the starboard deck, then we can look down below.'

'All shipshape, she's a tidy vessel,' Lt Vodo concluded as they stepped into the cockpit. 'Hang on, man, look at this.'

'What?'

Lt Vodo pointed out a pocket screwed to the port cockpit bulkhead. 'This is to secure a sail winch handle, but the handle's missing. It's not on the deck or anywhere else in the cockpit. And look, its twin on the starboard side has a handle in it, just as it should. Looks like bronze. It's a top-quality choice, though very heavy. We'll keep our eyes out for it below.'

Vodo pulled on the gloves Horseman gave him, took the handle from the pocket, then slotted it into a winch on deck and ratcheted it back and forth. 'Much easier than pulling on a rope. Let's take it below decks with us.'

'Yes, it would fit the bill as the murder weapon,' Horseman replied. He learned quite a bit about the function of various sailing tools during their search, but they didn't find the missing winch handle.

'Since I can't bag something that isn't there, I'll bag this handle and get the SOCO to throw all their tech at it. If it's clean, we'll hang on to it for matching, in case its twin turns up.'

'*Oi lei*, sorry I can't be more help.'

Horseman clapped Vodo on the back. 'You've been a great help, Timo. Have you got time for a quick bite to eat?'

***

Detective Sergeant Kelepi Taleca was frowning over the case file when Horseman returned to the station. Grey-haired Taleca had already passed retirement age, but the Training Division ignored the birthdays of valuable officers if they wanted to continue to serve. He was as skinny as ever and bounded up nimbly when Horseman greeted him. He held Horseman's hand and pumped it up and down for some time, his eyes moist, his grin splitting his face.

'Man, you still can't manage without me, and you a detective inspector for years? I thought my protégé would be able to stand on his own two feet by now! What's the matter with you?'

'Nothing at all, now that I've got you and the extra uniforms, Keli. Has anyone made you a cuppa yet? Have you eaten?'

'*Vinaka*, Joe, a cuppa would be perfect. As usual, my wife has packed my lunch box, and I'm just about ready to eat it. But what's your probationer DC Pareti doing? At the Police College, I trained him to make excellent tea, and as soon as he graduates, you start spoiling him by making the tea yourself?'

'It's just that when I'm restless, I enjoy getting up and making tea for myself. Helps me think. Actually, I can delegate quite well and will now demonstrate. Pareti? Let's have some tea, please, and round up the others. You can all gather around, eat your lunch and listen to what DI Singh and I have found out this morning. Invite the super to attend if he likes.'

Horseman ended up in front of the whiteboard, updating it as he related the events of the early morning. For once, Ratini drank his tea and listened without scornful interjections.

He ended his summary with the latest report. 'And last, hot off the email, the SOCOs found only a few calls on Ms Armstrong's mobile: two from Scala and one to him, and a text from Lt Connolly about the meeting they attended on Saturday morning. Apparently, she deleted everything daily. So they've sent it on to the Telecom experts.'

'Maybe she had two mobiles, sir. Or more.' Waqa said.

'That's possible, Lili. We do need to search Ms Armstrong's rooms. To conclude, everyone, this has been the most positive day we've had all week. What started as an effort to speak to Ms Armstrong's next of kin resulted in the arrest of Mr Scala following the discovery of what seems to be a major drugs haul. That find will deliver Alex Scala in handcuffs to our door around two o'clock this afternoon, and we can question him about his visit to Suva last Friday.'

DC Kau's hand shot up. 'Sir, isn't Scala our top suspect? I know we haven't got enough evidence to charge him with murder yet, but it's clear, isn't it? Ms Armstrong somehow suspected him of drug involvement, challenged him about it when they met on her boat. They argued, and he grabbed the winch handle, hit her over the head and then ran away.'

'Plausible scenario, Apo, and I hope you're right. But as you say, we need evidence. It's like rugby. You can throw yourself over the try-line, but if you haven't got the ball, what's the point? The ball is critical evidence linking the suspect to the crime. Let's not race ahead without it.'

His audience of rugby fans nodded sagely, muttering agreement.

'So, all our next actions follow from this morning's leads. My plan is to interview Scala, together with DI Singh and DI Vula. DS Taleca, you and Izzy Pareti can bring the High-Com driver in to explain his prints in the *Joshua*'s cabin. Apo and Lili, make a guard duty roster for the new uniforms at the yacht club. Show them the ropes. I've asked Ash to bring his SOCOs, a Customs officer and a detector dog to search the *Joshua* more thoroughly as soon as possible. Scala may have brought drugs on board last week, but drugs were the last thing on our minds on Tuesday. Keep your eyes out for their arrival.'

The detectives' eyes widened.

Horseman continued. 'Apo, I want you to get the divers back for a wider search, specifically looking for the twin winch handle. If we're lucky, the club skip won't have been emptied since Saturday. Consult the club manager about that—don't tip rubbish out all over their carpark. I'll be available to answer questions until Scala and Singh arrive. After that, DS Taleca will handle anything that crops up. By the way, have you tracked down the security guard on duty last Saturday evening?'

'Got his name, sir, but no phone number. He's never worked at the yacht club before. I'll try and get him through the security company.'

The DCs' faces were willing. More than willing, they were keen. Horseman thought now was the right time to put his request to Ratini.

'Super, I want to raise another matter. Would you prefer to discuss it here or in your office?'

'Oh, here, but be quick. Narcotics has asked me to provide extra staff for them on the back of the Savusavu interception this morning. I've already done them a big favour by releasing DI Vula, creating a shortage for your High Commissioner's case, which has international ramifications. So, I don't see how I can help them out anymore. All this robbing Peter to pay Paul has got to stop somewhere. I can't pull extra officers out of thin air, can I?'

'Well, my idea may help us all out, Super. As you say, the pressure from all quarters on my team is enormous, even with DS Taleca and the extra uniforms on board. DI Singh has told me crime is light in Labasa at the moment. That's why she's become involved in the ongoing enquiry with DI Vula into drug smuggling through Savusavu. Having met and got a sense of Scala this morning, she'd very much like to contribute to our case. We never considered Ms Armstrong's murder might have a connection to drug smuggling, but now it's a real possibility.'

'Hmm, you pointed out yourself, this is speculation, Horseman.'

'*Io*, sir. However, we've got evidence—the drugs. The lab will identify Scala's packets this afternoon, and then we'll know if we're dealing with meth, cocaine, self-raising flour or something else. What do you think about seconding Singh to us for the duration of the case, sir?'

'You two have been cooking this up between you for days, eh?'

'No, sir. Singh rang me about ten this morning to tell me they'd seized 120 packets of powder from *Pot of Gold*. We briefly considered whether she could work with us on Ms Armstrong's murder and whether the cases connect.'

'I accept the Armstrong murder needs more detectives, particularly at DI level, after your new leads this morning. You couldn't get a more level-headed and capable DI than Singh—I give you that. Why she wants to work with you, I don't understand. But okay, if her Labasa super agrees to it, I'll bring her on board. I'll even ring him myself. I hear they take long lunch breaks in Labasa and don't always come back to work afterwards, so who knows?' Ratini treated him to a suggestive wink.

Horseman reminded himself Ratini had agreed to Singh joining the team, and that was all that mattered.

35

Singh walked into the Suva Central Police Station with mixed feelings: elated to bring in her prisoner and proud of her role in his capture, even though hers was subsidiary to that of Sami the sniffer dog. She felt nostalgic to be at her old station, and regretful it was no longer her home. They were all waiting, their faces wreathed in smiles. Horseman came towards her, his hand outstretched.

She had to press her lips together to stop them quivering as she grasped his solid hand in hers, and blink rapidly to stop her eyes smarting. How could her body rebel against her mind at just this moment, after keeping control all morning? But when she looked up through a film of tears, her dear old team were also blinking. Then they clapped. Horseman put out his hand slightly to warn Lili not to rush forward to hug her former DS.

His smile was glad, but he only said, 'Welcome home, DI Singh. All the paperwork ready to process Mr Scala?'

Singh nodded. Her hand trembled as she handed over a bulging official buff envelope. Horseman opened the flap, slid the papers up a bit and flipped through them without taking them out.

'Go ahead, Singh, the sergeant's ready. I'll wait here until Mr Scala's safely in custody, then we'll go upstairs where the team can welcome you properly.' His voice flooded her with warmth. She'd often wondered if it was a mistake to take the promotion to Labasa. Professionally, she'd done well, but now she realised her heart was with Horseman, the first boss to treat her like a partner. Sometimes she felt he was up for something more, but was never sure. Now they were of equal rank, maybe he'd no longer regard her as out of bounds.

Scala made little fuss. He'd been allowed to pack a small bag under supervision before he left *Pot of Gold* in handcuffs. He resisted handing it over, even though Singh and others had watched him packing it. In the end, he complied, but still refused to be fingerprinted.

'I want to telephone my solicitor. I will not submit to any intimate bodily processing without his advice, as is my right. As your arrest procedure is therefore rendered incomplete, I will wait for my solicitor in an interview room.' Scala said.

Singh had spent quite enough time in Scala's company. She was glad to see his back retreating down a corridor to make his phone call. She smiled at Horseman, and they climbed the stairs to the detectives' floor. As she passed the super's office, the door opened and Ratini emerged, shook her hand and, supporting her elbow in a proprietorial gesture she despised, steered her the few familiar steps to the open office she'd worked in for years.

Her former colleagues showed their pleasure in cheers and claps, even those with whom she'd never worked directly. More precious to her were the grins and moist eyes of Horseman's team. DI Vula was there too, and Tanielo Musudroka, who'd now joined Ash Jayaraman's SOCO team.

Horseman relieved her of her backpack, and plump little Lili Waqa grabbed her around the waist in a fierce hug. When she'd greeted everyone, the circle parted to reveal the DC's table covered in a cloth and platters of pizza, rotis, fried fish cocktails, sliced dalo and sandwiches. After Ratini made an embarrassing flowery speech, they invited Singh to sit at the head of the table, and everyone else took a seat or stood behind the chairs after filling their plates.

Horseman sat on her right. The new probationer and Lili brought in tea as the others served themselves. Detectives who'd transferred to Suva since Singh's promotion to Labasa introduced themselves. Everyone wanted to hear more about the morning's raid in Savusavu, and while she was happy to oblige, Singh realised she hadn't eaten much, while most plates were empty. Then Horseman came to her rescue, as he so often had in the old days.

'DI Singh had an exhausting morning and has a demanding interview coming up. She badly needs a proper lunch. How about you tell her your stories now, while she eats and relaxes a bit? Lili, pour DI Singh a hot cup of tea.'

Everyone was apologetic and stopped quizzing her. Even Ratini seemed sincerely concerned. When Lili placed a cup of strong aromatic tea by Singh's hand, she gulped it with pleasure. '*Vinaka vakalevu* to you all for this wonderful welcome. To my great surprise, DI Horseman is right once again. I'm still quite hungry.'

Probationer Izzy Pareti's long arms reached over diners' heads and removed platters from the table. 'I'll consolidate these leftovers onto one plate and zap it in the microwave for you, Inspector Singh. You need a good, hot lunch.' With his other hand, he removed her own plate of lukewarm food and sped off to the kitchen.

Surprised, Singh said to Horseman. 'Your new probationer will go far. Tell me your plan for the interview while I finish my food.'

'No, Susie. Enjoy your lunch, such as it is.'

She sipped her tea and felt she'd come home.

36

Horseman grew more and more optimistic as he and Singh assembled the evidence they needed for their interview with Scala. They'd always enjoyed brainstorming an interview strategy together. But what he'd liked best about working with Singh was the natural rhythm they fell into during the interview itself. More often than not, interviews didn't go to plan, but with a glance or a lift of an eyebrow, they could change course in tandem without breaking their pace, or even worse, stalling the interview to confer outside the room. That always signalled to the suspect that the cops didn't know what to do next.

His phone buzzed as he was going down to the interview rooms. It was Musudroka, who'd rushed away to join Ash Jayaraman in the second search of the *Joshua*, with the detector dog. Horseman stopped Singh and switched the phone to speaker.

'Sir, Sergeant Jayaraman wants you to know we've already found a white powder residue around the water tanks. No packaged drugs yet, but we're not done. How about that, sir?'

'Fantastic, Tani. So fast!'

'This dog works like lightning, sir!' Musudroka sounded like an excited puppy himself.

'You're just in time. I'm heading to the interview room now. Congratulate Ash and ask him to rush that powder to the lab right now for immediate identification. We need it soon!'

'Already on its way, sir.'

Horseman and Singh entered the room where their chief suspect waited with his solicitor. Scala's beard and shoulder-length curls showed he'd wet his head and dragged a comb through his hair. Mr Fletcher Thomas wore a navy three-piece suit with a white shirt. Tiny white golf balls decorated his green tie. He stood courteously as the detectives entered and grasped their hands briefly as he introduced himself. He did not smile.

'Detective Inspectors, our paths have not crossed before, but you'll be aware I'm a partner at Thomas and Fareed Solicitors. I must begin with a protest that my client has been waiting here for hours and could not shower and change his clothes after a traumatic morning, not to mention hot.' His voice was calm and pitched low. He would not be one for melodrama, but he was blustering nonetheless.

'Mr Thomas, your client chose not to complete the check-in process for the holding cells by refusing to be fingerprinted until he spoke to you. He chose to wait here until you arrived. Mr Scala had the use of a toilet and washbasin whenever he asked. He's obviously rinsed his face and hair and been offered tea and something to eat.' Horseman glanced at the plastic jug of water, plate and paper cups on the table. 'Of course, you're entitled to make a formal complaint about his treatment. But it's best for everyone if you do that after this interview. Let's clear this matter up quickly, shall we?'

The solicitor cocked his head to one side as if considering.

Horseman continued. 'At least, that's my opinion. Do you agree, DI Singh?'

'Yes, I do. I suspect my morning's been even longer than Mr Scala's. I got up in the dark and drove from Labasa to Savusavu to lead the *Pot of Gold* operation. If we can clear things up quickly, let's do so.'

At a slow nod from Thomas, Singh switched on the recorder and made the preliminary announcements.

'First, I would like to express my condolences on the death of your former wife, Ms Helen Armstrong, the Australian High Commissioner. I had the privilege of knowing her a little in her official capacity. She was a most admirable and kind woman.'

'Thank you.'

'I was surprised to learn that you were her next-of-kin, Mr Scala. Divorced couples rarely take on such a role of trust for each other.'

Scala frowned as if confused and looked to Mr Thomas, who nodded. 'After our divorce, we kept our distance, but as time passed, we could become friends. To be frank, I think we both forgot that we were still each other's official next-of-kin. We were both healthy, and no situation arose where we needed a next-of-kin.'

'I see. You've come to Fiji a few times every year for a decade. Did you see your wife every time you came, in the six years she's been High Commissioner here?'

'Not always. I don't always have the time to come to Suva if my business is elsewhere in Fiji.'

'And your business is?'

'As well as competing in long-distance ocean racing myself, I provide various services to the international yachting sector. Such as brokering sales, delivering yachts all over the world, finding racing crew personnel, consulting on yacht overhauls—that sort of thing.'

Horseman turned to Singh. 'That sounds exciting, don't you think, DI Singh? Adventurous. A free agent.'

Singh smiled and nodded. 'Did you see Helen during your current visit to Fiji, Mr Scala?'

'No, I sailed direct to Savusavu.'

The solicitor pulled his eyebrows together in a frown. 'I must interject here. I see no relevance in this line of questioning about the Australian High Commissioner. My client was arrested in Savusavu after some unidentified packages were discovered on his yacht this morning. You said you wanted this matter cleared up quickly. I suggest you begin by asking questions relevant to that seizure and his arrest.'

Horseman smiled. 'Always useful to be clear about the background, Mr Thomas. As senior investigating officer for the murder of Ms Armstrong, I've been trying to speak with Mr Scala for a frustrating few days.' He turned to Scala. 'I thought I'd have to knock on your door in Australia, but then you astonished us by turning up in Savusavu.'

Scala looked unperturbed. 'My phone's battery was flat. Helen's death was a terrible shock. I couldn't summon up the will to go ashore to charge it. I'm not berthed at the marina.'

'I suppose you don't need to be. Inspector Singh tells me you've got a solar panel and a nifty little wind generator, too.'

'I was impressed. So please drop this fiction about the phone battery.' Singh said, all smiles.

'When did you last meet Helen?' Horseman asked.

'Several months ago, on my last visit to Fiji.'

'We understand Helen relied on your expertise to maintain her yacht. The *Joshua Slocum* hasn't left the Royal Suva Yacht club for a couple of months because Helen thought the engine was unreliable.'

'Yes, that's right. She'd got some quotes for a major overhaul and wanted me to check them over and test the engine myself. She didn't accept that the *Joshua* needed as much work as the engineers quoted for.'

'Did you call Helen when you dropped anchor in Savusavu? You understand we've applied for your phone records, but it takes us a day or two with Telecom Fiji, so I'm just speeding up the process by asking you directly.'

'Yes, maybe the next day.'

'Did you make an arrangement to inspect the *Joshua Slocum* during that call?'

'No. I offered, but she said she was flat out at work and would ring me back when she worked out a time.'

'And did she?'

'I'm not sure. As I said, I had problems with my mobile. What is this, anyway? These questions are not only intrusive, they've got absolutely nothing to do with my arrest.' Scala was nicely confused now. Horseman nodded slightly to Singh to finish him off.

'Blame me, Mr Scala. I've got a literal mind and need to draw a timeline with one event following another, step by step, cause and effect. I can't do that with you. If Ms Armstrong didn't ring you back because she was too busy, why did you come to Suva?'

Scala's eyes darted from one to the other. 'I didn't. I had business in Savusavu and expected to set sail for Suva when I knew she had some time to spare. Is there something wrong with you?'

Good, Horseman thought. Singh was getting Scala rattled.

Singh frowned. 'I don't know, Mr Scala, but there's something wrong with your timeline. Fiji Airways says you bought a ticket at Savusavu airport last Friday and flew to Suva at 1205 hours. Here's the passenger manifest.' She laid a print-out before Scala.

'But—'

'And before you say this must have been a fraud of some kind or someone impersonated you, here's a copy of your Visa card transaction, with the time-print.'

'No, this isn't true!'

'Well, the Twin Otter carries nineteen passengers, Mr Scala. But on your flight, there were only eleven. We can round up some of the others and show them your photo, or organise an identity parade, ask them to pick out anyone in the lineup who was on their flight. We're used to doing those routine checks, but it takes a few days to marshal everyone.'

'Do them, then! You can't accuse me on the basis of a Visa card transaction.'

The solicitor laid a calming hand on Scala's tensed arm. 'Let's call a break so that I can confer with my client, Inspectors.'

'Certainly, sir. I'll order tea and biscuits for you. Shall we say five minutes?'

'Twenty, please, Inspector. Mr Scala is understandably overwrought after the shocking experiences of this morning.'

'Very well. We'll return in ten minutes. Tell the constable on guard if you need anything, or if you're ready earlier.'

37

Horseman and Singh dashed back upstairs to check for news. 'I wish we had an interview room with a one-way mirror like on TV detective shows. It could be useful to observe these lawyer-client interviews. Don't you think, Joe?'

'Yes. Oh look, someone's left the Telecom report on Helen's mobile on my desk. Let's take a look—yes! Calls to Scala's phone on Friday and Saturday.' He passed the printout to Singh.

'Good! How d'you think we're going so far?' she asked.

'So-so. He can't work out why you're not grilling him about the drugs. I wonder if he'll make a statement.'

'If he admits to flying to Suva last Friday, he can't avoid telling us how he got back to Savusavu. Let's stick to our plan, but stay flexible. If Scala produces an alibi for Helen's murder, we'll charge him with Class A drug offences. If he doesn't, let's go with murder and see how he reacts.'

'A murder charge might well loosen his tongue, I reckon,' Singh predicted.

Horseman laughed. He wanted to hug her. 'It's great to have you back, Singh.' Indeed, he wondered how he'd got on for the last two years without her.

When they returned to Scala and his solicitor, Horseman noticed someone had treated the pair to china cups and milk in a jug, not to mention a matching china plate with biscuit crumbs. Fletcher Thomas must have connections at the station.

'Constable, can you clear the table, please? Leave the water and paper cups,' Horseman said. As the constable on guard hurried to comply, the detectives seated themselves, placing their document folders in front of them. Singh did the honours with the sound recorder.

'Let's continue, then,' Horseman said.

The solicitor cleared his throat. 'Mr Scala is very tired, and your question about his flight to Suva confused him. He now agrees that he purchased the Fiji Airways ticket and was on Flight FJA-43 last Friday morning.'

Singh laid out the airline printouts before Scala once more. 'Do you agree these papers are correct, Mr Scala?'

'Yes, they're correct.'

'Why did you come to Suva, Mr Scala?' Singh asked.

'I had business here.'

'Did that business include meeting Ms Armstrong?'

'No, although I did intend to contact her if I had time.'

'Did you speak to or meet your former wife while you were in Suva?' Horseman asked. 'Remember, in a day or two we'll have your phone records,'

'No.'

'What is the nature of your business in Suva?' he asked.

'Confidential, Inspector, and none of yours.'

Singh jumped in. 'You said you intended to sail *Pot of Gold* from Savusavu to Suva, Mr Scala. Why did you change your mind and decide to fly?'

'A client wanted to meet me to discuss potential services I could supply. He was only available that Friday afternoon, so I flew over.'

'Was your client a customer for the 120 kilograms of a Class A drug seized from your yacht this morning?' Horseman asked.

One corner of Scala's mouth twitched. Could it be amusement, triumph or arrogance? 'No, my client did not want to buy drugs. As I said, the meeting was commercial-in-confidence.'

Horseman continued. 'Oh, by the way, we got the results from our lab during your break. The packets seized from *Pot of Gold* contain cocaine.'

'I think your lab is wrong, Inspector.'

An alarm bell rang in Horseman's mind—the first warning that they could be heading in the wrong direction. He glanced at Singh.

'My timeline has still got a sizeable gap, Mr Scala. We're now agreed on when and how you travelled to Suva, but you've eluded us as to your return to Savusavu. Fiji Airways tells us you didn't fly back, and the Inter-Island Ferries tells us you didn't travel with them. So I give up, you'll have to enlighten us. When and how did you travel back to Savusavu?'

'I'm not here to pander to your curiosity, Inspector. Ask me a question relevant to my arrest for suspected drug smuggling and I'll answer.'

Horseman was worried. Scala was now confident, taking control, because they'd missed a turn, taken a track that led nowhere. Only one thing to do—bring out the big guns and rattle the man's cage. He signalled Singh.

'How about I give you some information, Mr Scala?' Horseman began. 'And then you'll see why we've been giving you these opportunities to explain yourself. After all, I suggested clearing this up quickly, and I suppose DI Singh and I could have been quicker. But so could you, Mr Scala.'

Suddenly, Fletcher Thomas looked up at Horseman, on full alert.

'First, impressed by Customs officer Sami's results this morning, I ordered our SOCOs to search the *Joshua Slocum* again, with a detector dog, who pointed the team to small traces of white powder around the yacht's water tanks. Those samples match the cocaine found on *Pot of Gold* exactly.'

The solicitor looked at his client sharply. Scala kept looking at Horseman, his face frozen.

'Now, Mr Scala, our search team may have poor olfactory ability compared to a dog, but one job they're expert at is fingerprints. They lifted excellent, clear prints from the yacht and matched most to the High Commissioner's guests or crew. But we haven't been able to match one individual whose prints are on a plate, a glass and elsewhere not long before your former wife was murdered last Saturday night.'

Scala's face unfroze and reddened. 'That's got nothing to do with me!' he shouted. Again, his solicitor placed a hand on his client's forearm.

'I was surprised you refused to surrender your prints when we welcomed you to Suva Central today. But it didn't matter because we obtained your prints from the Queensland Police rather quickly. We've just learned, again during your break, that the unknown person who ate a meal and drank a glass of wine with your former wife before she was brutally killed was none other than you, Alexander Scala.'

Scala's anger drained from his face. He was now white with fear.

Singh showed the Telecom printout to Scala. 'What's more, the Telecom report came through on Ms Armstrong's mobile phone while we were speaking earlier. You made two calls to her on Friday afternoon, at 3:17 and 3:40 in the afternoon. She answered the second, and you spoke for nearly two minutes. She called you on Saturday morning at 10:07. You spoke for 15 seconds.'

'So it seems you've been telling us lies, Mr Scala, maybe a full pack of them. What have you to say?' Horseman asked.

'Nothing. This is all a setup!' Scala now spoke quietly, deliberately.

'I'm afraid you leave me no choice but to arrest you on suspicion of the murder of Helen Armstrong. Inspector Singh, please remind Mr Scala of his rights.'

Mr Thomas kept his hand on his client's forearm; whether to calm or restrain, Horseman wasn't sure. 'Inspectors, I must confer with my client alone at this juncture,' he said, his tone neutral.

'Certainly, but five minutes only. Your client has just two choices, hasn't he? And I'm late for my rugby team's Thursday afternoon training session. We'll be outside the door. The constable will stay inside.'

The door shut. Singh whispered, 'I didn't think you'd go quite that far today.'

'I didn't either. But he'd go on with his denials and lies forever until the evidence shut him up. Don't you think, Singh?'

'Yes, but we've nothing else up our sleeve now.'

'He's frightened of someone—maybe his mysterious Suva contact, if he exists.'

The constable knocked on the door.

'Is he more frightened of a drug smuggler or a murder conviction? Let's see, Singh.'

Scala clenched his mouth and gritted his teeth as the detectives walked in and sat down. He glared, but not at them; he glared at the scuffed and stained tabletop. Was he rebelling against his solicitor's advice, or furious because he had no sane choice but to follow it? They would soon find out.

Horseman and Singh shuffled their folders on the table, and Singh switched the recorder on. Then all four participants were silent for longer than was comfortable for any of them. But Horseman knew he and Singh could hold out longer than the accused. He pulled his pen out of a pocket and placed it in the centre of his folder.

Eventually, Mr Thomas spoke. 'I believe my client is now prepared to explain the circumstances of his return from Suva to Savusavu following his business trip.'

'Good, let's hear it, Mr Scala,' Horseman said, folding his arms and leaning back in his chair.

Mr Thomas looked at Scala and nodded. His client's face changed as he reached his decision: the muscles relaxed, he lifted his head, his breath slowed.

'Good God, I've told you a heap of bullshit, trying to save my sorry skin. But do you really need me to identify my client?'

'Yes, how can we check your story otherwise?'

'Oh Christ! Here it is. The truth.' He inhaled deeply. 'My client was Henry Lam—he owns pharmacies in Fiji, Vanuatu and Samoa. He imports and exports pharmaceuticals. Recently, he got in touch, asking me to take a cargo to Australia for him in my boat. I said I could, for the right price. I'd delivered for him once before, a couple of years ago—that's when the traces of powder you found on the *Joshua Slocum* must have been deposited. But how? I only stored the cargo on the yacht for a few days because of a stuff-up by Lam's men. I can explain that later.'

'We'll look forward to that.'

'We—that's me and Lam—got most of the details ironed out on Friday afternoon, but I wasn't going to leave until half my fee was safe in my account. I'd have accepted hard currency cash, but that wasn't possible, Lam said. So I stayed overnight, rang Helen and we arranged to meet on the *Joshua* on Saturday afternoon for me to check out the engine once more and go through the quotes she'd got, help her make a decision.'

'Did you get your fee?'

'Yes, Lam paid. I went to the yacht club in the afternoon, tested the engine, analysed the quotes she'd left for me and had a nap in the cabin until Helen arrived.'

'When was that?'

'I'm not sure. Five-ish? The club bar was filling up. I didn't check the time when Helen arrived. Why should I? She was all dressed up for a ball, as dressed up as she ever gets, that is. She'd brought a picnic of smoked trout and salad, and we both had a glass of wine, which explains my fingerprints. I told her which quote I recommended and explained that I couldn't supervise the work as I had to return to Australia to pick up a yacht for delivery. She was happy enough with everything, so I left.'

'You say Helen was *happy enough*. Was something bothering her?'

'Oh, you know, she grumbled about the cost of the engine overhaul. Typical yacht-owner's angst.'

'Did you quarrel with your former wife?'

'No, we were well past that years ago.'

'Did you hit her?'

'Never. Helen's the only woman I've ever truly loved, Inspector. I'd never hurt her. Killing her—that's unimaginable.'

'Tell us about your movements after you left the yacht club.'

'I caught a cab to the airport, got on the private charter plane Henry Lam had organised. He wanted me to ride to Savusavu with the cargo I had contracted to transport to Queensland for him. I helped unpack the plane, caught a cab to the marina. The driver helped me load the plain cardboard boxes into my dinghy, and we puttered off to *Pot of Gold*. No problems.'

'You'll appreciate that we need more precise times for an alibi to hold up, Mr Scala. Did you speak to anyone, remember anything after you left the yacht club that would pin down the time?'

'Well, only the pilot of the plane and Lam's staffer who was at the airport. But the charter plane's flight times would be precise, wouldn't they?'

With Henry Lam behind the charter, Horseman wasn't so sure. 'I hope so. We'll get right onto that now. However, until we can confirm your claims, you'll remain in custody.'

'I will immediately request bail for my client.'

'You may do that through the sergeant on duty, as you know. However, I can't recommend bail when Mr Scala clearly has easy access to private charter flights and ocean-going vessels. Mr Scala will spend tonight here in the station cells. The magistrate will review your application tomorrow. In the meantime, DI Singh will assist Mr Scala with a written statement of what he's told us.'

'I strongly advise Mr Scala to delay making his statement until tomorrow, Inspectors. He's highly stressed because of the ordeal he's endured since early morning. He needs to rest and consider carefully the content of his statement.'

'No problem, Mr Thomas. The constable will escort you to the duty sergeant to be formally charged. Let's meet at nine o'clock, then.'

38

Just like on Monday, the Shiners were well into their practice game when Horseman jogged onto the sidelines. The boys stayed focused on the ball, yet none had missed his arrival. Somehow his presence had an impact—braced shoulders, faster reactions, renewed vigour. Their desire to impress worried Horseman. He didn't want the burden of responsibility the boys' hero-worship laid on him. He hoped that as they matured in the security of a safe roof over their heads, they would come to regard him as their coach and friend, rather than a hero.

All the same, he must show the same heightened attention to the boys' performance as they did to him. He resolved not to answer his phone during training. Could he be any good as the coach of the national teams? If he couldn't concentrate on a game for just fifteen minutes, the answer was no. So, let the next fifteen minutes be a test. If he failed to remain focused on the play for the rest of the practice game, that could be a sign he should decline the flattering offer without further consideration.

When Constable Lemeki blew the final whistle, Horseman pulled out his notebook and jotted down the common errors the boys made, then individual names and beside these, remarkable strengths to develop or faults to correct. He realised he needed to work on a training program with both the boys and the assistant coaches, who had fallen into the easy practice where teaching was a reaction to mistakes, rather than systematic instruction. And all this came from his own total focus on the play before his eyes for once.

The Shiners clustered around him, eyes anxious, hurling questions at him all at once.

'Joe, all of us are so sorry that Ms Armstrong is dead. Who killed her?'

'That bad man, he go to hell forever.'

'We love Ms Armstrong, she help us a lot!'

'Tell her family sorry from us, Joe.'

'You find that murderer quick, Joe!'

He held his hands up, and most of the jostling and shouting subsided. 'Shiners, *vinaka vakalevu*. Ms Armstrong's friends and colleagues at the High Commission will appreciate your condolences. You all have kind hearts. I was very late to training today because many police officers, including me, have been working hard to find our friend's killer. Constables Musudroka and Kau couldn't come to training this afternoon because they're still working, right now. Other police officers, too. I can't say when our hunt will be over.'

'But you're the best, eh, Joe?'

'*Io*, you'll crack the case!'

Most of the boys moved off to drink and sluice their heads at the grandstand taps. Horseman greeted the other volunteers, Lemeki's mates from Traffic, who told him of their dismay and shame that the Australian High Commissioner should be murdered in Fiji. They clapped him on the back in support, then joined Dr Pillai to unpack the boys' snacks.

Matthew Young, with Tina pulling on her lead, sauntered over to Horseman. As Tina jumped at Horseman, determined to lick his face, Dr Young said, 'It's amazing how reliable Dr Pillai has been for years. It's good the hostel can provide dinners now, though. Too much pressure altogether on him. Yet he still comes down to chat with the boys and keep his medical eye on them.'

'Raj is wonderful for the boys. He's the team's biggest fan, quite apart from his role as their doctor. By the way, are there any more results on Helen's tests to come in?'

'Not for Helen. We got the last toxicity results this afternoon—all negative. But the metal traces are definitely bronze. I'll finish off the full post-mortem report tonight and shoot it through to you. D'you have any leads on the weapon yet?'

'Did I tell you about the winch handle?'

'No—did the divers find one?'

'Not yet. I got Timoci Vodo to inspect the *Joshua* and tell me if any tools were missing—I wouldn't know. He spotted an empty pocket that should have a winch handle in it. Its pair's still in place, so if we can find it, we can match it. Oh, it's bronze, engraved with the boat's initials J.S. Of course, it's not certain, but nothing else with potential was out of place. The divers should be back tomorrow to widen their search area, now we know what we're looking for.'

'Promising, I hope they have luck.'

Horseman noticed Tevita hovering just behind them as they walked. '*Bula* Tevita, I didn't notice you there. Do you want to talk to me?'

'*Io*, Joe! Excuse me, Dr Young. Er, Joe, what's a winch handle?'

'What? You shouldn't have been listening, Tevita.'

'You two are pretty loud. I couldn't help hearing.' Tevita sounded wounded.

Horseman shrugged. 'It's none of your business. How do you like life with the other Junior Shiners?'

'Good, Joe! It's fun. I liked staying at the police garage, but it's great to have a housemother. Mrs Horseman is the best!'

Horseman chuckled. '*Vinaka*. She knows all the tricks boys get up to, so you'd better behave yourself.'

Again, Tevita looked hurt. 'Mrs Horseman is my friend, Joe. She needs help with the younger boys, and as I'm older, I try to look after them a bit. But now I'm so busy at the garage, and evening school, and training—oh look, the boys are lining up, don't wanna miss out!' Tevita jogged across to the queue at the trestle table.

'That boy's sure come a long way, but he's still fixated on you.' Dr Young said with a smile.

'Maybe he'll transfer his hero-worship to my mother. You know, he still sometimes sets himself up at Imperial Arcade with his shoe-shine box on the weekend. It's nostalgic for him, I reckon.'

'Nostalgic? A child living by his wits on the streets?'

'I agree, that was no life for a child. But now he's safe, he looks back and sees a fictitious freedom that he lost.'

'The kid's a born optimist. Maybe that's why he survived.' Dr Young shook his head in wonderment.

'Matt, we could test Scala's statement against a specific time of death for Helen. Have you narrowed that down from 'Saturday evening to early Sunday morning' in your final PM report?'

'A bit. As I said, it's compromised by allowing for an accelerated rate of decay in that sealed boat cabin for more than 64 hours. That's in daytime temperatures of over 30 degrees Celsius.'

'If only we'd found Helen earlier!' He would always regret this failure.

'You did very well, mate. It's her colleagues at the High Commission who should be on their knees begging for forgiveness! As a fellow Aussie, I'm ashamed of their lack of cooperation. Anyway, what's done is done. But I could narrow the time of death a bit. I'll go through my calculations again before I send the report.'

'If Scala's telling the truth, he might just have an alibi, damn him.'

'What's your gut tell you?'

'He could be guilty, but I need more to convince me. He only admitted the drug smuggling when I arrested him for murder, so I don't believe a word that comes out of his mouth.'

'That doesn't mean every word he says is a lie.'

'Exactly, but it's hard sorting the lies from the truth. Hey, I'm meeting Susie at the Holiday Inn for dinner. Why don't you come along? She'd love to see you.' For some unaccountable reason, he felt himself blush. He hoped it wasn't visible.

His friend looked quizzical. He'd noticed then. 'Thanks, mate, I'd better get the post-mortem report wrapped up, as I said. Look, if the timing's critical for Scala's alibi, I'll consult a pathologist mate in Brisbane who's an expert on environmentally induced accelerated decay. That will probably delay my final report until tomorrow. But given what you've said, it's much more important to narrow the time of death range as accurately as possible. Tell Susie I'm so glad she's in Suva, and she'd better reserve an evening for me before she leaves.'

39

'Scala's got to be guilty, Joe!' Singh protested in too loud a stage whisper. Fortunately, the tables next to theirs in the Holiday Inn were empty, and the jazz band was playing in the bar.

'I'm with you a hundred per cent on the drug smuggling. Seizures from yachts sailing from the west coast of South America across the South Pacific are now commonplace, so we know that's a standard route for the Colombian cartels, and a successful one. But I'm not so sure about the murder—not yet. Not until we get some evidence.'

'Joe, he's got means and opportunity. Motive isn't so clear, but only because I think he's got more than one!'

'Such as?'

'First, ongoing resentment towards his former wife and jealousy of her success, which presents a stark contrast with his own disbarment and disgrace. On top of that, if Helen found out about his drug smuggling, or even suspected and told him she'd report him to the police—well, that could easily tip him into violence, even if he didn't intend her to die.'

Horseman nodded. 'I agree that's possible, maybe even probable, but everything that makes us suspect him is circumstantial. We've no evidence yet that Scala was the one who struck Helen twice on the head.'

Singh ignored him and continued. 'I can also imagine a financial motive. The life of a professional ocean-racer and yacht deliverer may not yield a high income, let alone a secure one. Maybe Scala asked Helen for money and she turned him down. He lashed out.'

'I agree, the only motive for smuggling drugs is money. If the missing winch handle was the weapon, the killer didn't plan the murder.'

'Another thing, don't you think the Telecom report on Helen's mobile was odd? So few calls and texts? Deleting every day?'

'Yes, but then she's in her sixties, and her colleagues stress her discretion and caution about security. I know my mother loves chatting for hours on end, but only in person. She uses her mobile for making arrangements, household business, things like that. So I don't know if we can read much into Helen's sparse data.'

'Oh well, my parents don't have mobiles at all, so maybe not much.'

Horseman spotted the waiter approaching with their main courses and gestured to Singh, who was about to reply. The young man served her grilled tuna and a medium-rare rump steak for Horseman, placing a generous bowl of chips and a salad between them. When Horseman thanked him, he said, 'It's an honour to serve you, Josefa Horseman,' and left them.

'Isn't the fish fresher in Labasa?' Horseman asked Singh, with a grin.

'No, I thought it would be, but it's not. You can't beat Suva or Lautoka for fish. On the other hand, I'll probably never order curry in Suva again. Honestly, Labasa curries are scrumptious—superb, actually. Especially the goat. A cousin of mine, who has a farm outside Labasa, is a veritable goddess of the goat curry. Which reminds me, you've never taken up my invitation to come and try the Labasa cuisine.'

Horseman knew she was just teasing but felt guilty anyway. 'I intended to do just that, but I don't know where the time's gone.' His reply sounded lame, even to him.

'You mean you haven't thought about it once,' Singh chuckled.

Horseman grinned. 'Let's eat while we think about our next steps.'

His steak was succulent and tender, the chips and salad crisp, and he felt more agreeable as he put down his knife and fork.

'My goodness, my tuna was lovely!' Singh said.

'You looked like you were enjoying it. That look of pure concentration you get, it's priceless.'

Singh lifted her chin haughtily. 'Excellent food deserves nothing less.'

'True. I was thinking: the most urgent job is to find out when the plane chartered by Lam took off. Private planes still have to lodge flight plans with Civil Aviation. A drug smuggler would have no qualms about giving the passengers false names, though.'

'None at all. And on Saturday evening, if Nausori has no flights scheduled, the control tower probably wouldn't be manned at all. Who'd ask questions about a plane taking off from an airport?' Singh asked.

Horseman shrugged. 'No one. So you think the flight might be under the radar, literally?'

'It's possible. The monsters in these rackets are ruthless.'

'We need to talk with Siale Vula and Narcotics about this, Susie. I hope your work with them will give us an in. They're really cagey. I understand why, but they're difficult to work with.'

'I don't have the big picture at all—I'm on a strictly 'need to know' basis with Narcotics. But I hope what we have to tell them may provoke gratitude. I'll give it my best shot.'

'But we can't do that this evening. Okay, what do you say to this? Tonight I'll find out what we can about that charter from the official records and chase up the pilot if we can get his name. You handle the Savusavu end with an officer on the ground you trust. Any witnesses you can dig out, especially the taxi driver, any airport staff, anyone who observed the driver and Scala loading his dinghy. Kelepi and the DCs can follow up any blind alleys in the light of day—and there'll be plenty, I'm sure. Tomorrow, we put pressure on Scala for more precision on that flight. Then we find Lam.'

'If he's still in Suva.'

'Wherever he is.'

'Joe, that's the most ridiculously overambitious to-do list I've ever heard! If we ticked off half of that, it would be a miracle!'

'*Oi lei*, miracles happen, Singh. We're the good guys. I asked you, "What do you say?" I'm waiting for an answer.'

She paused, watching him while she considered her answer. Then, her green eyes sparkled. 'I say let's order dessert and get some sugar on board while we fine-tune that list of yours. Then back to the station and we can start from the top.'

40

One of the good things about the Civil Aviation Authority of Fiji was that real people answered the phone twenty-four hours a day. Well, maybe twenty hours. Indeed, with passenger jets delivering hundreds of holidaymakers to Nadi and Nausori airports at night, there were few hours when the gateway airports rested. And while they were open, there were people on deck at the CAAF.

'*Bula*, this is Detective Inspector Joe Horseman. I'd be grateful if you could help me with a top priority investigation.'

'*Bula*, Inspector Horseman. I'll help if I can. But, you know, we're a skeleton staff at night unless there's a scheduled international landing or takeoff. What do you need?'

'I need to know if a charter aircraft took off from Nausori last Saturday night in the early evening. Can you look up your records for me, please?'

'Well, it's not my job. The record clerks who work the day shift should handle that. But I can access the records, so if it's urgent police business, I'll do my best, sir.'

'Do local private charter planes need to submit flight plans?'

'CAAF does need to approve flight plans, yes. What time are you looking at, Inspector?'

'I'm not sure. Probably between six and eight o'clock at night.'

'Okay, I'll check Nausori now. Let's see ...'

Horseman willed the record to materialise on the man's screen.

'Well, there was one flight that departed Nausori at 1915 hours. Palm Air Charters, to Savusavu.'

'*Io*, that could be the one I'm looking for.' Singh was hovering. Horseman gave her a thumbs-up and a grin.

'Landed Savusavu 2003 hours. Aircraft was a Cessna. Then it returned to Nausori.'

'Do you have the pilot's name?'

'*Io*, it's George Tabua.'

'And the passengers?'

'For inter-island flights like this, only the principal passenger, that's usually the charterer, needs to be listed. That's the case here."

'I see. And who was the principal passenger?'

'It says here—Voreqe Bainimarama. Do you think this is a joke, sir?'

Horseman sighed heavily. 'We'll soon find out. Were there any other charter flights from Nausori last Saturday night?'

'No sir. Only that same plane landed back at Nausori fifty minutes later.' The poor man sounded awed and baffled at the same time.

'*Vinaka vakalevu*, you've been most helpful. Can you email me that information without too much trouble?'

'*Io*, sir, I'll take a screenshot. Just shoot me an email requesting the flight details and I'll send it right away.'

As soon as Horseman took down the address, he typed a terse message and sent it. He looked up at Singh. 'The principal passenger on that charter flight plan was the Prime Minister of Fiji.'

Singh's eyes widened, her mouth opened, then she laughed her surprising, hearty laugh. Horseman, whose initial reaction had been profound irritation, joined in after a shocked moment.

Singh's laugh subsided to a broad smile when Horseman said, 'Probably a prank, I agree, but tomorrow we'll check with the Prime Minister's protection officer. That will be simple enough. Getting the charter flight confirmed so easily was too good to be true. The identity of the passengers is something I'll quiz the pilot about if I can get hold of him. George Tabua at Palm Air Charters, based at Nausori. I'll look him up right now.'

'I'm making tea right now. Would you like one? Take a break while I tell you about my discoveries.'

'Yes, please, to both those offers.' Horseman pulled the phone book from a shelf. There was a quarter-page display ad for Palm Air, complete with a post office address, a smiling picture of the proprietor, George Tabua, beside a small plane, and both landline and mobile numbers.

As Singh placed a mug of strong tea by his hand, he swivelled the book around. 'It looks like the pilot last Saturday night was the company's proprietor. Maybe he's a one-man band. Do you recognise him?'

Singh bent over the page, frowning. 'No, but the name seems vaguely familiar.'

Horseman pulled a chair up to the side of his desk. 'Well, sit down and tell me your news before I call Mr George Tabua.'

'I was lucky, too. My trusted colleague in Savusavu foolishly answered my call and agreed to find out what was happening at the airport around eight o'clock last Saturday night. He's going to talk to taxi drivers tonight and the marina staff too. But my guy thinks it'll be more productive waiting until tomorrow to chat to the yachties and any airport staff. He says the airport would have been deserted at eight o'clock anyway—the last scheduled flight left early afternoon. So, a promising start, I think.'

'A great start on what you said was an overambitious list. I'd like to try the charter pilot before we pack up for the night. If you want to wait, we could share a taxi home to the flats. But you've had a gruelling day, so why don't you call it a night now?' he ended, feeling awkward.

'I'll keep you company.' She smiled. 'I'll research Palm Air's media mentions while you're on the phone.' She took her tea to the table she'd been given and switched on the computer.

To Horseman's pleasant surprise, George Tabua answered his phone on the third ring. Horseman switched the phone to speaker mode and waved to Singh. 'This is Detective Inspector Josefa Horseman, Suva Central station. Mr Tabua, I'm investigating your charter flight departing Nausori at 1915 hours last Saturday, landing in Savusavu a few minutes after 2000 hours. You were the pilot of that flight, weren't you?'

'Um, *Io, ovisa.*' The deep voice sounded confused but not fearful.

'And the prime minister chartered it, according to the flight plan you submitted to CAAF. I'm assuming that was in Mr Bainimarama's private capacity? Perhaps you're a relative of his, or a friend?'

The same deep voice uttered an innovative sequence of Fijian swear words. 'Sorry, sorry, sir. No, you're wrong. I just put down that name as a joke. Those morons in CAAF don't even look at the details, but the poor pilot's in big trouble if the form's not filled in completely. Am I in trouble with the police about this?'

'Mr Tabua, it's an offence to provide false information on an official government document. If you think for a moment, I'm sure you're intelligent enough to realise that. The crime is called fraud—I'm sure you know that, too. However, if you cooperate with me in supplying the correct information now—the information you should have put on the form in the first place, I'll consider excusing you this time, as I'm sure this is your first offence.'

'Um, er, *io, ovisa.*'

'So let's begin again. Who hired you to fly to Savusavu?'

'Oh, he's a regular customer. He likes to guard his privacy, actually.'

'I see. Do you own this neat plane I see in your advertisement in the phone book, Mr Tabua?'

'*Io*, sir. I have a loan, but I've paid off most of it.' His voice swelled with pride.

'Do you employ other pilots?'

'No, I'm a one-man band. I don't make much money, I do my own maintenance and repairs, but my Cessna and I provide for my family.'

'You've done well, Mr Tabua. Congratulations.'

'*Vinaka vakalevu*, sir.'

'Mr Tabua, you know well that the CAAF has approved and registered your Cessna as airworthy, and approved and registered you as a commercial pilot in Fiji. Are you going to jeopardise your wonderful achievement and your family's prosperity because you refuse to fill in your flight plans truthfully? Just because your customer likes his privacy?'

The pilot remained silent.

'People like to call officials morons when they have to complete time-consuming forms and do tests. I believe you understand that there's only one reason for all the CAAF forms and tests and licenses you must deal with, and that's safety.'

'*Io*, sir.' The pilot's voice was now soft and afraid.

'I'm going to ask you the CAAF questions once more. I need the truth and the promise you won't fill in any more CAAF forms with false information.'

'*Io*, sir.'

'Who hired you to fly to Savusavu last Saturday at 1915 hours?'

'South Pacific Pharmaceuticals, sir.'

'I believe Henry Lam is the proprietor of South Pacific Pharmaceuticals.'

'*Io*, sir.'

'Was Henry Lam a passenger on that flight?'

'No, sir, he did not fly this time. Um, ah, Mr Paula Balavu was the passenger.'

'The son of Ratu Sitiveni?'

'*Io*.' The pilot sounded like a man who had given in. Good.

'I believe there was another passenger, too.'

'*Io*, Paula told me to wait for him. He arrived on the tarmac in a taxi. I don't know his name. He was European, sounded like an Aussie. A polite man.'

'You carried some cargo, too. What was the cargo?'

'*Io*, sir. A number of cardboard boxes, I didn't count them. I didn't notice any labels. Paula and me helped the Aussie unload the boxes onto my trolley, and they wheeled them to a taxi. I took my trolley back and they drove away.'

'*Vinaka*, Mr Tabua. One more thing. I need you to come to Suva Central Station tomorrow to make a written statement about what you've just said. How about ten o'clock?'

'*Io*, sir. I promise I'll be there.'

'Ask for DI Horseman at the front counter. If everything is satisfactory, it may be possible to overlook your fraud as a first offence.'

'*Vinaka vakalevu*, Inspector Horseman. You're a good man.'

'I don't know that I can agree with the pilot, Joe,' Singh said when Horseman hung up, her voice full of reproach. 'You terrified him.'

'So he should be terrified! What if the plane had ditched into the sea and the CAAF had no clue as to who was on board? And neither did the passengers' families?' He realised he'd raised his voice, but he was annoyed that Singh supported the criminally negligent pilot. He had considered his questioning sympathetic.

There was no one left on the detectives' floor. They said goodnight to the uniforms downstairs, flagged a cab, and sat in silence on the brief trip to Seaview Apartments. Horseman insisted on carrying Singh's small trolley suitcase into the lobby.

He set her luggage down and touched her on the arm. 'Susie. It's wonderful you've come to save us. I couldn't be more grateful. Happy, too. You've done sterling work bringing in Scala and right through the day until now.'

'It can get a bit slow in Labasa sometimes. Quite often, actually. You know I love days like today.'

'Yes. This murder case is growing tentacles, but I'm hopeful now you're here.'

'Don't shout at me again, then.'

'What? When did I shout at you?'

'When I criticised you for threatening the charter pilot.'

'No, Susie, I didn't shout, maybe raised my voice a little. I was astonished you defended him. If Henry Lam's a regular customer, that pilot's probably well aware of what he's carrying and crooked to his core. Anyway, if I did shout, I didn't mean to, and I'm sorry.'

'Forget it. I understand you're overstressed, Joe. You could be too personally involved in the High Commissioner's murder. Try to get a good sleep.' She smiled, but not warmly.

The open lift pinged them impatiently. They stepped in and rode in silence together to their separate floors.

FRIDAY 20th July

41

Horseman's reprimand, if that's what it was, had knocked Singh off balance. So had her reaction to it. Perhaps it wasn't possible to pick up the easy collegiality and, yes, friendship, from where they'd left it two years ago. Why had she criticised his phone interview with the charter pilot? Horseman saw his threats as a tactic to get quick results. They'd done that. And the threats had not been deceptive: Tabua could expect to lose his pilot's license, at least for a time, over falsifying his CAAF flight plans, even if the authority didn't take the matter to the police.

Had she not also overreacted by criticising when he counted on her support? If he'd overreacted by shouting, it was due to overstress. His role as SIO in the horrific murder of a woman who was the fairy godmother to his charity must be unbearable. Still, it wasn't like him to resent her comments, which he'd always considered, even when he ended up disagreeing. She wanted to talk it over with him, but the moment was not right now. Better to begin their working day as if nothing had disrupted their previously easy relations.

Apparently, Horseman had reached the same conclusion. He gave her a broad smile as she walked into the detectives' floor to find him talking to Kelepi over a cup of tea. They stood beside an extra table squeezed in along a wall for group meetings and meals. '*Yadra*, Singh! Can I pour you a cup? You'll want to hear what Kelepi's just told me.'

'*Yadra*, Joe, *yadra* Keli. Absolutely, you can pour me tea, and I can't wait to hear from Keli.' She shrugged off her backpack and set it on her desk. She sat at the tea table, and Horseman poured from the capacious aluminium teapot, taking pride of place in the middle. Singh added milk herself and turned to Kelepi, eyebrows lifted. 'Ready when you are, Keli.'

The detective sergeant took a long slurp of his tea and sighed in satisfaction. 'DI Singh won't be surprised to find out that the High Commissioner's driver, Vuki Maya, hasn't told us the whole truth. When your probationer, DC Pareti and I told him we found his fingerprints in the *Joshua*'s cabin, he protested that he'd never been inside. Then he admitted he'd sometimes carried boxes and bags to the yacht for Ms Armstrong but had always left them in the cockpit. He claimed the SOCOs had made a mistake.'

Kelepi shook his head in disbelief. 'After a bit of pressure, he admitted that he'd occasionally carried stuff into the cabin for her, but not recently, and always in Ms Armstrong's presence and at her specific direction. He plays the innocent boofhead, but that one is wily. He knows we can't tell how recent his prints are, so he's telling us a story that's plausible and fits the physical evidence. Don't get me wrong—I can't see him as the murderer, not yet. But I'm certain Mr Vuki Maya knows more than he's saying. He could be scared of someone or simply doesn't want to become involved. Don't worry, revered Inspectors, I'll give some thought to what might make him open up.'

'*Vinaka*, Kelepi,' Horseman said, glancing at his watch. 'Singh and I must dash off—we're meeting with DI Vula to check how large Scala and Lam loom on Narcotics' radar. We hope to get a new lead or two that way. Can you keep the DCs on task down at the yacht club? We're desperate for a sighting of Scala, the driver, or any High Commission staff whose prints were lifted from *Joshua*'s cabin. We've interviewed all staff, except the guard on duty last Saturday night, who's the most vital of all. But we also need to talk to every member and guest at the club last Saturday. They all have to sign in, so it's doable. Talk to the taxi drivers too, if you can track them down.'

'*Io*, Joe. I noticed that the few photos Lili Waqa's showing could be improved. I'd like to get Photography to produce a few folders with quality A-4 enlargements of all the people you've mentioned.'

'Please do that. Should've been done already, but a great deal happened yesterday. Okay, do that first, and the DCs can update the case file under your watchful eye while you're waiting.'

'Leave all that with me. Good luck!' Kelepi replied.

***

Singh was happy to be speaking with DI Siale Vula. They'd worked together on the notorious Dev Reddy murder. She was then a sergeant, but DI Vula had respected her ideas and was unfailingly pleasant. She could not say the same for the Narcotics officers she'd come across.

This morning, Vula leapt out of his chair and greeted them both warmly. 'Our cases meet again!' he said. 'It's great to see you in Suva again, DI Singh!'

She shook his hand. 'It's just Singh. Joe's briefed you about Scala?'

'With a broad brush, yes. I'm grateful to you both for the intel and yesterday's op in Savusavu—well, all I can say is 'Wow', Singh! What a formidable organiser you must be to get that one up overnight.'

Singh sensed Horseman was bored with all the mutual admiration, so she got to the point. 'Unfortunately, Scala might have an alibi for the High Commissioner's murder. We're seeking corroboration today. We're hoping you can tell us about pharmacist Henry Lam, Paula Balavu, possibly Lam's associate, and pilot George Tabua of Palm Airways. Are they persons of interest for Narcotics?'

'Henry Lam certainly is. I've collected a pile on Lam, which I've printed out, and I'll email you a folder of documents when I've added a few more. Do you want a quick summary?'

'*Vinaka vakalevu.*' Horseman replied. Singh held out her hand for the manila folder.

'Where do I start? Henry Lam is a 48-year-old Fijian of mixed descent, mainly Chinese, who qualified as a pharmacist at Auckland University, opened his first retail pharmacy in his mid-twenties in Lautoka. He now has four retail pharmacies in Fiji, one in the Solomons, one in Samoa and another in Vanuatu. He also established a wholesale warehouse in Nadi to supply all his shops.'

'The ideal set-up for a drug smuggler, or manufacturer,' Horseman said. 'If we confirm Scala's alibi, he won't be facing a murder charge anymore, but he's confessed to drug smuggling for Lam. I need to focus on the High Commissioner's murder, so I'm happy to hand over Scala to Narcotics to manage the case, with Singh as liaison. But I'm only happy if I can be sure Narcotics will prosecute him. And I'll be deeply disappointed if Singh's evidence isn't enough to prosecute Lam on a charge that will stick.'

Again, Singh thought Horseman's tone was overly firm.

Vula lifted his eyebrows in surprise. 'Man, our hopes are the same. Shoot me all the relevant statements when they're done. I'll put what you've said to our super this morning.'

'We're interviewing Scala again in half an hour. Would you like to join us?' Horseman asked.

'Would I ever? If my chief will spare me, I will.'

'*Vinaka*, Siale. See you in Interview Room 2 at nine o'clock. If possible, could you search the names Paula Balavu and George Tabua through your files before then? We could use anything you've got on either of them. Any fact may lead to Ms Armstrong's murder.'

Singh saw the strain on Horseman's face as he tried to live up to his image of the ideal SIO, leading his team to greater heights through his personal example. Even though this was only the seventh day since the High Commissioner's murder, Horseman looked defeated, or rather, that he had failed. Not for the first time, she reflected that there were excellent reasons for the custom that detectives did not work on cases where the victims were family or friends.

42

Back in Interview Room 2, waiting for Vula, the battered wooden table and brownish stains on the wall did nothing to lift Horseman's mood. He feared the likely outcome of this interview; Scala would avoid the charge of murdering his ex-wife. Even though Horseman now believed Scala was probably innocent, he still feared what would follow. He feared starting again; he feared the futile, endless work of chasing other leads until they too petered out. He feared failure; he might as well face that.

Vula entered and sat at the end of the table, near Scala. He apologised for holding them up, but looked pleased. Singh and Vula both appeared eager and confident. Singh was crisply professional in a plain pink blouse tucked into a black pleated skirt, her glossy hair scraped back into a disciplined ponytail. When he sat beside her, she smiled at him with lifted brows, her hand on the sound recorder.

Horseman nodded. Singh pressed the button and recited the preliminaries.

'Mr Scala, have you anything to add to what you told us yesterday afternoon?'

'No. My solicitor, Mr Thomas, has prepared a statement for you.' Fletcher Thomas handed over a stapled two-page printed document, impossible for three detectives to read simultaneously.

Singh picked it up, nodding at Horseman to carry on the interview while she skimmed.

'Mr Scala, the Civil Aviation Authority of Fiji records show Mr Lam's chartered Cessna took off at 1915 hours or quarter-past seven in the evening. How does that sound to you?' Horseman asked.

'Very likely. It was just after dark.'

'Was it dark when you left the club?'

'Dusk. I don't have to tell you how quickly the night falls here.'

'True. Do you remember the name of the taxi driver who took you to Nausori airport?'

'No.'

'Anything distinctive about the driver or the cab? We want to track this driver down since he might possibly help confirm your story.'

Scala frowned. 'All right, for what it's worth. He was an older guy, short grey hair, went on about his army days. I wasn't listening. The cab was an old Mazda but clean enough.'

'Thanks. You'll have to tell us what's new in your statement. Our police station isn't set up to provide photocopying services.' Horseman said.

'I wanted to explain the drug residue detected on the *Joshua Slocum*. I admit that I did carry some drug packets packed around the water tanks—that was the first run I ever did. Helen and I were separated then, but it was before our divorce and property settlement. And of course, many years before she became High Commissioner to Fiji.'

'I see. Where were you living then?'

'On board the *Joshua*, based in Queensland, trying to carve out a freelance ocean-going yachting career for myself. I didn't get much work at first, and I was desperate, so I accepted an offer when I was in Honiara in the Solomons after a race. Someone asked me to deliver a parcel to Coffs Harbour on the New South Wales coast. Which I did. Helen, of course, knew nothing about it. My personal habit destroyed our marriage; that and the death of our son. If she'd known I was smuggling, she'd have killed me. Now I wish she had.'

'Yours is a common story, Alex. What happened in Coffs Harbour?' Singh prompted quietly.

Scala looked at her, grateful. 'All went to plan. The quantity was small, the Customs inspection was cursory, and the contact was waiting.'

'How did your yacht end up in Suva?'

'When our property division was settled, Helen took the *Joshua Slocum* because she loves the boat and I needed something faster if I was going to race seriously—I mean, for the big prize money.'

Scala had stared at the table throughout his last speech, his head bowed. Horseman needed no convincing of Helen Armstrong's upright character. Did that mean he could believe Scala's claims on other matters, namely, his own actions? Decidedly not.

'Are you dropping the charge of murder against my client? Surely the CAAF evidence of his flight from Nausori is a watertight alibi?'

'Not yet, Mr Thomas. To be frank, because of the heat in the yacht's cabin, Ms Armstrong's body suffered accelerated decomposition. This means the pathologist's preliminary estimate of the probable time of death covered quite a wide range. At my request, he is re-evaluating his estimate with a view to narrowing the times. He is also consulting a colleague in Australia, a specialist in human decomposition. I'll let you know when we get his final post-mortem report.'

The solicitor nodded, displeased.

'Whatever time Helen died, I swear it was after I left the *Joshua*. I left her alive and well!' Scala shouted, close to tears. Fletcher Thomas placed a restraining hand on his arm.

'In that case, we can only wait, under protest. However, my client has recalled some information that I believe will be of great interest to you in the separate matter of the import and export of prohibited drugs to and from Fiji. I've advised him to keep that information to himself unless the police assure us his cooperation will be reflected in any charges that may be laid in connection with the raid on *Pot of Gold* yesterday.'

Scala swept his arm away from his lawyer. 'Cut the crap, Fletcher. This is my only chance. I owe the bastards who exploited me nothing!'

Mr Thomas interjected. 'I demand a break for my client.'

'No, I want to get this over with. I know what I'm doing, Fletcher!'

Scala looked distressed, his weather-beaten face aged, his eyes red, his hair a mess from running his hands through it again and again.

Mr Thomas frowned, clenched his lips together, then shrugged.

'Please go ahead, Mr Scala,' Singh urged.

'I've worked for Henry Lam more than twice. I should have had the brains to realise once I'd done one job, I couldn't ever refuse another. But I was arrogant. You'll laugh at this, but I believed that a former rising barrister like me could be a free agent!'

'None of us is laughing, Alex. We've heard this so many times.' Singh responded.

'I want you to throw the book at the two criminals who are behind one racket operating here and on other islands, too. They are Henry Lam and Ratu Sitiveni Balavu, both evil to the core, which is why you may never bring them down.'

Vula's eyes widened. 'Ratu Sitiveni? The chief?'

'Yes, a greedy crook, who poses as a champion of youth employment schemes for his bailiwick!' Scala's voice rose again in derision.

'I understand it was Paula Balavu who flew with you to Savusavu last Saturday evening and helped you with the cargo,' Vula said.

'Yes, he's Sitiveni's son, and completely under his father's control. I suspect he's a decent kid at heart, but he has no choice in what he does. I can give you chapter and verse on the roles of father and son in more operations than I care to count.'

'Have you any corroborating evidence of your accusations?'

'Some, but probably not enough. I've been stupid enough to keep a record of my ventures, carefully hidden. Of course, I have data from my navigation instruments on *Pot of Gold* and my logbook. I will hand these over to you if you're interested.'

'I'm very interested, Mr Scala. My colleagues in Narcotics will be too. I'll arrange for a longer interview with you after I've briefed them.' Vula glanced at Horseman.

'Please go ahead with that, DI Vula,' Horseman said. 'I'm solely concerned with the High Commissioner's murder case. Is there anything more you can tell us about that, Mr Scala?'

'I've racked my brains to remember anyone I saw at the yacht club as I left. There were people about, but I really can't remember. I focused on getting a cab in a hurry.'

Horseman looked at the solicitor. 'Well, let's end this interview now, Mr Thomas. We need to find this cab driver and put pressure on Telecom to get Mr Scala's phone data to us today. Their police liaison section doesn't work all hours like us.'

Scala leaned forward, insistent. 'Believe me, I do want to help. I've admitted my crimes. But I must convince you of the truth. The truth is that I didn't kill Helen. She was alive and well when I left her. You should be grilling that weird Russian boyfriend of hers, not me! There, I've given you a tip!'

'Are you referring to Professor Orlov at USP?'

'That's the one! He even came out on the *Joshua* when I was skippering. What a hide!'

'Let's get back to the sequence of events at the yacht club on Saturday, please.'

Scala's outrage subsided. 'When I left the *Joshua*, the light was starting to fade. I knew I should hurry out to the car park, where I hoped to pick up a cab dropping someone off. There were no cabs in the car park, so I rushed out onto the road and hailed one almost immediately. It was dark when we arrived at the airport.'

'Thank you, Mr Scala. I must be off to track down the taxi driver.' Horseman pushed his chair back, nodding to Singh to wind up the interview. He was too angry at Scala to remain in the same room as the scoundrel a second longer. When would Matt come through with the time of death?

43

The detectives had only just got back upstairs when the phone rang. Singh answered and listened.

'Joe, the pilot's waiting downstairs. I'm happy to take his statement, if you like.' Horseman was surprised, wondering why she'd want to take that over. Didn't she trust him? Then he shrugged. 'Sure, see if you can get anything more out of him, particularly about Paula Balavu.'

'Would it be okay if I sat in on this one, too?' DI Vula directed his question to Singh, who looked to Horseman, her eyebrows lifted.

Horseman paused. 'Good idea, Siale,' he said. 'I suspect he's not connected to the High Commissioner's murder, but we've got to eliminate him. After that, Narcotics will want to follow through on him.'

'*Io*. He could be quite a lead. *Vinaka*, Joe.'

'No problem, man.'

At last! Horseman settled at his laptop and saw that Dr Young's final PM report had landed in his Inbox. He opened the attachment and read avidly. Nothing seemed different from the Interim version, except—he scanned furiously—yes, the time-of-death estimate had narrowed significantly. Or he hoped it was significant. He called the pathologist.

'*Vinaka*, Matt. I got the final report. Just need you to talk me through it. I can't make a mistake here—this is the acid test for Scala's claim to an alibi. I only wish it wasn't so close.'

'Yeah, it's pretty rare, isn't it? Let's check. By the way, my colleague in Brisbane was super-helpful. He drew my attention to two recently developed formulas for calculating the acceleration of decay due to high environmental temperatures in confined spaces like we have in that boat cabin. I've checked the ambient temperatures over the time period and got a result. Of course, it's still an estimate, but you've noticed the reduced range of the minimum and maximum TODs.'

'Sure, now the earliest's at half-past seven and the latest's at half-past ten. That lets Alex Scala off the hook. But will that earliest estimate stand up in court?'

'It damn-well should, mate. I'll swear my head off in court, and so will old Prof Winter in Brisbane. Can you verify Scala's where-abouts?'

'Sure can. The CAAF have a Cessna chartered by Henry Lam leaving Nausori at 1915 hours last Saturday. The pilot has identified Scala from a photo lineup and has stated he was the second passenger on the flight. Scala had to get to the airport from the yacht club, and even if we can't find the taxi driver, he must have left at half-past six at the latest, possibly earlier.'

'That's definitely too early. No question. How do you know he was on the yacht at all?'

'Fingerprints on the plate and glass, freshness of food remnants collected. His story's coherent once we slowly stripped away his stupid lies, one by one.'

'What's your gut feeling, Joe?'

'As it seems to be a sudden crime of passion, I could see him lashing out in a fury. I can't see him planning to kill Helen. While I'd love to wind up the case, I'll drop the charge of murder this afternoon. He'll remain in custody on the drug smuggling charges, though. At this stage, he's desperately trying to earn favourable treatment as an informant on those.'

'Is he now? Sounds totally untrustworthy to me.'

'You bet. We only got back to verifiable facts because he was ter-rified of being tried for murder. So we have to look again at all the people who left their fingerprints in the *Joshua*'s cabin. Could the killer really be one of her colleagues?'

'Seems unthinkable, doesn't it?'

'But someone killed her. And we'll find him. Or her.'

'How's Susie bearing up?' Dr Young asked.

'Better than me, man. Better than me. How about I take Tina for her walk tomorrow morning? I'll pick her up at seven.'

'She'll be waiting on the verandah for you, her ball in her mouth.'

44

Horseman texted Singh, suggesting an early lunch at the Arabica, a café she'd loved in her Suva days. He wanted to get her ideas now he'd struck Scala off the list of suspects. Well, he'd been the only suspect investigated for the past two days. Despite urging caution on the team, he'd privately put his money on Scala as the killer, too.

He hated failing, he hated losing a lead just as much as he'd hated losing possession of the ball to the opposing team. The only thing to do was to get the ball back. That meant going after another lead. As his old coach had said, the game was up to him. He put his notebook and laptop in his satchel, slung it over his shoulder and headed out. He craved a decent coffee.

At midday, the narrow streets west of the station bustled. Tucked away in a quieter back lane was Arabica, his ideal refuge. The business processed beans grown in Fiji's highlands and sold them to American specialist outlets whose customers sought single-source organic coffee varieties that their friends hadn't yet discovered. But in a tiny café in one corner of the colonial spice warehouse, locals could taste the best coffee in the world, in Horseman's patriotic opinion. The owner, Didi, had succumbed to demands from fans of Arabica's product to include a few tables in the old warehouse for tasting events. Later, he added a regular coffee menu. Now he served sandwiches, scones and biscuits made and delivered by his mother daily.

'But this is as far as it goes,' Didi had protested. 'No tea, no food menu. No kitchen. The only thing we cook here is coffee beans!'

The roasters were on. Horseman inhaled the heavenly scent like a desperate addict, waved to Didi and made a beeline for his usual table in the corner. Seated next to the enormous plate-glass window, he wouldn't miss Singh coming up the quiet lane, which at this time of day was like a shady chasm. He opened his laptop and placed his notebook beside it.

He'd got his notebook up-to-date by the time he spotted Singh hurrying up the lane, leaning forward to support her backpack, which usually contained everything she and her colleagues might need at work in the field. For her, it was a dress-down day. Her perfectly ironed *bula* blouse ran riot with yellow and orange hibiscus and set off her royal-blue cropped pants. He enjoyed watching her stride along, overflowing with keenness and energy—the very qualities that eluded him these days.

Singh grinned as she caught sight of him. She pushed against the warped old hardwood doors and gazed around. Didi placed Horseman's espresso on their table and rushed to greet her.

'*Bula* Susie, DI Singh! Man, you haven't been here for years! Have you transferred back to Suva?'

'*Bula vinaka*, Didi. Just a temporary secondment. It's wonderful to see you again. I've missed your coffee so much.'

'But not me? The story of my life,' Didi grumbled, his eyes twinkling. 'Latté, Susie? Sandwiches and rock cakes for you both?'

'What a memory! Yes, please.'

'Did you and Siale get anything out of the pilot?' Horseman asked as Singh sat down.

'Sort of, in a negative way. But you first. Has the final PM report come through?'

'Yes. The earliest time of death is half-past seven Saturday night. I spoke to Matt, and he's prepared to swear in court that Helen did not die any earlier.'

'So Scala's off the hook. Hmm, what do we do next?'

'I was hoping you'd have some ideas.'

The waiter delivered Singh's coffee, along with a plate of thick sandwiches.

After a minute or two's silence, Singh swallowed, then sighed with satisfaction. 'I'd forgotten how good Didi's mother's corned beef and cucumber sandwiches were.'

Horseman was content to see her happy. 'When you're ready, tell me what you 'sort of' got out of George Tabua.'

Singh pointed to her cheek and sped up her chewing. When she'd swallowed, she said, 'Predictably, he denied all knowledge of the contents of the boxes he transported for Henry Lam. He could easily be lying, but it's also perfectly plausible that he assumed boxes from a pharmaceutical company contained pharmaceuticals. But that's not relevant to our case.'

Singh took a few sips of coffee. 'More important, I'm as sure as I can be that the pilot has no connection to the High Commissioner's murder. And I'd be surprised if Henry Lam did either. With Scala cleared of that charge, my gut tells me that his drug smuggling has nothing to do with his former wife's death.' She took another bite of her sandwich.

'I tend to agree. Putting that possible connection aside for now, what we need is more clues.'

'I'd like to suggest something, but I can't be much use, Joe. I only started on the case on Wednesday night. You're expecting too much of me.'

'Sorry. We'll find out at the case review if anything has come from turning the yacht club upside down. That job must continue. With so many people coming and going, someone must have seen something. But we've got an untapped new source, and that's Helen's office and apartment at the High Commission. Hugh Forester, First Secretary, opposed a SOCO search, but if the Scala lead didn't pan out, he would reconsider. I want to call in that half-promise and set that search in motion this afternoon. What d'you say, Singh?'

'I say, when do we start? Two raids in two days? What could be more fun?'

Horseman chuckled. 'Calm down, Susie. This is not a raid. I'm expecting your charming conversation and discreet behaviour to win over the diplomats, who regard the Fiji police as a rough-and-ready lot. The only examples they've seen so far have been me and the DCs.'

'Okay, I'll try. I'm looking forward to meeting them.'

The waiter approached. 'Another coffee for you both? How about rock cakes to go with it?'

Horseman raised his eyebrows in assent. 'We've still got to eliminate Professor Orlov, who's got no time for the police. Kelepi's sure the driver knows more than he's saying. I think both of them are unlikely suspects, but we've got to be sure. That only leaves Helen's colleagues.'

'Unless our victim had a secret life no one knew about.'

'Sure, and her office and apartment may reveal something. Again, we need to keep an eye out for what's missing. Staff and colleagues have been in and out of those rooms until two days ago, when they were supposed to be locked.'

'You don't seem to trust the people at the High Commission,' Singh observed.

'I don't. I haven't got a handle on them yet. Maybe you can tell me what makes them tick. I hope so.'

'I wouldn't count on it. You've hobnobbed with high society through rugby. I'm only a poor farmer's daughter, remember?'

'Barely. While I'm checking what's happening at the yacht club, could you get caught up with everything from the High-Com on the case file? I need fresh eyes on what we've already got.'

'I'll be delighted to have a change of scene from Scala and the drug racketeers.'

'Put your feet up while you're doing that if you can. You must be exhausted. I already sent an email to Hugh Forester asking for a meeting this afternoon. True to form, he hasn't replied. I'll ring the office manager now. Should've done that in the first place. Excuse me, Singh.'

While he was speaking on the phone, the waiter brought their second coffees and a basket covered with a checked tea towel. Horseman folded the cloth back and offered the basket to Singh with a bow, who laughed as she took a rock cake, bursting with plump sultanas. 'Practising my manners,' he said in explanation.

They bantered while polishing off the cakes. Horseman felt his face relax in a surge of optimism. Singh hadn't asked to work with Vula on the drug smuggling case as he had feared. When she referred to Helen's murder as *our* case, he couldn't believe his ears. He knew he was working better since she'd joined him. But how long would it be before her own superintendent called her back to Labasa? As they stood to leave, he admired the loftiness of the old spice warehouse, its century-old hardwood columns. This old place reassured him that some good things stayed around. If only Singh would.

45

Lili Waqa and two uniforms were waiting by the marina gate, chatting with Ilai, the security guard, as Horseman walked over from the car park. They looked pleased to see him, and he realised how he'd neglected them over the past few days. The DCs thrived with constant feedback. He felt satisfied that DS Taleca would now give them that. He shook hands with Ilai, who looked almost benign today.

Waqa said, 'Apo and Izzy are at the scene with DS Taleca, sir. He wants us to join him.' Ilai watched while a uniform opened the gate and headed off to the clubhouse. As they walked along the pontoon, Waqa held up a green A-4 folder in front of Horseman. 'Sir, DS Taleca's photo folders made quite a difference. They're so cool! Already one of the yacht club members thinks she saw Alexander Scala on Saturday afternoon!'

'Really, Lili? Well done. When?'

'Around two. He passed the bar and went into the men's toilet. Does that fit?'

'It does. He was on the *Joshua* for hours, he must have needed the toilet. By the way, Scala's alibi holds up, so he's no longer a suspect.'

Waqa's disappointment showed in her slumped posture. 'Do you think I need to re-interview the staff and members we've already spoken to? I'd rather not start again, but if the photos help them remember ...' She trailed off, with a worried frown.

'We'll talk about that when we're all together,' Horseman said as they came up to the *Joshua Slocum*, still surrounded by police tape.

Although it had only been a few hours since they'd last seen each other, DS Taleca shook Horseman's hand hard. '*Bula vinaka*, boss, has DC Waqa told you about her breakthrough?'

'All because of your professional visual aids, she claims. Excellent work. That's only the beginning, too. Go back to those you've interviewed and re-interview those at the club from six to ten in the evening using the photo line-up. That time window should reduce the numbers quite a lot.'

No one showed displeasure at this tedious task. They were a solid bunch. 'Have the divers finished up?'

'*Io*, sir,' Kau replied. 'They brought up a screwdriver, a spanner and three rusty knives of different sizes. Nothing resembling the winch handle I showed them. Do you want me to pass them on to Sergeant Jayaraman?'

'*Io*, give him a call if all the SOCOs have left, too.'

'They have,' Kau said.

'If the SOCOs can identify any of them, it could be useful. I guess the sea immersion will have removed prints and so on, but I'm not a SOCO. Sergeant Jayaraman can work magic sometimes. Anything more from the rubbish skip?'

'Nothing like a winch handle, sir. The uniforms all deserve medals. Ilai arranged for them to have hot showers in the club bathrooms. The boys were very grateful—good towels and soap, shampoo laid on. They changed into boilersuits for going through the rubbish, so they had their clean uniforms to get into after they washed.'

Everyone chuckled. The club manager wouldn't have tolerated stinking constables on guard duty, and no one could blame him, Horseman reasoned.

'Have you found the security guard from Saturday night?'

Kelepi spoke up. 'Nothing yet. I'll call the company again. And I've held off a second chat with the driver, Vuki Maya. I need something to shake him out of his complacency. If all the staff and members here on Saturday evening can see the photo line-up, maybe Vuki's glossy A-4 will spark a memory.'

'Is that your plan for this afternoon, DS Taleca?'

'*Io*, with your permission, boss.' Kelepi brought his hands together as if in prayer.

'Granted. You can have Waqa and Pareti for that. I still want one uniform on the marina gate and another near the *Joshua*. Kau, you can come to the High-Com with me.'

46

The downpour began just as Horseman, Singh and Kau pulled up near the steps to the High-Com offices. The flag still flew at half-mast above the Residence. They were ten minutes early for their appointment with Hugh Forester, now Acting Australian High Commissioner to the Republic of Fiji. By unspoken agreement, all three sat still, praying the deluge would be brief.

Apo Kau broke the silence. 'I can't understand why Dr Orlov didn't want to speak to me, sir. He said straight out, before he knew what the call was about, that he would only talk to you. Then, when I said DI Singh was the only detective inspector available, he agreed to see her. Did I say something wrong?'

Singh leaned forward from the back seat. 'I was listening and you said nothing wrong, Apo. If anything, you came across as too humble. Just be your natural, confident self.' She sounded quite maternal. She must have missed her first probationers when she moved to Labasa.

Horseman said, 'Here's something I've observed about anti-authority types like Dr Orlov. Their resentment doesn't extend to the top. Now, if the President rang him up, he'd be standing to attention and saluting the phone.'

The others laughed. 'Apo, you go along with DI Singh. You can collect Dr Orlov's fingerprints. See what you both make of him.'

'Do you think there's anything in Scala's 'boyfriend' accusation? Just jealousy?' Singh asked.

'I don't know. Tell me what you think after the interview.'

They sat in silence for another minute, watching the rain ease. Then, as suddenly as it had started, the rain stopped altogether and the sun shone, turning the bitumen car park into a stage wreathed in vapour from a smoke machine.

'Let's go, DI Singh. Apo, wait in the car until I radio you. Three cops, even in plain clothes, might startle the diplomats.'

DC Kau chuckled.

Horseman led Singh through to the reception desk and introduced her to Losana, who was clearly impressed, toning down her usual warmth and enthusiasm under the influence of Singh's reserved official presence. Horseman had thought Singh's insistence on going back to her flat to change after lunch was totally unnecessary. She was neat and looked great. But he saw a natural deference in Losana's reaction to Singh's navy-blue suit, striped business shirt and her hair twisted into a French roll. He reminded himself that he should never question Singh's dress choice.

'Mr Forester has arranged for a few other senior staff to join your meeting,' Losana said.

'Good,' Horseman smiled. Although Horseman knew his way, Losana walked a step ahead of them and tapped on the familiar door bearing the brass plaque, First Secretary.

Hugh Forester emerged from the bunch of people around a drinks trolley: Chief Inspector Bob Browning, Lt Pat Connolly and Walter Friend, Third Secretary. Horseman was intrigued that Mr Phillip, who'd introduced himself on Wednesday as the Pacific Secretary in the Foreign Affairs Department, was also present, still in his black suit. What had prevented his returning to Australia with the others?

'Good afternoon, DI Horseman. I appreciate your coming to report on your progress.' He held out his hand to Singh, who introduced herself to everyone. 'What will you have to drink, Inspectors?'

Drinks in hand, they moved to the conference table. 'I've asked Losana to take notes,' Forester said as she sat beside him and opened her laptop.

Singh placed her own notebook and pen on the table. Forester frowned and looked at Horseman. 'The floor is yours, Inspector.'

'Thank you, Mr Forester. We've had a hectic two days, but with the secondment of Inspector Singh and others to our team, we've made progress. As you know, Alex Scala became a suspect on Wednesday. A few hours ago, we confirmed the alibi he offered for

Ms Armstrong's murder. For the time being, he remains in custody on other charges. New leads are being pursued. The SOCOs have now finished at the crime scene, and the labs have analysed most of the evidence. I would have preferred to examine Ms Armstrong's office and apartment two days ago, but I held off at the High Commission's request. However, now we need to go ahead with the search. We can't do that without your willing consent, which I now request.'

The High-Com staff looked at each other. 'When do you propose to conduct this search? You'll understand it will disrupt our work in a time of great upheaval,' Hugh Forester said.

'As the search of the *Joshua* has just finished, specialised search and forensics officers are available this afternoon. I suggest we start immediately. I'm afraid murder is always a highly disruptive crime, but I make no apology for leaving—' He nearly said no stone unturned, but stopped himself just in time. '—nothing to chance in my investigation.'

Forester nodded to Chief Inspector Browning. 'Your opinion, Bob?'

'On Wednesday, I said the relevant rooms would need examining if Mr Scala was cleared of suspicion. That has now eventuated, so I agree with DI Horseman that the search should go ahead without delay.'

Forester turned to Lt Connolly on his left. 'It's upsetting, but the sooner it starts, the sooner it will be over.'

'Mr Phillip?'

'I understand your concerns about privacy, Hugh. However, as an outside observer, I can take a wider view. Australians would expect their representatives in Fiji to do their utmost to help the police find the High Commissioner's murderer. Suspicious souls might ask, "What have they to hide?" Don't you agree?' The mild-mannered man sounded and looked vaguely surprised.

'Does anyone else wish to speak?' Forester asked. No one replied. 'I invite you to go ahead with the search today, Inspector. A High Commission staff member in each room will observe the process and record any items the police wish to take away. I assume you have recording procedures of your own?'

Such an ignorant question annoyed Horseman, who glanced at Singh. 'We do indeed, Mr Forester. Sometimes photographs are enough. As for digital evidence, these days we save material onto memory sticks, so we won't need to take your equipment away. For key documents, we prefer to take photocopies, if you allow us to use your machines. We'll produce a list of any property we need to examine further and require an authorised officer of the High Commission to counter-sign it. This is quite an everyday procedure for us.' She smiled reassuringly around the table. 'If you'll excuse me, ladies and gentlemen, I'll get this going at once.' She gathered her things and left the room, looking every inch the inscrutable diplomat herself.

47

Half an hour later, Horseman checked that each room met the conditions Forester had set for the search. In Helen's office, Singh hovered near the door. She ducked outside when she saw him. 'I thought I'd keep an eye on what they're pulling out, direct the photocopying,' she whispered. 'But I'm not sure I'm needed. They're competent. Has Ash got enough direction, d'you think? I was thinking I could check with Dr Orlov if we could come this afternoon.'

'Let me get the lie of the land,' Horseman whispered back, opened the door and went in.

After a minute's observation, he could see Losana was more than a staff witness. As the High Commissioner's assistant, she told Ash and his technician the whereabouts and function of any records he might wish to look at. Indeed, as someone who had worked for the High-Com years longer than Helen had, she had set up some of the storage systems herself.

'Ms Armstrong was happy to fit in with most of my arrangements,' she told Horseman.

'I bet she knew she was lucky to have you manage the records,' Horseman smiled. 'I'll leave you to get on with it. DI Singh will be here to watch and learn. Please ask her if you're not sure whether we need a closer look or a record of any specific items. *Vinaka*, Losana, Ash.'

'See you later, then,' Singh said.

***

Helen's apartment was hidden behind a timber-panelled wall at one end of the big reception room of the official residence. Horseman couldn't help pausing for a few seconds to gaze over the back verandah at one of the best views in Suva. The serried hills faded from lush green to misty purple; the sinuous shoreline of curving bays was edged with sunlit sand here and there. And then the sea, for him the star of the show, spotlit here and there by shafts of sunlight piercing the iron-grey clouds.

DC Apo Kau opened the door to Horseman the instant he knocked. He wouldn't have noticed the High Commissioner's private door except for the polished brass knob. A subdued Lt Connolly met him just inside. The comfortable living room had its own verandah—the same view in a smaller frame. Books and newspapers lay on low tables beside cane sofas, a pair of reading glasses marking Helen's place in an open journal. Two SOCOs knelt beside a large antique sideboard, sifting through the drawers. They looked around, nodded and returned to work quickly.

Lt Connolly dabbed at her eyes with a tissue. 'Sorry, Inspector, it's just being in Helen's apartment again. Seeing her books and things, I realise now she's not coming back. She loved living in the old house. For her, it was a privilege.'

Horseman couldn't think what to say. He still couldn't understand why she'd kept vital information to herself from the beginning of the search. Now Helen's colleagues were under suspicion, she and Vuki were the ones he trusted least.

'I understand this is hard for you, Pat. Why don't you take a seat while you keep an eye on the search?'

Lt Connolly sat down. 'Thanks, the bedroom and study are through that door.' She pointed to the other end of the room. 'I can't bear to watch them going through her clothes, her private things.'

'The SOCOs understand and respect that. Do you know if she kept any private papers here?'

She sniffed and shook her head. 'I assume she did—I mean, we all do. She was very, um, discreet. I guess *diplomatic* is the word.' Her tiny smile lasted a second.

He opened the door and saw Chief Inspector Bob Browning standing at an open filing cabinet with Horseman's old DC probationer, Tanielo Musudroka. Horseman would ask Musudroka about what they were saying later, knowing Tani's tendency to joke and chat. Browning turned around and smiled, looking quite relaxed. Maybe Horseman was too on edge, too suspicious of trustworthy people. Maybe not.

The office end of Helen's roomy bedroom accommodated a desk, office chair and open shelves as well as the filing cabinet. Another SOCO emerged from the bathroom. He introduced himself as Joeli Tanibo. He was solid, forty-something, with a friendly smile. Horseman was happy to see chatty Musudroka had supervision. He called Kau to come through.

'Man, this must be the tidiest, cleanest place I've ever searched,' Tanibo said.

'You knew they'd cleaned it on Monday morning?'

'No wonder! The office waste bins are all empty, the bathroom and kitchen too.'

'I didn't know there was a kitchen. Where is it?'

'It's just a cupboard behind sliding doors in the living room panelling. Clever. I don't think it's used much. Kettle, toaster, microwave, sink with a few cupboards. Neat, though. I've just come from the bathroom. It's roomy, with a laundry next to it.'

'We can't undo the cleaning, Joeli. You know your job, but I suggest you pay attention to any crevices, take out drawers and look underneath, all of that. Private notes the High Commissioner may have tucked away might be the most useful finds of all. We don't know yet.'

'Leave no stone unturned, sir. That's what you always told us!' Musudroka butted in with a chuckle.

'You're right, Tani. Look at the space between stones, too.'

He asked Kau to come with him to the bathroom and laundry. 'Did you tell the SOCOs the apartment was cleaned on Monday?'

Kau frowned. 'No, sir. I assumed Sergeant Jayaraman had briefed them, and they had all the info they needed. Sorry.'

'Assume nothing, Apo. It doesn't hurt anyone to hear things twice. I need you to play a more active role in this search than you seem to be. Lt Connolly is here to see fair play, but I want you to look over the SOCOs' shoulders, ask questions. Tell them to check underneath drawers and furniture, niches and gaps, everywhere. Keep moving between the living room and bedroom. It doesn't matter if they find nothing, but I need to know they've looked.'

Anxiety flashed across Kau's round face. 'Sir, they're all senior to me. I can't do that.'

Horseman patted him on the shoulder. 'Course you can. You're the only detective here; you represent me, the senior investigating officer. You have the responsibility here.'

Kau looked doubtful. 'I'll try, sir.'

'You can do it, Apo. DI Singh and I are depending on you, and I know you won't let us down.'

***

Back in Helen's office, Horseman and Singh consulted Ash about how to split up the material they wanted to look at. Most of it was digital, on memory sticks, together with two small boxes of photocopies. They decided Horseman would take all of this to the station. Ash would take only a few personal, handwritten notebooks to his lab for forensic examination before the detectives read them.

'Why can't we take photocopies?' Singh asked, holding up the plastic evidence bag containing them. 'Surely these notebooks are the most likely of all the documents to contain revealing material. Whatever Ms Armstrong wrote in them, she chose not to consign those words to a computer. That's what I want to read first!'

Ash was familiar with the protests of detectives and smiled. 'That's just it, DI Singh. The photocopying process can compromise deposits of other material on the pages. Let us see what we discover first. It will be quick to match a hair, skin or fingerprints from Ms Armstrong. Just imagine, if we find anyone else's DNA on those notes, that could be significant. You might even be grateful to us much-abused SOCOs.'

Singh laughed. 'You're still wonderful, I'm glad to see, Ash. Of course, you're always right. Be quick, though!'

Horseman pulled his vibrating mobile from his pocket and saw it was from Ilai at the yacht club. He answered, puzzled. After a few moments, he felt unsteady and dropped onto a chair. He couldn't speak. He finally gasped the words, 'Say that again.'

48

Horseman stared at his mobile for a moment, wondering how it got into his hand. He saw the name Ilai, heard a confused voice ask, '*Bula, bula*, Inspector Horseman? Are you there?' Then a cool hand took hold of his other hand, curled it around a cup of water, raised it to his lips. He drank a mouthful, noticed Singh guiding his hand.

Losana bent over him, her hand firm on his shoulder, her brow furrowed. 'Do you need to lie down, Inspector? Let's get you onto the floor. You're probably just a little bit faint.'

He looked from his phone screen up into Singh's incomparable eyes, the green of sunlit water over sand. In that instant, he knew where he was and what had happened. He also knew what he wanted, saw his path ahead in a flash, felt Singh by his side. But that would have to wait.

'Have some more water, Joe.' She let go of his hand, allowing him to handle the cup himself. He took a careful swallow, then straightened up and gulped the rest down.

'Can you speak now, Joe?' Singh asked.

He shook his head, looked around and realised there were five people watching him intently. 'Yes, yes. I'm fine. Sorry about that—the news was a shock.'

He raised his mobile to his ear again. 'Ilai, I'm sorry, something demanded my attention, but I'm back with you now. Tell me again from the beginning, please.' As he listened to the tale of horror once more, he felt a heavy stone sink down his gullet and lodge above his stomach. It hurt like hell.

'I'll come right away, Ilai. Is he with you?'

'No, DS Taleca and the arresting constable, Antoni, took him to the station. The other uniform stayed here to guard the *Joshua*. But

I reckon you've got your man now, haven't you? No need for guards anymore!'

'Not so fast, Ilai. I'll be with you in ten minutes. *Vinaka vakalevu* for letting me know.'

'No problem, sir. But DS Taleca and Constable Antoni aren't back yet, so you'd best go to the station.'

Horseman braced his hands on his chair to push himself up, but he was fine. More than fine, he'd burst from the murky swamp into fresh air, full of energy.

'Apologies, everyone. Thanks for your concern. There's been a development. DI Singh and I must dash away. Ash, can you supervise the apartment search and give DC Kau a lift back, please? I need the vehicle.'

'No problems, sir! Leave it all with me.'

***

Horseman, Singh, Kelepi Taleca and Constable Antoni sat around a table upstairs on the detectives' floor. The sound of the rain hammering on the corrugated iron roof drowned out conversation.

'Now, from the beginning, Constable. You'll have to shout!' Horseman yelled.

'Sir, I was near the *Joshua* on guard around three o'clock when I heard splashing to the west of the boat, quite close to the shore. I saw a person surface and dive back down. He was wearing a mask and a pair of shorts, no diving equipment, but he had a bag attached to his belt. He dived three more times, moving further west and away from the shore each time. I thought he was gathering shellfish or sea cucumbers, but I kept track of him. In the end, he swam back to shore. I radioed DS Taleca, who told me to detain the swimmer as he reached the beach. That wasn't difficult, he was only a teenager and tired from all that diving. I saw he had something in his net bag, and he showed me, quite pleased with himself. It was something like the winch handle you told us to look out for, sir. I thought he must be the High Commissioner's killer, come back to get the weapon and dispose of it better.'

Antoni spoke confidently, proud he had done the right thing. 'Go on, Constable,' Horseman prompted.

'*Io*, sir. I radioed DS Taleca to report, stepping away for privacy, and the kid took off. He must have heard what I was saying in spite of my precautions. I ran after him and handcuffed him, and a minute later, DS Taleca turned up.'

'Did you ask his name, arrest him, tell him his rights?'

'*Io*, sir. He said his name was Tevita, and he knew you. I arrested him on suspicion of murder. DS Taleca said I'd done well, and that we all needed to go to Suva Central station. We waited for a police car to pick us up from the yacht club. It began to rain and the kid was shivering. I asked if he had any clothes with him, maybe a bag he left on the rocks. He said no.'

'Do you confirm this, DS Taleca?'

'*Io*, as far as my involvement went.'

'Have you had a chance to record the events in your notebook, Antoni?'

'Not yet, sir. But I've made my statement to the duty sergeant. DS Taleca helped me with that.'

'Are you satisfied with Antoni's statement, DS Taleca?' Horseman asked.

'*Io*, I don't think we need to keep him any longer, Inspector.'

'I agree. You certainly acted quickly, Antoni. When does your shift end?'

'Six o'clock, sir.'

'You can go home now, Constable.'

***

'*Oi lei*, Keli, help me understand. Why in heaven's name did you arrest Tevita?'

Singh shot him a warning look, then got up and left.

'You heard, boss. The rascal ran away. Antoni caught him and cuffed him to prevent a repeat performance until I got there. Correct procedure, eh?'

Horseman rubbed his face and got a shock to see his hands trembling. He clenched them into fists.

'*Io*, but arresting him for murder? Because he picked up a tool from the bottom of the bay? That's leaping over about twenty steps of procedure, Keli, and you know it better than anyone!'

'But you know, immediately undoing what a probationer has done incorrectly isn't the best training method. Especially in front of his prisoner.' Taleca replied.

'True. But to put Tevita through the whole booking process at the station? That's going much too far. The kid must have been terrified!'

'He was quiet.'

'Rigid with fear, I'd say.'

'He didn't seem so. He cheekily asked us to call you, because he was helping you with Ms Armstrong's murder case.'

Horseman sighed heavily. 'That'd be right. He's done it before.'

'What, Joe? You wouldn't send your delinquents out scouting for you? Not even you would take such risks!'

'No, I wouldn't. And they're not delinquents. Tevita's been washing cars in the police garage for a few years now, goes to night school, and is heading for a job as a police driver when he's old enough. I meant he's taken it into his head to assist the police before—remember the Jona case?'

'*Io*, io, that poor fishing observer whose head ended up in a shark's belly!'

Horseman nodded. 'Tevita decided to help and ended up a captive in a brothel full of smuggled Chinese prostitutes.'

'Ha! That did have its funny side. So he's that boy!'

'*Io*, and he's obviously up to another misguided caper. After training yesterday, I was filling Dr Young in on the murder weapon when I realised Tevita was right behind us. Now it's obvious he heard us, has found out what a winch handle is, and has gone looking for it to help me.'

Singh came back with a tea tray. 'He could be trying to prove himself to you.' She put the tray on the table. 'I'll let that brew for a few minutes.'

'Those rascals idolise you, Joe,' Taleca said.

'I've done nothing to encourage that, Keli. Now it's my fault the kid's charged with murder! I need to see him right away.'

'I don't think that's the best idea at the moment,' Singh said. 'We've all had a shock, and what we need is tea and coconut biscuits.'

Singh's tone brooked no argument. Taleca whipped out his notebook and wrote up the events of the afternoon. Horseman followed suit. When Singh judged brewing sufficient, she poured milk into all three cups, followed by scalding brown tea and passed the cups around. 'Add your own sugar, gentlemen,' she invited.

'Ginger nuts are better,' Taleca remarked, having dunked his coconut biscuit and looked on in dismay as it broke into crumbs like so many floating islands.

'Let's be positive. I agree with Joe about Tevita, but finding the winch handle, if it is indeed the murder weapon, is a step forward, isn't it?'

'Yep, it is. Where is it?' Horseman asked.

'Bagged, tagged and on its way to the evidence store,' Taleca said.

'When you've had your tea, please get it back and let me look at it. Then take it to the SOCO lab. Take a taxi voucher if there aren't any cars.' Horseman tried to repress his resentment of Taleca.

'*Io*, Boss.' Taleca made a note in his book.

'What about the super?' Singh asked. 'I think he should know about this.'

Horseman drained his cup, reached for the big aluminium teapot and poured himself another while he pondered. 'Sorry, anyone else for a second?' They both wanted another, so he poured.

After another extended pause, Horseman spoke up. 'I'm with Singh. We should brief Ratini next. Persuade him of Tevita's innocence and get him released.'

The others nodded. 'I'll get that winch handle, then,' Taleca said, not at all apologetic. Horsemen knew Taleca had never supported his Junior Shiners project, but allowing Tevita's arrest to stand was sheer prejudice.

'Keli, I think it's time to make a decision about the driver, Vuki Maya. I agreed earlier that we should wait for the right moment, but we need to narrow our list of suspects down fast. So please use all your tricks to put pressure on Maya.'

'All, boss? Really?'

'*Io*, you have my full permission.' Horseman didn't smile.

Together, Horseman and Singh cleared up the tea things, planning how they would tackle Ratini.

49

'What a breakthrough! Well done to all concerned!' Ratini grinned, to Horseman's consternation. His senior officer had reverted to his normal mode of dress, looking like he'd been interrupted while digging in his garden. He was in worn jeans with grubby knees and pockets, a faded floral *bula* shirt. His hair, barbered in honour of Wednesday's meeting at the High-Com, was still neat, but patchy grey-and-black stubble had regrown on his cheeks, chin, and neck.

'*Vinaka*, sir, if the tool retrieved by Tevita proves to be the murder weapon. But after a week in the sea, it's unlikely to have the victim's biological material on it. Taleca's taking it to the SOCO lab as we speak.' He glanced at Singh.

'Sir, DI Horseman and I both feel Tevita's arrest was a procedural error by a young constable, who understandably panicked when Tevita ran away. We would certainly like to question Tevita without delay. But we don't expect to have any evidence to detain him further today.' Singh said.

'But he ran away! He says he has no family, but that must be a lie. He will run away again! These street kids are like the mongoose, scuttling into their holes in an instant.'

They had both agreed to leave the persuasion to Singh, but Horseman couldn't bottle up his outrage. 'That's sheer prejudice, sir! Exactly what Tevita and his mates have to put up with every day of their lives. I know Tevita well. He's a reliable member of the Junior Shiners rugby squad, and yes, he grew up on the streets, where he worked as a shoe-shine boy from an early age. He doesn't talk about his past, but I've seen horrific scars on his legs and body when the boys sluice themselves down after training.

'Tevita's been working in the police garage, cleaning vehicles, for a few years now, and goes to night school. His supervisor, Sergeant Walo, speaks well of his work and will recommend him for training as a police driver when he's old enough. He's just moved into Junior Shiners House, where he's under supervision. If he's released on bail, he will not bolt, I can guarantee.'

'You know him? That explains your support of the boy, but I will not tolerate insubordination or emotional outbursts from my staff.' Horseman could not tolerate a lesson in etiquette from the rudest man in the station, either. But he pulled his head in after a warning glare from Singh.

Horseman continued. 'I agree with your concern for the security of any accused, Superintendent Ratini. You may not know that Junior Shiners House employs a house-mother, whom Tevita greatly respects. She's Sala Horseman, the well-known former President of the Fiji Nurses Association. Mrs Horseman will certainly agree to supervise him when he's not at work or his evening classes. Tevita will willingly comply with her curfew and whatever reporting orders the police require.'

Ratini frowned for a while, and Horseman hoped Tevita was in with a chance. 'Do you mean the accused is on close terms with the entire Horseman family?'

'Just my mother and me, sir. Please listen to my reasons for being certain Tevita is innocent.'

'Well, no one could ever claim that I didn't listen,' Ratini said with unjustified pride.

'First, if he was the murderer and threw the weapon as far as he could south-west, why would he come back to retrieve it? The police divers didn't find it in two days of searching, and they weren't coming back. The weapon's not vital to the case now. Even Tevita would guess that sea and sand would eliminate any biological evidence within a week, so why?'

'*Oi lei*, Horseman, you should know it's psychology: the criminal returns to the scene of the crime. In this case, it's the scene of the weapon.' He smiled condescendingly at his own cleverness.

Horseman forced his mouth to smile, his head to nod, for Tevita's sake. 'Second, sir, what possible motive could Tevita have to kill Ms

Armstrong? She visited them twice at training, shaking hands and talking to each of them. Only a week ago, she gave them all new rugby socks. She also attended a match and chatted with the boys afterwards. They all understand she's leased us Australian land to build the hostel, saving them from life on the streets. Every boy is beyond grateful. Why would Tevita kill her?'

'Who knows? These neglected kids can have twisted, sick minds. You can argue it's not their fault their bad parents didn't look after them, but that can't change the outcome.' He nodded sagely. 'Here's what will happen. One: Horseman, as Tevita's father-figure and patron, you can have no role at all in the police investigation of the boy's involvement in Ms Armstrong's murder. None at all. Two: you will continue as SIO of the wider case, but DI Singh will conduct Tevita's investigation. Three: Tevita will remain in custody for his own safety until he is cleared of suspicion. We can't have enraged friends of Ms Armstrong breaking into the hostel to take their revenge, can we? Especially with Mrs Horseman's safety at risk, too.'

'That scenario is so extremely far-fetched we can dismiss it,' Horseman protested.

Ratini raised his hand and wagged one finger at Horseman. 'In the interest of Tevita's welfare, he will remain in the station lockup here. Four: As I can't trust you to respect your senior's wishes, Horseman, you are not to visit Tevita except in the company of DI Singh and a police guard. No, no, don't look so furious, man. What would you do on these private visits? I know very well: coach him in his interview answers, write his statements, and ask for his loyalty. The list goes on. I understand you want to help your protégé, but it's breaking the law, and I won't have it, Horseman. I think that's about it, Inspectors. Are you both clear? Any questions?'

Singh glared at Horseman, so he complied. 'That's clear enough, sir,' he said.

Singh smiled at Ratini. 'I can see that's a workable procedure, sir. I'll do my best to produce the right outcome.'

Ratini looked so self-righteous, Horseman longed to punch him. 'I know I can always rely on you, Susie. It's wonderful to have you back in Suva again.'

Singh's sweet smile must have gratified Ratini, but it produced a sharp pounding in Horseman's chest. He realised he got jumpy when any man flattered Singh. He was just so scared that his love would be unrequited. Well, he'd better try treating her like the precious gem she was, hadn't he?

50

Singh was happy enough with how the meeting with Ratini had gone, apart from Horseman's too-intense attempts to persuade Ratini of the ludicrous nature of Tevita's arrest. Joe's arguments were sound, but he could never manage to keep his diehard loyalty to the Shiners out of his voice. Singh reckoned Ratini saw that as a weakness to zero in on. And man, did he love Joe rising to his bait.

But on this occasion, to her dismay, she thought Ratini was correct. While Constable Antoni had gone too far to arrest Tevita on suspicion of murder, the boy must explain to the police his possession of the winch handle, whether or not it turned out to be the murder weapon. Absolutely, he must. Taleca's total support of Antoni's arrest puzzled her. In Taleca's place, she would have no hesitation in downgrading the potential charge when they got to the Suva Central station. Wasn't that what a supervisory role was all about, giving young officers feedback on their actions? Perhaps she could chat to Taleca later and find out more.

Despite all that, she agreed with Ratini that Joe should have no role in investigating Tevita. He was just too close. Tevita's history was the most shocking and sad of all the Junior Shiners, yet he'd inspired Joe to make a rugby team of the shoe-shine boys of Suva. She understood Tevita's cheeky cheeriness appealed to Joe, no matter how embarrassed he was by the boy's dog-like devotion. She wished Ratini hadn't relished knocking Joe back, but he'd been right this time.

'Joe, I'll consult you on Tevita's case at every step, don't worry about that. I agree he's innocent, but he and the tool he found could both advance Ms Armstrong's case, don't you think?'

'I do, Susie. But locking him up is cruel. I don't think he'll cope.'

'It'll be tough on him, but he's survived much worse, hasn't he? You just won't get anywhere by opposing the super on this, you'll only hold up the investigation and delay Tevita's release, too.'

Joe held her gaze and eventually nodded.

'I want us both to talk to Tevita now, together. Ratini permits that.'

'You're not going to comply with his idiotic conditions, are you?' His tone was incredulous.

'Yes, I am, in Tevita's interest. I'm on your side, Joe, but I'm also on the side of the law.' Maybe she'd come across as pompous—she hoped not.

'And you think I'm not? How could you doubt me, Singh?' He shot her a glance full of hurt, full of sorrow. She longed to comfort him, but she was at work. So was he.

'I don't doubt you, Joe. But you're too close to Tevita to be objective, you must know that. Now, let's get ready to talk with him.'

***

When they entered the tiny cell with the constable who would report to Ratini, they'd agreed on a plan which the super could not object to—if Joe followed it. Singh prayed that he'd stay calm.

Horseman had dashed to the roti vendor outside the station and bought a big paper bag of the hot savoury wraps. He sat beside Tevita on the hard, narrow bunk, gave the boy a pat on the back and offered the bag.

Tevita's face lit up with a radiant grin. 'You come, Joe! I said you would! *Bula vinaka*, Sergeant Singh!'

'*Bula vinaka*, Tevita.'

'She's DI Singh now, and she's come back to Suva to help us find Ms Armstrong's killer. It won't be long now she's here.'

'But Joe, listen to me. Stupid constable, he told them I killed Ms Armstrong! Me! I love Ms Armstrong, she gave us the land! Divers, they couldn't find the winch handle, but I find it, Joe! I watch them search away from the shore, but I look west, close in. I was going to give it to you, but constable arrest me first!'

'We understand, Tevita,' Singh spoke slowly, softly. Now she had two outraged males to reassure. 'This is how we're going to divide up the work. DI Horseman must continue to hunt down Ms Armstrong's killer. He'll visit you when he can.'

Tevita nodded and sniffed a noisy and prolonged sniff. Singh continued. 'I'm going to find out exactly what you were doing at the time Ms Armstrong died, and try to prove it. That's the best way to get you out of here. Always tell me the truth, or I won't be able to help you. Do you understand?'

Tevita's mouth was full of chicken roti. He forced himself to swallow, wiped his mouth with the back of a hand and nodded vigorously. '*Io*, DI Singh. I will tell truth.'

'I'm going now, Tevita. Remember what I said. Help DI Singh by telling the truth.' Joe grasped the boy's hand in a prolonged handshake and patted his shoulder. '*Moce mada.*' Then he left without looking back.

Singh thought this first meeting couldn't have gone better. Talking and eating together had calmed both man and boy. Would the stress of the interview room and the recorder panic Tevita again? She waited until he'd eaten his second roti, then asked, 'Tevita, let's talk now. Would you like to go upstairs to an interview room? Or we can stay here and talk while you finish your rotis.'

Tevita stopped chewing and looked up in consternation. 'DI Singh, I reckon I'm a proper police witness now. I like interview room. More better, eh?'

***

Singh opened the door to Interview Room 3. Tevita sat beside Sala Horseman, who readily agreed to take the role of responsible guardian for his interview. The boy seemed subdued, aware again that he was under arrest for murder, not the star witness he'd imagined. Izzy Pareti took the chair beside Singh and made the introductions.

'Mrs Horseman, did you see Tevita last Saturday?' Singh asked.

'Yes, he was at the hostel when I left at three o'clock to visit my daughter and her family. I didn't see him again until the next day, when we were all busy preparing for our grand opening.'

'Tevita, where were you last Saturday evening, 14th July?' Singh asked.

'After dinner at the hostel, I was walking around Suva on my own and saw sunset. I like the lights, the dark, the shops.'

'Did you see anyone? Buy anything? We've got to find someone who remembers you from sunset to later in the evening.'

Mrs Horseman gave Tevita a nudge. 'Don't keep any secrets, Tevita.'

The boy stared at the floor. 'Mrs Horseman, I was with a girl, I think she's my girlfriend. I hope she is. Maybe. But I don't want to say. All the Shiners they will laugh at me, tease me. I don't like that. I don't want to tell anyone about her.'

'*Oi lei*, something as simple as a girlfriend!' Mrs Horseman said, shaking her head.

'Where did you go with her?' Singh asked.

'Um, to church.'

Singh's heart raced. Maybe this would come out right, after all. 'Which church?'

'Her church. It's the Church of God, way up the hill in Rewa Street. She likes to go to that church as much as she can. I only see her there. On Saturday we went to choir practice, Bible study and worship service.'

'She must be a lovely girl. What's her name? How did you two meet?'

'She's Mere. We meet two months ago at the church free-food van on Victoria Parade. She works on the van. She invited me to church, so I go along. She's very pretty.'

Singh smiled at Tevita. 'I think you've got a watertight alibi that will get you released tomorrow. I'd like to talk to you a lot more, but for now, just tell me Mere's full name and address and the times when you were with her at church last Saturday. I'll go and see Mere and take her statement—'

His eyes widened in alarm. 'No, no, don't do that! You can't! Mere will dump me!'

'What, Tevita? Why on earth?'

'I'm arrested for murder! She won't want to see me again. I know she's too good for me.' Tears rolled down his cheeks, which he wiped with a filthy piece of towel.

'Tevita, Mere likes you, and she'll want to help. She'll understand the police sometimes make mistakes, and she'll want to put that right. She'll tell the truth to set you free.'

Singh wondered if Mere would turn out to be yet another instance of Tevita's wishful thinking. It was all too possible.

Tevita sniffed. 'Maybe Mere didn't see me on Saturday night.'

'Didn't you sit next to her at these church meetings you told us about?'

The boy shook his head. 'No, the church is always crowded.'

Singh smiled. 'Don't worry, Tevita. I'll see Mere and the pastor, and we'll work it out. You'll need to sleep in the lockup tonight, but I expect Mere and the pastor will help me get you out tomorrow.'

Mrs Horseman patted Tevita on the shoulder. 'Well done, my boy. I've brought dinner for both of us. We'll eat together in the lockup, then I'll help you with your homework.' Tevita beamed.

'I've got to play against Dudley High School tomorrow at three o'clock,' he said.

SATURDAY 21st July

51

After taking Tina back to Matt's after their early morning romp on the foreshore, Horseman joined his friend for breakfast on the deep verandah while Tina flopped into her basket and snoozed.

When Horseman related Friday's whirlwind, Dr Young frowned. 'Hell, mate, that's tough. I'm no lawyer, but it sounds wrong to me, too. More coffee?'

'Yep, more coffee and of course Tevita's arrest was wrong. Singh thinks Ratini was right to exclude me, and maybe he was, but she hopes to get him out today. Mum came to the rescue—she's acting as his responsible adult, she's brought him a decent meal and coached him through his night school lessons. That should distract him from his situation a bit.' He drank the hot, strong coffee gratefully.

'I reckon so. Thank God for your mum, Joe. What are you up to today, apart from the game at three o'clock?'

Horseman shook his head while spreading a dollop of marmalade on another thick slice of toast. 'I won't be able to stay for the whole game. I'll be there early to pep them up, though. We don't know when the Church of God pastor will get to the station, so I've told young Maika he'll play if Tevita doesn't get out in time.'

'Maika's a good pick, he's got a lot of potential,' Dr Young agreed. 'But what a dark horse Tevita turned out to be. Good on him, attracting the notice of a nice girl!'

'Yep. Singh found Mere last night, and Tevita's account is exaggerated, but not fabricated. Mere's already made her statement.'

'What else is on your list for today?'

'In ten minutes, Apo Kau and I are off to USP to fingerprint Dr Orlov and press him to open up about his presence on the *Joshua Slocum*. Singh was down for that, but now she's taken over Tevita.

Then I'll go to the station and examine the mounds of material we took from the High-Com yesterday afternoon. How much I can get through in one day, I don't know.'

But he feared it would be very little unless he pulled all the DCs off the yacht club interviews. Perhaps that would work. 'What about you?'

'A day off. Shopping, the game, then dinner with Gloria later.'

'This is getting serious, then?'

'No. We enjoy each other's company in our leisure time, but we both have demanding jobs. We're good friends. She's amazing, so different from anyone I've ever known. But I don't know if I want something permanent ever again, after Talei. Maybe I'm one of those birds who mate for life.'

'True, you and Talei were a couple in a thousand. But Talei died more than ten years ago, Matt. What would she want for you?'

Dr Young shrugged. 'You're hardly one to be dispensing marital advice, mate.'

Horseman stuffed the remaining toast in his mouth and crunched quickly before he could confide his changed feelings for Singh. 'You're right. I'll be off.' Apo Kau pulled up in a police car. Horseman got himself out of the soft old cane chair without using his hands to push off, feeling much better. He gave Tina a pat and said, 'Thanks for breakfast, Matt. Really picked me up.'

'See you at the game!'

***

Dr Orlov came to the door when the car turned into his gravel driveway. Overhanging trees and flowering creepers made his single quarters appear secluded. When they entered the quiet gloom of the spartan living room cum study, Horseman thought it was just the sort of place he himself would enjoy coming home to. The old ceiling fan wobbled as it rotated at high speed.

'I was surprised to get your call, Inspector Horseman. I thought you'd be looking into the High Commissioner's ex-husband, like I told you.'

Horseman knew very well he was fishing, but what the heck? 'We've scrutinised Mr Scala's actions, and cleared him of any suspicion of killing Ms Armstrong.'

Dr Orlov lifted his eyebrows. 'Really? Are you sure?'

'Completely. As I mentioned on the phone, you are now the only visitor to the *Joshua Slocum* whose fingerprints we don't have. We need to eliminate you. I've brought along Detective Constable Kau to save you a trip to the police station.'

'I'm amazed those diplomats allowed you to fingerprint them. I imagined they'd all protest about the police invading their sovereign soil and claiming diplomatic immunity.'

'No, they didn't. They understood it's necessary, quick and painless. I hope you do, too.'

'All right. I don't like it, but it seems you give me no choice.'

'You do have a choice, Dr Orlov, and I really appreciate your cooperation.'

While DC Kau, with gentle patience, guided Dr Orlov through the process, Horseman asked, 'Have you thought more about the date of your last visit to the yacht?'

'As I told you last Tuesday, I can't remember. But it seems like a long time ago.' Dr Orlov replied.

'Would you have written it in a diary, recorded it in a digital calendar?'

'How can it matter now?' Dr Orlov's resistance puzzled Horeman. Was this a ritual with him, or was he concealing something?

'It could matter quite a lot. I won't know until the lab compares your prints with the ones collected from the yacht. But in the meantime, I need to ask you what you were doing last Saturday evening.'

'Someone's been talking about me, eh? I knew it! Who?' His face contorted with fury.

Aha, Orlov had as good as admitted he'd been hiding a secret, one he knew someone would discover. Horseman hadn't a clue what that secret could be, but Orlov didn't know that.

'Dr Orlov, I would urge you to tell me frankly now what rumours or accusations are circulating about you. Be honest now, and I may find Ms Armstrong's killer faster. No matter what you've done, telling the truth will reflect well on you.'

'Bah, that's what the voice of authority always says.'

'It's true in Fiji, Dr Orlov.'

The professor was edgy; he fiddled with the neck of his polo shirt and then ran his fingers through his shoulder-length hair, tucking it behind his ears. 'Muggy today, isn't it? Would you like a Coke?'

'Yes, please, if it's no trouble. DC Kau?'

Kau nodded his thanks, and Dr Orlov jumped up and left the room. He came back quickly with three cans and two glasses. They all drank from the cans in silence. Horseman never drank Coke if he had a choice, but today the icy sweetness hit the spot.

'*Vinaka*, that's better. So, have you remembered what you did last Saturday evening?'

'When, precisely?'

'Begin at half-past six, please.'

Orlov's prominent Adam's apple bobbed as he swallowed. 'I left here around then to walk to a party at a colleague's apartment on campus. About a five-minute walk. I was there until around midnight, I think. Then I walked back here.'

'Was it a big party?'

'No, about twenty guests.'

Horseman smiled in a way he hoped was encouraging. 'Good, good. I'll need a list of guests, just to confirm that. Phone numbers and addresses too, please. A university staff party, was it? Do all the guests live on campus?'

'Not all staff, no. Some students were there, too. Some live in halls of residence. I don't know the addresses of the others.'

'No, you wouldn't, of course. Never mind, we can get those details from USP records. But I would be really grateful if you could write down the names and departments of the USP people.' He nodded to Kau, who handed Orlov his open notebook and a pen.

'Take your time, sir. We can wait while you're thinking,' Kau said.

'Hell, I won't bloody remember while you two are staring at me!' Orlov sounded irritated. He sprang up and moved to his desk, leaving Kau's notebook on the coffee table. Kau exchanged a glance with Horseman while they sipped their drinks. Orlov brought back a scrawled list of ten names. 'Surely that's enough to confirm my alibi?'

Horseman smiled. 'Thank you, Dr Orlov. If we could wait a bit longer while you check on the date you were last on Ms Armstrong's yacht, I may not have to trouble you again.'

Orlov sighed heavily and returned to his desk. Horseman pushed himself out of his sagging chair, raising his voice so Orlov could hear. 'Dr Orlov, my leg is cramped, I need to walk about your room for a minute. Do you mind?' That should hurry the professor up.

Orlov grunted. Horseman marched around the room, not noisily but not soundlessly either.

Before long, Orlov brought Horseman a sticky note with a date. 'It's not as long ago as I thought, 17th March,' he mumbled.

'That must have been her last sailing party on the *Joshua*,' Horseman said.

Orlov scrutinised him, his eyes wet.

'Thanks for clearing that up, Professor. We'll be in touch. And thank you for my first Coke in an age.'

52

DS Kelepi Taleca agreed with Horseman that the young DCs needed a break from the repetitive grind of questioning the Royal Suva Yacht Club's members and visitors. The most fruitful time to resume in earnest would be at five o'clock, when the regular Saturday night crowd would begin to gather.

Waiting for them at the station at nine in the morning were hundreds of routine admin folders that were unlikely to contain nuggets for the murder case. Still, they had to check them all. Taleca distributed the files on the memory sticks among the young detectives, whom he trained and closely supervised. For Izzy, this was a completely new task. Lili had some experience, but not enough to work independently. After Horseman pointed out what they were looking for and Taleca showed them how to search systematically, they celebrated with tea and biscuits, then threw themselves into the new task with enthusiasm.

Horseman delegated the job of checking out Orlov's alibi to Apo, who was getting to be something of a human sniffer dog himself.

He reserved the physical records for himself. After all, whether computer printouts or handwritten, they'd probably be more productive. He took the cardboard archive box to his desk for a preliminary sort. He arranged the photocopied files in priority order and sat to look through each. He put the list of files on his right to tick off as he finished each one. It was then he remembered the evidence bag of handwritten notebooks, which Ash had taken to examine for deposits of human material. When they'd dropped off Orlov's fingerprints at the SOCO lab earlier, Ash was out, and Horseman had forgotten to enquire if the books had been examined yet. He rang Ash immediately, only to find he was still out. All he could do for now was leave another message.

Someone had labelled the manila folders clearly. He was grateful. He leafed through three before giving in to his rising anxiety that this task was insurmountable. No, of course it wasn't insurmountable; just one folder after another, one folder at a time. But he'd only ticked off four files when the phone rang.

He recognised the velvety bass tones immediately. 'So pleased to find you able to take my call, Joe. Usaia Tuilau speaking. I understand you're run off your feet. I won't ask how your investigation is going, but it must be a great deal of pressure.'

'*Io*, Ratu, we're pursuing the High Commissioner's killer every hour we have. We'll get there.'

'Joe, I'm getting questions from the Board about whether you've had time to read the draft contract they authorised.' Horseman smiled to himself. Courtesy would forbid the chief from checking up on Horseman except on the board's behalf.

'*Vinaka vakalevu* for your interest, Ratu. I've read it more than once. I simply haven't had the time to give it due consideration. So I haven't been able to make a decision yet.'

'The board understands your position completely. Do you have any queries I could clarify for you at this stage?'

'*Vinaka*, not yet, Ratu Usaia. It's all pretty clear.'

'Good. Remember, there's room for flexibility, Joe. You're the Board's first choice. However, I won't keep you from your urgent work. We have every faith in you. God bless.'

After signing off on only another three files, he knew office work was not the most effective use of his time today. Better to channel the restlessness he couldn't suppress into activity. Few of the High-Com staff would work on Saturday, and if he could meet them off campus, they might be more talkative. After a little more thought and a few phone calls, he slung his satchel over his shoulder, had a word with DS Taleca, and left the station.

He strolled the couple of blocks to the bay and continued on to Suva's biggest and busiest Saturday meeting place, the City Council market. In spite of the grey skies, the produce laid out on official benches or cloths spread on the ground bounced the light around as if hit by sunbeams. The outlandish colours of tropical fruit and vegetables made him smile. He loved the abundance, the variety, the freshness ... what wasn't there to love? Perhaps the half-starved dogs lurking in the shadows, the over-eager barrow boys, the boys with no barrows who begged shoppers to let them carry their purchases and the enduring puzzle of shoe-shine boys in a city where most people wore sandals or flip-flops or went barefoot.

He kept his eye out for Losana as he bought vegetables and herbs, papaya and pineapples. This could not be done quickly, as vendors and shoppers alike often thrust out their hands for him to shake. He gladly responded, but a greeting was often not enough for his fans. Men in particular sought his opinion on the current Suva rugby competition, the mistakes of umpires, the Pacific Cup, the Hong Kong Sevens. Enjoyable as this could be, Losana had said he could speak to her at the market or not at all, as her daughters' netball games would fill her entire afternoon.

He caught sight of her at last, with her husband and three daughters in netball uniforms, all good-looking and well-groomed like their mother. A boy trailed the family with a half-full wheelbarrow. Losana introduced Horseman, who spent a few minutes chatting to Losana's husband until she said, 'I told you I need to speak to Inspector Horseman for half an hour. I'll meet you at the pineapple juice stall. Make sure you've finished the shopping by then, slow coaches!'

'How about upstairs—it'll be quieter,' she said to Horseman.

The upper level was the territory of the spice wholesalers. As they ascended, the mixed scents became more intense: the immense cones of ground cumin, cayenne, turmeric, nutmeg, garam masala, and more looked as spectacular as they smelled. They found a bench between two stalls and sat. The hospitable vendor poured tea into two plastic cups and presented them on a tray, which Losana rested on her knees. 'Losana is our valued customer, always welcome,' the vendor informed Horseman.

'Did you discover something important yesterday, Inspector?'

'We don't know yet. Everyone's busy checking the digital documents today, and the physical evidence is still with the lab. How's the mood at the High Commission?'

'The search unsettled people. They're worried, but they don't really know what about, that's my impression. We're still coming to terms with Helen's loss. She was a vigorous leader, a big personality.'

'How can Mr Forester step into her shoes?'

'Exactly, we all think of him as second-in-command. The usual policy is for Foreign Affairs to appoint a new High Commissioner from another mission, or from the headquarters in Canberra. Then the new appointee is the boss from the beginning. I think Mr Forester wants to be the High Commissioner here. But it's not usual for someone to be promoted in-house.'

'Would he have the support of the other staff?'

'I doubt that matters to Canberra, but I'm just admin. Don't get me wrong. He's competent, conscientious, and fair with the staff. As for his diplomatic effectiveness, I wouldn't know.'

'I was curious about Mr Phillip joining our meeting yesterday. Why did he stay behind when the others left?'

Losana shrugged. 'I don't know exactly. To help with the aftermath of Ms Armstrong's death, I suppose. That's more or less what they said. The others flew back yesterday morning. Hugh wanted to go with them—asked me to book him an air ticket. Which I did. Then, last thing yesterday, just as I was getting ready to go home after all the police had left, Hugh told me to cancel it.'

'Did he say why?'

'Not really—only that he was needed here. Just between us, I wonder if Mr Phillip is the next High Commissioner and Hugh has to show him the ropes. I don't think he'd be happy about that situation.'

'Anything's possible, isn't it?'

Losana laughed. '*Io*, wait and see. Sorry I couldn't be more help.'

'*Vinaka*, Losana, you've filled in one or two blanks. That's a win for me.' She stood, and the spice vendor took the tea tray from her. As Losana went down the stairs, Horseman remained on the bench, thinking. Then he went to the fresh spice stalls and bought a handful of ginger root, and fifty grams each of whole nutmegs and vanilla beans. Could he tempt Singh with a curry-from-scratch tonight? They had to talk. Before he could tell her how he felt about her, she should know about the choice he'd have to make sooner rather than later.

53

Horseman shut his fridge door after stowing the last of his fresh food. As usual, what seemed modest quantities in the market somehow grew into enough to feed an entire rugby team in his little kitchen. He stood up, stretched his calves and hamstrings while inhaling the dizzying herbal aromas stirred by the ceiling fan.

He grabbed his mobile to call Singh, but saw he'd missed a call from Ash Jayaraman.

'*Bula* Ash, I thought you were enjoying a rare weekend off.'

'Man, so did I. But Tanielo called to say you'd dropped off Orlov's fingerprints, so I told him to check them against the *Joshua Slocum* data immediately. And Orlov is the last piece in my jigsaw puzzle! His prints match the only remaining unidentified prints we lifted from the yacht's cabin.'

'Wow, that's quick!'

'That's the tremendous advantage of having a full set of elimination prints on file. Speed!'

'Ash, is there any way of knowing how old prints are?'

'No, not yet. The yacht was clean. Hardly any dust. But a light dust over varnished timber usually won't remove prints, even if the surface looks clean. I can't help you there. I've got more for you, though.'

'Great! What?'

'Did you notice anything distinctive about the winch handle Tevita fished out?'

'No, I saw it through the evidence bag, nothing surprising, wet and sandy.'

'It has the initials JS engraved on its head, just like its twin,' Ash said. 'Sea immersion and abrasion cleaned it thoroughly. The engraving's fine but quite deep. We've managed to extract minute blood deposits, but too small and degraded for DNA analysis. They do confirm the handle was the weapon, if that were ever needed.'

'Identifying the weapon's good, but who wielded it?'

'Can't answer that, Joe.'

'*Vinaka*, Ash. Did you find any other mobiles at all?'

'No.'

'Have you finished with the handwritten notes from Ms Armstrong's office?'

'Oh yes. Only her own fingerprints, so she must have kept them strictly private. Shall I send them over to Suva Central?'

'Please do. I'll be back there in fifteen minutes. *Vinaka vakalevu*!'

Before he left, he sat down at his desk and called Singh. He relaxed at the sound of her friendly voice.

'Hi Joe. I've just been talking to your mother. She should be with Tevita now, having lunch. The pastor was held up, but he promises to be here very soon.'

'It's a good thing I arranged for a reserve to play in his place, then.'

'Joe, I loved seeing Shiners House—I couldn't believe the quality of the building. And the boys are so proud, so happy. Congratulations to you, Joe. What a fantastic achievement! I had no idea your project was so ambitious.'

'I'm happy with the result too. But you know there's an army behind it.'

'No, just one police detective, everyone says so.'

'Susie, things are happening fast. We need to fill each other in. I met Losana at the market today and ended up buying a lot of nice ingredients, which I need to cook while they're fresh. Can you come here for dinner tonight or lunch tomorrow? I bought a lovely walu fish—too big for my oven, so it'll have to be a fish curry.'

'Surely you don't have time?'

'It'll be late, I guess what happens at our last campaign at the yacht club isn't predictable. But we've got to eat—and talk.'

'Well, I think Sunday lunch would suit me better, whatever happens later today. I'm not leaving the station until I see Tevita off the premises.'

'Great, I'll get the curry done tonight, and it can do some self-improvement until Sunday midday.'

'Sure, I'll come to the yacht club if I can this evening.'

'*Moce mada*, Singh!' Already, he felt more positive.

***

Back at the office, Keli, Lili and Izzy still focused on their computer screens.

'Anything yet?' Horseman asked.

'Nothing you could call a clue, but we're getting to know the work of the Australian High Commissioner rather well,' Keli Taleca said laconically.

The others chuckled. 'Quite eye-opening,' Izzy said.

'Great, we do need our eyes open!' Horseman replied. 'What about you, Apo? Any luck with Orlov's alibi?'

'Sir, I've spoken to six guests at the party Orlov went to last Saturday night. I've no doubt the party happened, and he was there. Is six enough to cross him out as a suspect?'

'*Io*, I'll join you and you can tell me more about it. Guys, have you had lunch yet?'

The team shook their heads.

'It's lunchtime, then. Go outside, have a walk, a decent meal, come back in one hour, refreshed for the hard work of Saturday night at the yacht club. I won't keep Apo long.'

'It's weird, sir. The USP teachers on Dr Orlov's list all sound so wary when I introduce myself. I mean, they're so highly educated, I can't understand why they're scared to speak with a police officer. I thought they would know better.' Kau's perturbed eyes fixed on Horseman.

'Professors are no different from street sweepers, Apo. If a cop approaches them, they immediately think of all the things they've done wrong and wonder which one this cop knows about.'

Kau smiled. 'Really? There's another thing, sir. The professors are all men, who say the party was for colleagues. The students are all girls, and they say the teachers invited them to get to know them better. Something funny going on, sir?'

'Not funny, depressing, Apo. A small minority of university teachers are dishonourable—sleazebags, in fact. They seduce girl students with flattery and promises of special help in their studies. Sometimes this might be coaching, but usually just giving them extra marks they earn by sleeping with their teachers. I discovered this practice twenty years ago when I was a student myself. I hated it then and hate it now. Sometimes teachers employ girl students as maids, like Dr Orlov does, and give them the maid's room that comes with their campus quarters. The girls are in and out of their teacher's home, and no one thinks anything of it.'

'That's totally wrong, sir!'

'I agree, but not a crime. These shameful predators know what they're doing. You'll find the foolish girls are all eighteen and willing participants in an arrangement that brings them material benefits. It doesn't surprise me to find Dr Orlov is one of them. Still, if you believe the other guests, we must cross him off the list.'

'*Io*, sir. I understand now why they all sounded a bit afraid.'

'One by one, we cross them off, and that's progress. We're down to the High Commission staff now, aren't we? One of Ms Armstrong's colleagues must have killed her.'

'Are you sure, sir?'

'*Io*, there's no one else. Off you go to lunch now.'

'What about you, sir?'

'I'm meeting one of our diplomatic suspects for lunch—Lt Connolly. I just hope she'll be more open outside the High-Com. I'd like you to phone some of the guests at the Bastille Day Ball, especially Ms Armstrong's friends who kept an eye out for her there. They're likely to have noticed Lt Connolly. Get approximate times from anyone who saw her if you can. By the way, has DS Taleca released you for the game at three?'

'Not sure. Can you have a word with him, sir?'

'*Io*, you'll be back in time for the assault on the Saturday regulars at the yacht club. The boys will be proud that you're there. I'll have to leave at half-time. Is Tanielo going?'

'Sergeant Jayaraman's loaded him with lab tests. But he can go when he finishes them.'

'Great—the Shiners will play better with both of you cheering them on.'

<h1 style="text-align:center">54</h1>

Lt Connolly got out of a taxi at the Suva Bowling Club and gazed around her. She wore a longish, full skirt and a sleeveless cotton top in an Asian fabric. Horseman thought *batik* was the name he'd heard. The opposite of her white navy uniform. When she saw him approach, she smiled with relief.

'Hi, Pat. Have you been to the Bowling Club before?'

'No, what a fantastic spot, right on the water!'

'Yes, the facilities are basic,' he said, waving at the concrete slab with a bar at one end, the rest open-sided under a corrugated iron roof. 'The food's basic too, but the setting's unbeatable. It's a local secret I like to introduce to chosen expats.'

'I'm glad I passed the test! Thanks.'

White-clad players sat on benches alongside the greens, keenly appraising the play and waiting for their turn. 'I'm told bowls is a game of strategy and tactics,' he said. 'I might try it when I get older.'

'My grandparents are still keen players. They're in their eighties and are fiercely competitive about the game.'

They sat at one of the chunky wooden tables. Horseman handed Lt Connolly a menu. 'They feature Chinese dishes and the usual snacks. What do you feel like?'

'Ooh, let's see. Fish with ginger, please. Steamed rice. What about you, Inspector?'

'Please call me Joe. I'm rather peckish, actually. I'll go for a hamburger. They do them Aussie-style here, with beetroot.'

'Oh, I'm homesick for a proper hamburger! I'll change my mind and join you.'

'Will you join me in a Fiji Bitter, too?'

'Sure, if they have glasses.'

Horseman went to the counter to order, marvelling at how the naval attaché's personality changed with her clothes; from starched and buttoned to relaxed and flowing. But she knew they were both still on the job. How should he broach the murder? Maybe he should give her the chance to bring it up. Which she did as soon as the waiter brought their beers.

'Any progress on Helen's case?'

'Yes, new information is progress, even though we're not at the end yet.'

She cocked one eyebrow. 'I heard there's been an arrest.'

'Oh, who said that?'

'We have our sources at the High-Com,' she smiled.

'We've detained someone who's helping us, yes. But he's not Helen's murderer. Pat, how did Helen and Hugh Forester get along? They come across as rather different personalities.'

'They are, or were. But they seemed to work together without problems. And a Head of Mission and First Secretary do need to work closely together. Hugh's efficient, intelligent, personable—what else can I say?' She laughed.

Their hamburgers arrived, and they ate in silence for a few minutes. Horseman sensed she was about to tell him something.

'What else could you say? Maybe ambitious?' he prompted.

'You're right, Hugh's ambitious, very much so. That's no problem in the diplomatic service, but people must wait their turn, or at least seem to do so.'

'Too keen, is he?'

The naval attaché smiled, arching her neck back, catching the cool air off the sea. 'What a lovely spot this is. So unusual to have a dry neck in Suva without air-conditioning. Um, I won't beat about the bush, Joe. I've decided to tell you something that I probably should have already. It may have no relevance, but I've observed enough of your investigation now to accept what you say, that only you can be the judge of relevance.'

'Tell me, Pat. Take your time. I'll shut up and eat my hamburger.' He puzzled over why she was flattering him.

Lt Connolly drank more of her Fiji Bitter, dabbed at her mouth with her paper serviette. 'Those of us who live on campus at the

High Commission need to guard our privacy. It's hard to observe one's neighbours, which is inevitable, and keep that knowledge from affecting our working relationships as colleagues in a hierarchy. Helen was more aware of this than anyone and avoided personal relationships with staff outside work. She was always friendly, but never a friend. She had an outgoing personality and easily made friends outside our walls, even outside diplomatic circles.'

Including some unworthy of her, Horseman reflected, thinking of Dr Orlov.

'I was a slight exception, probably because I'm a woman, and I'm seconded from the navy for only two years. She took trouble to show me the ways of Foreign Affairs, and we got on easily. And of course, we had sailing in common. Anyway, it's hard for me to come to the point, but I will.'

Horseman spread his hands. 'Take your time, it's always helpful to understand the context.'

'Hugh's wife, Justine, and two children seemed to be a lovely family. Their kids were the only ones on campus, but their lives were full of school and sport, and they looked happy. At social occasions, Justine was a bit shy and reserved, but pleasant. When Justine and the kids went to Australia in the school holidays, their immediate neighbour told me how nice and quiet it was. Not because of the noisy kids, but because Hugh and Justine had regular blazing rows, real shouting matches that the weatherboard houses did nothing to muffle.

'I once ran into Justine in the supermarket. Her face had bruises badly covered with makeup. She told me she'd tripped on the uneven pavement and fallen flat on her face. Possible, of course, the downtown footpaths are dire. I agonised, but decided to tell Helen in the end. Helen thanked me, saying she was aware of the Foresters' domestic conflict. She didn't say anything more to me, but a while later I saw Hugh leaving her office looking upset, no, angry. Four months ago, Justine and the children went to Canberra on another holiday and haven't returned. Hugh's always blandly polite when people ask him how they are or when they're coming back to Fiji. Of course, his family is none of our business.'

Lt Connolly ran a hand through her hair, glinting red-gold as it caught the sun.

'On Friday afternoon, the day before she was killed, I went to Helen's office to check on where and when to meet for the FAWG meeting at the university on Saturday morning. The door was slightly ajar. I was about to knock when I heard Hugh's raised voice. "You're happy to ruin my career just for that?" He sounded more incredulous than angry. I should have left, but I confess I chose to eavesdrop.'

Horseman nodded. 'Please go on, Pat.'

'Helen replied, her voice also a bit loud, but calm and firm. "You have the right to know, Hugh, that I can't recommend you as a suitable candidate for ambassador." Hugh's reply was icily sarcastic. "So, you've never known ambassadors who were alcoholics, incompetents, philanderers or worse? Who could imagine being without sin was an essential requirement for the job?" He may have had a point, from the stories one hears. There was another exchange, but I couldn't hear what either of them said, so I scuttled around the corner and back to my office. When I saw Helen on Saturday, she didn't mention Hugh, and I could hardly ask.'

'Thanks for your frankness, Pat. The source of that information won't need to be made public, but I'll need to make a note of our conversation for the case files.'

'My conscience is clear now. Thanks for introducing me to the Suva Bowling Club.'

They stood up and strolled to the road, where Horseman hailed a taxi for Lt Connolly. At last, someone at the High-Com had a motive. Hardly credible, though, was it? The second-in-command killing the chief because she wouldn't give him a job reference? No, there had to be something more, or someone else.

<h1 style="text-align:center">55</h1>

From around four o'clock, the first regular Saturday nighters trickled through the doors of the Royal Suva Yacht Club. Most were solitary men in shorts who, after ten minutes on the verandah watching the late races and boats being hauled to and from the water, drifted to the long bar and ordered their first beers.

After a morning at the station, fruitlessly sifting through the High Commissioner's files, the young DCs were happy enough to be back at the club for what Horseman called their last-ditch assault. They whooped with excitement when Horseman confirmed the winch handle Tevita had found belonged to the *Joshua Slocum*. They'd outright cheered when Apo got back from Dudley High School at four o'clock, incoherent with joy. Before the match, Horseman had urged the Shiners to play their best for Tevita. Inspired, the Shiners won the match against Dudley High, who ranked second in the Juniors competition. Now, he tried to gee up the young DCs.

'Detectives, all three of you are familiar now with the club members who spend all their leisure time there; those for whom it's home. Greet them and be friendly, because they may point out your actual targets tonight, or even introduce you. Because this afternoon, there'll be many members you haven't met, members who only visit the club on Saturdays. Security guard Ilai tells me these members roll up from four onwards and many stay until eleven o'clock, when the club closes.'

'A lot will be staggering out drunk,' Izzy said with a laugh.

'If they're drunk, don't let them drive, put them in a taxi,' Horseman replied. 'Remember, many haven't been to the club since the High Commissioner was killed last Saturday evening, although they'll all know about the murder by now. You may already have spoken to some of them on your cold calls. Tonight's our best hope of triggering their memories. Tick their names off the list, chat a bit, loosen them up, ask everyone the same questions, and sit down with them to look through your photo lineup folders. We won't be repeating this operation. Today is our last and best chance to find someone who saw the killer.'

'*Io*, sir!' they chorused.

'Any questions, any doubts whatsoever, immediately call DS Taleca, who'll be here at the club throughout the evening. I've got to leave right now, but I'll be back.' Taleca, Lili, Apo and Izzy formed a circle, bowed their heads and prayed for God's help, just like rugby players did before their games, from the Shiners to the national team in the World Cup. Horseman turned back when he noticed, a little late, but he joined in the *Amen*. They would all need both luck and help from the Almighty.

***

He badly wanted to read Helen's handwritten notes discovered in her office. They should have arrived at the station by now. And when he walked through the station door, a keen constable waved him over and handed him a sealed package from the SOCO lab.

After scanning each ordinary school exercise book, he understood that Helen's unofficial notes were categorised: the first book she'd used for notes on staff at the High-Com, the second for notes on Fijian institutions and individuals, and the third for observations about other diplomatic missions and personnel. His pulse quickened. Man, this was a gold mine he couldn't wait to plunder. He could be a character in a John le Carre espionage novel, entrusted with deadly secrets by his brave agent in the field, secrets that could save the free world.

Abruptly, he pulled himself back from the brink of fantasy. Whatever the High Commissioner had been doing, she had already died. He was a simple police detective tasked with finding her killer. He knew each notebook had potential, but the most relevant was likely to be the notes on High-Com staff. The book covered the last few years, but not the entire period of Helen's tenure as head of mission. Leafing through, he saw Helen commonly used initials or abbreviations to identify individuals. With so many Australian staff serving short terms, he couldn't easily distinguish who was currently at the High-Com and who had moved on.

Still, Helen's frankness piqued his interest and made him smile.

'does he think the next step up from Third Secretary is World Dictator?'

'industrious and intelligent—needs support in social settings to help her gain confidence'

'a born diplomat, but must pull his finger out and learn to write concise reports. I don't have time to read his meaningless waffling.'

'entitled Pacific princess can't accept a hierarchy unless she's near the top'

Horseman knew he wasn't here for his pleasure or to satisfy his curiosity by prying into Helen's private notes. He searched the book to pick out the staff they'd interviewed. One near the beginning must be about Losana: LOS—clever, discreet and the most organised on staff: promote to Office Manager asap.

Even so, it was harder than he'd hoped. He needed to give it his undivided attention at home to uncover any insights that threw new light on the case.

He put the books back in the evidence bag and slotted it into his satchel. He'd head home and concentrate on the notebooks. But first, he'd let the team know his whereabouts. He went to the radio desk and called DS Taleca.

'Keli, how's it going? I'm about to leave the station. Do you need any help at the club? Over.'

'No, boss. Our numbers are about right to handle the patrons here. No one can escape. But I was about to call you. First, the casual security guard from last Saturday night is here again. Over.'

'At last! What's the story?'

'It was his first shift at the club, so he doesn't know people here. He hasn't got his own mobile and relies on his cousin to pass on messages. Oh, and I believe his story he was sick through the week, as he's still got a nasty cough.'

'Can you talk to him yourself, Kelepi? Show him the photo line-up?'

'Will do. And something more—young Lili's just got a positive on the photo lineup!'

'*Oi lei*! Who?'

'Vuki Maya, the driver. A club member noticed the Mercedes first, the diplomatic number plates second, and the man getting out of the driver's seat third. Over.'

After asking about the times and confirming Maya's address, Horseman radioed, 'Well done, everyone. I'm on my way to talk to the driver. By the way, I forgot to tell you all to take the day off tomorrow. See you on Monday. Out.'

56

Horseman turned left off Prince's Road towards Suva's water reservoir, then up a winding track leading to a sizeable settlement of incomers to the capital who'd looked for work and mostly found it. Over the last few decades, it had become a well-organised community where inhabitants could lease suburban-sized plots and build their own homes. He soon found Vuki Maya's neat house, abutting the street so that he could devote maximum space to the lush food gardens behind and to the side. He got out of the car and called out to two boys working in the side garden.

'*Bula*, boys, I'm Inspector Horseman, Fiji Police. I've come to meet Mr Vuki Maya. Am I in the right place?'

'*Io, ovisa*!' the boys yelled, with broad grins. 'Come in! We'll tell our father,' the elder said, handing his garden fork to his brother and wiping his hands on his shorts before running off.

In less than a minute, the driver appeared around the side of the house, his brows lifted in surprise. He held out his hand to Horseman, and they shook.

'What's happened, Inspector? I heard one of your hostel boys was arrested for the murder of Ms Armstrong.'

'True, true, Mr Maya, but he didn't kill her. He did find the murder weapon, though.'

'Oh, that's a good start, isn't it?'

'Indeed. But we want to bring the investigation to a good end, and quickly. It's been a week now since Ms Armstrong died a violent death. I haven't had the chance to talk to you at length. Can I speak to you now in your home? If that's not convenient, I can drive you to the police station and we can talk there. And drive you back home, of course.'

The driver shifted from one bare foot to the other, weighing up his options. 'Sir, my home isn't ready for visitors, and the women are cooking. But there are some chairs out the back if that's suitable ...'

'Perfect, Mr Maya.' The driver led him to the rear of the house, where a lean-to porch offered a roof and timber framework enclosed by mosquito netting. One edge of the netting lifted like a tent flap. Inside were a couple of chairs, several stools and a small table. This would be where the men would gather to gossip over a *yaqona* after a day's work.

'*Vinaka*, Mr Maya, what a nice retreat you've made.'

'*Vinaka*, please call me Vuki.'

Horseman nodded and smiled. 'I don't want to take up too much time, but I want to ask some questions about last Saturday. Where did you drive Ms Armstrong last Saturday, Vuki?'

'Nowhere, sir. I polished the car to take her to the FAWG meeting, but she wanted to drive herself with Lt Connolly. I expected to drive her to the Bastille Day Ball, but after she got back from FAWG, she told me she'd be going early to have cocktails with friends first. She asked me to drive Lt Connolly, Mr Forester and Mr Friend to the Grand Pacific in the evening, whatever time they wanted. After that, she said I could sign off for the rest of the weekend. She was always considerate like that.' He pulled out a ragged handkerchief and wiped his face.

'Apologies, sir. My gardening hanky,' he said with an embarrassed half-smile.

'No apology, please. Your garden is flourishing. You must be self-sufficient.'

'Most of the time we are, and often have extra to give away.' They both gazed at the productive beds of root crops, greens, corn, tomatoes and more.

'But you didn't sign off, did you, Vuki? You drove an official car to the yacht club on Saturday evening. A witness saw you standing beside the car.'

'What? How?'

'Vuki, you seem like an honest family man. But I'm afraid you're not. You lied to us about going aboard the *Joshua*. My officers are talking to everyone who was at the yacht club last Saturday and showing them photos, including yours. One person picked you out, remembered you hovering around a nice Mercedes with diplomatic plates, strolling back and forth, getting in, sitting in the driver's seat, then getting out again. He watched you for a while because he thought your behaviour was suspicious. Please tell me what you were doing there.'

The driver's mouth hung open for a long moment. Then he pulled himself together and answered. 'I was worried about Ms Armstrong. That story about cocktails with friends—I was suspicious. I heard she was meeting her ex-husband on the yacht, and I wanted to make sure she was safe.'

After all Helen's efforts to keep her private life private, her driver had heard that. But then, Horseman knew the speed and power of rumour in Fiji could never be exaggerated.

'What did you see while you were watching?'

'The usual comings and goings until I saw Mr Scala leaving in a hurry about six-fifteen, carrying a holdall. He hurried through the car park and hailed a taxi. So I thought Ms Armstrong would be safe, with him gone. Maybe she had gone to drinks with friends after all. So I returned to the High Commission and drove Mr Forester and the others to the Grand Pacific, where I left them at half-past seven. After that, I came back and I did sign off, sir.'

'I'm surprised Mr Scala didn't recognise the Mercedes.'

The driver shrugged. 'It was twilight. He was looking for a cab, not a Mercedes.'

'Vuki, you've been wrong in keeping this from the police, but the best thing you can do now is come with me to Suva Central station and make a full statement. I'll give you a cab voucher to get you home.'

'Could I do that tomorrow?'

'No, now is best. Then it will be over.'

The driver nodded, accepting the inevitable. During the first part of the trip, negotiating the winding gravel track back to the water reservoir, Horseman pondered Vuki Maya's behaviour in silence. In these breathtakingly beautiful islands, was there a single soul who would admit to a mistake, regret their action, and make amends by telling the whole truth? Without the police prising the truth from them with irrefutable physical evidence?

When he rejoined Prince's Road, even though he was probably wasting his breath, Horseman made a final appeal to the driver's conscience. 'Vuki, please try to remember the events of last Saturday carefully, both your own actions, and what you observed, conversations you heard. The best way to help your kind employer, Ms Armstrong, is to tell me everything. You know, it's a wonderful blessing to clear your conscience.'

Vuki Maya looked at him and nodded, but said nothing.

***

After Maya had left the station, Horseman still felt uneasy, suspecting the driver knew more than he was saying, just as DS Taleca had. It was good to have Scala's alibi confirmed again, but that wasn't necessary, and he'd hoped for more. He checked his phone and discovered a missed call from DS Taleca.

'What have you got, Keli?'

'Something unexpected from the guard, boss. He picked out Mr Forester from the photos.'

'*Oi lei*! Really?'

'Around eight o'clock. He says a European man, dressed in a formal black suit, asked him to open the gate for him, said he was meeting friends for drinks on their cruiser before going to a grand ball. The guard shouldn't have let him in, but he's new, and the gentleman was European, all dressed up and so friendly, the guard thought all was well. He doesn't remember Forester coming out, but he said he got called away from the gate several times. What do you think?'

'I'm gobsmacked, Keli. Forester? The driver just said he dropped him at the Grand Pacific around half-past seven. Can you take a statement from the guard at the yacht club? I could bring him into the station, but then he'd lose pay. And we mightn't find him again if we let him go after his shift.'

'Will do. I've even got the right forms, boss.'

'*Vinaka vakalevu*, Keli. Incredible as it seems, this could be a breakthrough. And there could be more before the night's over!'

SUNDAY 22nd July

57

Singh didn't know what to expect. Over the years, she'd shared many restaurant meals and takeaways with Horseman, but he'd never cooked for her before, least of all Sunday lunch. She didn't want to read more into the occasion than there was, so she agonised a bit over what she could contribute. In the end, she bought a six-pack of his favourite Fiji Bitter and some chocolate brownies from the Republic of Cappuccino.

When she arrived, Horseman was juggling various pots and pans. He opened the door with a tense smile, then dashed back to the stove, dismissing her offer to help with a wave of his free hand. But before long, he placed the centrepiece fish curry on the table, along with rice, chutneys, papadums, and vegetable dishes, raw and cooked. He stood back and surveyed the table with an endearing pride before pulling out a chair for her. She uncapped two of the beers she'd brought and put them on the table before she sat.

For a while, they devoted their attention to the food. And it was scrumptious. Obviously not an elaborate Indian-style curry banquet, but the simplified, casual Fijian adaptation, which she rather preferred. She supposed she shouldn't be surprised; Horseman had told her his mother, Sala, refused to let her only son become the spoiled, useless pet of his three older sisters and taught him the same domestic skills her daughters had learned. Expected him to use them, too.

'Joe, this is all so wonderful! The fish curry—mouth-watering.'

'*Vinaka vakalevu*! But I must tell the whole truth—Mum made the chutneys.'

They drank their beer and helped themselves to more of the food, which they ate rather more slowly but with just as much enjoyment.

'Talking of the whole truth, what did you get out of Vuki Maya last night?' Singh asked.

'You heard?'

'I'm a detective! Actually, I rang Keli Taleca and he spilled the beans.'

'I shared Keli's belief that Vuki was withholding something. The man claims he was worried about Helen. He knew Scala was in town and suspected Helen was on the *Joshua* with him. So he parked at the club and kept an eye out. He saw Scala leave alone around quarter-past six. That fits with Scala's statement.'

'And Forester?'

'After I sent Vuki Maya back home, Keli told me another club member identified Maya, and the casual security guard picked out Forester. The guard spoke to him and allowed him into the marina around eight o'clock. Forester told the guard he was going to drinks with friends on a cruiser. Keli took statements from both witnesses. I'm still getting my head around the idea that Forester might have killed Helen. What do you think? I mean, I accept it's possible. But I'm inclined to wait until tomorrow, take him by surprise at work.'

'I'm surprised too. I'm sceptical of the coincidence that Forester was on another boat, though. Aren't you?'

'At first I was. But there have to be quite a few boats among the diplomatic corps—they're young to middle-aged expatriates, afflu- ent, connected. I ended up thinking it wasn't unlikely at all. What is more suspicious is that Maya dropped Forester at the hotel at half-past seven, and he turns up at the yacht club at eight o'clock. And why hadn't Helen already left for the ball by eight?'

'Maybe she was waiting for Forester.' Singh asked.

'Why? They could talk at the ball if either of them wanted to.'

Singh frowned. 'Did he call her?'

'The last call received on her mobile was from Scala, on Saturday morning. Oh, by the way, Ash said they found no mobile phones at all in Helen's apartment or office.'

Horseman pushed his chair out and gathered up the bowls and plates and took them to the kitchen, a couple of steps away.

'I suppose she didn't like using them.' Singh sounded doubtful. 'Here, let me help.' She put the remaining bits and pieces from the table onto the empty rice bowl and handed them through to Horseman.

'*Vinaka*, but not today, Susie. I've got a surprise.'

Singh subsided back into her chair. What was coming? She went out to his balcony, transfixed by the view, even under the leaden grey sky. Far superior to hers on the first floor.

'Okay, dessert is served,' he called, sounding excited. When she got back to the table, he whisked a cover from a glass bowl. 'My attempt at *gulab jamun* custard, but with pineapple instead of *gulab jamun*.'

Singh leaned in and inhaled a delicate spicy aroma. 'Yummy, nut-meg?'

'Fresh from the market yesterday and grated by me. Not to mention the vanilla bean I simmered the milk in. There, no more bragging. It's the eating that counts.' He spooned the smooth concoction into two small bowls, setting one in front of her with a flourish.

The cold creaminess was truly superb. Even her tradition-bound mother would approve, for she herself sometimes substituted diced fruit for the fiddly fried dumplings when she was short of time. Her mother would draw the line at using vanilla instead of rosewater, but Singh thought the substitution was inspired. She lifted her chin, closed her eyes and savoured the perfection.

'Are you all right, Singh?' His voice was laced with anxiety.

She opened her eyes, embarrassed. 'Yes, of course. Pure self-indulgence. You've surpassed yourself, Joe.'

'Help yourself to more, then,' he said, nudging the serving bowl towards her.

'*Vinaka*, but really, I couldn't. Indulging is one thing, overindulging is another. Hey, I forgot. I brought something too. If you're making coffee later, that might be the time.' She went to the kitchen where she'd left the white paper bag from the café. She cut the brownies into smaller pieces, found a plate and brought them to the table.

'Now's not the time, but when we've digested a bit, maybe ...'

'Why not now?' Horseman took one and bit into it, mocking her own closed-eye indulgence tactic. 'Republic of Cappuccino, are they? Brilliant! I'd better get the custard back in the fridge and make the coffee.'

They worked so naturally together as detectives, but Singh felt awkward skirting around him in the tiny kitchen as they cleared up. She knew he did, too. Brushing against each other, arms colliding, feet stepping on toes—what was happening here? When they touched, his solidity reassured her. She wanted to lean against him, head to toe. His body was true to his inner nature: good, reliable, honest. He was consistent from skin to heart, without deceit or surprise. She trusted him as she trusted no one else. This was what she wanted, wasn't it?

Horseman chuckled. 'We're literally treading on each other's toes. Susie. I'm ordering you to the sofa while I make our coffee.'

She laughed, transferred the brownies to the coffee table and went out on the balcony again. The clouds had lifted, and shifting sunbeams lit the sea here and there. She felt like the sea, touched by bursts of happiness that were fleeting, shifting.

He brought the coffee and sat in the single armchair. He poured the coffee into small cups. 'The beans are from the Arabica.'

'I expected nothing less from you, Joe.' They didn't speak while they sipped the rich, strong brew.

'Another cup?' he asked.

'Yes, please.' She stretched her arms above her head and yawned. 'Sorry, Joe. That was the best lunch I've ever had. If you ever got sick of the Force, you'd make a sensational chef.'

Horseman laughed out loud. '*Oi lei*! I couldn't stand it. But there is something I want to tell you, Susie. I've promised not to tell anyone, but it affects you, and I know you can keep a secret.'

If only you knew how well, she thought. 'I'm all ears. What is it?'

'The Rugby Union Board has offered me a job. A wonderful job—national coach. The Board understands I can only seriously consider it after we find Helen's murderer, of course. It's fallen into my lap, Singh. I haven't considered leaving the police, certainly not spoken to anyone about it. I realise now I've never thought about a career. One day follows another. I just keep doing this job, which satisfies me, in spite of a hundred disadvantages. Now it's time to change my attitude and think about what I really want.'

Singh took his words in like a punch to the gut. She couldn't breathe or think. She sipped her coffee while she recovered.

Horseman stared at her. 'I know, that's how I felt. But now I've adjusted to the idea. And I need to tell you, because if I did decide to take the job, there'd be a DI vacancy in Suva. I know you're doing big things in Labasa, but I sense Suva suits you better. Have I got that wrong, too?'

'No, you're right. If there was a chance of a transfer to Suva, I'd jump at it. But Joe, my preference can't be a deciding factor for you. I couldn't forgive myself if it were. You must decide what's best for you. If that suits me too, then that's a lucky coincidence.'

She realised the implication of what she'd just said. 'But Joe, please, I take that back. I would never want to see you leave the police. CID is a much better place with you there. In fact, I can't wait for you to be promoted so your influence can spread wider! When that happens, I could still transfer to Suva. If we're thinking about careers, that pathway would be my dream for both our careers.'

His brows knitted in puzzlement, or so it seemed to her. 'You really care about your police career, don't you?' he said. 'That drives the truth home to me, the truth that I never have cared, not really. I care about my cases, some much more than others, but not about my so-called police career.'

'Maybe you should pay attention to what you care about, Joe. That will help you decide what to do.'

He nodded a few times. '*Vinaka*, I will. Perhaps I've underestimated how fierce some people's dedication to their careers can be. If career ambition is the most important thing in your life, you might hate someone who deliberately blocks your career path. Maybe you could be driven to kill that person.'

Singh grinned. 'I hope you're not thinking of me!'

Horseman laughed. 'I'm keeping my eye on you! No, I just couldn't take Hugh Forester's only known motive too seriously—thought if he did kill Helen, there must be some other reason than her blocking his promotion to ambassador. Speaking as a dedicated careerist, what do you think?'

'That's more than enough motive, Joe. Especially for a spur-of-the-moment attack. Not for me, I hasten to add, but for someone with a temper and a few drinks on board, definitely plausible.'

'I'll challenge Forester tomorrow morning. Susie, I'm so grateful to you for getting Tevita out of that lockup. And just in time to watch the second half of the game, which the Shiners won against Dudley, by the way. He should never have been arrested, but it's ended well, thanks to you.'

'I enjoyed that small triumph, Joe. Ratini's claiming credit, but never mind that. I must go now and put my feet up. *Vinaka vakalevu.*'

'If you must. But please take some leftovers.' He got three take-away boxes from the fridge and put them in her hands, enfolding them. For a moment, she thought he would kiss her, hoping he would. But he smiled instead, then opened the door.

MONDAY 23rd July

58

Although Horseman had spent all Sunday evening analysing Helen's handwritten notes on her staff, he wasn't further ahead. There was nothing that he could connect to her death in any way at all. He realised also that the notes were self-censored, through the abbreviations, code and what was left unsaid. Clearly, the author had been aware the notes might be read, even though she kept them in a locked drawer of her desk in her own office.

But with a reported sighting of Forester at the yacht club on the evening of Helen's death, he had ample justification for turning up at the High-Com with a polite request for the Acting High Commissioner to explain himself. He'd get there early, before Forester was likely to have left for an off-campus meeting. Horseman had just put his coffee cup in the sink when his mobile rang. It was Ash Jayaraman.

'Thanks for sending the notebooks across, Ash.'

'No problem. I'm ringing to tell you my technician forgot to send the journal over, too. Do you still want it?'

'Journal—I didn't hear about that. Where's it from?'

'Hang on, let's double-check the label. Yes, from the bedroom of the residence. The bedside cabinet, bottom drawer, locked. As you know, I was searching the office building, but you were in the High Commissioner's flat, weren't you?'

'I was, but I'd returned to the office building before I got called away early, remember. Ilai from the yacht club rang to tell me Tevita got arrested after he found what you proved was the murder weapon. I wonder why Apo didn't tell me. Anyway, more potential evidence means all is not lost.'

'You thought all was lost? Not like you. How come?' Ash sounded concerned.

'No matter how much more we know about that Saturday, no matter how much circumstantial evidence we've found, we're still looking for a critical link to Helen's killer.'

'That's always how it goes, though, Joe. Isn't it? You'll get there.'

'I'm worried that I won't this time. That Helen's murder will just end up as a cold case.'

'Don't let fear paralyse you, though. Let that fear spur you on. I've got a bundle of stuff to send to Suva Central. I'll add the journal addressed to you and get it off right away.'

'*Vinaka*, Ash. Tempting as it is to read the journal first, I'm off to the High-Com now, to bail up Forester in his office before he's off to his first meeting of the day. I'll pick it up when I get back.'

***

A small evidence bag was waiting behind the station reception counter on his return. Horseman thanked the constable who handed it to him, and hurried up the stairs to the detectives' floor.

Superintendent Ratini's door flew open as Horseman passed. 'In here, Horseman!' Ratini barked.

Wondering how he'd offended his superior this time, Horseman turned back and joined Ratini in his office, trying to be pleasant.

'*Yadra*, sir, I'm pleased you're in. Is now a good time to bring you up to date on the case?'

'Of course it is! You've kept me waiting long enough. Your team are all here with nothing to do but catch up on paperwork! That's because their leader went missing in action!'

Horseman aimed for a reassuring cheeriness. 'Necessary work, sir. Our yacht club blitz over Friday and Saturday meant no documents were registered, no diary actions or notebook entries were completed, let alone transferred to the computer. The case file's behind, but no worries, we'll catch up by the end of today.'

Ratini rubbed his stubbly jowls, emitting an off-putting hawking sound. 'That's them, okay. What about you?'

'Sir, I've been to the High-Com, following a new lead we found during the weekend. The security guard we've been looking for turned up and reported speaking to Mr Forester at the yacht club last Saturday evening. He admitted Forester to the marina within the time period Helen was killed. I met Mr Forester this morning, smoking an e-cigarette while waiting for his official car, but he said he didn't have time to talk to me. I'll keep trying.'

'Hmm, be careful there.'

Horseman held up the evidence bag. '*Io*, sir. And I've just received from the SOCO lab what appears to be Ms Armstrong's private journal, discovered on Friday in a locked drawer in her High-Com flat. I'm going to read it now.'

'That's taken a while to get here, hasn't it?'

'Fewer SOCOs to examine it for fingerprints on the weekend, sir.'

'*Io*, let me know if anything useful's in the diary. We've got to wrap up this one. I've got the Deputy Commissioner breathing down my neck!'

***

Ash had correctly classified the book as a journal. It contained dated entries of varying length from the beginning of the year, with no titles and little underlining. Although Helen hadn't written in it daily, she'd done so often enough to give Horseman the impression she'd valued the book as a repository for her thoughts on issues both at work and beyond. But the feeling he was invading Helen's privacy even by handling her book troubled him, so he called Lili Waqa to photocopy the pages with entries—approximately sixty, but they were small.

He found a few coloured highlighters to follow Singh's effective habit of colour-coding. His prime focus was Forester, who would be yellow, but he reminded himself to keep an open mind. When Waqa returned with the copies and a mug of tea, he was ready to start close reading. After an hour, feeling wrung out, he summarised the text he'd highlighted.

Back in January, Helen noted staff complained about loud arguments coming from the Foresters' house. She told Forester this had to stop, particularly for the sake of his children. He'd agreed, claiming his wife's unhappiness in Fiji caused her outbursts. After more complaints in February, she called Forester in again and also went to see his wife, who had bruises on her arms. Justine denied her husband was responsible, but Helen doubted her. In March, Lt Connolly told Helen of Justine's black eye, and at the end of March, Justine and the children went to Canberra for the Easter school holidays and hadn't returned to Fiji.

Forester's annual performance review came up in April. Helen wrote of her distaste for getting involved in staff's personal lives, but reminded Forester about Foreign Affairs' preference for diplomats with stable domestic lives. A few weeks later, she herself heard Forester shouting in his house as she passed it on her way to visit the Second Secretary. She had no idea who he was shouting at.

Once or twice, Helen wrote of the drawbacks of the enclosed life at the Australian compound. She wished her High Commission was like the little Japanese embassy, with a couple of floors leased in a downtown office building, the ambassador's residence up in the hills, and staff housed in rented properties scattered throughout Suva.

In June, Helen was astounded to learn of rumours that Lt Connolly often visited Forester's house. None of her business, she concluded, but she wished staff would stop telling her such things. She wondered if the rumour was true. Her last entry was on Wednesday, 11th July.

Horseman was disappointed. While the journal confirmed much of what Lt Connolly had told him, it also made her own report less reliable. Could Forester and Pat have been having an affair? If Hugh had ended it, or if he'd not responded to her visits to his home, should her tip-offs about him be suspect because they were made by a scorned woman? Helen had clearly thought so.

If only Helen had written of her interview with Forester on Friday afternoon, the day before the ball, the day before her life ended.

59

Horseman knocked on Ratini's door, but the super was out, so he sent a text instead. 'Ms Armstrong's journal confirms Forester had a grievance with her. Evidence supports police questioning, but not arrest.'

After a word to DS Taleca, he shouldered his satchel and went for a walk along the seafront. Maybe the rising breeze would help his mind work better. Forester's tendency to shout in domestic arguments hardly pointed to him being a murderer. Assaulting his wife was another matter; a crime that Helen suspected but could not prove. Even so, she could recommend against his promotion for any reason she saw fit.

While Horseman thought this motive a weak one for murder, he remembered yesterday's talk with Singh. She was deadly serious about her career, in contrast to him, and she was convinced the motive was strong under the right circumstances.

If his career was Forester's all-consuming passion, it was entirely possible that in a rage, he could kill the person who calmly announced she was about to destroy it. But did he? At this point, it seemed unlikely they'd ever prove it. If Forester agreed to explain his presence at the yacht club's marina gate last Saturday evening, he could find support for any claim he made without too much trouble.

He'd reached the market without even noticing. Monday was a quiet day here, and the roti seller was grateful for his custom. He perched on the seawall to devour the comfort food. Not that he felt comforted today, but it filled a hole nicely.

He watched a game-fishing boat and a yacht heading across the bay from opposite directions towards the yacht club. He remembered Ilai telling him the *Joshua Slocum*'s neighbour, *Seeker*, was away on a diving charter. He'd keep on walking to the club and see if *Seeker* had returned.

Ilai was on duty at the marina gate and waved Horseman over. After an enthusiastic handshake, the guard asked, 'Did you get anything from Saturday night?'

'We did, Ilai. That campaign was productive. It hasn't delivered our killer quite yet, but we're closing in. We finally caught up with last Saturday night's guard, which was useful. I'm wondering whether any resident boats that've been away for the last week have returned to their berths yet.'

'*Io, io*, I can help there. *Seeker* docked yesterday, back from a week's charter. She's *Joshua Slocum*'s neighbour, so if you're going on board the *Joshua* again, you'll meet the owners anyway. The Andersons are polite people. They live on board when they're in Suva.'

'*Vinaka*, Ilai. I'd certainly like to talk to them.'

The *Seeker* was a seaworthy-looking yacht with two masts. Its deck was chock-a-block with scuba equipment, which two men were loading onto a trolley parked up against the stern.

Horseman introduced himself, reaching up to shake hands over the stern rail. 'I'm leading the investigation into the terrible murder of your neighbour, Ms Armstrong.' The welcoming faces transformed with strain and sorrow.

'I'm Chris Anderson, the skipper, and this is divemaster and deckhand Berenado Tukapi. My wife, Lina, is cleaning out below decks. It takes us a full day to restore order after a charter.'

The skipper peered from under his towelling hat, his eyes tearing. 'We didn't hear until we arrived back yesterday afternoon. Unbelievable! Helen—we've known her for years. A good sailor, friendly too. And to think she was lying in the cabin, already dead when we took off early Sunday morning!' He turned his head to gaze out to sea.

Berenado nodded and crossed himself. '*Isa*, poor dear, a lovely lady.'

'Did either of you see Ms Armstrong on Saturday evening?'

Both men nodded vigorously. Anderson said, 'Yeah, once or twice. All three of us were in and out all day loading stores for the charter. I saw Alex arrive around mid-morning, and we discussed *Joshua*'s engine problems for a bit. Helen got here later in the afternoon, don't know exactly when. Did you speak to her, Nado?'

'*Io*, passed the time of day. She was all dressed up, told me she had a diplomatic function to go to straight from the club. She was cheerful, looking forward to getting her boat in working order again. The diplomats were missing her sailing parties, she said.'

'I last saw her sometime after six when she was waving Alex off as he left. It was starting to get dark. He was in a hurry, but Helen and I chatted for a bit after he left. I told her about our dive charter to the Rainbow Reef off Taveuni and then on to Kadavu Island. Just pleasant conversation—she was always so interested.' Chris broke off, took off his hat and wiped his face with it. 'I never saw her again.'

'I don't know when Hugh came along, but I was loading the air tanks and buoyancy vests onto the deck when I saw him hopping on board. Strange, he was in a fancy suit,' Berenado added. 'I made a joke about it and he laughed and said he was going to a grand party the French embassy was holding for their national day.'

Horseman held his breath, frozen in suspense. The deckhand lifted his brows, expecting him to say something. 'Did you see Helen then, too?'

'Well, not exactly, but I heard her call out from down below. "Hugh, you'd better come down." I'm not sure of her exact words, but something like that.'

'Was she expecting him, do you think?'

Berenado considered this question. 'I didn't think one way or the other at the time, but now you ask, maybe she did sound a bit surprised.' He shrugged. 'But really, I don't know.'

'We were hungry by the time we finished loading and cleaned up, so all three of us went to the club café for burgers and chips. No beers, unfortunately, as we'd be diving the next day.' Chris said. 'We were quick. On our way back, we ran into Hugh leaving—he was passing our yacht. It was drizzling, and he had his umbrella up.'

'Did you speak?'

'Yes. Just pleasant goodbyes and good wishes. As you do, you know,' Chris replied.

'Oh, I remember now. I asked where Helen was, and Hugh said she'd gone ahead,' Nado added. 'I didn't think anything of it, as I saw all the cabin lights were out.'

'You don't think Hugh—do you?—no!' Chris Anderson was floored when he made the connection.

Horseman said, 'We're still investigating. But you've filled in a gap in our timeline of events that Saturday. I'm sorry to interrupt your work, but could you come to the station with me now? It's urgent. I must get your statements on the official record straight away, just as you've told me.'

The two men glanced at each other. 'Anything to help. If Joe Horseman says it's urgent, we'll step up. Give us a few minutes. Lina will come, too. Women notice more, don't they?'

60

As Horseman and the *Seeker* crew entered the station, Singh and DC Kau were hurrying down the stairs.

He briefly told them about the new evidence. He asked Singh to inform Ratini, then get Taleca and Waqa to help take statements from the Andersons and Tukapi. He would head straight for the High Commission with Apo Kau. 'Get us the best car in the pool for the rest of the day. If there aren't any, grab a cab.' Kau raced off.

'Singh, please stress to Taleca that these witnesses are VIPs and need to be treated as such.' She gave him a reassuring pat on his arm. 'Got it! Good luck!'

***

Horseman jumped in the car and Kau drove off. He called AFP Chief Inspector Bob Browning's mobile number, praying he wasn't in some top-security planning meeting. Browning answered.

'Bob, I need your help. Witnesses have just placed Forester arriving and leaving Helen's yacht alone during the critical period. They own the yacht berthed next door, they know Forester and spoke to him. They've been away on a week's diving charter and only learned of Helen's murder yesterday. It's enough to arrest Forester on suspicion and detain him for questioning. I'm on my way to the High Commission to do that now. Where do I stand?'

Browning swore profusely. 'Sorry, that wasn't directed at you, Joe, just the situation. I'd better tell Geoff Phillip. Speak asap.'

Each second dragged as Horseman waited and Kau navigated the heavy traffic as schools disgorged hordes of children onto the streets.

At last, as Kau turned onto Prince's Road, a hundred metres from the High-Com entrance, Horseman's mobile rang. An unknown number. He took the call and switched on the speaker.

'Geoffrey Phillip, Pacific Secretary, Foreign Affairs. We've met a few times, DI Horseman. Bob's briefed me. I'm afraid Forester isn't here. In under an hour, he's flying on the Fiji Airways flight to Sydney, then on to Canberra. He's probably checked in already.'

The news knocked the breath out of Horseman, along with the hope building in him since he met the Andersons.

Phillip continued. 'The High Commission will certainly not oppose your action should you decide to detain Hugh at the airport. However, it would help, in our opinion, if Bob and I were also present to counsel Hugh about his best interest.'

'And what would your counsel be, Mr Phillip?'

'Cooperation, Inspector. We have more to discuss. See you soon.'

Horseman drew in air and saw a chink of light. 'I think that's cause for cautious optimism, Apo.'

'*Io*, sir. Let's pray.'

'You pray and drive, I'll radio the airport police.'

Luckily, they were pointing in the right direction. The 'back road' to the airport was longer but quicker, and Horseman normally enjoyed leaving the suburbs behind in the climb up the backbone of the Suva peninsula, then through dense rain forest, descending to the bright patchwork of the fertile floodplains of the Rewa River. Today, he saw nothing. He remained in radio contact with the airport police and even with Ratini, who grudgingly approved Horseman's unilateral action.

What preyed on his mind most was his fear that Forester would escape questioning, escape arrest and escape conviction through the operation of diplomatic immunity, a concept Horseman had not previously had to deal with. He'd heard traffic police say that vehicles with diplomatic number plates parked wherever they pleased in the centre of town—at bus stops, across entranceways—knowing they couldn't be fined. He didn't even know if those tales were true.

Much more serious was the potential claim of diplomatic immunity by Forester. And more complicated. The Australians supported the Fiji Police investigation of Helen's murder, but they'd delayed every step, especially the police search of their sovereign bubble. Was all that reluctance due to Forester's manipulation? Maybe, but Horseman doubted it. The diplomats could not have foreseen one of their own as the prime murder suspect. When the news broke, how strong would be their urge to protect Forester? Once he was in Australia, where would the Fiji Police stand?

They crossed the Rewa Bridge to Nausori and the flat delta lands, which hosted Suva's airport. Only ten minutes away. Horseman radioed the airport police again.

'We tried to detain him at the gate, sir. But he showed us his diplomatic passport and said we could not stop him boarding the plane. He insisted and just barged through our staff. We didn't want to create a disturbance, sir.'

'What's happening now, officer?'

'Forester's on board, sir. Business class. We've ordered the captain to delay takeoff until you arrive, but he's not happy.'

'Don't give way on that. Mr Forester must not leave Fiji. It doesn't matter how upset the pilot is. Do not give way, officer.'

'Siren, sir?' Apo Kau asked.

'Absolutely!'

Siren blaring, they sped to the Airport Police office in under five minutes. A constable waited nearby, holding the gate to the runway open and waving the car through. The Fiji Airways Boeing was stationary and the front steps were still in place.

61

'Park in front of the nose, Apo.'

They got out. 'Got your handcuffs?' Horseman asked Kau, who pulled them from his pocket, grinning. 'Only if he resists,' he added.

Horseman and Kau held their ID badges out to the wide-eyed flight attendants at the top of the steps. A pilot stepped through the cockpit door.

'We're here to detain a passenger, Mr Hugh Forester, and escort him from the aircraft,' Horseman said.

'Go ahead, we need to take off,' the pilot said. 'Where's he sitting, Mara?'

'Seat 4A, sir. This way.'

Forester wore the same blue linen suit as in the morning. He glared at Horseman. 'You have no right to order me off the plane. I carry a diplomatic passport.'

'I understand that, Mr Forester. Your passport does not stop the Fiji Police detaining you for questioning. It's much better for you to come with us so the plane can take off.'

'I disagree. How is it better for me?'

'We can't question you on the plane, Mr Forester. Please think of the other passengers and your own privacy.'

Horseman straightened and spoke to Mara and the hovering pilot. 'Please announce that a police operation is in progress, which passengers are not permitted to photograph.' Mara's eyes widened and she retreated to the attendants' booth. The passengers in the surrounding business class seats craned their necks. One got up, pulling out his phone. Horseman told him to sit down before leaning over Forester again.

'If you don't comply with my request, I'll arrest you on suspicion of murder. Surely you don't want to leave the plane in handcuffs, sir?' Kau took the cuffs out of his pocket, letting them rest on his open hand.

Suddenly, Forester leapt to his feet, grabbed a briefcase from beside him and shoved it at Horseman, who passed it to an attendant standing behind. The diplomat stepped into the aisle, every muscle of his face contracted as he fought for control. He shook off Kau's restraining hand, scowled at the hovering pilot. Horseman told Kau to retrieve their prisoner's cabin luggage as he moved beside Forester and escorted him down the steps. At the bottom stood two hefty airport police officers, an anxious airline official and a short distance away, a white Mercedes with Vuki Maya at the wheel.

When the flight attendant handed Forester's cabin luggage to Kau at the top of the steps, Horseman had a sudden thought.

'Have you got any luggage in the hold?' he asked Forester.

Forester shook his head angrily. 'No.'

'Please check that with Fiji Airways, Constable. The plane can't take off until all Mr Forester's property is unloaded.'

The Mercedes' rear doors opened, and Geoffrey Phillip and Bob Browning got out. Straightening their jackets, they strolled across to the little group surrounding their First Secretary. Horseman met them halfway.

Phillip greeted Horseman with a grim smile. 'You succeeded, Inspector.'

Browning offered Horseman his hand. 'Nicely done, Joe.'

'You agreed we would attend Hugh's interrogation. Where can we do that?' asked Phillip.

'We could use a small room in the Airport Police office here. But I'd prefer to go to Suva Central Station. Are you Mr Forester's legal representative, Mr Phillip?'

'No, Bob and I would be additional, representing the interests of Mr Forester not only as an Australian citizen but also as a diplomat.'

Not to mention the interests of the Australian government, Horseman thought.

Browning handed his mobile to Horseman. 'Joe, I took the liberty of advising your Fiji Deputy Commissioner of your success in apprehending Forester. He'd like to speak to you.'

Horseman took a step or two towards the group of Fiji Police and listened to his senior officer. 'Joe, well done. How sure are you that Forester killed Ms Armstrong?'

'*Vinaka,* sir. Almost certain, say 95 per cent. I haven't put our fresh evidence to him yet. It's circumstantial, but compelling.'

'I trust your judgement, Joe. This one's complex, though—victim and accused from the same diplomatic mission, eh? Who would've thought it?'

Horseman made a noncommittal noise. The Deputy Commissioner continued. 'We don't want this spattered all over the media; neither us nor Australia. I've spoken with Bob and Geoff, and decided that it's best Mr Forester be confined to the Australian High Commission compound. You will have all reasonable access for questioning and searching. The Australian Department of Foreign Affairs will make sure Mr Forester does not leave the compound. Effective house arrest.'

There was no point bucking this; the arrangement was actually better than some alternatives Horseman had imagined.

'*Vinaka,* sir. I can live with that. What about his transport now?'

'You might not like this. Mr Forester will travel in the official Australian High Commission car with Bob and Geoff.'

Horseman inhaled. Suck it up. '*Io,* sir. We'll follow them, in case Forester leaps out the door, or something. Does Superintendent Ratini know this yet?'

'Not yet. Don't you worry about that, however. I'll inform him now. This is a most grave situation, Joe,' Tauvaga's voice quavered.

'*Oi lei*, I agree, sir. I believe Forester's getting desperate.'

The constable ran up but waited until Horseman ended the call. 'Sir, Mr Forester didn't check in any luggage.' Horseman thanked him before returning the phone to Browning.

***

When Apo Kau pulled into the High-Com car park, behind the official car, Horseman felt his muscles relax. His anxiety had wound him up tight.

He wasn't invited in. Affable Bob Browning explained Forester needed to calm himself, eat something and rest before being interviewed. Moreover, he himself, Geoffrey Phillip and a High-Com consular lawyer wanted to counsel Forester for this interview.

Browning locked eyes with Horseman. 'Believe me, Joe, Geoff and I will not advise Hugh to restrict himself to "no comment" answers. We will do our best to convince him to stick to the truth. We won't be writing a script for him, and we won't be coaching him. But in the end, we can't control him.'

'I understand, Bob. I hope Mr Phillip and the consular lawyer do too.'

They agreed to meet in the neutral space of a conference room in the High-Com office building at seven o'clock, when all staff would have left.

'That allows us to go to training, Apo. Even if we're a bit late. Tevita will get a kick out of that.'

Kau laughed. 'I can already hear him bragging to the other Shiners about being locked up.'

'*Io*, he'd do better keeping quiet about it.'

'Would you like to help interview Forester, Apo?' Horseman asked.

'*Io*, sir, that would be cool. But you'll want DI Singh, won't you?'

'I will. But if Forester can have a retinue of advisers, so can I, don't you think? Three on each side of the table is fair.'

'*Vinaka vakalevu*, sir. It would be an honour.'

'Nonsense, Apo. You're an able DC, soon to be a DS after the next sergeant's exams.' Kau's cheeks darkened in a blush. Horseman knew he would deeply disappoint Kau if he decided to quit the police. He knew that shouldn't be a factor in his decision, but loyalty could never be taken lightly.

62

All was jubilation at Albert Park when Horseman arrived, just a little late, with Singh and Apo Kau. Even those Shiners who regarded Tevita as a bit of a pain cheered him wholeheartedly. In a mood to celebrate, the boys couldn't summon up much fighting spirit, so this training session was more youthful fun than aggressive tactics. That didn't matter for once.

Horseman wanted to speak to Singh, but there was no chance. She'd only come to cheer on Tevita. He would've been discourteous to decline the boys' invitation to sit with them on the grass and share their dinner of boiled dalo and corned beef fritters. Dr Pillai had picked it up from the hostel, adding oranges from his own trees. The Shiners' laughter and exuberance, the way they bounced up again after terror and heartbreak knocked them down—well, they lifted Horseman's spirits.

The boys hung about the field before ambling off in twos and threes, most of them heading straight home to Junior Shiners House. Tonight, no Shiner would prowl the dangerous backstreets seeking a hidden corner to lay his head. Horseman was grateful. Grateful to so many people who'd helped, but most of all to Helen Armstrong, whose dead body still lay in the hospital's mortuary. Crusading police officers made him uneasy; he believed in blind justice. But pursuing Helen's killer was as close to a crusade as he'd ever been.

***

Forester was composed and curiously expressionless. His hair was damp, his short-sleeved white shirt well-ironed. Browning and

Phillip had also changed into casual clothes, but their faces wore marks of stress. Phillip introduced Janice Gisbourn, Forester's appointed legal advisor.

DC Kau switched on the digital recorder and made the preliminary announcement, each person present stating his or her name and title.

'Mr Forester, please tell us where you were at six o'clock on Saturday, July 14th?' Horseman asked.

'Oh, I can't be precise about the time, but I was probably getting ready for the Bastille Day ball at the Grand Pacific.' Forester's voice was relaxed, even.

'When did you leave the High Commission for the ball?'

'Oh, look, Inspector, you know very well I've already made an official statement accounting for my movements.'

Horseman smiled. 'Let's just go through that again, if you don't mind.'

'Surely the driver has confirmed that he drove Lt. Connolly, Mr Friend and me there shortly after seven o'clock?'

'Indeed, he has, Mr Forester. The problem is, witnesses on board the *Seeker*, berthed next to the *Joshua Slocum*, saw you arriving and departing from their neighbour that Saturday evening. One of them spoke to you as you arrived around eight o'clock. You told him about the ball when he asked about your formal dress. We know Ms Armstrong was on board because the witness clearly heard her call out to you from the cabin to come on board.'

Forester placed his clasped hands on the polished table in front of him.

'When the witnesses returned to their boat after eating at the yacht club, they passed you heading back towards the marina gate. You exchanged pleasantries: you wished them well for their week-long charter. Mrs Anderson is certain the time was 8:40. She looked at her watch because she was keen to get back to readying their yacht for departure the next morning.'

Forester leaned back in his chair, stony-faced.

'Mr Tukapi actually asked you where Ms Armstrong was, assuming you were going to the ball together. You told him she'd gone ahead. No one doubted this because the cabin lights were off. You had considerable presence of mind to switch the lights off, I must say. Or was it because the sight of her dead body horrified you?'

Forester said nothing.

His legal advisor spoke for the first time. 'Please leave us, Inspector Horseman, while I confer with my client.' Her voice was low and pleasant.

After ten minutes, Ms Gisbourn asked the officers to come back in. With a stiff smile, she said, 'I request we adjourn this interview until tomorrow morning, Detective Inspector Horseman. My client needs time to consider his response to your questions.'

Horseman's gaze shifted to Forester, who appeared relaxed, still leaning into the back of his chair. 'Mr Forester, I recommend you simply tell us the truth now. I promise you we'll look favourably on your full cooperation.'

Forester nodded politely. 'Good night, Inspector.'

'Nine o'clock tomorrow morning?' Ms Gisbourn asked.

TUESDAY 24th July

63

Horseman was already at his desk in the station before eight o'clock, preparing for whatever might happen during Forester's interview. He was well aware he was just killing time—he couldn't focus on anything for more than a few minutes. Surely, Forester had no choice but to confess, in the light of the *Seeker* crew's evidence.

Singh joined him half an hour later, looking fit for presentation to royalty in her blue tailored suit and cream blouse, with her lustrous hair tamed in a severe bun. Horseman grinned, 'Good morning, Singh. Don't look askance at my cargo pants, I'll change into my *sulu* and tie before we go to the High-Com.'

Apo Kau arrived just as Horseman's mobile rang. He switched to the speaker. 'Bob Browning here, Joe. Can you come right away? A maid found Hugh dead in his house.'

His hopes for the case vaporised in an instant. No justice for Helen now.

'Have you called a doctor?'

'No, you're our first call.'

'Good. I'll get Matt Young to come.'

Singh and Kau stared at him, mouths open, eyes wide.

'No need to change now,' Horseman said. He pressed his lips together.

Browning was waiting with the guard at the High Commission front gate and hopped in the back of the police sedan. 'We'll go straight to Hugh's house. Turn right instead of going to the car park.'

'Dr Young will only be a few minutes behind me.'

'Good, the guard will direct him.'

In front of the house, a hedge of brilliant-coloured crotons defied the horror within. Kau fished gloves and overshoes out of the kit bag. A uniformed maid sat at the verandah table, her head buried in her hands, her shoulders trembling. She looked up as the police climbed the steps.

'Kau, please calm her and ask her about what she did, what she saw, and what she noticed this morning. No need to hurry her. Have you got any water for her?'

'*Io*, sir.' He pulled a bottle from his bag.

Through the floor-to-ceiling louvres, the human form lying on the floor was visible under the softly whirring ceiling fan.

They filed through the door and into the living room in silence. A couple of Fijian carvings were on the floor, and papers were scattered around the dining table. Had there been a struggle? Despite the open louvres, the ceiling fan wafted a mild, sickly smell about. The memory of the noxious stench of Helen's decomposing body in the yacht whacked Horseman in the guts again, and his stomach lurched.

He swallowed and looked down at Hugh Forester, lying on one side, his hands curled to his chest, his legs apart as if in mid-stride. He was still in the white shirt he'd worn to their meeting the night before, and a pair of striped boxer shorts, stained around the crotch. His visible skin was pale, with a bluish tinge in his face, especially in his lips. Reddish drool and maybe vomit had dried on the large pandanus mat where he lay. The same reddish drool caked his mouth and spattered the white shirt.

They paced around carefully. 'There are envelopes on the table,' Browning said. 'One's addressed to you. Looks like suicide?'

Horseman nodded. 'I'll wait until Dr Young gets here before opening it.'

Singh disappeared into the kitchen at the back. 'Come here, Joe.'

Several vials like eye-drop bottles lay on the tidy sink. They seemed to be empty. 'What are they?'

'I'm not certain, but they could be refills of Vape fluid.'

'You mean e-cigarettes? I saw him smoking one outside the office building just yesterday. And last week, too. He said it was his secret vice.'

Singh nodded. They heard Dr Young speaking to Bob Browning, so they returned to the living room.

The pathologist was kneeling beside Forester, his bag open. 'Good morning, Joe, Susie. Terrible times! He's been dead for several hours. Symptoms of asphyxia, maybe caused by drug overdose.'

'You'll see bottles in the kitchen that look like Vape refills. Is that possible?' Singh asked.

'Yeah, if he took enough. Nicotine alone is unusual, maybe other toxins are involved, but the lab can tell us precisely.'

'What about the papers and ornaments on the floor?' Horseman asked.

'Seizures are common with this type of poisoning—it's not quick. He could have done it himself while fitting. Without the disturbed items, would you think suicide likely?'

'Looks that way to me. There are notes on the table,' Horseman replied.

More knocks on the door heralded Alisi, the photographer and Ash with Musudroka and three other SOCOs.

'We've got to stop meeting like this, sir,' Musudroka greeted Horseman with a grin. Singh shook her head, and Ash said, 'Not now, Tanielo,' firmly. Horseman was pleased Musudroka's new boss was still working on his former probationer's excessive joking.

After a brief examination, Ash allowed the detectives to take the letters, sealed in evidence bags.

Horseman and Singh joined Kau on the verandah, leaving the technicians to their work.

'Do we need to talk to our witness further, Apo?' Horseman asked.

'No, sir. Leti has been very clear.'

'*Vinaka*, Leti. You may go. I'm sure you could do with a cup of tea.'

'I'm happy to help, sir. God bless you.'

After Leti left them, the police team sat at the verandah table to open the unsealed envelopes. Horseman opened the one with his name on it, passing the other two to Singh and Kau.

To: Detective Inspector J. Horseman

I have chosen not to submit to further questioning, arrest or trial in relation to the death of Her Excellency Helen Armstrong It is better for my family, the Australian High Commission and my country that I end my life before any of those events happen. I went to the yacht that fateful Saturday night to persuade Helen not to block my application for an ambassador's post. I begged her, but she coldly told me she would not change her position. I lost my temper and in my frustration, lashed out with a tool close by.

I did not intend to kill Helen and deeply regret my impulsive action. When I realised she was dead, I panicked and tried to cover my tracks. The rest you have discovered.

Hugh Lawrence Forester

Singh wiped tears away. 'How is his wife going to bear this? I don't think I can read it out.' She passed the letter to Horseman.

My darling Justine,

I confess I betrayed you, our children, our families and our country when I accidentally killed Helen in a fit of temper. Out of cowardice and fear for you, I could not tell the truth afterwards. You and the children will create a new life and future without me. I am so sorry to have brought you shame, you who are such a private person. I encourage you to change the family name if you wish, to protect yourself, Naomi and Charles from public association with me.

I am sorry for all my shortcomings as a husband, but believe me, I love you three more than my life. Please, always tell Naomi and Charlie that I love them

Hugh

Kau passed his envelope to Horseman. 'His letter to Mr Geoffrey Phillip is similar to yours, sir. He also asks Mr Phillip to intercede with the Department of Foreign Affairs to provide his widow with financial benefits in line with his status as acting ambassador when he died in the line of duty. Isn't that odd?'

Horseman shrugged, read the letter and passed it to Singh. He sat still for a few moments.

'What now, sir?'

'We'd better call on Mr Phillip. To save time, I'll ask him to photocopy the letters to him and Mrs Forester. I'm certain he'll prefer to notify Forester's family, but I'd better offer. Then it's back to the station to report to Ratini and await Matt Young's verdict. Do our paperwork.'

'I feel a bit sorry for Mr Forester,' Kau said. 'I don't know, those letters ... Do you, sir?' Kau's round face and glasses made him look far too young to be a policeman.

'It's always sad to see a dead body, but no, I don't. What Forester says is plausible, but we only have the killer's version of events. I still don't know what happened on the yacht, why Forester went there. Was the winch handle really lying in the cabin? As the yacht hadn't sailed for months, surely it was more likely back in its pocket in the cockpit? In which case, Forester must have picked it up on his way in, or left the cabin to fetch it during his altercation with Helen. Either way, his assault, and there were two blows, remember, was a deliberate act. If he'd lashed out without thought, he'd have struck her with his fist, wouldn't he? We'll never know now.'

Forester had cheated him out of the truth.

<h1 style="text-align:center">64</h1>

Horseman felt he'd been washed out, put through the wringer and pegged up to dry when Matt Young rang to tell him Hugh Forester had died from a lethal dose of nicotine, self-administered. Ash confirmed the lab had identified Forester's fingerprints and no others on the Vape refill bottles, which contained a total of 80 millilitres of nicotine.

He sensed the others were relieved by Forester's suicide, particularly Ratini, who was fearful of the unknown of diplomatic entanglement. Horseman could understand that they just wanted the gruelling case wrapped up, but he hated Forester, not just for killing Helen, but also for denying him full knowledge about what had happened. He ordered everyone on the team to go home at five o'clock and not show their faces at the station until nine the next morning.

After they'd gone, he pottered around reorganising the case file and busying himself with tasks the detective constables should be doing the next day. But the time had come when he must tell someone his decision, make it real. And the only person who knew he had a decision to make was Singh. He shut the computer down, tidied his desk, went to the basement where he had a shower and put on his tailored *sulu* and long-sleeved shirt. A tie would be overdoing it, but he grabbed his navy jacket. The south-east breeze could be cool these July evenings.

The Holiday Inn waterfront terrace was quiet. He had no trouble getting an outer table. As he waited, he sipped his Fiji Bitter and tried to relax. She arrived on time, fresh and beautiful in a loose patterned skirt and black slinky top. She paused to have a word with the barman, then waved, her smile broadening as she joined him.

'Feeling any better now?' she asked.

The waiter served Singh's Fiji Bitter, pouring it expertly into a tall glass.

'Yes. I'm just realising Forester's suicide rattled me.'

'I know. I haven't worked on the High Commissioner's case much, but even so—'

'I feel he's cheated me of the truth. I've been thinking back to the beginning, when I didn't suspect him at all. From the start, he was delaying, which I just put down to diplomatic caution. More than delaying, the man lured me down blind alleys, cast suspicion on others, distracted me. None of it was obvious to me. What sort of detective am I? And when I was almost there, he blows the whistle on the case. I feel he's won.'

'I could talk for five minutes proving to you that's utter rubbish, but I don't want to argue. Let's talk about something else.'

'The menu?'

'Good topic. After Ratini ordered in pizzas for lunch—what a surprise by the way—I'd better have something more nutritious. Maybe a Caesar salad.'

'I'm sure he only did that—the pizzas—in an effort to please you, Susie.'

The waiter appeared and Singh gave her order.

'Fish and chips for me, please,' Horseman said.

'I can't help thinking it couldn't have worked out better for the High Commission,' Singh said.

'True. Forester's suicide is convenient for them.' His mind flipped to full alert, and he banged his beer bottle down. 'But that doesn't make them complicit. You're not suggesting that, are you?'

Singh stared at him. 'Relax, Joe. Sheer speculation. Both Matt and Ash pulled out all the stops to complete every possible analysis, and it all pointed to suicide.'

'I wouldn't put it past Phillip to have a cosy chat with Forester about his patriotic duty, though.'

'I hope you're joking!'

'We'll never know. That's what Forester's done by killing himself.'

The waiter brought their food and served it with aplomb, along with another beer for Horseman and a glass of Riesling for Singh.

They faced the sea, whipped into small waves as the evening breeze strengthened. They tucked in hungrily.

He couldn't bring himself to broach the topic of the future, but he had to. This might be his last chance before she had to return to Vanua Levu. How much did he want his vision at the High-Com to materialise? Maybe an inviolate dream was safer. But no, that was the way of delusion.

She shivered, pulled a pashmina from her bag and threw it around her shoulders. Was this woman always prepared for any eventuality? Now, man, do it now!

He put his jacket on. 'It's cool, isn't it? Do you want to go inside for dessert?'

'I'm easy. There's hardly anyone on the terrace, it might be crowded inside.'

But the waiter found them a table for two, hemmed in by potted palms, far enough from the cool jazz band not to have to shout at each other. How did the waiter sense Horseman had something of the utmost importance to say?

'Have you made your decision yet?' Singh asked. For a panicked split-second, Horseman forgot he'd told her about his offer from the Fiji Rugby Union.

He nodded. 'I have, and in the end it wasn't difficult, thanks to your advice. Susie, I'm taking the national coach job. That's where my heart's leading me. And whatever ability I may have, too. I've done the best I could as a detective, but I think as the years go by, the life is getting me down. And in this last case, I've got so sickened by all these people who've stalled us, each one out to save his own skin, who couldn't care that a wonderful woman was murdered and her killer might never be discovered.' He held Singh's gaze as the waiter served their coffee and petits fours.

Singh's eyes welled. Was she so disappointed in him? But he couldn't stop, had to share how he felt, and he could only do this with her.

'I hate the evil drug dealers taking over our islands, and that's eating me up from the inside out. I mean, Scala, what a despicable pirate! And he was a barrister? I can't spend my time with these excuses for human beings anymore. You're different, Singh, stronger.

The worse the criminals, the more energised you are to hunt them down. Maybe I used to be like that, but not now.'

'Joe, it's called burnout. You'll bounce back.'

'The only thing I want to bounce now is a ball. And work amongst inspiring young people who'll give their all to be better and better, then the best, even if it's only a game. Anyway, I've never understood why people say *only* a game. A game's a model of what's fair, skilled and law-abiding. More so than police work too often.'

'What are the terms like?'

He loved her for cutting to the chase. Loved her for everything. 'Generous, but my contract with the Rugby Union will only be for three years. I mightn't have a job after that. I doubt the police force would want me back. But you know—I had a kind of vision a few days ago.'

Singh frowned. Damn, he shouldn't have said that.

'Vision?' she asked.

'Yep. A flash through to the future. As certain as the sunrise tomorrow. I saw that it didn't matter whether I continued as a detective or took up the national coach offer.'

Singh kept on frowning. She already must think he'd lost his mind.

'It didn't, um, doesn't?' She sounded bewildered.

'No, because if you're beside me, it doesn't matter what job I do for a living—our living. And if you're not beside me, it matters even less.'

Her eyes welled again, a tremulous smile hovered around her lips.

'Am I making any sense?' he asked.

'I think so.'

'I fell in love with you on the boat to Paradise Island when you showed me your colour-coding system. And if not irretrievably then, certainly when you pushed up your sunglasses and I looked into your green eyes. I was just too stupid a nincompoop to know it.'

Singh's tears spilled over and rolled down her cheeks. She dabbed them with her starched cotton napkin.

'I feel the same, Joe. I realised when I walked into the station last Thursday, delivering Alex Scala to you.'

'What? Really?'

She nodded slowly, now grinning her wide grin. He couldn't believe it. Was this really happening? He reached across the table and took her hands in his.

'Susie, to be practical, after wasting years being blind, and as we're both just a tiny bit closer to forty than thirty, I can't see any reason to wait any longer—unless you want to, of course. Will you marry me as soon as we can arrange it?'

'Yes, Joe, I will. If you'd waited much longer, you might have forced me to suggest that myself. But I love that you spared me the humiliation.'

'What say we drink our coffee and go home, Singh?'

'Let's do that. Oh, I'll get the waiter to put our cakes in a box.'

Horseman laughed out loud, delirious with joy.

FRIDAY 27th July

65

Singh sat with the DCs in the Holy Trinity Anglican Cathedral, watching solemn guests arrive for the funeral of Her Excellency Helen Armstrong. Formally dressed foreigners, probably diplomats, filed between Fijian soldiers and sailors, resplendent in their dress uniforms. There were police officers, nurses and school students in uniform, too. The High Commissioner's judicious spread of Australian aid and her genuine personal interest had benefited all of them.

Perhaps the uniformed contingent who loved Helen most were the Junior Shiners, who filed past in their spotless but faded tan rugby jerseys with the black shoe motif and their new black socks. Sala Horseman sat with them up ahead of Singh.

She could only guess at how the High Commissioner had touched most people in the church, who were not in uniform. Fijians of all ages carried their Bibles and woven fans: the men dignified in *sulus*, jackets and ties; the women stately in long black dresses. Many Indians wore light suits or white saris.

Her mind strayed to whether to wear a traditional crimson sari for her own wedding. She couldn't ask anyone's advice yet—they were keeping their engagement secret until tomorrow. Anyway, maybe she should decide by herself.

Suddenly, everyone around her stood. She started out of her daydream and hastily followed. The organ and choir struck up a slow version of the national anthem. A soldier in scarlet tunic and white *sulu* carried the sky-blue Fijian flag before the President of Fiji, followed by the Police Commissioner and the Commander of the Defence Force. Singh sat next to the aisle, and now craned her neck.

Ahead of the coffin wafted the sweet floral scent of gardenias, frangipani and the unique Fijian *mokosoi*. Mr Phillip and DCI Browning were the front pallbearers, next were men she didn't know, and Joe was at the back with Lt Vodo. She'd never seen Joe in his scarlet tunic and white *sulu* before, and this might be the last time he wore what must be the most flattering police uniform in the world. She gazed at him expectantly but he kept his eyes ahead, as he should.

While the eulogies, the heartfelt hymns, the glowing tributes and prayers flowed on, Singh felt how sad it was that Helen had not one of her own family at her funeral. It was possible her criminal ex-husband was at the back with a prison guard, of course, but he hardly counted.

Finally, the haunting sorrow of *Isa Lei*, the Fijian farewell song, brought tears to the eyes of the entire congregation. Joe and the other pallbearers shouldered their burden again and marched down the aisle. This time, he spotted her and held her gaze for a few seconds. They would be together again when his duties were done.

Welcome gift for Fiji Fan Club members

I hope you enjoyed this book. Like other *Fiji Islands Mysteries* readers, you may have also enjoyed discovering Fiji. My years in these beautiful islands inspired me to write this series.

When I published *Death on Paradise Island*, I began a blog which has evolved to include Fijian food, customs, history, sport—whatever occurs to me. I was so delighted with readers' responses, I compiled the best into an illustrated e-book with hot links to cool music and videos, too. *Finding Fiji* is a short, subjective collection that enriches readers' enjoyment of my novels.

Finding Fiji is exclusive to Fiji Fan Club members, so I invite you to join us today. Each month, I'll send you some news about my books and Fiji. I'll also share the latest crime fiction promos. As a welcome gift, I'll present you with *Finding Fiji and* my prequel novella, *Death of a Hero: How it all began.*

Join the Fiji Fan Club here: bmallsopp.com

Enjoy this book? You can make a big difference.

As an indie author, I don't have the financial muscle of a major world publisher behind me. However, I do have loyal readers who loved my first book and took the trouble to post reviews online. These reviews brought my book to the attention of other readers.

I would be most grateful if you could spend a few minutes posting a short review on Amazon, BookBub, Goodreads or your favourite book review site. Just a line or two will encourage potential readers to try a new author.

About the author

B.M. Allsopp writes the *Fiji Islands Mysteries* series. She lived in the South Pacific islands for fourteen years, including four in Fiji, where she worked at the University of the South Pacific in Suva. She now lives in Sydney with her husband and tabby cat. You're always welcome at her online home: www.bmallsopp.com.

Glossary and Guide to Fijian Pronunciation

bula – hello
bure – house, detached resort accommodation
lali – wooden slit drum
masi – cloth made from beaten mulberry bark
moce – goodbye or goodnight
moce mada – see you later
io – yes
oi lei – wow! /oh no!
ovisa – police officer
ratu - chief
sulu – wraparound skirt worn by men and women
vakalevu – very much
vinaka – thank you
yaqona – kava (the plant, its roots, ground powder and drink)

Acronyms
DI – detective inspector
DS – detective sergeant
DC – detective constable
DCI – detective chief inspector
SOCO – scene of crime officer

Spelling
The Fijian alphabet is based on English but it is phonetic,
so each sound is always represented by only one letter,
unlike English.

Vowels
a as in father
e as in let
i as in Fiji
o as in or
u as in flu

Consonants
Most consonants are pronounced roughly as in English,
with the following important exceptions.
b = *mb* as in member eg. bula = mbu-la
d = *nd* as in tender eg. dina = ndi-na
g = *ng* as in singer eg. liga = ling-a
q = *ng* as in stronger eg. yaqona = yang-gona
c = *th* as in father eg. maca = ma-tha

The Fiji Islands Mysteries

DEATH OF A HERO: HOW IT ALL BEGAN
FIJI ISLANDS MYSTERIES PREQUEL NOVELLA   (ISBN
978-0-6488911-2-3)
*Meet young Joe Horseman. How much will he risk to save his dead
hero's honour?*
When Horseman finds his rugby captain's corpse, he vows to help
investigate. But the police refuse to pass him the ball.

DEATH ON PARADISE ISLAND
FIJI ISLANDS MYSTERIES 1   (ISBN 978-0-9945719-4-6)
*An island paradise. A grisly murder. Can a detective put his rugby
days behind him to tackle a killer case.*
DI Joe Horseman knows he'll have to up his game when guests at an
island resort witness a young maid's corpse wash ashore.

DEATH BY TRADITION
FIJI ISLANDS MYSTERIES 2 (ISBN 978-0-9945719-3-9)
Must DI Joes Horseman sacrifice his chance to catch a killer?
Horseman can't wait for his American girlfriend to join him in Fiji.
So he sets a deadline to crack a murder case in the remote highlands.
But dangers loom through the mountain mist.

DEATH BEYOND THE LIMIT
FIJI ISLANDS MYSTERIES 3 (ISBN 978-0-6488911-0-9)
Can a landlubber detective combat evil on the high seas?
DI Joe Horseman stares into the eyes of a severed head fished out of
a shark's gut. But did the tiger shark kill Jona?

DEATH SENTENCE

FIJI ISLANDS MYSTERIES 4 (ISBN 978-0-6488911-4-7)

A notorious convict is free. The public wants him dead.

When Dev Reddy is released, the Fiji media whip up an outcry in Suva. As protest threatens to escalate to riot, DI Joe Horseman fears Reddy's parole may be a sentence of death.

DEATH OFF CAMERA

FIJI ISLANDS MYSTERIES 5 (ISBN 978-0-6488911-7-8)

A TV reality hit. Players dying to win.

Champion, the TV game show sensation, is shooting a new series in Fiji. When a young finalist dies, DI Joe Horseman must unpick Champion's tangle of ambition, fantasy and greed to stop a killer.

DEATH OF A DIPLOMAT

FIJI ISLANDS MYSTERIES 6 (ISBN: 978-0-6488911-9-2)

A VIP diplomat is missing in Fiji. DI Horseman's dream becomes a nightmare.

When a High Commissioner fails to turn up at a grand opening, DI Joe Horseman must dig into her life in the elite circles of Suva. He exposes criminal networks reaching to the highest in Fiji.

More details and buy links at: bmallsopp.com/books

Acknowledgements

During my years in Fiji, I was fortunate to be invited to the Australian High Commission where I enjoyed warm hospitality and marvelled at the views from the verandah of the old colonial Residence. I assure you that the horrifying events and the characters portrayed in this book are entirely fictitious.

I'm grateful to Professor Donald Rothwell of the Australian National University for his advice on diplomatic immunity, to Commander Piers Chatterton HADC, RAN, for telling me about the role of a naval attache, and to Carolyn Carter for sharing her experiences at another Australian diplomatic post in the Pacific.

I couldn't write about police work in Fiji without the help of Mr Waisea Vakamocea, retired senior officer of the Fiji Police Force, who patiently answered my many questions when I was writing my first *Fiji Islands Mystery*.

Thanks also to my editor, Troy Lambert, a fine crime writer himself, who gave me much insightful advice, most of which I followed. Maryna Zhukova of MaryDes once more created a fantastic cover, even including some bougainvillea at my request.

As for the volunteer advance readers of Horseman's Cavalry who pointed out remaining errors and told me how much they enjoyed the story, I can't thank them enough. All errors of any kind are my responsibility.

Finally, I thank Peter Williamson for his advice on nautical matters, his patience through reading draft after draft, his enthusiasm for my writing and constant support.